DAWN OF LOVE

In a gentle voice he said, "Why are you so shy, love? You mustn't fear me."

"I fear no one."

He leaned nearer and pulled her toward him, leaving kisses along her skin and over the curve of her ear.

Jessica felt the warmth flow through her in spite of herself. Though she pulled away, she wanted the kisses to continue . . . she wanted his powerful arms to tighten about her.

Mysteriously, he understood her contradictions and tangled his fingers in her hair to guide her mouth to his. Allowing his tongue to trace the curve of her lips, Jessica felt her skin glow from the inside out. And lovingly she opened to him so that he could taste all of her sweetness. . . .

THE TRYST

Lynda Trent

AN ONYX BOOK

NEW AMERICAN LIBRARY

PUBLISHED BY
THE NEW AMERICAN LIBRARY
OF CANADA LIMITED

Copyright © 1986 by Dan and Lynda Trent

ⒷⒷ ONYX IS A REGISTERED TRADEMARK OF NEW AMERICAN LIBRARY

SIGNET, SIGNET CLASSIC, MENTOR, ONYX, PLUME, MERIDIAN
AND NAL BOOKS are published in Canada by The New American
Library of Canada, Limited, 81 Mack Avenue, Scarborough,
Ontario, Canada M1L 1M8

First Onyx Printing, October, 1986
2 3 4 5 6 7 8 9
PRINTED IN CANADA
COVER PRINTED IN U.S.A.

To Roy and Dawn Dalrymple for friendship, farsed chicken, lemonwhyt, and no complaints.

And a special thanks to all the staff of the Rusk County Memorial Library in Henderson, Texas, for their help, and to Linda White in particular for finding answers to all our very unusual questions.

Nothing is so firmly believed as what is least known.
    —Michel Eyquem de Montaigne
    (1533–1592)

Prologue

Hargrove Castle, 1570

LADY DEVONA HARGROVE shifted her weight uncomfortably on the stool and tried to focus her attention on her ladies' conversation. Her swollen belly rounded beneath her silk gown, which was stiff with gold embroidery and seed pearls. She had been chambered for two months and was overly tired of seeing the same faces. But nothing was to be done for it. Until her babe was birthed, she must keep to her chambers and the company of her women.

With a sigh, she rose and walked awkwardly to the window. Although a late-spring storm blew sheets of water against the leaded glass, she could see the thin spires of the church in the distance. Melancholy spread through her. In the churchyard were the half-dozen small graves of her infants, and inside the church lay a more recent child. Her only son to survive infancy was buried there with his father's fathers. Young Robin had seemed so healthy. She had had such hope. And now once again she waited the birth of a child and worried that she might never even hear its cry.

"Lady Devona," called one of her ladies, "we have

a dispute. Mistress Anne thinks Sir Edmond Kenton is the most skillful at archery, and I think the honor goes to Lord Randolph. What think you?"

"My lord husband has a most gifted eye," Devona said absently, "yet Sir Edmond has won the last few contests." What if I cannot give Randolph a child to grow to adulthood? she fretted silently. What then?

"Come away from the window, my lady," called another of her ladies, who was more perceptive. "The storm is causing you melancholy and might mark the babe."

"How could a storm do such a thing?" Devona asked testily, yet she turned away. "Perhaps a dog or lizard might mark it, but the storm is such that nothing is out and about."

"Play me a game of primero," Mistress Anne suggested. "I have the cards here." She produced a pack of playing cards from a carved ivory box she had just removed from an oaken chest.

"I tire of primero," Devona complained, pacing to another window.

"Maw, then. I hear 'tis becoming all the rage in London."

"Very well, maw it is." Devona sat back down on the stool and watched Mistress Anne sort out the thirty-six cards used in the game. At times she wondered who was set to amuse whom. At once she felt guilty. Mistress Anne was the widow of one of her husband's poorer cousins and had been her lady-in-waiting for most of the eight years of her marriage. Devona reminded herself to be more charitable.

Above the noise of the storm the ladies heard the sound of someone's footsteps running by the door. The hum of their conversation paused, each hoping for some diversion, then picked up again as the steps receded down the corridor.

"The servants need disciplining," Devona observed. Since her chambering, she feared the housekeeper had become lax in her duties.

Mistress Anne shuffled the cards and nodded. "Mistress Tibb is a foolish woman if you ask me. I care not for her at all."

Devona ignored her. A rivalry between the two women had brewed for years, and neither would admit anything good about the other. Secretly Devona agreed with Mistress Anne, but the housekeeper was the daughter and granddaughter of Hargrove housekeepers and was grooming her eldest girl as her successor. There was no simple way of removing the woman. "You begin the play," Devona said.

Suddenly the heavy oak door to her chambers burst open and slammed against the wall. In the doorway stood the startling apparition of a large man in tattered clothes and matted gray beard. His frenzied eyes raked the room as the ladies shrieked and huddled together. Wild lightning flared and thunder crashed deafeningly as his gaze found Devona. From outside the room came calls of men and the sounds of more running feet.

"In here!" Devona screamed. "He is here!"

The intruder rushed forward with a lumbering gait and shoved Mistress Anne aside. He clapped his bony hands over the swell of Devona's unborn baby and forced her to meet his crazed eyes. "Babes will be born," he hissed in a voice unused to conversation. "Twin babes!"

Devona shrank back but the wall prevented her retreat. "Randolph!" she screamed. "Randolph, he is here!" At that moment, the search party ran into the room, her husband leading the way.

The madman spoke quickly. "I tell you true, woman. You bear twin girls!" His thin lips pulled back to show his rotted teeth. "One of them will be fair. As fair as a spring morn."

The man was quickly restrained, and as his captors began dragging him away, Devona slumped into her husband's arms. But before he could be hauled through the doorway, he continued, "The other will be mad! As mad as I am!" Then he let out a cackling laugh that seemed to reverberate wickedly in the stone room. "As mad as I!" he repeated as he was whisked out of sight.

Devona trembled as if chilled to the bone, and would have fallen had not Randolph's strong arms supported her. She raised her terrified eyes to his. "You heard him, husband."

"He's but a daft old man," Randolph said uneasily. "He has been crazed since his youth."

"But he often knows the future!" she protested. "I have heard you say many a time that Leopold the Mad knows more in his small cell than a yeoman at large in the parish."

"It was but the raving of a madman."

Devona pushed away his arms and steadied herself against the wall. "Twins, he said. We have mentioned how great the babe grows. It could well be two!"

"Or it could well be also that Goody Throckmore is off in her calculations. Mayhap you are nearer term than she thought."

Slowly Devona shook her head. "I think not."

Randolph frowned and glanced at the clustered women who watched them with round eyes and whispers. "My brother is mad. Everyone knows that. He has been confined in his cell most of his life."

"A prophecy or a curse?" Devona persisted. "In the end, does it matter which?"

" 'Tis neither, wife!" Randolph Hargrove tried to

silence her with a scowl. "Would you give credence to the words of a man who no longer even knows his own name?"

A dull ache began in her lower back and moved slowly down her thighs. Devona leaned against the wall, ignoring its dampness. "Still, he has been right before." The first birth pain sliced through her and she doubled, her arms about her middle.

"My lady?" Randolph turned to Mistress Anne. "This unpleasantness has brought on the child. Send a man to fetch Goody Throckmore."

"Hurry!" Devona added as another, stronger pain began. She knew from other births that the babe was coming quickly. "Help me to my bed, love."

Randolph put his arm around her and led her to the tall feather bed in the center of the room. Already one of the ladies had turned back the cover, and another was folding a sheet to use as a birth pallet.

Devona halted and, in a voice too low to be overheard, said, "What if Leopold is right?"

Randolph glanced at the door through which his men had dragged his protesting brother. "There is nothing we can do. Who can tell what a child will grow to be?"

"There was a clue," Devona persisted, catching her breath against the labor pains. "He said one would be fair. The dark one, if there are two, will be the tainted one."

Randolph looked long at her. "Then if two are born, we must rid ourselves of the dark one."

Anguish paled Devona's face. "How can we? After so many disappointments, how can we rid ourselves of a healthy babe?"

"How can we allow one to grow who will be like Leopold?" Randolph countered, jerking his head toward the door. "It would be better to have no child at all than to raise another as unfit for the world as he is."

Mistress Anne returned and briskly took Devona's arm. "Come. Goody Throckmore is sent for and will be here shortly. Lord Randolph, you must leave." When he hesitated, staring down into his wife's eyes, Mistress Anne said, "Quickly! There are things to be done."

Reluctantly Randolph left the room. The door was slammed behind him. He paced the antechamber for a few minutes before stopping at the rain-lashed window, through which he sightlessly looked across the field toward the church. Surely Leopold was wrong, he reasoned. He was only a madman. But somehow he had managed to escape his cell and find Devona in this maze of rooms and mutter his prediction. Or his curse. As Devona said, it little mattered which. A madman's curse could be the same as a true prophecy.

He ran his hand over his brown hair, and worry creased his face. Leopold had been deranged for almost as long as Randolph could remember. At first it had only been slightly evident, but then the sickness progressed and became obvious. At last the family had deemed it necessary to lock Leopold— whom they referred to as "the Mad" to differentiate him from their father—away and name Randolph as heir to the considerable estate. On his father's passing, he had inherited a fortune as well as the care of Leopold.

The prospect of having to raise a child that was doomed to insanity disturbed Randolph. The best decision would be to rid themselves of the baby before it was old enough to be a real person. His thoughts squeamishly turned from the idea of how the vile deed would be accomplished, because he knew there was no one to do it but himself. A pillow over the tiny face and the matter would be ended.

He closed his eyes as the first of Devona's birth screams rent the air. He must remain firm in his decision.

The midwife, swathed in somber colors as befitted her important station, waddled into the room, a few crumbs of tansy cake still clinging to the stray hairs on her chin. She nodded perfunctorily at Randolph, then entered the lying-in room. Randolph caught a brief glimpse of Devona, robed in a chaste black gown as a proper wife should be, and lying on the bed. Then the door was shut and he was along again.

He considered returning to the boisterous company of his men, but instead he lingered by the window. Devona was usually quick in birthing, and if a babe must die, it would be better to see to it before word of live twins spread. But perhaps the birth would not yield twins at all.

He glanced at the rain-shrouded church where he had buried his only son a few months before. His grief was still raw. Perhaps Devona would give birth to a boy. He needed a son, for there was no heir to carry on his family line.

Again Devona screamed, and Randolph knelt on the rushes to pray for a live son.

Hours passed before he heard the faint wail of a child. Randolph jerked around toward the door. The babe was born! Without waiting to be summoned as was proper, he shoved open the door to see Mistress Anne receiving a squalling baby from the midwife.

When Goody Throckmore saw Randolph, she began gesturing for him to stop. "Out!" she commanded. "You've no business in a birth chamber."

"The babe," he said stubbornly. "Is it a boy?"

"Nay, 'tis a lass, and we're not done yet." She shoved the door shut, narrowly missing her master's nose.

Randolph scowled. What did the old crone mean by that? He had almost convinced himself that Leopold was wrong.

Within minutes, the cry of another newborn rent the air. Randolph closed his eyes and prayed more fervently than ever before in his life that the second born was a fair-haired son.

Goody Throckmore opened the door and gestured for him to come in. Mistress Anne stood there with an uneasy smile, a baby cradled in each arm.

"Greet your daughters, Lord Randolph," she said hesitantly.

Slowly Randolph approached and looked from one tiny face to the other. Then he wheeled to face Devona, whose large eyes were dark with fear. Turning back to the babies, he looked more closely. "They are identical!" he exclaimed.

Devona struggled to rise to her elbow. "Are you certain? Surely one . . ."

"Identical," he repeated. "And both fair of hair!"

Goody Throckmore, who alone was unaware of Leopold's prediction, shrugged with indifference. "Crib hair. Mayhap it will change as they grow older. But both are alive and healthy, my lord. You can thank me for that."

Randolph stared down at the newborns as one of the women whisked the midwife off into a corner to relate what had happened. Slowly Randolph turned to his wife. "One is exactly like the other," he said in a tired voice. "Both are fair."

Devona held out her thin hand. "Give thanks, husband. A great sin has been spared you."

Randolph could only nod. "I will give prayers for the next month as atonement for my intentions." Then, with a forced smile, he said, "Perhaps Leopold may still be wrong."

Devona regarded her twin daughters with concern. After a long pause she said, "We will name one Jessica after your mother, and the other will be Madeline for mine."

With a sigh Randolph said, "Which will be which? And how can we tell if we have the right name to the right twin?"

"I suppose in time we will learn to tell them apart," Devona replied.

In the corner Goody Throckmore looked from her informant to the babies, then shuffled out. This was gossip too rare to hold back. Within the hour everyone in the castle knew about Leopold the Mad's prophecy.

1

JESSICA LEANED LOW over the neck of the galloping horse and breathed deeply of the bitterly cold February wind. A bird's song could be heard over the thudding hooves and she could see occasional patches of snow in the bordering wood. She raced over the acres of wasteland, too full of the exuberance of being alive to care that her pale hair was escaping her snood and whipping about her face, or that at the maturity of twenty, she was well beyond the age for such adventures.

She passed yeomen and tenants on their way to the fields to gather cattle dung for fuel or to do other chores that took them from their hearths. On recognizing her, they tugged at their caps but she saw the disapproval in their faces. A woman should be home seeing to proper women's work, not flying about the countryside astride a horse.

Skirting the woods in a curving sweep, Jessica reined the animal back home. Dawn had already pearled the sky and was deepening to blue. Everyone would be up by now and her absence noted.

She rode into the stableyard, the horse prancing

and snorting in his eagerness to run further, but Jessica easily controlled him. Having ridden since early childhood, she prided herself on being able to ride any horse on her father's estate. After she dismounted, she fluffed her billowing green skirts and handed the reins to the approaching stableman. He made no effort to conceal his disapproval.

"You be late today. Folks been asking after ye."

Jessica glanced toward the square lines of the castle. "Papa?"

The man nodded. "He's been here twice asking for ye. I had no choice but to tell him you'd taken out Charger."

Jessica sighed. Another lecture would be forthcoming. Bidding the man a good morning, she crossed the barnyard, where the last of the field hands were finishing their bowls of porridge. The maids bobbed her a curtsy as they ladled the last of the steaming gruel from the breakfast pot, and Jessica nodded in acknowledgment. It was even later than she had thought.

As she hurried up the broad steps into the entrance chamber, she tried to smooth her thick hair back into its binding, but the wind had tossed it into rebellion. Giving up, she removed the snood and tossed her hair so that it cascaded in rippling golden waves down her back. Her father preferred it loose and perhaps this would help to pacify him.

Her parents were waiting for her in the hall. From years of practice, Jessica easily gauged her father's temper and decided it would be best to greet her mother first. She rushed to Devona's side with a wide smile she hoped would be disarming.

"Where have you been?" her father demanded from across the room.

"I took out the new Barbary for a ride," she replied. "Surely the stableman told you that."

"He did indeed. A sorry plight it is when a father must ask a stableman the whereabouts of his own daughter."

"That horse is half-wild," her mother put in reproachfully. "He's a man's horse!"

"I handled him with no trouble. Charger just likes to run. I had a very pleasant ride."

"Alone! You rode alone! Jessica, I've told you again and again it isn't proper." Randolph Hargrove glared at his daughter.

"Oh, Papa," she laughed. "Who would dare harm me? As a daughter of the castle, I'm safer than anyone else in the parish."

"That's not the point and you are well aware of it," Devona snapped. "It was bad enough when you were a child, but now you're a grown woman. If you must go for a ride, you should ride pillion as your sister and I do, not just take off on your own like . . . like a hoyden!"

"No one saw me. At least none of the gentry."

"The field workers saw," Devona moaned. "That's just as bad. You must have been seen by several this late in the morning."

Jessica glanced at the window. "Is it so late? The days are lengthening so quickly I lost track of time."

Randolph called to a servant, "Go to the solar and fetch Lady Madeline." Without question, the serving maid rushed away to do his bidding.

"You haven't waited breakfast for me, have you?" Jessica asked.

"No. We ate a full hour ago."

"Then why are you sending for Madeline?" Jessica noticed both her parents were still frowning. Had she done something else as well? She racked her brain but could come up with no new misdemeanors. At least not any she hadn't already been scolded for or that were likely to be discovered.

"Must you question my every move?" Randolph roared. "May I not send for my daughter without answering to you?"

Jessica held her tongue. Her parents seemed uncommonly agitated over her early ride. Had they learned she had bribed Mistress Anne to finish her embroidered dress panel? No, that was in her mother's area of discipline and her father was taking the lead today.

The sound of approaching footsteps drew Jessica's attention, and she looked toward the door as Madeline entered. As always, the young woman wore a spotless gown, and her long blond hair, a perfect replica of Jessica's, swung in well-brushed waves to her hips. Jessica's frown deepened, and she again tried to smooth her tumbled hair.

With her eyes humbly downcast, Madeline bobbed a curtsy to her parents. "You sent for me, Father?" she asked in dulcet tones.

Not for the first time Jessica felt a pang of resentment and glared at her sister. Madeline always affected that faint lisp when speaking to their parents or any other adult of account. Yet when they were alone, her voice was as normal as Jessica's.

Randolph's expression softened. "Yes, child. Your mother and I have news." Glaring at her twin, he added, "Now that Jessica has finally returned, I may tell you."

"News?" Jessica asked. "Is there a fair on the way?"

Madeline waited silently, the perfect picture of a dutiful daughter.

"Can you think of nothing but pleasure? No, this is much greater news."

"War? We've declared war on Spain?"

"Hold your tongue," Devona ordered sharply. "Our good Queen Elizabeth has declared war on no one."

"A messenger arrived at first light this morning. Betrothals have been arranged for you both."

"Betrothals?" Madeline asked, forgetting to lisp.

"For both of us?" Jessica gasped. "Who?"

"You have well to ask the names that will mean so much to you for the rest of your lives. You, Madeline are to marry Lord Nicholas Garrett, Earl of Wyndfell. Jessica, you are to wed Sir Edwin Fairfax."

"I've never heard of Lord Nicholas Garrett," Madeline murmured, her deep blue eyes wide.

"Sir Edwin?" Jessica exclaimed. "I'll never marry that old woman in breeches!"

"Enough!" Devona commanded.

"You'll wed him, daughter, and be glad you did," Randolph told her. "I've negotiated for months to bring off this match."

"But he's old! And his rank isn't even up to ours. That sort of thing isn't done these days."

"It is when news of a girl's headstrong nature has swept the countryside," Randolph retorted. "You've already ended two good matches by your untoward actions."

"You cannot continue to blame me for that," Jessica objected. "One was as ugly as a boar and the other simpleminded!"

"And both rich! They were good matches!" Randolph shouted.

"They were no better than animals! And Sir Edwin is worse. He's old enough to be my grandfather!"

"If he were not a recent widower, we would have failed there too. He has the experience to handle you, whereas a young man might not."

"You sound as if he is a . . . a bearward!"

"Don't dare shout at me!" Randolph drew back his hand to strike his daughter, but she didn't flinch. He dropped his arm.

"Appearances matter little," Devona said in an effort to soothe her least favorite daughter. "With Sir Edwin you will have a prosperous life."

"And my betrothed?" Madeline ventured at last. "Is he also old?"

Randolph regarded her fondly as he stroked her hair. "No, poppet. Lord Nicholas is young still. Not a callow youth, but a man nearing his thirtieth year."

"And is he rich?"

"Would I marry you to a pauper? His family income isn't what it once was, I'm told, but he has a fine lineage and a name even older than our own. His elder brother went through a bit of his inheritance before he died, but Lord Nicholas has assured me you will never want for anything. Besides, your dowry is a fortune in itself."

Madeline sweetly bowed her head in compliance.

"Where is this paragon?" Jessica demanded. "Why have we never heard of him?"

"*I* have heard of him. His father was a friend of my youth. We were sent to the same castle to be nurtured and trained as men. I met the elder brother of your betrothed at a gaming table when I traveled through Yorkshire."

"Yorkshire?" Jessica exclaimed. "That's almost across England!"

"News of your escapades travels wide," he said dryly. "No nobleman in the vicinity was willing to chance marriage with you, and your reputation even tainted that of your poor sister."

Madeline glanced reprovingly at Jessica, who glared back.

"Then why not let me go to Yorkshire and be well

rid of me?" Jessica retorted as tears born of hurt stung her eyes. She tossed her head to keep her emotions in check. She wouldn't give them the satisfaction of making her cry.

"Your betrothal was arranged first. I thought it better that way. Also, Madeline's intended is of a great family whom I would not offend."

"You think they would be offended by me?" Jessica held her head high. "I am not so very terrible." Her parents never thought ill of Madeline. "Most of the misadventures of which I have been accused are not my doing at all!"

"Now, Jessica, don't start maligning your sister again," Devona reproached, going to her other child. "This is a day for rejoicing, not false witnessing."

Madeline smiled angelically at her mother but flashed Jessica a warning glance from the corner of her eyes.

With an effort Jessica controlled herself. True, she was given to wild rides at dawn, but she loved horses. And she had on more than one occasion walked barefoot in the dew and even stripped down to her chemise and swum in the river, but only when she was sure no one was around. The bad things, however, the truly bad deeds, were none of her doing at all.

Madeline smiled in her closed-lipped way, as a proper lady should. "When will I be married, Father? Will I meet him before?"

"No, child. He lives so far away that a previous meeting is out of the question. I have arranged for you to exchange miniatures. You will sit for yours starting this afternoon, and I'm sure his will come by messenger in the near future. I can tell you this, however: his father and his brother were tall, handsome men. I doubt not you'll be pleased."

"And I, Papa? Will I too, be pleased?" Jessica asked in a small voice, knowing full well that her father didn't care.

"You will be married." Randolph's voice took on an unconsciously harsher note.

"A woman must be married." Devona spoke the obvious. "You can't remain a maid forever."

"Queen Elizabeth has!"

"Her majesty is the queen," Randolph snapped. "You are but an impertinent chit. Now, go to your chamber and fetch your sewing. I have business to be about."

Jessica lifted her chin, ready to defy him, but then she turned and ran from the room as tears gathered and brimmed in her eyes. Behind her she heard her father deploring her unladylike ways, but had she left more sedately, everyone would have seen her cry.

By the time Madeline joined her in the solar, Jessica was dry-eyed and more angry than hurt. Madeline sat on a stool and picked up a corner of the Turkey-work cloth she was sewing with Devona.

"Mother will be up soon. We were discussing the plans for our weddings."

Jessica snorted and jabbed the needle into her embroidery, tangling the silk thread.

"My wedding is to be first," Madeline continued. "Yours will follow in a month."

"Not if I've any say in the matter."

"Well, you don't. Father said you will take this match or have no other."

Jessica narrowed her eyes at her sister. "What does that mean?"

Madeline looked away and was silent.

"Don't play meek with me! What did he mean?" A woman had to marry or be like Mistress Anne and live out her days as little more than a servant. In Jessica's case it would be worse, for Mistress Anne was at least a widow.

"He was speaking of the curse. Everyone knows about it," she continued when Jessica paled. "Just because Leopold the Mad is dead now doesn't change anything."

"Don't call him that." Jessica recalled the poor old man she had seen crouched in a corner of the tower cell. He had seemed more pitiful than dangerous to Jessica, who had often bribed his keeper to see that he was kept cleaner and better fed. When he appeared sane, or almost so, she reflected that in his brighter youth he might even have been comely. "He was our uncle," she reminded Madeline.

"Yours perhaps."

Jessica slapped her sewing down in her lap. "Would you care to explain that?"

"Everyone knows one of us is doomed to madness," Madeline said with feigned sweetness. "They all whisper 'tis you."

Jessica's eyes widened. She, too, had overheard such rumors, but had believed they were spoken to keep her in line as a child. "But I'm not mad!"

"Aren't you? What other lady do you know who rides rampant over the countryside? Why, you even sit astride. It's falling out of fashion, as you well know. Not only that, your tongue does ever race ahead of your brain."

"I'm sorely vexed! Especially by you."

"And you shirk your ladies' work."

"Can anything be more boring than a chamber full of ladies discussing ways to prepare a warden pie? Pears don't make for fascination in my opinion. Or the newest Italian stitches. Or the most recent cut of a French hood."

"I find these things fascinating. But then," Madeline said as she carefully drew her thread through the heavy cloth, "I'm not mad."

"Neither am I!"

"They all think you are."

"I was not the one who drowned the maid's cat in the pail of milk!"

"He did look rather poetic, didn't he?" Madeline mused, her eyes becoming dreamy as she recalled the incident. "A cat drowned in fresh milk. How appropriate."

"How cruel, you mean! And it was not I who plucked Mama's best laying goose, and it still alive!"

"I needed those feathers, as you well know, for the pillow I was making for Father. That ridiculous goose will grow more feathers."

"The point is, you led everyone to believe *I* did these things."

"I never told them you did."

"Maybe not in so many words, but those glances and sighs spoke volumes!"

"It's your own fault. If you were as gentle as I am around our elders, no one would accuse you."

"Ha! I'll stand accused before I demean myself by becoming a simpering 'Bartholomew's baby'!"

"There are worse things than being thought doll-like. Being mad, for instance."

"Stop saying that!"

"Listen to how loudly you are speaking. Your words must carry several rooms away. Is it any wonder people say that about you?" Madeline's voice, though she had dropped her lisp, had not raised at all.

"What else did Papa say? About my wedding, I mean." Jessica fought to speak more decorously.

"He said if you'll not have Sir Edwin—if you chase

him away as you did the others—then he will have you locked away."

"Locked away?" Jessica whispered. A cold hand seemed to be tightening around her throat. "I don't believe you."

"He mentioned *Uncle* Leopold's cell. I believe you're familiar with it?"

Jessica stood abruptly, letting her handwork fall to the rushes. After a long stare at her sister, who continued to sew with a small smile curving her lips, she turned away and walked numbly to the window. She leaned her forehead on the cool glass and looked out at the patches of snow. Soon the grasses would be strewn with a blanket of vivid wildflowers. Would she by then be fastened away in that horrid cell with its single open window and soured straw? She shuddered. "I will go through with the betrothal," she said.

"That's good, Jessica," her mother said, coming in the door. "It is the only wise move."

Jessica turned and saw the truth of Madeline's words on her mother's face. They exchanged a long and wordless look.

"Oh, Jessica!" Madeline's tinkling voice exclaimed. "You've dropped your embroidery and the thread is snarled. Here. I'll set it right for you."

Slowly Jessica returned to her stool as the other women of the castle began to drift in to start the day's work. Jessica's thoughts seemed frozen at the prospect of her future.

Although the weddings for each of the twins would be a month apart, the betrothal ceremonies were set for the same day. Due to the distance involved, Lord Nicholas Garrett had sent a knight, Sir Raymond Chadwick, to be his proxy. Madeline was all smiles and sweetness as she stood by the handsome, broad-shouldered young man and repeated her vows to the chaplain.

Then it was Jessica's turn. A wave of nausea gripped her as she forced her feet down the aisle, her hand resting on her father's uplifted palm. Ahead of her stood the man who would soon own her, body and mind.

Sir Edwin Fairfax was of average height and bony thin. His skin stretched across his balding forehead and puckered into wrinkles around his mouth. Blue eyes that seemed to have faded from so many years of use were sunken behind wild gray eyebrows. His body twitched and his veined hands trembled as if he could scarcely wait to have her alone in his bed.

The rosy glow of healthy youth paled from Jessica's smooth cheeks as her eyes met her prospective groom's. Once these betrothal vows were made, only death or proof of kinship could dissolve them. She was positive the Fairfax family was no relation to her own. That Sir Edwin might conveniently die was too much to hope for, as the wedding date was set for early May and it was already late February.

She stumbled as she took her place at the altar and her father placed her hand in Sir Edwin's. The old man's skin was as dry and lifeless as ancient fabric. Jessica closed her eyes, trying to control herself.

The chaplain glanced uneasily at her, and Jessica was mortified to realize that he, too, must think her insane and likely to do something strange or cause someone harm at any moment. Nervously the minister cleared his throat and began to repeat the vows her sister had just taken.

"Do you, Lady Jessica Hargrove, daughter of Randolph Hargrove, come to this altar of your own free will?" He looked at her in trepidation.

Jessica's deep blue eyes found her father's, and she stared at him until he, too, moved uneasily. At last she answered, "I do."

"And you, Sir Edwin Fairfax of Stonebroke. Do you also come freely and desiring this union?"

"That I do right willingly," the old man cackled.

Jessica caught the inside of her lip in her teeth to keep from running.

"Will you honor this woman? Will you protect her and keep her for your wife?"

"I will indeed."

"And you, Lady Jessica, will you honor this man as your husband and give yourself only unto him forever?" The words were almost run together in the chaplain's haste to have the ceremony finished.

Jessica swallowed and held her trembling breath. Forever was a long time. "I will," she replied at last.

The chaplain also released the breath he had been holding. "I bind this couple in the first of their vows. Henceforth, they are betrothed and promised one to the other in the sight of God and of man. Have you a ring?"

Sir Edwin fished in the pocket of his greasy jerkin and produced a set of three rings which he handed to the minister.

With practiced fingers the man released the rings from their woven design. One narrow ring he placed in God's name on Sir Edwin's smallest finger. Another he placed first on Jessica's thumb, then her next two fingers in succession in the Trinity's name, and finally on her third finger. The last ring he kept as proof of the betrothal. On the day of their wedding the three rings would be rewoven into the lover's knot and placed permanently on Jessica's finger.

She looked down at the gold ring. It was too large for her and only the joint of her finger retained it.

Had it been made to measure for a larger hand? His dead wife's, for instance?

Jessica clenched her fist and her eyes darted about the family chapel. She didn't want to marry this awful man. He was fearfully old and he smelled! She risked a glance at him. Perhaps he was so old he would not be interested in claiming his conjugal rights. But his leering grin soon dispelled that hope. She didn't hear any of the brief sermon that followed, and when Sir Edwin smacked her wetly on the lips she felt disgust rise in her throat.

Later that evening, after the betrothal dinner, the girls returned to their bedchamber for the night. Madeline chattered for an hour in her excitement. Finally Jessica blew out the candle on her side of their bed and pulled the covers tightly against her chin. She was exhausted from the ordeal. Sir Edwin Fairfax, who had consumed too much mulled wine, had been anything but a gallant knight. It was all Jessica could do not to insult him in front of her parents and the other guests.

As Madeline continued to babble about how grand it would be to marry the Earl of Wyndfell, Jessica dropped off to sleep. Fitful though it was, her slumber did provide some refuge.

Nicholas Garrett sat easily on his large bay horse, a breeze furling his black hair across his tanned forehead. Below him, the land dipped in a gentle dale and rose again to hold Wyndfell, his ancestral home. He never tired of looking at the thick, silvery-gray walls and turrets that were so unexpectedly his. As a younger son he had never thought to be lord here. By all rights his brother Walter should have held it and passed it down to his children, but Walter lay in his untimely grave, having left no heirs save Nicholas.

He nudged his horse forward and trotted down the hill to splash across a shallow stream, then rode up the green slope toward the castle's keep. As he drew closer, he took note of the numerous repairs that were needed. Some of the lichen-encrusted walls were weakened from age and sieges of a more violent time, and although it didn't show, Nicholas knew the north tower's roof was rotted away, as well as the floor beneath. Years of neglect had taken a toll on the proud castle.

Walter had been given to gambling to such an extent that it was an addiction rather than a pastime. As a result of his unlucky cards, a large amount of gold was owed to a neighbor, Sir James Swineford. In the years that Walter was lord over Wyndfell, not one farthing had gone toward its upkeep. Precious few had even shown up on New Year's Day, when the servants were traditionally given coins to buy new clothing or livery. Some of his servants were ill-clothed indeed.

He crossed the heavy drawbridge that spanned the silvery moat that was fed by the meadow's stream. As the stream was supplied by several fresh springs, this moat wasn't muddy as most were. The various designers of Wyndfell had, over the centuries, kept an eye toward beauty as well as function.

Nicholas nodded to the guard in the gate room and rode into the cobbled bailey, his horse's hooves ringing loud on the stone surface. Although numerous outbuildings lined the wall, the open area was ample to turn a coach-and-four. If there were a coach. When the new conveyances had become fashionable in London, Walter had bought one, but within the month he had gambled it away.

Casting an eye toward the sun, Nicholas thought of Lady Madeline Hargrove, who by now was his betrothed. He wasn't especially eager to get married, but the lady came equipped with a most generous dowry. A fortune, in fact. There would be more than enough gold to repay the debt to Swineford, repair Wyndfell, and make investments that would increase rapidly. As skilled as Walter had been at wasting money, Nicholas was at gaining it. If he must marry to get the necessary foundation, then so be it. Besides, he needed to marry and get sons. Otherwise on his death Wyndfell would go to his younger brother, Thomas, who was a match to Walter's irresponsibility. Nicholas only prayed Lady Madeline would be passably fair and not ugly or shrewish. Yet if she was as plain and dull as yesterday's porridge, he was determined to have her—and her dowry.

He dismounted and tossed the reins to a stableboy who ran out to meet him. Wyndfell towered over him, casting a cool shadow over the courtyard. It was old, and castles were losing fashion to manor houses, but Nicholas loved every stone of his estate.

He entered and crossed the hall to the winter parlor, where huge stained-glass windows splashed vivid colors over the rushes. A woman in heavy black wool sat beside the hearth as if she needed the low fire for warmth.

"Good day, Lady Jane. Where are your ladies?"

The woman looked up, then back at the fire. "Greetings, Lord Nicholas. I sent them away. Their chattering tired me."

He bent to lay another log on the fire and studied his sister-in-law's profile. Since her husband's death three months before, her health had declined and she appeared to have aged years. "Have you eaten?"

"I wasn't hungry."

"You must take care of yourself. Will you starve from melancholy?" His voice sounded harsher than he intended, for he had never seen Walter bestow much affection on his wife, and he couldn't understand why she was suffering so. Jane seemed determined to make her dead husband into a saint.

Jane regarded him reproachfully. "Had you lost your mate, you would grieve as well, I should think."

"I will send a maid to bring bread and cheese. White meat may be eaten even during a religious fast."

"I want nothing." Her voice, always calm, was flat.

Nicholas stroked his close-clipped black beard as he paced to the window. "The primroses are in bloom. Will you walk out to see them?"

"Perhaps later. I was about to go to the chapel and pray for Walter."

"Again?" he asked tactlessly, then silently cursed himself. He should be glad Jane had been such a devoted wife.

"Have you forgotten how he died?" she asked in mild dispute. "To die by his own hand has placed his soul in perilous danger. Already he may be beyond redemption." She stood and went to Nicholas and put her pale hand on his arm. "I want to thank you again for persuading the church to let him be buried there. Had it not been for you, he would lie at the crossroads with a stake in his heart." She shuddered.

"The chaplain is not above bribery," Nicholas said gruffly. "Not when he so badly needed new vestments." Nicholas hoped Jane didn't know he had sold his second-best horse to pay that bribe. Jane, like all true ladies, was gentle to a fault and needed to be protected from the harsh realities of the world.

She smiled and her fine skin creased in the precursor of wrinkles. Her somber eyes, however, mirrored only heartache. "I'll pray for you, too."

Nicholas watched her walk silently from the room.

In an earlier age, he thought, she might have taken the veil following her husband's death and entered a life better suited to her. But since the Reformation, many of the convents had been disbanded. And, besides, the Garretts were Protestant. Regardless, he couldn't imagine Lady Jane ever marrying again.

Once more his thoughts traveled to his future bride. Would she be kind to Jane? As mistress of the house, this Madeline would rule in the women's areas just as he ruled over the whole.

He knew so little about this woman with whom he would spend the rest of his life. Was she pretty or plain, gentle or overbearing? By the size of her dowry, he assumed she was the only daughter of a wealthy man. Not only was the amount impressive, but the value of her future inheritance as listed in the marriage agreement was enough to make his head swim. Occasionally he had wondered why her father would be willing to give such a prize to a man he had never met, and one who lived so far away. On the other hand, his father and her father had been close friends. No doubt that explained a great deal.

Nicholas went back into the hall and climbed the tower's steep steps. One of his first improvements would be replacing these perilously worn steps with a real staircase in the hall, one that would sweep up to the second floor in luxurious comfort and be gaily painted with blue or green risers and fine red railings. He had many grand plans for Wyndfell.

He climbed up to the roof and stepped out onto the sentry walk, surveying the area. Of the several gardens that lay around Wyndfell, most were overgrown with weeds. Beyond the rose garden lay the maze, now a jumble of yew, and beyond that the orchard. Almost hidden from view was the vegetable garden. Surrounding it all were meadows and parks where grass grew thick beneath ancient trees. At a distance an oak thicket, its trees oddly shaped due to generations of pollarding, harbored the swine herd. Past that were wasteland and the common fields of the nearby village. Further to the west was his nearest neighbor, Sir James Swineford.

A commoner by birth and a bastard by origin as well as by nature, Swineford had never been Nicholas' friend. Rumor had it that Nicholas' own father had sired him. Whether the rumor was true or not, Swineford preferred to believe *he* was the true eldest son, and thus coveted Wyndfell for his own. As a young man, Swineford had been knighted on the field in France in Queen Elizabeth's service. Nicholas heartily wished he had stayed there on the French sod, for many of his family's troubles could be traced back to Swineford.

He and Walter had been gambling cohorts and it had been Swineford who encouraged Walter's weakness to the point of destitution. Much of the gold that flowed from Wyndfell had puddled in Pritchard Hall, the manor Swineford had inherited from his mother. Walter had fallen so far into debt to Swineford that until Nicholas had made this match with the wealthy heiress of Hargrove Castle, he had feared that he might lose Wyndfell to his enemy. Swineford was the source of Walter's downfall into debt and had even been with Walter the night of the man's suicide. Nicholas didn't believe Swineford had pulled the trigger of Walter's pistol, but he was willing to wager the man wasn't totally blameless in Walter's death. A word here, a threat there. Walter had not been a man of strong fiber.

Nicholas clenched his fists as he gazed westward. He would see Wyndfell pulled down stone by stone before he would let it fall into Swineford's hands. A muscle tensed in Nicholas' lean jaw as he swung his head toward the south. In two months he would journey to get his rich bride and he would be secure in his home. His keen dark eyes tried to pierce the distance as he again wondered what she would be like.

2

THE SNOW OF March fell silently beyond the thick leaded windows. An occasional gust of wind penetrated the casement and lifted the heavy tapestry that screened the stone walls. Madeline shivered and drew her sable-lined cloak more closely around her. "Cover the window, Jessica. 'Tis freezing in here."

Reluctantly Jessica drew the thick cloth over the glass, leaving the room lit only by candlelight. The sharp, frosty scent of snow was replaced by the mustier odor of old rushes and candle wax. Since her betrothal and her father's threat of locking her away, Jessica had been on her best behavior. She knew her only escape was marriage; even Sir Edwin was preferable to a mad cell.

Jessica absently fingered her betrothal ring as she sat on a padded stool by the fire. Without the other two parts, it was merely a twisted band of gold, curved so that it would interlock with its companions, and engraved with an alien-looking vine design. She had wrapped thread about it to keep it on her finger, but it still hung loosely on her knuckle. Madeline's betrothal ring, however, seemed to have been made to her measure. Even in the dim candle-light, the stone in her ring, a garnet which was clasped in the petals of a golden rose, glowed a sensuous red like a drop of wine.

"Sir Raymond has returned," Madeline said as Jessica took up her dulcimer and began to play. "Father said he will be here for several weeks."

"Who?" Jessica asked as she tried to play the stanza of a tune musicians had played last Twelfth Night.

"Sir Raymond Chadwick. Surely you recall him. He stood proxy for Lord Nicholas at my betrothal. He's come to work out details on the dowry or something of the sort."

"Yes, I remember now." She strummed a note, then stilled the strings to try another.

"I think he is most handsome. Don't you?"

"Have you received Lord Nicholas' miniature? I didn't know it had arrived."

"I'm not speaking of Lord Nicholas, silly. I mean Sir Raymond. Do you not find him comely? I'm sure that Lord Nicholas chose the most handsome of all his knights to stand in for him."

Jessica recalled the sandy-haired man. He was of a muscular build, though not very tall, and he had kind eyes. All in all she agreed with Madeline, but it would gall to tell her so. "He seemed pleasant enough."

"I thought he was quite good-looking."

Jessica found the correct note and played the lilting strains of "Can She Excuse My Wrongs?"

"That's a sad song, for my taste," Madeline objected. "It's about a man whose love is spurned. Play something more cheerful."

The tune suited Jessica's mood. She knew that no man would ever "for her sake die contented," although her ancient intended was nearer the grave

than the baptismal font. She repeated the stanza
again.

"If you don't start sewing, you will never finish
your wedding dress in time, let alone your linens.
Think how embarrassed you would be if some servant had to sew your dress at the last minute. That
would be as bad as purchasing the contents of your
bridal chest from some vendor."

Jessica shrugged. "There is time yet."

"What a dour bride," Madeline scolded. "The way
you mope about, one would expect a funeral dirge
rather than a wedding in the offing. Take up your
needlework. Mother will return soon from inspecting the dairy and you've nothing to show for the
morning's work."

Jessica laid aside the dulcimer and took up the
cloth she was embroidering. Because of her distaste
for the necessary needlework, she had learned to
sew quickly. In half an hour she had accomplished
almost as much as Madeline's careful stitching of an
hour.

The door opened and both women looked up to
see a knight enter and bow to them respectfully.

"Sir Raymond Chadwick," Madeline exclaimed. The
man was even more virile than she remembered.
"Do come in. Draw up a stool by the fire. The pas-
sageways are freezing."

"That they are, my lady," the man said. "Yet here
in this chamber, I find spring in bloom." He gestured to them both.

Madeline blushed in pretty confusion. Jessica studied him with frank interest. His compliment seemed
almost flirtatious, as though he was trying too hard
to be gallant. She turned back to her quick stitching.

Madeline, all pink cheeks and smiles, carefully drew
the green thread through the Turkey-work chest

covering. "Do you like this design? It will grace my new home at Wyndfell."

Raymond Chadwick leaned nearer to view her work, thankful that he knew for sure which twin was which. "It's lovely, Lady Madeline. Wyndfell will be honored by such fine needlework."

"Tell me about my new home," she urged. "Is it a castle or a manor?"

"It's a grand castle, my lady. Quite ancient, and dating, in parts, to Norman times."

"Oh," Madeline said in disappointment.

"But it has been added to over the past centuries and is fine in its line."

Jessica thought of her own future home. Edwin Fairfax's castle was scarcely more than a single tower surrounded by a battlement. Because he was below her father's rank, she had never visited there, but from the outside the place was little more than a ruin. "Madeline, did you instruct the kitchen maids to make the new batch of candles?"

"Not yet, dear sister," Madeline answered in her sweetest voice. "I've been so busy here." Again she slowly drew the thread through the cloth. She was a study of demure domesticity.

"Mama told you to supervise them early this morning," Jessica reminded her.

"I will soon. I am speaking with our guest now, and sewing my trousseau."

Jessica stood up. "The candle-making can't wait or it will not be finished before we run short." Jessica was irritated by the attention Raymond Chadwick was lavishing on Madeline—attention she thought a bit out of place since his Lord was engaged to Madeline. Yet perhaps she was annoyed because he reminded her that the emissary of Madeline's betrothed was of equal rank to her own intended. Jessica was the daughter of a viscount and felt she deserved better.

Behind the veil of her unbound hair, Madeline gave her sister a venomous look. "In time, sister." Her voice was gentle, in contrast to her expression.

Jessica swept silently from the room. As usual Madeline's chores in addition to her own had fallen on her shoulders. If the candle-making was not ordered, Jessica knew she would somehow be blamed even though Madeline was at fault.

As soon as Jessica was gone, Madeline leaned forward eagerly. "Tell me, Sir Raymond, what of my intended? Is he well?"

"He is." Raymond averted his eyes and seemed deeply interested in the fire.

"Have you brought me his likeness?" she prompted.

Raymond drew a deep breath. This was the moment he had waited for. "No, my lady," he said with exaggerated hesitation. "Lord Nicholas did not commission one."

"Did he not? Why ever would he fail to do so?" She sat back in amazement and stared at the man.

"Begging your pardon, my lady, but Lord Nicholas instructed me to tell you that you must take him on his title alone. He says you should be glad to marry above your station and not put any emphasis on appearances. He did, however, make much over your miniature and pressed it to his lips again and again."

A slight frown puckered Madeline's forehead. "Is he not young and handsome and of noble bearing? Why would he not wish me to see his likeness?"

"He is young, my lady. Not yet thirty years."

"And the rest?" she persisted.

Raymond drew a deep breath and followed it with a long sigh. When he remained silent, Madeline insisted that he answer. She was making this much easier for him, he thought. "Ask me not, for I am a knight who is bound by his oath of honesty and his pledge to protect the virtuous."

Madeline laid aside her sewing and put her hand on Raymond's sleeve. "Then you must tell me in truth, sir knight. What is this man who will be my husband?"

His eyes met hers and he hesitated, drawing his lies about him like armor. "Since the day I stood by you at the betrothal in Lord Nicholas' stead, I have respected you and thus I will tell you what you ask, but you must promise to keep this knowledge a private matter. Lord Nicholas must never know."

"You have my word. Now tell me." Madeline's impatience was growing and her anxiety was evident from her tone.

"He is young enough, as I have said, but dark of both appearance and nature. His face is not of a handsome turn, nor is his frame. It was the accident in his youth. His back is not much twisted, nor his left leg very short. In a cape it scarcely shows unless he moves about."

"A cripple!" Madeline gasped.

"Fear not. He will be able to get sons. Already half the children of the castle and parish have the dark hair and black eyes of the Garrett strain."

"Half?" she whispered.

"Most of the mothers were willing enough. The others . . . well, my lord has the ways of a man suited to the plunders of war."

"He is cruel?" she demanded.

Raymond shifted uneasily. "I never said that, my lady."

"Nor do you deny it! Does my father know of this?"

"How could he not? Was he not familiar with old Lord Walt? They say the apple falls near the tree."

Madeline's blue eyes flickered with repressed emotion. How dare her father treat her thus! She was his favorite, his darling. Why, old Sir Edwin Fairfax would be better than this monster! "Tell me, in truth, kind sir, of the castle. Is it grand as you have led me to believe?"

Here Raymond could be more truthful. "As I said, its lines are excellent. The chambers are light, yet situated for warmth." He paused and she inclined her head nearer. "The roof, however, is another matter," he said in a low voice.

"It leaks?" she whispered.

"Not any longer, my lady." He motioned with a thumbs-down gesture.

"It's not fallen in!"

"Only in one tower to the extent of being uninhabitable."

"Are there tapestries and wall cloths to make the hall gay?"

"Sold for debts, my lady."

"And are there goblets of silver, plate, brass?"

"Gone before the tapestries, my lady."

Madeline sat back in stunned silence. Her cheeks were pale and looked as rigid as alabaster.

"It is not rare for a man to marry wealth to increase his coffers," Chadwick told her gently. "You will be the wife of an earl, the mistress of great land holdings."

"He kept his land and sold off that which would make my life bearable," she said in a curiously still voice.

"Many another man has done worse. 'Tis not as if all the work will be upon your lovely shoulders."

Madeline looked at him sharply.

"There is another mistress in residence, the young widow of Lord Nicholas' brother," Raymond explained.

"How young?"

Raymond shrugged. "I am no judge in such matters."

"I gather she has no offspring with black eyes and hair?"

"Not yet, my lady."

Their eyes met and held for a long moment. Madeline drew a sapphire ring from her right hand and gave it to the man. "Here, my friend, this is your reward for honesty. As I promised you, I'll tell no one of what you've said. You have done me a great service. I must remain here for a short time to think on what I have heard; then I will meet you in the gallery to learn more of my fate." Her eyes darkened like grottoes of deep water. "I must think on this."

Raymond stood and bowed solemnly. "Forgive me, lady, for telling you such unpleasantness, but I thought you should know."

"I cannot thank you enough, Sir Raymond. Give me leave now. I will join you soon."

Raymond bowed and left, pulling his heavy cloak about him while he hurried through the biting cold of the corridor. His breath frosted around his pale beard and he shivered. This winter had been unusually harsh. He thought of the dread portents that had come to his ears. Fearful happenings of stars falling from the sky, of suns seen together in the heavens, of a rain as red as blood and another that turned into toads as it struck ground. All the commoners were filled with dire predictions and all agreed that the turn of the century, just ten years hence, would surely be the end of the world. Raymond shivered again and ran toward the doors of the gallery.

The long room was golden from the glow of many candles and a huge fire that blazed at each end. Tapestries of hunt scenes and fables covered the row of windows to shut out drafts. Raymond hurried to the nearest fire, trying to capture its warmth.

His thoughts went back to the woman he had just left. Although the sisters were identically beautiful, he greatly preferred Madeline's gentle ways. He would give a great deal to kiss those coral lips and inhale her flowery perfume, but he wasn't sent to dally, rather to destroy.

Before leaving Wyndfell, he had received the message he had expected and, as was prearranged, had swiftly ridden over the lands belonging to Nicholas Garrett and onto James Swineford's holdings. For most of his adulthood, Raymond had been secretly employed by Swineford and had spied covertly on the master of Wyndfell. It had been Raymond who told Swineford of Walter Garrett's passion for gambling. More recently he reported that the new lord was about to wed a rich bride.

After Raymond explained how he would assist with the marriage preparations between Nicholas Garrett and Madeline Hargrove, Swineford suggested a plan for pulling apart the betrothed couple. Raymond was in complete agreement. If Nicholas Garrett could not pay his debts, he would have to sell Wyndfell. Then Swineford could snap it up, thus tripling his own lands and gaining his father's ancestral home as well. Swineford was uncommonly galled by the label of bastard, though he had fathered enough of his own.

On the way to Hargrove Castle, Raymond had thrown Nicholas' miniature and his bride gift into a river. After arriving, he had been unusually fortunate to find himself alone with Lady Madeline. Now that he had explained Wyndfell and Nicholas Garrett in his own false terms, Madeline must be well-nigh beside herself and firmly set against the marriage. He was very pleased at how well everything was going, for once Swineford owned Wyndfell, Raymond was promised a house and land as well as a pension.

The door to the gallery opened and Madeline entered, her face composed and her eyes demurely downcast. With her gliding walk she joined Raymond at the fireplace and held her slim fingers out to the warmth. Raymond had always admired women with delicate hands. They showed good breeding and a life of elegant ease.

After a moment, Madeline said, "I have been giving thought to what you have told me, Sir Raymond. Are you certain Lord Nicholas is as . . . as ugly as you described him?"

"If anything, my lady, I was kind," Raymond affirmed.

"And his temper is truly so deplorable?"

"Again, I have been charitable to him. A quality I fear my lord totally lacks in himself." In the filtered light of the gallery, she was even more beautiful than before. When Raymond realized he was staring at her, he quickly averted his eyes.

Madeline was silent for a while. When at last she spoke, her voice was faint as if she were overcome by the prospect of her fate. "If what you say is true, perhaps I should break the betrothal."

"Would that I could spare you the pain. If I could, in honesty, plead my master's course, I would. However, I cannot."

She lifted her eyes to his, and after a long glance, lowered her dusky eyelashes shyly.

"If I may be so bold," Raymond said to strengthen

his case, "a delicate flower such as yourself should not be subjected to the storms of Wyndfell."

"Is the weather also at fault there?"

"I refer to the storms that rage within the keep, my lady."

"I see." She left the fire and strolled along the length of the gallery, Raymond by her side. "You know, of course, there would be much turmoil if I were to break the betrothal. Nor would it be a simple task. I don't suppose I could prove Lord Nicholas to be promised to another?"

"No, my lady." Even her voice, he noticed, was beautiful, and her movements were the epitome of gracefulness.

"The only other honorable way to put aside the pledge is if I were his kinswoman, which I am not." She kept her voice low and her features calm, though the fury inside her was building.

"I am aware of that, my lady. Perhaps your father would hire a solicitor to falsify your records of lineage."

"As my father is a part of this duplicity, he would oppose such a thing. I would have to think of some other way."

Chadwick had not thought his plan through carefully enough and was at a loss as to what to suggest. As he studied the distress that marked Madeline's lovely features, he wished that he were of more noble blood and could somehow take Nicholas Garrett's place as this woman's husband. "If there were a way I could help you, I would."

Somewhat suspicious of this man, Madeline decided to test his loyalty to his master. "Would you?" She turned to him, her eyes widely innocent.

Raymond's heart expanded at her beauty. "That I would," he replied, meaning every word. "For one sweet smile I would move the stars for you." When she looked at him like that, he could scarcely keep his hands from her, let alone think.

Madeline's lips lifted in a smile and a dimple appeared in one cheek. "You have the pleasant words of a courtier, sir. They fall most sweetly on my ears."

"They are not mere pleasantries. I mean them every one."

She lowered her glance and began to walk again. "Do you?"

"I do indeed." If only he could ever have hopes of winning the love of such a prize, Raymond would have done anything. He had never seen such a beauty.

"Then perhaps," she said, pausing once more and gazing up at him, "perhaps you can help me get my mind off this dilemma. I am sorely vexed now and can think on it no more at the moment."

"I'll do whatever you wish."

Madeline stepped nearer so that her skirts billowed around Raymond's legs and her breasts grazed the front of his doublet. She heard him draw in his breath with a surprised gasp. Not showing she heard, Madeline put her hands on his chest, fingers spread as if measuring its breadth. "Have you a wife, Sir Raymond?" she breathed.

"No. No wife."

"Are you promised?"

"No, my lady." He seemed to be having great difficulty breathing.

Again Madeline favored him with a dimpled smile. "I believe you and I can work out a way so that I don't have to marry this monster. Do you not think so?"

Raymond opened his mouth to stammer a reply. When he did, Madeline pressed her lips firmly against his. For a stunned moment Raymond stood as if frozen, and Madeline wondered if she had made a tactical error. Then his arms roughly encircled her, and he kissed her with all the fervor of a stableboy. When he groped for her breast, Madeline sighed with relief. Men were so easily manipulated, she reflected. She had no doubt that if she needed his help, he would do exactly as she said. Although Raymond Chadwick was only a knight, he was more of a man than any she had ever met. As for her father, if he had indeed matched her to a cruel cripple, she would get even.

Jessica looped the last of the warm, still-malleable candles over the wooden drying rack. They hung like creamy icicles and her movement caused them to sway. The maids were drawing the nearly empty pot of wax from the fire so it could be stored until the next day of candle-making. Jessica looked in the cupboard to check the amount of materials on hand, then when the pot was on its proper shelf, locked the cupboard door.

The cold gusts rattled the thick, nearly opaque kitchen window. The glass in this room was not cut in diamond-shaped panes, but rather small, ill-fitting squares. If not for the huge fire that always burned in the monstrous hearth, the room would be as frigid as the castle's corridors.

Taking a deep breath against the cold, Jessica instructed the maids as to their next task and hurried out. Snow clutched at the dark rose velvet of her gown and clotted her yellow brocade kirtle. The wind cut through the layers of cloth and made her eyes smart as she ran for the nearby castle door. Once inside, the wind was blocked, but the short corridor was nonetheless clammy and cold.

The hall itself was warmer and Jessica lingered by

the welcoming fire. Winter was her least favorite season and she looked forward to spring.

The molten landscape in the hearth shifted and a long stick reminded Jessica of the shape of the tower that made up most of Sir Edwin's castle. By the time wildflowers covered the green, she would be a married woman. At twenty she had been expecting to be a bride for several years, but she couldn't reconcile herself to the groom chosen for her. He was worse than the two previous suitors she had successfully eluded.

The blustering wind blew a mournful sigh through the open windows in the chamber above, and Jessica lifted her head as her thoughts searched the rooms on the upper floors. When she was a child she had believed such sounds must have been Leopold the Mad in his cell. Now she knew it was only the wind, for her uncle was resting at last in his grave.

Jessica was not eager to sew her trousseau, and in procrastination walked to the narrow turret stairs, climbing them swiftly, when another low moan echoed off the stones. One hand swept up her skirt, while the other lightly touched the damp walls for balance.

The steps circled up in a tight coil to the second floor. A landing, worn and dipped by countless feet, led to a narrow corridor. At the end, Jessica saw the door to Leopold's cell, open to the winter. Shivering with cold, she approached it, and as she rested her hand on the heavy metal latch, she looked around the tiny room. An old pallet lay in the moldering straw against the wall. Remains of a broken table and a chair were strewn across the room. In the wall the single window still gaped open with shards of glass sprouting from it. No one knew why Leopold had suddenly broken his furniture and shattered the window. Not only was the cell high above the ground, but the window was much too small for an adult to squeeze through.

Jessica looked around the room and breathed shallowly against the stench that still permeated the cot and straw. She understood why he had done it. If she had been caged here, especially for as many years as her uncle had been, she would have done anything to escape. In the end it had worked, for his violent throes had caused his heart to stop.

She reached out and touched the tips of her fingers to the wall where Leopold had scratched undecipherable runes. Was this the cell where her father planned to lock her away if she didn't marry Sir Edwin? Surely her own papa couldn't really mean to do this! Yet he *had* been Leopold's jailer for more years than Jessica had lived, and they had been brothers.

Incongruously she thought how Leopold, when the menservants carried him into the hall to be prepared for burial, had actually looked serene.

Looking upon him, one would not have guessed he was insane, but rather some poor relation. How mad had he been, Jessica found herself wondering, when her father locked his elder brother away those long years ago? As mad as she was?

Fearful dread gripped her and she slammed the heavy door shut to block out the sight of the cell. The noise echoed down the corridor and she ran back toward the fire and the security of the hall.

In her absence her parents and Madeline had entered the hall, and they whirled to face her as she ran down the stairs and into the room. "Where have you been?" Devona gasped, her jewel-bedecked hand to her throat, glancing from her daughter to the stairs she dared not climb herself.

"The door to the cell was open," Jessica explained,

"and the wind was moaning through the window. I closed the door."

Devona turned away and moved closer to the fire. "You shouldn't go up there. A servant would have done it."

Randolph scowled darkly at Jessica. "We have looked everywhere for you. Explain this!" He thrust a handful of cloth at her.

Jessica took it from him, her eyes confused. Slowly she smoothed the thick folds and exclaimed, "The Turkey-work covering! Who has ruined it?"

"That is what we want to know," Randolph snapped.

Jessica held the cloth to the light and her lips parted as she viewed the extent of the damage. Not only were the fine stitches clipped and frayed, but everywhere there had been a face, the fabric had been cut and gouged. "Who did this?"

"Don't you know?" Madeline asked solicitously.

"Your scissors were found in the folds," her mother replied dully.

"Mine!" Jessica whipped around to stare at her.

"There is no need to feign innocence," Randolph replied with disgust. "We know you did it."

"I would never do such a thing!"

"Then where have you been for the past few hours?" Devona asked as she turned to face her daughter. "Surely you haven't been up in that cell so long."

"Certainly not. I only went up to close the door in order to stop the draft. I had been supervising the candle-making."

Madeline's sorrowful eyes met hers, then turned to their mother, who tilted her head forward and covered her mouth as if she were hearing dreaded news of a death.

"I had Madeline oversee that chore," Devona said.

"But she didn't do it," Jessica protested. "She sat sewing in the solar and when that knight, Sir Raymond, came in, she still sat there as if he were her equal and due her attention. In order that we have candles tomorrow, I did her chore."

"Poor Jessica," Madeline sighed, "how easily you lie these days."

Jessica stared at her sister. "You know I'm not lying."

Devona took the cloth on which she and Madeline had spent so many hours sewing. "It's ruined beyond repair. How could you, Jessica? This was to go in Madeline's bridal chest."

"But I didn't! Madeline must have done it herself." At her accusation, Jessica heard Madeline gasp. "You were in the solar. I was down in the kitchens."

"No, sister, it was the other way around."

"Would Madeline ruin her own needlework?" Randolph roared.

"We sewed for hours on this cloth," Devona protested. "She would never ruin her own work."

"She must have, for I certainly didn't!"

"Dear Jessica, I forgive you," Madeline said gently, putting her hand on her sister's arm.

Jessica jerked away and glared at her. "You did it! Tell them you did this."

Tears welled in Madeline's eyes. "I know you didn't mean to, that betimes you lose control. I blame you not."

"Shed no false tears on my account," Jessica snapped.

Randolph put his arm around his favorite's shoulders. "There now, child. Don't weep. Your chest will be full to overflowing, you'll see."

"Jessica," Devona said, "you'll give Madeline that

embroidered window covering you finished last month in the place of the piece you ruined."

"That's my prettiest cloth!" she protested. "Mama, I didn't cut up the Turkey-work. I swear it!"

"Perhaps," Madeline suggested, "Jessica is envious because I am to wed an earl that Father says is kind and handsome and she is to have a mere knight and him in his dotage. Father, can we not switch husbands? Then Jessica will be happy. I will gladly wed Sir Edwin if you but say the word."

"Nonsense, daughter. Why, the betrothal has even taken place and the wedding dates have been set. You will marry the Earl of Wyndfell as was arranged. As for your sister"—he swept a baleful glance at his other daughter—"she will behave herself or she will see even more of Leopold's cell."

Jessica paled but she held her tongue with an effort. To speak now would do much more harm than good. She clasped her hands tightly together as her family left, her father's arm still about Madeline. The knot in her middle tightened until she thought she would be ill. Her only hope lay in escape through marriage. Slowly she sank down on a stool by the fireside and stared into the embers.

3

NICHOLAS RAN HIS hand over the sleek dappled gray coat of the new horse he had just purchased. She was a beautiful jennet from Spanish stock, and although she stood several hands smaller than his own large bay, she was equally well-proportioned, with long graceful legs and a tapered muzzle.

"You'll do my lady proud," he observed with satisfaction. He had sold several prime sheep to buy the mare and her red leather trappings, but had done so willingly, for he knew any woman would ride this animal proudly.

He fed the horse a handful of hay and patted her again as he left the box stall. Nicholas was no stranger himself to pride and he would have beggared himself to make a good showing to his bride. Everyone knew that love wasn't to be hoped for in the beginning of a marriage, but first impressions would set the tone of the years to come. He didn't want Lady Madeline to be embarrassed by his lack of wealth. In fact, he had not revealed the state of his monetary affairs to anyone. Only a few knew the truth.

His steward, who was a man not much older than

Nicholas and a friend from his childhood, was aware that little gold was left in the coffers. The bailiff, a fatherly sort who had once owned and lost an estate of his own, might guess. But the rest of the servants assumed the Garrett fortune sprang like grass from the ground and would never be depleted. Otherwise they might be tempted to leave his employ or shirk their duties.

As he strolled out to the enclosed courtyard, a short man came to meet him. Nicholas' ready grin appeared, making his even white teeth gleam in contrast with his dark beard. "Sir Raymond! You've had a good journey?"

"As pleasant as possible, my lord. Your lady has finally sent you a token." Raymond reached in the pouch he carried and took out the miniature he had kept from Nicholas since his first trip to Hargrove Castle. "She has sent her likeness."

Nicholas took the tiny portrait, studied it, then grinned more broadly. "God's bones, she's a comely lass. I was wondering at the delay in receiving her miniature."

"I believe another was done but it was found lacking."

"This girl doesn't appear to be lacking in any quarter."

"She's more woman than girl, my lord," Raymond dared. "Had I not been told her age was twenty, I would assume her to be more . . . mature."

Nicholas looked at the man. "Is she not as young as I was told?"

"To be sure," Raymond replied hastily. "To be sure, she is."

Again Nicholas studied the smiling portrait in his hand. "Does this picture do her justice?"

"I couldn't say my lord."

"Nonsense. You've seen her face-to-face, heard her voice, observed her nature. Is this a true likeness?"

"I would say it flatters her somewhat. Only a little, but somewhat."

The earl's dark eyes penetrated the knight's as if he would probe out all the details in his servant's brain. "And her manner—is it pleasing?"

"How may I answer? What serves one man's taste may be offensive to another."

"Offensive!"

"I did not say so of the Lady Madeline," Raymond hurried to add. "Merely that one man's opinion may not match another's."

"What of *your* opinion, Sir Raymond? Is she shrewish, lame, given to fits? I can see she isn't pocked, but has she good teeth and a sound body?"

"Aye, my lord, she has her teeth and is not prone to fits. She will be able to bear you sons, if I am any judge in the matter."

"What of her temperament?"

Raymond hesitated but a moment. "She is as pleasant as springtime, master."

"Thank you, Sir Raymond. You may go." Nicholas watched the man bow and walk away, then looked at the picture of the sweetly smiling young woman. Perhaps she wasn't as fair as she had been painted. Few women were. She might even be older than her touted years. But she couldn't be much older or Raymond would have told him, and she could be much plainer before she reached a point of ugliness. As for her temperament, she was nobly born, and no true lady was actually shrewish though her tongue might be sharp. All she would need in that case was a strong husband to show her the correct behavior. He knew women instinctively wanted to please men because his own father had told him so. The rest was merely a matter of instruction. Smiling again, Nicholas crossed the courtyard to his castle.

At the door he met his younger brother, Thomas, and greeted him cheerfully. Although he had never been close to his younger brother, Nicholas had gained a new sense of magnanimity when he gained his inheritance of the title of earl. He had decided to mend his fences with Thomas. "Sir Raymond has returned, and look what he brought," he said, holding out the portrait.

Thomas, a smaller and less virile copy of his brother, looked at the tiny painting. "She is more than fair, Nicholas. With those features to look forward to, and gold as well, you must be flying like a lark."

"I am at that. I'll admit I was concerned when her likeness wasn't forthcoming as promptly as promised, but it seems the first painter had a clumsy hand. 'Twas well worth the wait."

"We can only hope she is healthy and as gentle as our Lady Jane."

Nicholas hid his concern. He, too, hoped that was true. "Sir Raymond says she is the picture of health and kindness itself." These weren't Raymond's exact words, but Nicholas was certain they were what he had meant. Raymond Chadwick was a bachelor and not accustomed to complimentary phrases, that was all. To show he bore no ill will to Thomas' doubts, Nicholas said, "We must find you a wife next, brother."

"With no land and no home of my own?" Thomas scoffed. "No one but a yeoman's daughter would have me."

"No home? We have Wyndfell." Nicholas struck the walls with his palm as if the place were a living being. "Often two or more families have lived here.

There would be plenty of room for you and a family of your own."

"And what would I do for money, dear brother? Beg at your gate?"

"Don't be a damned fool, Thomas," Nicholas said testily. "You have an income from your sheep. True, it's not grand, but if you stayed away from cards and dice it would more than sustain you. There's the same gambling sickness in you as there was in Walter. If you had a wife, mayhap you'd leave off gambling, and maybe wenching as well."

"Never, brother. I've never met the woman that could make a puppet of me. Nor have you, I wager." Thomas did not appreciate his brother's tone, which he found patronizing, but he was determined to get along with him. After all, Nicholas did control the family purse strings. He handed back the miniature. "This pretty poppet will grace our castle and no doubt will present you with a lusty son every year." He scowled. "But in time you'll again be in the haystack with Big Bet."

"Bet was Walter's leman, not mine." Nicholas glared at Thomas and wondered why he had let him take the gloss from his day.

"That's a pity. Bet knows her way around a haystack," Thomas said with a grin, knowing he had upset Nicholas, "and she has a passel of black-eyed babies to show for it."

Nicholas sighed to think of the number of bastards his brothers had sired between them. A startling number of peasants' bairns bore a resemblance to the family in the castle. "Don't let me detain you longer. I'll go in to Lady Jane." Although his words were civil, his tone was not and he strode away before Thomas could speak.

He found Lady Jane in the gallery, gazing out at

the winter-glazed fields. "My lady," he said cordially. "Are you warm enough in here? I thought to find you in the parlor."

Jane smiled up at him, her fine skin wrinkling at the corner of her lips. "Greetings, Lord Nicholas. I thought to have a turn or two. The winter grows so long and I miss my walks in the garden."

Nicholas looked out at the panorama of gardens, orchards, and the river beyond. In other seasons, the aspect was beautiful, but now with the last snow melting in soiled slushes, and spring not yet arrived, the view was somber.

"Sir Raymond is back and he brought Lady Madeline's likeness." As always when he spoke to his sister-in-law, his voice was soft and kind.

Jane took the offered portrait and he noticed how her hands had grown thin and waxen, as someone's who had been ill for a long time. She still wore her somber mourning clothes though he felt she should give up her grief and go on about her life.

"She's beautiful," Jane said in her calm voice. "One can see at a glance that she will make the most loving of wives."

"Thank you," he said, pleased. Jane always knew the right thing to say. "I can only hope to be as fortunate in my choice as was Walter," he added gallantly.

"Poor, dear Walter," she sighed. "I tried so hard to make him happy." She looked earnestly at Nicholas. "Do you suppose I ever did?"

"Of course," he lied.

She shook her head sadly. "You are ever my champion, dear brother, but we both know better." She smiled faintly. "Perhaps by spring I may ask Walter for myself."

"None of that talk," Nicholas objected, his deep

voice outraged at the idea. "You know 'tis unlucky to speak in that way."

"Is it? At times I have a knowing," she replied as she gazed back out at the mauve-and-gray landscape. "I see Wyndfell as it looks in the spring but I cannot see myself."

Nicholas frowned at the fey note in her voice. "You'll be here," he said gruffly.

Jane summoned the ghost of her old smile. "Of course I will be. Someone must befriend your new bride. We can't have her left here with only you and dour Thomas for company, can we?"

His expression cleared at her attempt of levity, but when she again turned to the window, he felt a deep foreboding.

During the second week in March, a warming trend melted the last patches of snow from beneath the protective boughs of the yews and everyone hoped the winter was through for another year. The winds began to blow steadily from the south, whipping the bare tree limbs about as if nature were trying to arouse the sleeping plants for the beginning of a new cycle. Peasants and yeomen took to the fields in great numbers, splitting rails for the repair of fences, trimming the evergreen hedges, and preparing the soil for the spring planting.

Since the incident with the ruined Turkey-work, Jessica had been taking great pains to appear as ladylike as possible, for she feared the consequences otherwise. Even in her riding, she had made concessions by sitting demurely sidesaddle. But when she was certain no one was watching her she would kick her mount into a headlong gallop. Riding was her only pleasure and she was determined not to be robbed of it.

The end of the month drew near, and the weather began to mellow into true spring. "Mothering Sunday," the one day a year when apprentices from all over England dressed in their blue coats and flat wool caps and left their cobblers' benches, printing presses, and the like to visit their mothers, came and went. April approached with unerring sureness and with each passing day Jessica's nerves became more and more taut, for her wedding loomed but a month distant. She was constantly torn between the dread of marrying Sir Edwin, who was proving himself a lecherous suitor, and the threat of being locked away, at least temporarily, if she didn't marry him.

On Holy Thursday Raymond Chadwick returned. As soon as he made his presence known in the castle, he sought out Madeline. She and Jessica were in the forest gathering flowers to decorate the castle's well in honor of the day. Jessica had wandered a short distance from her sister in search of the more delicate lady's-smocks.

When she heard a man's voice greet Madeline, she raised up to glance over the bush that separated them. Seeing it was only the emissary from Wyndfell, she went back to picking flowers.

"Greetings, Sir Raymond," Madeline said in her gentle lisp as she looked about to see if Jessica was still close by. "How fares my groom?"

"As well as may be, my lady. He sends his greeting and bids me kiss you in his stead."

When the silence beyond the bush grew long, Jessica glanced toward it in curiosity. She could see nothing. Then she heard Madeline say, "How is my lord's health?"

"The recent rains have made his limp more pronounced, but he has passed the winter in moderately fair health."

Jessica leaned back on her heels in surprise. What limp? Sir Raymond sounded as if he were talking of a man who was lame.

"I have given much thought to what you told me before. Surely he is not as ugly as you say?"

"Why would I lie? 'Tis to my advantage to fill your head with his praise so you will near love him before you meet. Only my honesty has kept me from this deception. My lord is as ill-featured and as cruel-tempered as I have said. If these words I speak ever reached him, I would fear for my life. As you can see, therefore, my fate is in your small hands."

"Would he do you harm for merely speaking truth?" Madeline exclaimed.

Jessica shamelessly leaned nearer the concealing shrubbery. This wasn't at all the way their father had described Nicholas Garrett.

"Lord Nicholas has done worse for less cause than this."

Madeline's voice grew faint as if she might be overcome. "I still cannot believe my father would give me to such a man."

Jessica tried to peer through the bush in her effort to hear better.

"I know not what to say," Raymond began cautiously. He was becoming concerned that she still doubted his false words.

Suddenly Jessica lost her balance and tumbled forward with a crackling of brush.

Raymond was at once on his guard and had unsheathed his sword to defend Madeline and himself. When Jessica stood and brushed the leaves and dirt from her skirt, he scarcely looked less discomfited.

"Jessica!" Madeline gasped. "I didn't know you were there."

"Where else would I be?"

"You could have returned to the castle for all I knew."

Jessica noted that Madeline was blushing profusely. She was probably embarrassed that Jessica had overheard the description of Lord Nicholas. "I could not help but hear what was said," Jessica offered in compassion. "Surely Papa doesn't know."

"He must," Madeline said brusquely; then, far more gently, "After all, Father agreed to wed me to this man. He must have seen him at some point."

"Lord Nicholas is a powerful earl," Raymond reminded them. "He is sought after by many."

"Why then would he agree to take the daughter of a viscount?" Jessica asked.

Raymond shifted uncomfortably. "There is the question of dowry."

"So," Jessica said thoughtfully, "he seeks to line his purse."

"With the dowry Father has promised, he may line his entire castle," Madeline remarked dryly.

"Are not our dowries identical?"

"What a silly goose you can be," Madeline scoffed. "My dowry is suitable for the bride of an earl. Yours is appropriate for a mere knight."

Jessica held her temper with great difficulty. She was angered by the news of her smaller dowry, and why her sister must insult her as well was beyond her comprehension. "Take these," she said, dumping her flowers into Madeline's basket.

"Where are you going?"

"Back to the castle. I have something to say to Papa." She stalked away, too annoyed to see the tender look Madeline bestowed on Raymond or the languishing one he returned.

Gathering her skirts, Jessica ran up the knoll that was crested by her family castle. Humiliation racked her as she thought about her father's additional show of favoritism. Just because she refused to fawn and simper like Madeline, she was treated inferiorly.

She burst into her father's closet just as he was discussing the day's business with his steward. "I must talk to you at once," she demanded.

Randolph looked at her with distaste but motioned for his steward to leave. "Well? What do you mean by bursting in here like this?"

"Papa, is it true that you have settled a larger dowry on Madeline than on me?"

"Yes, it is."

"For what reason?"

"Madeline is a good and dutiful daughter. She has no unnatural temper as you do. She has rarely come to this chamber except when bid do so by your mother."

"Is your privacy so sacrosanct that it warrants this unfairness?"

"Certainly not. That was merely one example in many. I wanted her to have the best possible husband, and for that one must pay. To attract an earl costs considerably more than to get a knight."

"Especially one so old!"

"He is still vigorous enough to get sons. An older man will be better able to control a willful woman and more apt to overlook certain deficiencies."

"I am not deficient!"

"Nor are you a biddable lady. You should thank God and all the angels that you were given this chance for a husband. Especially after you drove away the other two men who asked for you."

"They were but fortune hunters—like this fine but penniless earl."

Randolph's eyes widened at the word "penniless" but then he shrugged. "Why should I give credence to what you say? There has been no sign of miserliness in his gifts, and his knight wears clothing of a fine cut, as do the men who accompanied him. When I met Lord Nicholas last summer, he was astride a fine horse, wore expensive clothes, and did not stint on the food we were served."

"You met him? Face-to-face?"

"Of course. I wouldn't marry Madeline to a perfect stranger." He was watching Jessica as if her words were not entirely rational. "Where did you get the idea this man is penniless?"

"It matters not," she sighed. "All that really matters is the fact that I must marry old Sir Edwin and that you have shamed me in the size of my dowry as compared to Madeline's."

"You should never have been so crass as to ask her what I settled upon her. You shame yourself. As to your own sum, Sir Edwin's name also was not cheap. News of your unsettling behavior has spread throughout the countryside, and I had to pay dearly for this match."

"I am surprised you did not betroth me to some man from as far away as possible," she retorted to hide her hurt.

"I tried. None were willing."

Jessica felt as if he had hit her squarely in the stomach. She stood staring at him, not trusting herself to speak.

A light tap at the door drew Randolph's attention. "Yes?"

A liveried servant came in. "Sir Edwin Fairfax is here, my lord. He wishes to see Lady Jessica."

"She will be down immediately. Have Sir Edwin wait in the arbor."

Jessica remained staring at her father.

"Go to him," Randolph instructed. "Do not keep him waiting."

"If he has to wait, mayhap he will die of old age," she snapped, but then did as she had been told.

The arbor, which lay beside the castle's outer wall, curved over a paved walk. At this time of year the leaves were newly green, giving the sweet air an emerald hue. Up until now this had been Jessica's favorite garden, but henceforth she knew she would always associate this spot with old Edwin. He was waiting for her on a long bench, his wrinkled face as out of place here as a fungus of death. When he saw her, he lurched to his feet.

"Sir Edwin," Jessica said coolly.

"My dear," he responded, capturing her hand and placing a wet kiss on her knuckles.

Jessica jerked her hand away. "You wished to see me for some reason?"

"What lover would not wish to see his bride? I find I cannot keep my eyes from you." He reached out to draw her near.

"Nor your hands, I fear. Kindly do not compromise me in my father's garden." She pushed his groping hands aside.

Edwin chuckled. "I prefer a wench with spirit. It makes for good bed sport."

"I am no 'wench,'" Jessica stated proudly. "My people fought beside Edward the First and were knighted in the field."

"Rumor has it that some of your female ancestors were also nighted by Edward Longshanks. I hope you follow their lusty lead."

Jessica glared at him. His mention of her backhanded royal strain was scarcely a revelation to her. Plantagenet gold hair was a hallmark of her family. "I'll thank you to be civil in my presence."

"Come, I meant not to fash you. Let us walk, shall we?"

She strode off through the green tunnel, miffed to see that Sir Edwin was keeping up with her brisk pace. The arbor branched and curved, taking her farther from the castle. At the end of the vines she stopped to view the rolling hills she had known since birth.

"Yonder lies the church," Edwin said. "In a few short weeks we'll journey there, you and I."

"I am well aware of that."

"I'll make you a good husband," he crowed in keen anticipation. "I've sons in my loins yet."

"You've made that clear. I wonder that you need more sons after the passel bestowed upon you by your former wife."

He grinned as if she had paid him a compliment. "A man can't have too many sons nor too young a wife." He looped his arm around her waist and pulled her to him with surprising strength.

"Unhand me!" she demanded, shoving against his thin chest. Her healthy young muscles broke his embrace, but not before he cruelly slapped her buttocks. "I'm returning to the castle. You may come and see me again when you show me proper respect."

"I'll show you respect," he said as he jerked her back around.

Before Jessica could stop him, Edwin thrust his bony hand into the bodice of her gown and grabbed at her breast as he ground his wet lips against hers. With a strangled cry, Jessica fought him, but this time he was better prepared. He thrust against her so that she fell to the ground with Edwin on top of her. The impact knocked her breathless and she struggled to stay conscious as the sky and grape leaves threatened to dissolve into blackness.

Edwin pinned her beneath him and yanked her skirt up to shove his free hand beneath her petticoats. Pain from his questing fingers and the pebbles being ground into her back jerked Jessica to consciousness. With desperate force she shoved against the old man and rolled to one side. Edwin tumbled from her and she scrambled to her feet.

Grabbing the nearest object, a gardener's hoe, she began striking at the man. Fortunately for Edwin, she held the metal-edged blade and the blunt wooden end bounced off his shoulders. He yelped like a wounded animal and rolled away, trying to fend the blows with his arms.

Jessica felt hands grabbing at her and she cried out in fear before she recognized her father and two of the gardeners trying to restrain her. "Papa!" she gasped in relief. "Sir Edwin tried to . . . to . . ."

"Control yourself!" Randolph ordered.

One of the gardeners had her about the waist and her father held her wrists as the other gardener wrenched the hoe from her hand. Tears blinded Jessica and she had no idea how long she had been crying. As she quit struggling, the gardeners released her cautiously but Randolph retained his hold, his fingers biting into her flesh. Jessica tried to hide her tear-stained face but her father showed no mercy.

"What is the meaning of this disgraceful exhibition?" he demanded.

"Sir Edwin tried to force—"

"I but kissed her, my lord," Edwin interrupted. "A chaste kiss such as is proper between a promised couple. She became a termagant!"

"It was far more than a kiss! He put his hands all over me! Down my dress and beneath my skirt and—"

"Begging your lordship's pardon, but I would never

do such a thing. I have too much respect for you to be unseemly toward your daughter."

"He's lying!" Her skin still ached from his rough touch. "He would have taken me right here in the grape arbor!"

"My lord, I'm astounded!" Sir Edwin gasped. "I cannot believe my ears!"

"It's true, Papa! He would have used me most cruelly," she sobbed.

"Enough, daughter! You confound me," Randolph exclaimed. "Take you, indeed! Give the man credit of having fair intelligence. You say he attacked you, but where is there a tear in your gown?"

Jessica looked down but the fabric of her gown was still whole. "My back," she said frantically. "You can see where I fell to the ground."

"She was dusty when she met me," Edwin lied to her father. Turning to Jessica, he continued, "You were picking flowers in the woods. You must have fallen there."

"I didn't fall—I was thrown down!" Jessica peered imploringly into her father's face, but found only iron resoluteness.

Edwin crept sideways in his eagerness to leave. "My lord, in view of what has happened, I feel I must break the betrothal. I mean, a man can't have a wife that would take a hoe handle to him every time he kisses her. Because I so adored your daughter, I discounted the rumors I've heard of her lunacy as jealous gossip. But her irrational behavior today has convinced me the gossip is true. I would be unable to sleep for fear of my life."

Randolph glared at the servile old man, then back at his daughter. The two gardeners exchanged uneasy glances as if they wished they were far away from the scene. Having no option, Randolph ground out, "Very well, Sir Edwin. You are hereby released by my consent from your betrothal to Lady Jessica." His angry eyes bored into his daughter's.

"If I may say so, my lord, I would lock her away before she does someone harm."

When Randolph didn't answer, Edwin bowed hastily and slunk away. Only when he and the gardeners were gone did Randolph Hargrove release his daughter.

She rubbed her sore wrists where the vivid imprints of Randolph's fingers were already darkening to purple. Her chin quivered, but she fought desperately to keep from shedding further tears.

Neither spoke as the silence seethed between them. Jessica braced herself too late for the blow that sent her sprawling. The gravel cut into her palms as she tried to break her fall. Drawing herself to a half-sitting position, she waited defiantly to see what he would do next. As her father, he had the right to do anything to her short of murder, and she was no stranger to beatings.

To her surprise and relief, he glared at her a minute longer, then turned on his heel and strode back through the arbor. Jessica let her muscles relax and tears streamed from her eyes to bead on the dusty ground.

When she was able to control herself, Jessica stood and brushed the yard rubble from her gown, keeping one eye cautiously on the castle. Her cheek stung and was tender to her touch, but she held her head high as she retraced her steps. Although her father was angrier than she had ever seen him, a part of her refused to believe that he would really lock her away. Oh, he might have her shut up for a few days to frighten her into submission, but Jessica knew her mother wouldn't condone it, and she was the real ruler of the castle. In a matter of days she would be released.

Jessica entered the castle and moved quietly through the hall. If she could reach her chamber and bathe her wrists and cheek in cool water, she would feel better. Until then she didn't want to see anyone.

As she passed her parents' chamber door, she heard their voices speaking her name. Pausing, Jessica waited to hear her fate.

"It was disgraceful," Randolph growled. "Thank God you were spared the humiliation of such a scene."

"She actually struck him?" Devona exclaimed.

"With a hoe! Then accused him of trying to rape her! What man in his right mind would take a maid in broad daylight in her own father's arbor?"

"She must be mad indeed," Devona murmured in a dazed voice. "I assume Sir Edwin broke off the betrothal?"

"Of course he did! I'll be fortunate if he doesn't have her up on charges of assault."

"His pride won't allow that. Randolph, we must lock her away. I know you've fought it, but we must."

"There seems to be no other way," Randolph replied tiredly. "Perhaps for a week or so . . ."

"No. Not for a week—forever."

Jessica's body jerked and bile rose in her throat.

"She is as mad as your brother. For everyone's sake, she must be restrained."

Randolph was silent for a long time. "I will see to it at once."

"Not yet. If we fasten her away before Madeline's wedding, the guests will talk of nothing else. We can't have Lord Nicholas know there is a taint in our family."

" 'Tis Madeline he will wed, not Jessica."

"All the same, he mustn't know. Nor must Jessica

know what we plan to do with her, else she may try to run away."

"A woman alone? Impossible. No house would take her in, her with no servant or companion. She would be treated as a common whore, a walking mort."

"She is our daughter. We cannot allow her to be treated like that, nor can we let her roam free in the castle now that she is becoming violent."

"You speak well of the truth." His voice was tired and curiously old. Jessica wanted to leave the door and hear no more of her fate, but she seemed rooted to the stone floor.

"I will have the window replaced in Leopold's cell and order the rushes and bedding changed. I can do this when Jessica is busy with other tasks, and she will never suspect." Devona's voice was also sad and weary. "I suppose Sir Raymond reported all is still well with the marriage plans for Madeline?"

"Yes. The only hitch is that Lord Nicholas will be detained until almost the day of the wedding. He and Madeline will have little time to get to know one another before the ceremony."

"A shame, but it can't be helped. They will have ample time afterward." Following a long silence, Devona spoke again, with great reluctance in her tone. "As soon as the earl and his retinue leave, we will take Jessica to the tower."

After a pause, Randolph replied, "It will be as you say. What a pity I did not end our sufferings that day in this very chamber. We would have been spared so much."

"How could you?" his wife soothed. "They were so alike. What if you had taken dear Madeline by mistake?"

Jessica had no idea what her mother meant, but

her future was all too clear. Trembling, she hurried to the chamber she shared with Madeline and shut the door before either of her parents could discover her in the corridor.

So little time was left! Jessica went to the window and pushed open the single small pane. When the last of the wedding guests departed, she was to be locked away in that odorous cell. She wasn't mad now, but she knew she soon would be under those conditions. She had often wondered how poor Leopold had managed to survive as long as he did. The cell was stifling in summer and had no source of heat in winter. Not to mention the servants who had treated him like a menagerie beast and who must have tormented him on the sly.

Yet there was no escape in leaving Hargrove Castle. If she found rape by Sir Edwin unbearable, she could never face the nightly rape by a series of strangers that she would have to subject herself to in order to earn enough gold to live. No, she was no harlot. She even doubted she would be able to run far enough away to become one, if that was her desire. Her father would be watching her as a hawk does a rabbit. If she were to miss a single meal, her father would have his men scouring the countryside for her.

In defiance, she tore off her betrothal ring and threw it out the window. She almost wished she could follow it. Still, there were a few more precious weeks of freedom. Some avenue of escape might still open.

4

JESSICA WATCHED AS Madeline took one of her prettiest dresses from her brass-bound chest and motioned for her maid to comb her hair. "Why are you going to such trouble? No one is here to see you but our family." She smoothed the skirt of her own clean but sun-faded pink velvet.

"I enjoy looking my best," Madeline said, swatting at the maid for pulling her tangled hair. "Besides, Sir Raymond is here."

Jessica shrugged and drew her ivory brush through her thick golden waves. "What of it? He is only the emissary of your betrothed."

"It's a matter of pride. What think you? Is the gold locket or the pearl brooch prettier with this gown?" Madeline held first one, then the other to the low bodice of the moss-green dress.

"The brooch. And that dress is cut much too low for day wear."

"I don't think so. Besides, I will soon be a married woman and have to cover my bosom all the time." Madeline pouted prettily at the mirror.

"Likely you'll catch fewer colds," her sister observed dryly. "Head rheums aren't the most attractive diseases."

"You might have loaned me your Eastern hyacinth to wear as protection. You aren't as susceptible to colds as I am. Last winter I reeked all season of vinegar and mulberry syrup."

"It wasn't so noticeable. Besides, I doubt the jewel has the power to prevent disease."

"Then why would you not lend me yours?"

"You lost your own and would likely have lost mine as well. I may not believe in it, but I think it's a pretty ornament." Satisfied that she looked passably well, Jessica sat on the flock bed she shared with Madeline and leaned her cheek against the carved bedpost. "Aunt Catherine and her retinue arrived this morning. She is the first of the wedding guests. Only think," she sighed, rolling onto her back, "in another week you will be a married woman."

"You are rumpling your dress," Madeline chastised automatically, then peered thoughtfully at her own reflection.

Jessica spread her arms and gazed up at the familiar ceiling. Only one more week of freedom for her. In the past few days, however, she had formed a plan. The castle would be packed with relatives and acquaintances for Madeline's wedding. Even yeomen and tenant farmers would turn out for the event. With luck, Jessica planned to steal a servant's dress and smuggle herself out in the confusion. She was adept at sewing and house management, though she disliked both, and could possibly find work in a distant manor if she passed herself off as the orphaned daughter of a housekeeper. The plan was extreme and fraught with danger, but the alternative was unthinkable. Her most difficult task would be finding a manor or castle where a new servant was needed.

"Are you daydreaming?" Madeline asked impatiently. "I said I hear the dinner bell ringing."

Jessica slid off the bed and glanced at her reflection in passing. Next to Madeline she looked like a poor relation, but at least her dress was aired and pressed. Besides, she thought Madeline overdressed for a meal whose only guest was their mother's sister. She secretly hoped her parents would send Madeline back up to change into more appropriate attire. Not that they would, of course. As far as they were concerned, Madeline was more perfect than ever these days.

The servant was still ringing his silver hand bell when Jessica and Madeline joined their parents and aunt in the vestibule. Jessica politely curtsied to her aunt, Madeline did the same, saying, "Dear Aunt Catherine, how nice to see you." Her sweet lisp was back on her lips, Jessica noticed.

"There's our bride." Her aunt beamed. "Such a pretty girl. Both of you," she added.

Jessica wondered if her mother had confided their family problems to her sister. "Was your journey pleasant?"

"Adequate," her aunt replied, her eyes searching Jessica's face cautiously.

She knew, Jessica deduced from her aunt's expression. As unearned guilt swept over her, Jessica hid it by lifting her chin proudly.

From beyond the door to the hall, the sounds of stools and benches scraping on the stone floor beneath the rushes and the scuffling of the servants as they made ready for the meal drew everyone's attention. Then, as if by signal, Randolph opened the door and ushered in his family. Again furniture bumped and scraped as everyone stood up in deference to the nobility.

Jessica went to her usual seat on the dais beside her father. Madeline, in honor of her aunt, gave her the seat beside her mother. Below the raised table of the family, the double row of trestle tables extended to the far end of the hall. Halfway down each stood the ornate silver salt cellars. Above them were seated the steward, the family chaplain, the gentlemen ushers, and Devona's ladies-in-waiting. Beyond, half-hidden from the main table, were the servants of the castle who weren't assigned to the kitchen, some tenant farmers who had come to transact business with the steward, and a couple of dust-stained travelers who happened to be passing by and had asked to be fed.

The hum of too many incoherent conversations flowed about her, and Jessica found she was nervously clenching her cold hands in her lap beneath the damask cloth. She couldn't allow herself to be locked away! Her plan for escape *must* work. Mentally, she went over her list of candidate maids and chose two who were about her size and height. Surely one of them would be out of her chamber long enough for Jessica to slip in and take a plain gown. She studied the women seated below the salt, noting their flamboyant gestures. Passing as the daughter of a servant would entail more than a mere change of clothes.

The steward rose and tapped his white wand for silence. At once all conversation halted and heads bowed as the chaplain stood and said grace. Jessica repeated her own prayer until she heard the usual closing phrase of blessing for Queen Elizabeth and the country. At the amen, the conversation resumed as if there had been no pause.

Under the pretense of sipping her malmsey, Jessica studied the way the common women ate, using either hand and wiping their lips on their sleeves. She wouldn't enjoy it, but she could do that. They also talked with their mouths full and laughed uproariously with the men and each other. Jessica decided that whether necessary or not, she wouldn't give up all her manners. That was asking too much.

The carver presented Randolph with a farsed hen and he gave the nod for the man to begin spoiling it. Two serving lads brought in a roasted goose to be reared, and the meal was under way.

Jessica dipped her fingers in the offered silver bowl and dried her hands on the linen towel presented by another servant. Daintily she started to eat the delicate white meat. Beside her, Randolph motioned for his official taster to begin taking the say to see if the food was poisoned. Jessica thought this was a silly custom, since the entire family was already eating that same fowl.

She dipped her smallest finger in the salt dish and conveyed it to her plate. From the corner of her eye she saw the lowborn women doing much the same over the coarser fare on their trenchers. There was so much to remember, and she had never paid much attention to the commoners' habits before.

When Randolph was finished, the butler made a deep bow to him and ceremoniously carried away the large salt cellar. Jessica hastily dipped her fingers in the bowl to rid herself of the sticky fruit juice of the last course and dried her hands as the chaplain again stood and gave thanks for the meal. When his amen was sounded, the din resumed amid the clatter of stools being pushed aside above the salt and benches below it. In the past hour Jessica had learned a great deal. She decided to spend the next few hours in the kitchen observing the maids.

Madeline smiled at Sir Raymond, who had been seated at right angles to her side of the table. As her betrothed's emissary, he had a favored position opposite Mistress Anne, her mother's primary lady-in-waiting, or decayed gentlewoman, as Devona sometimes referred to her.

Chadwick returned her smile, though his thoughts had been drifting in a dismal direction. As yet she had not firmly decided to break the betrothal. Since that afternoon in the forest when Jessica had overheard them, he and Madeline had had little opportunity to talk. Each time he tried to bring up the subject, she said that she was still thinking and wasn't ready to discuss it. With the wedding day almost upon them, Chadwick was growing very uneasy. But his nervousness was not solely due to his fear that he might fail in his mission. Every time he was near Madeline, he had to fight his arousal. The woman was exciting at the very least, if not outwardly enticing. Had even a slim possibility existed that she would truly be interested in him, he would have begun to court her, but such thoughts were folly. He would concentrate on achieving his goal or prepare to suffer the wrath of Sir James Swineford.

"Your father sets a fine meal," Raymond said in a low voice as he escorted Madeline to the door after the meal. "Would that Wyndfell could boast of such. Unfortunately, my lord is miserly in addition to his other faults."

Madeline glanced back to be certain no one could overhear her. "It is time we spoke more of this, sir knight. May I show you our parapet?"

She led him through the castle's winding corridors

to a set of spiraling steps within the far turret. "Stay near, I beg. I've not much head for heights."

Raymond obediently pressed his body nearer hers and Madeline smiled, for she had fearlessly climbed these steps all her life, but Sir Raymond didn't know that. "The view is quite spectacular," she said when he looked around to see if anyone was watching them.

"No view could be as sweet as the one I have now of your swanlike neck," he ventured.

"Why, sir! You'll have my head spinning," she flirted shamelessly. With quick steps she led him upward.

The stairs ended on a broad landing that led past an unused guardhouse and out onto the parapet. Madeline stepped up to the stone walkway, remembering to cling to Raymond's arm as if overcome by trepidation.

To one side lay the narrow courtyard and castle proper, to the other rolled a breathtaking view of field and woods. Madeline sighed happily. "Someday this will all be mine," she said as if she were thinking aloud.

Raymond's eyes narrowed speculatively. He was besotted by her, but never so much as to ignore monetary considerations. "What of your sister? Will not half go to her?"

"Poor Jessica is not as healthy as she seems," Madeline confided. "I will be vastly surprised if I see her when next I come to Hargrove Castle."

"As ill as that?"

Madeline nodded. "I've no other brothers or sisters. They all lie beneath the church, as will dear Jessica." She summoned her ever-ready supply of tears and turned so that Raymond could see her damp cheeks.

"Here now! You're crying," he exclaimed.

"Am I? It's only that I pity my sister so. Oh, Sir Raymond, whatever will I do? I'm cruelly betrothed to a man any lady would hate—and me an heiress to a great fortune."

"Surely something can be done about it. Perhaps if you speak to your father and tell him that you do not wish to marry my master."

"As I told you before, that would never do! My wedding guests are already arriving. To call it off now would bring great shame to me and my family." She glanced at him. "And surely Lord Nicholas would retaliate, would he not?"

"Aye, that he would." Chadwick, who wasn't adept at logic and reasoning, hadn't fully considered the scope of the earl's reaction to losing his bride.

Madeline hid her smirk by burying her face in her hands. "How dreadful even to consider it!"

"There, there. Surely we can think of something," Raymond soothed, patting her shoulder awkwardly.

Turning, Madeline pressed herself into his arms. He looked down at the courtyard hastily and edged back into the shadowy doorway. Madeline put her arms about him as if in great need of comfort, then eased him into the empty guardroom.

"Oh, Raymond," she sighed, using the familiarity of his name like a silken weapon. "You're so strong, so handsome. If only I were betrothed to you. How happy I would be."

Raymond swallowed hard, then remembered to breathe. "Lady Madeline, I . . ."

"Forgive me. How could I have been so forward! The words have been so often in my mind that they slipped free of their own accord." She looked suitably mortified.

"No, no. You mistake me. I was about to say that I,

too, wish it were true." Suddenly Chadwick's fear of Nicholas' retribution was overshadowed by the realization of his fantasy.

Madeline gazed up at him, her blue eyes round and her lips parted as if in surprise. "You do?"

"I shouldn't say this, but you have rarely been out of my thoughts since the day you allowed me to kiss you in the gallery."

"That was dreadfully bold of me," she encouraged.

"My lady," he said hoarsely, all too conscious of the way her breasts pressed against his chest, "I think I love you."

"Oh!" she exclaimed happily. "Is it true?"

"Yes. Yes, I *know* I do."

"Raymond!" She threw her arms around his neck and pulled his head down to kiss her.

At first he was reticent, half-afraid she would be offended or that someone would ascend the narrow stairs. Then he succumbed to her considerable expertise and kissed her roughly, his mouth grinding over hers.

Instead of pulling away, Madeline met his violence with a greedy purr. His tongue plunged into her open mouth and she sucked it wantonly. Lust boiled in his veins and he was hard-pressed not to rip her gown as he thrust his groping hand inside to fondle her breast. Madeline undulated her body to give him better access and moaned when he pinched her hard nipple.

"Madeline," he groaned. "Give me the strength to stop before it's too late."

"No! Don't stop. If I must be given to a monster," she said passionately, "let me at least have this day of love."

With shaking hands, Raymond released the fastenings of her dark green gown, revealing the pale yellow of her kirtle beneath. He pulled roughly at the back lacings to remove the kirtle as well. When it billowed to the dusty floor with the gown, Raymond massaged Madeline's full breasts through the thin chemise as she untied her petticoats.

His breath was ragged in the silence as he jerked the bodice down to reveal twin pink buds. Her breasts were larger than he had thought from the tight-bodiced kirtle, and they peaked firmly in his palms, urging him on.

Madeline stepped free of her petticoats and started to untie the ribbon that held her long chemise. With a growl Raymond snapped the ribbon, leaving a vivid mark on her pale shoulders. Madeline moaned with excitement as he thrust the cloth away from her, leaving her in her white silk stockings and silver-buckled cloth shoes.

With pretended modesty, she tried to conceal her ripe breasts and the nest of her womanhood, but Raymond was past subtleties. Yanking her to him, he pinned her arms behind her slender back, forcing her breasts to jut forward. Madeline rolled her head back in ecstasy as he forced her to stillness and nipped painfully at first one nipple, then the other. Only when her breasts were wet and glowing from his kisses did he force her to the floor.

Madeline rolled onto her back on the pile of her garments and watched hungrily as Raymond ripped down his breeches and untied the points that held up his trunk hose, not bothering to remove his doublet. Raymond's engorged member rose to meet her, and Madeline's eyes flickered with greed.

He spread her legs with no ceremony and thrust deeply inside her. Madeline cried out, not from discomfort, for the act was not new to her, but from extreme pleasure. His brocade doublet scratched her sensitive breasts and made her arch toward him to intensify the exquisite agony. He savagely pounded her again and again, and Madeline uttered a guttural groan as ecstasy ripped through her in waves of pleasurable pain. Never had she been taken with such force, such bestial need. And she loved it. Raymond gave a grunt and spent himself deep inside her, then collapsed upon her in heaving gasps.

"Oh, my dear," Madeline murmured with pretended coyness. "What have we done?"

Slowly Raymond raised on one elbow and stared at her angelic face. "I ... I couldn't help myself," he stammered between breaths.

"Hush," she whispered silkily. "For true, I love you more than ever."

His expression was incredulous, and he could think of nothing to say.

"After this I could never wed another," she continued. "You're the only man for me."

"You'd ... you'd marry me?" he exclaimed. "Me?"

"Oh, Raymond! You've made me the happiest of women. I will be honored to be your wife." She threw her arms about him and hugged him close.

"But your father ..."

"We mustn't tell him of our plans! Truly we mustn't. Just trust me, dear one. Everything will work out beautifully." She beamed up at him, the bewitching dimple playing in her cheek. And how beautiful, indeed, she thought. Raymond was not only a satisfying lover, but kind and caring as well. He had risked a great deal for her and she was grateful.

Raymond was captivated, body and soul. Not only had he broken the betrothal, but he had won the bride in the bargain.

*   *   *

Jessica walked quietly through the back regions of the castle, alone for the first time in days. She had tried to sneak off to the maids' quarters several times, but people always seemed to be with her or near her, and she couldn't tell them to leave without arousing suspicion. Evidently her parents thought she would do something to cause the wedding to be canceled and had told Madeline and the maidservants to watch Jessica constantly. Her steps faltered as she realized that what she was about to do would likely be viewed as insane if she were caught. But the wedding was set for that very afternoon and this was her final chance.

Once she had assured herself that none of her servants had traced her, Jessica slipped into the maids' chamber. Quickly she moved around the room, pulling first one garment, then another off the wall pegs where they hung, and holding them to her to check for size. Most were far too large, and she had no time for alterations.

Moving into another room that led off the first, she stepped over the straw pallets to inspect these garments as well. All the servants owned at least one change of clothes, and a few hooks held two extra dresses. To Jessica's relief, she found the peg that held the clothes belonging to the girl being trained as the cook's helper. She was about the right size and Jessica was sure these clothes were hers because of a curiously shaped patch on one skirt. Taking the other blue dress, Jessica looked around guiltily. Never in her life had she stolen anything. To salve her conscience, she dropped three shillings—more than enough to replace the dress—in the pocket of the patched gown.

Lifting her skirts, Jessica tied the servant's dress beneath her kirtle and fluffed her gown back in place. With no mirror, she couldn't see whether it was well hidden, but her nervous hands told her the extra bulge about her hips would likely not be noticed beneath her voluminous kirtle and overgown.

She was about to leave when she heard the door to the outer room open. She pressed her body against the wall and prayed that whoever it was would not enter the inner chamber.

From the next room she heard the plain voices of two of the maids and a quick laugh as one replied to the other's sally. Jessica closed her eyes and willed with all her might that they would leave.

One of the voices seemed to be nearing but the other called her back. "You've no time to go nosing about in there," she said.

"But this is a good chance to see if my Rob gave that little slut a token."

"Don't be daft. One posy looks like another. Besides, the groom has come. I saw his retinue approaching as we came down here. If we don't get back to work, we'll be missed for sure."

"All right," the nearest voice said reluctantly. "But she had best not be seeing my Rob or it's sorry she'll be."

"Come along. You can fight her for him later."

Jessica heard footsteps cross the floor; then the door slammed. She let out her caged breath. She could have offered no possible explanation for her presence here. If the maids had seen her, she would most likely have been locked away at once, wedding or not.

She forced herself to stay put for several moments. Then she crept into the larger room and hurried to the door. Opening it a crack, she saw the maids' skirts disappear around the far corner that led to the kitchen. Taking a deep breath, Jessica stepped out into the hall and briskly walked back the way she had come. Suddenly the servants stolen gown seemed enormously bulky and she feared anyone might notice it beneath her skirt.

Every time she met someone, she slowed her pace and tried to appear as though she had nothing on her mind except the afternoon's wedding. Luckily the castle was in such a turmoil of last-minute preparations that no one noticed her at all.

On reaching her chamber, Jessica shut the door and leaned against it as she fumbled to untie the purloined gown. As she had planned days before, she rolled back her top flock mattress, laid the dress on the one beneath, and pulled the first one to cover it. As she again smoothed the satin coverlet, she heaved a sigh of relief. The dress would be safe here until that afternoon. She could slip away from the wedding guests, change clothes, and be gone before her parents had finished toasting the bride and groom.

As she nervously awaited the wedding ceremony, curiosity about the mysterious Lord Nicholas Garrett overcame her. Could he really be as ugly as Sir Raymond had said? Surely her father would never have given his favored Madeline to such as that. Unable to curb her curiosity, Jessica left her chamber and slipped down to the ladies' parlor that overlooked the courtyard. If Sir Raymond had lied, she wanted to tell Madeline not to worry. This seemed to be the least she could do, as her disappearance would likely turn the wedding feast topsy-turvy in a matter of hours. Although Madeline had done much to cause hard feelings between them, Jessica now knew that many of the problems had originated with their parents. It wasn't Madeline who insisted that she be locked away. It was her father, and her mother in

particular. Before nightfall, she would be well gone
and away from it all.

Pushing open a diamond-shaped window, Jessica
leaned out. The retinue was still milling about in the
courtyard, so she searched for some man who might
fit the unpleasant description. As she scanned the
crowd, her attention stopped on her parents and the
man who stood next to them. She straightened in
surprise as the stranger turned his head toward her.
Their eyes met, and he paused in his gestures as if
he might be feeling the same curious stirring she
was. He was tall, well-built, and startlingly handsome. Hair as black as a raven's wing blew over his
forehead and shone in the sunlight.

Jessica drew back slightly as her mother greeted
him with a polite kiss. There could be no mistake.
This was Lord Nicholas Garrett, Earl of Wyndfell.
Again he glanced from her parents toward Jessica,
and this time he grinned, showing strong white teeth
in his black, close-cropped beard.

At this distance, Jessica knew that only the cut and
color of her dress would distinguish her from Madeline, and that Lord Nicholas must believe her to be
his bride. Her suspicions were confirmed as he swept
his velvet hat across the steps in a gracious bow.
Before her parents could follow his line of sight,
Jessica quickly withdrew into the room.

The door opened and Mistress Anne entered. "Lady
Madeline? I've looked everywhere for you." She
squinted at Jessica in nearsighted confusion.

" 'Tis I, Jessica," she corrected. "You seek my sister?"

"Everyone is searching for her," the older woman
complained. "The groom is here at last, late by several hours, and now no one can find Lady Madeline.
'Tis most distressing. We must leave for the church

in an hour and she has neither met her groom nor started to dress."

"Don't be vexed. I will help you find her." Not only did Jessica want to see her sister to reassure her that Sir Raymond, for some strange reason, had lied about Lord Nicholas' appearance, but she needed the wedding to take place on time so she could make good her escape. Jessica thought how fortunate Madeline was, for Lord Nicholas was more handsome than any man she had ever seen.

Jessica knew all the castle's hiding places, having used them herself at one time or another, but Madeline was nowhere to be found. She ran out to the stables, thinking perhaps her sister had gone for a ride, but the head groom had not seen her all day. Madeline was unlikely to be in the other outbuildings that rimmed the castle wall, but Jessica looked anyway, even peering into the smelly brewhouse and equally smelly mews.

The courtyard was crowded to overflowing with strange men wearing the green livery of Wyndfell, a gold griffin emblazoned on their breasts. Commoners from all over the parish crowded the gates and were already lining the road to view the wedding party. The Hargrove servants ran about with more alacrity than was usual, cheerfully shouting orders to one another. Delicious smells wafted from both kitchens, as the cooks had been at work for days in preparation for the enormous wedding feast.

When Jessica entered the hall, her mother rushed up to her. "Where is Madeline?" she demanded in a harried voice.

"I've not seen her. Is she still not found?"

"I have the servants searching for her," Devona said with obvious concern. "Where could the girl be? Her groom grows impatient, as well he might. We are nearly ready to leave for the church and she is nowhere to be found." Devona looked disdainfully at Jessica. "What are you wearing! Go change into your best dress. Quickly! We cannot wait for you once we find Madeline."

Jessica glanced down at the dress. In her worry about stealing the servant's gown she had forgotten to change for the wedding. "I'll go, Mama. And don't worry about Madeline. She wouldn't miss her own wedding."

Jessica hurried back to her chamber, hoping that Madeline had returned of her own accord and was already dressing. Jessica dared not delay the procession to the church and draw attention to herself. Today of all days she must be the model of propriety. But when she got there, the room was empty. If the wedding was postponed, their parents might change their plans and lock her up anyway. A deep frown furrowed her brow.

She knelt by her trunk and started to take out the gown she reserved for Sundays and festivals, then paused as she looked thoughtfully at Madeline's trunk. A new and daring idea began to form. No. That was too dangerous even to consider.

As she started to unlace her gown, Jessica remembered one place she had not thought to look. Most likely no one else had gone to the parapet either. The chances Madeline would be there were almost nonexistent, but as she was nowhere else, Jessica decided to take a quick look before changing.

She ran down the corridor and up the stairs that curved up to the parapet. No one ever went up there, but Madeline had liked the place as a child.

Jessica glanced in the empty guardroom and stepped out onto the sentry walkway. On one side, far below, the courtyard teemed with jostling bodies.

Toward the front of the castle, the roadway was almost as full. Everyone was crowding to see the groom and his retinue. By leaning over the parapet, Jessica could see toward the back of the castle, where the skirt of grass sloped sharply down to the thick woodlands. In the distance were two very familiar riders.

"Madeline!" she shouted out. "Come back!"

Madeline drew up her mount and Sir Raymond looked back toward the parapet where Jessica was waving frantically. Madeline laughed and blew her sister a kiss before sending her horse plunging after Sir Raymond. In moments they were swallowed by the woods.

Jessica stared in stunned amazement. Suddenly everything made sense. The sly looks Madeline had cast toward Sir Raymond, her numerous comments about his good looks, the lies he had told about Lord Nicholas. They had been courting each other all along! And now they had eloped!

For an instant Jessica started to run to tell her father so he could go after Madeline, but she stopped. If Madeline was set on eloping with one man when she had another waiting to take her to church, she would never go through with the wedding anyway. And if she didn't, Lord Nicholas was sure to take revenge on her family. Breaking a betrothal would cause bad blood between the houses, but to stand a groom up at the very altar would be tantamount to declaring war.

Thoughts crowded into Jessica's mind as she looked from the busy courtyard to the empty green. Resolutely she made her decision. With no time to waste, she gathered her skirts and ran back to her chamber.

5

AS SOON AS she reached her bedchamber, Jessica kicked the door shut behind her. She hastily removed her gown and kirtle and stuffed them in her trunk. Then she stripped to the skin and washed herself hastily. Now that her decision was made, she dared not pause to think. Her plan was a desperate one, but not only would it see her safely away from Hargrove Castle, it would save her family's good name.

She pulled Madeline's fine lawn chemise over her head and tied the pale blue ribbon at the low neck, then tied the ribbons that held the ends of the sleeves to her wrist. Next she chose, from among Madeline's silk stockings, the ones with a clock design embroidered in gold. She pulled them on, smoothing out the wrinkles and securing the tops with silver-buckled velvet garters. Quickly she yanked the ribbon from her hair and brushed her tresses until they flowed in gleaming topaz waves below her waist. As a bride she would be expected to wear her hair unbound and her head uncovered.

As she stepped into the turquoise velvet kirtle that Madeline had encrusted with gold embroidery, the door flew open, and Jessica's heart stopped. Mistress Anne and three of the maids burst in.

"Lady Madeline! There you are!"

"Yes, Mistress Anne," Jessica said, quickly swallowing the lump in her throat and remembering to keep her voice soft.

"You naughty girl! Where have you been?" The woman motioned for the maids to come to Jessica's aid.

It had occurred to Jessica that Madeline would need a good excuse for her absence, so she was ready for the question. "Forgive me. I have been looking for my betrothal ring. I took it off yesterday while bathing and now it is gone. I've looked everywhere."

The maids pulled up her kirtle and helped her draw the sleeves over her arms. As one laced the dress up the back, another took the canary-yellow overgown from the chest. The third helped Jessica step into the heavily embroidered glove-leather shoes, then buttoned them at her ankles.

"Your mother is frantic," Mistress Anne continued as she took the hairbrush and began stroking it through Jessica's hair.

Jessica slipped on the overgown and held still as the maids fastened it before pulling tufts of her chemise sleeves through the slits in her kirtle. Mistress Anne gestured at the door and a serving girl entered with a garland of flowers. Devona was close upon her heels.

"Finally!" her mother scolded. "Where have you been? Never mind. Just hold still while I put these flowers in your hair."

Jessica couldn't have moved if the castle were burning down around her. If her mother even suspected she had taken Madeline's place, she would be un-done forever.

Devona scarcely looked at her daughter as she fastened the garland atop Jessica's head so that it trailed down, entwining with her fair hair. "Where is your sister?" she demanded.

Jessica's eyes widened before she realized what her mother meant. "I know not, Mother," she said with Madeline's sweet lisp. "I assumed her to be down in the hall."

Devona sighed as she patted a nonexistent wrinkle from Jessica's gown. "That girl will see me in an early grave. Pray that she does nothing to embarrass us until the guests are gone!"

With an effort, Jessica bit back the retort that sprang to her tongue.

"You're beautiful," Devona said affectionately. "What man seeing you would not fall in love?"

Jessica gave her Madeline's closed-lip smile and lowered her eyes shyly.

"Come along. Quickly, love, quickly! Everyone awaits your arrival. Don't pull up on your dress like that. It's supposed to be cut that low. Good heavens, child, one would think you'd never had it on before."

Jessica quit trying to make the bodice rise to a more discreet height and let her creamy breasts mound above the fabric. Narrow white velvet rib-bons had been basted to the sleeves and the skirt of her overgown, and she fingered one nervously as she followed her mother and Mistress Anne down to the hall.

The din was overbearing, but Jessica paused as she came in sight of the gathering, and a hush descended on the throng. With all eyes on her, she regally lifted her chin, hoping that no one would notice how much it was trembling. There was no turning back.

Beside her father stood the handsome man she had seen from the window. He had changed from his traveling clothes into a deep garnet velvet jerkin over gold netherstocks. His cloak was so dark a blue as to be almost black and was encrusted with gold embroidery, seed pearls, and jewels. It appeared to be lined with pale cream satin. Across the chest he wore a heavy gold chain of exquisite workmanship. As before, their eyes met and held and Jessica grew short of breath from the sensation in the pit of her stomach. Fear gripped her and she had to lock her knees to keep from turning and running upstairs.

Then Nicholas Garrett smiled and walked to the foot of the stairs without once taking his eyes from her face. Slowly Jessica came down to meet him, and when he held out his hand to receive her, she willingly obliged. His hand was firm and warm as it closed over her fingers, and she couldn't take her eyes from his. The irises were velvety black and the skin at the corners of his eyes was wrinkled as if he smiled often. His forehead was smooth and his skin sweet-smelling. His beard was clean and well-trimmed.

Randolph joined them and said proudly, "Lord Nicholas, may I present my daughter Madeline, your bride."

Nicholas' teeth flashed in a look of adoration that moved Jessica's soul and she could only stare at him as if stunned. Slowly she sank into a formal curtsy; then he raised her to her feet.

"My lady, I am honored." His voice was mellow and deep in a tone that stirred sleeping fires within her.

"The honor is mine," she murmured softly.

"Well done," Randolph boomed. "Now to the church."

Jessica let herself be swept outside. Two of her

young male cousins rushed forward and caught the white bride's laces that dangled from her skirt and sleeves. With broad grins and jests, they led her forward and down the steps to the courtyard. An older boy, the son of her Aunt Catherine, walked ahead, quite serious about his role as leader of the bridal procession. In his arms he bore the large silver cup, trimmed with sprigs of gilded rosemary, and filled with spiced wine. Behind her, Jessica heard the group of musicians fall in and begin playing a lilting tune.

She kept her eyes on her cousin's heels and hoped no one would notice that she wasn't who she seemed to be. For once the physical likeness that usually resulted in her being blamed for Madeline's misdeeds was working in her favor. A new and dreadful thought suddenly struck her. Suppose Madeline hadn't eloped at all, but was only going for a ride to delay the wedding? She might return at any minute! Jessica felt faint from fear. Perhaps she was indeed mad to have concocted this scheme. But it was much too late to change her course.

As she passed, the tenants, yeomen, and peasants doffed their woolen caps and their wives and daughters curtsied. Jessica remembered to keep a smile on her lips, but inside she was shaking violently.

Behind the band of lutes, viols, and flutes walked the bridesmaids, mainly comprising her cousins, as Madeline had few friends. Several of them carried the heavy bride's cake. With them walked Lord Nicholas. Jessica could feel his eyes on her back with every step. In his belt he wore a bunch of rosemary, supposedly gathered by his bride, as a token of his manly attributes. Jessica assumed her mother or one of the maids had picked the rosemary, since Madeline had evidently been hiding out for some time.

Following the groom were her parents, walking with a man she guessed to be Nicholas' brother, due to his resemblance. Sir Raymond had said that Nicholas' parents were no longer living, so this brother must be his only family representative. Jessica was profoundly thankful her parents were so far away, for she wasn't at all sure she could fool them on close inspection. Following her parents was her bevy of cousins.

As the gray walls of the church drew nearer, she stared at them as if she were being drawn to her death. Of all the stupid ideas she had ever had, this was by far the worst. She was led up the steps and into the cool shadows of the nave. The music sounded louder as the procession followed her inside. Because her father had already given Madeline away in her betrothal ceremony, they proceeded directly into the chancel, where the parish vicar and a dean were already waiting. Jessica had never noticed the central aisle was so long, nor the church so cold. Beneath her feet lay slabs of stone engraved with the names of her ancestors and her brother who had died before her birth. She studied the familiar words to keep from looking at the altar.

The musicians quieted and Jessica felt the warm presence of someone beside her. Gazing up, she found herself looking again into the eyes of Nicholas Garrett. He smiled and took her hand, squeezing it gently as if to reassure her. Jessica faintly returned his smile, knowing he would probably run her through with his sword, if he knew of her terrible deception.

The dean began the service, his slightly nasal voice reaching over the shufflings and coughs of the crowd. At the end of his address, the vicar said in a singsong voice, "Do you, Nicholas Garrett, Earl of Wyndfell, Viscount of Penshire, knight of the order of St.

Michael and St. George, take this woman as your wife?"

"I do," Nicholas' voice range out firmly.

"Do you promise to honor her and love her, protect her and keep her for as long as you shall live?"

"I do."

The vicar turned to Jessica. "Do you, Lady Madeline Hargrove, of Hargrove Castle, come to this marriage of your own free will?"

Jessica thought of the cell that awaited her at Hargrove Castle. "I do," she said with resolution.

"Do you promise to honor this man and obey him in all ways, to care for him and be his helpmeet for as long as you do live?"

"I do." This time she remembered to use Madeline's gentle tone and to lower her eyes demurely.

"You have brought the ring?" the vicar said to the groom.

Nicholas took it from his own smallest finger, and taking Jessica's right hand, he placed it first on her index finger, then the next two, saying, "In the name of the Father, Son, and Holy Ghost, I thee wed." Then he placed the ring on the third finger of her left hand.

Jessica looked down at the golden ring, fashioned like two clasped hands holding a large garnet full of fire. Faintly she heard Nicholas say, "With this ring I thee wed, with this gold I thee honor, with this dowry I thee endow."

The vicar nodded. "Before God and all this company, by the authority invested in me, I now pronounce you man and wife."

It was over. Jessica blinked at the enormity of what she had done. If Madeline rode up now, would Jessica be the legal bride? Or would Madeline, since Jessica had married in her name? There was no time to ponder this dilemma because Nicholas pulled her to him and pressed his lips against hers. She opened her eyes wide at the soft touch of his beard and his warm lips. The sweet scent of his breath was still in her mouth as he gazed down at her in proud possession. Nothing else seemed to exist as she drowned in the gentleness of his eyes.

Then the crowd rushed forward and Jessica shrank against her new husband as the young men grabbed for her bride's laces and pulled them off so they could twine them about their caps. Nicholas good-humoredly let them jerk at the white ribbons, but when one grasped Jessica's sleeve, Nicholas pushed him aside.

"Enough," he bellowed in his deep voice. "Would you strip my bride at the very altar? Back, I say." Although he still grinned, the crowd eased back. The power he commanded was clearly evident to all.

Jessica glanced up at him thankfully. She had seen more than one bride leave the church in rags and tatters. Devona came forward and pressed their joined hands as she looked fondly from one to the other. Jessica turned away quickly and bent her head so that her hair half-hid her face.

Randolph began handing out wedding gifts of scarves and gloves to the older guests and brooches to the younger ones, as Nicholas had before Jessica came down to the hall. When all were satisfied, he motioned for the bride and groom to lead them back to the nave.

Nicholas inclined his arm to Jessica and she hesitantly placed her hand upon his wrist. As they walked back into the large chamber he said, "Are you always so quiet, little one? Surely this match was not against your will."

"Oh, no, my lord. I daresay no bride ever went more thankfully to the altar."

He glanced at her curiously, but she didn't elaborate. "I am amazed not to see my man Sir Raymond Chadwick here. Have you seen him today?"

"Only from a distance," she answered truthfully.

"I understand it not. Shortly after I arrived, he sent me a note which I assume was meant to explain his absence. Unfortunately, Sir Raymond is almost illiterate and the note was incomprehensible. I made out your name and a few other words, but I have no idea what the note was meant to convey. Did you send him on an errand?"

"Not I, my lord."

"I suppose his departure must have been of some importance for him to have left thus, but the mystery will have to wait until I see him." Nicholas' expression softened as he thought of his bride. "But no matter. You are all I need to fill my mind this day. Truly your miniature did you little justice."

She looked up at him and remembered to smile with her lips closed, for everyone was watching them. "You flatter me, my lord."

"No, I speak the truth. You are more beautiful than I was led to believe."

Jessica laughed and a dimple appeared in her cheek. "And you are far more handsome than I expected. Tell me, have you a fierce temper?"

"A temper? No more than any other man, I wager. Did Sir Raymond not tell you I am a saint among men? A paragon of knighthood?"

"Not in quite those words."

"Then I made a poor choice of envoy, for I believe such lies to be the rule in matchmaking."

"Did he say such flattering lies about me?"

Nicholas bent his head toward her. "No words could adequately describe your beauty and sweetness."

Having never been called sweet in her entire life, Jessica blushed.

In a lower voice he said, "Be not afraid of me tonight, love. I promise to be gentle with you and teach you love rather than harsh duty."

Jessica almost stumbled. Tonight! She had never once considered that she would have to go to bed with him.

Nicholas was delighted with his bride, who was so pure and sweet that she was nearly overcome by the mere suggestion of physical love. He vowed to be gentle with her and teach her to enjoy lovemaking as much as he did. Not for them the rough coupling merely to get children, but rather the languorous delights of heaven on earth.

By the time they reached the nave, the bride's cake had been divided and set out on several trestle tables. Nicholas broke off a piece of the nearest cake and held it to Jessica's lips. Numbly she ate it and then offered a piece to him, but it could have been sawdust for all she knew.

Would she actually have to bed this stranger? If so, she was truly undone. While she wasn't yet eager to wed, she knew she might be someday, and without her virginity to offer, she would never be able to marry anyone. She studied Nicholas covertly. Could he be duped? And if so, how? For the guests to "bed" a newly married couple was no longer in vogue, but she had no doubt at all that he would insist on his conjugal rights. Even as she thought this, he threw back his head and let his booming laughter ring out at one of the guests' bawdy jests. Jessica jumped and took a step backward.

He was a big man, this husband of hers. Not only

was he unusually tall, but his shoulders were as broad as the length of an ax handle and his hands could probably span her waist. His voice was deep and hearty, and not a little frightening. And he had a tremendous amount of charisma that even Jessica found a bit awe-inspiring. Before today, she had prided herself on never having met her match. Now she wasn't so sure.

The remainder of the bride's cake was broken up and passed around. The married couples and young men ate their portions, but most of the unmarried girls hid their share in a pocket or pouch. That night the girls would place the cake under their pillows so that they might dream of their own true loves.

Randolph motioned for the boy to bring forward the silver cup of spiced wine. "The knitting cup," he proclaimed jovially. "Drink to your future."

Nicholas held the cup so that his hands covered Jessica's. She couldn't take her eyes from his as he guided it to her lips. With the honeyed wine sweet in her mouth, she presented the cup in turn to her husband. When he drank a large swallow, he grinned at her.

"Drink hale," Nicholas roared as he passed the cup next to Randolph. To Jessica he said, "See how the cup is handed about the nave? Everyone is eager to bear witness to our marriage."

She nodded, thinking they would be even more eager if all knew which of the twins was being feted. She hoped desperately to be gone before her secret was out. "My lord?" she asked uncertainly. "How long will we bide here before journeying to Wyndfell?"

"Not less than a week," he reassured her. "I know how it is with brides. They are hesitant to leave their homes and all they hold dear."

"A week!" She could never hope to fool her parents for so long. Only the sheer audacity of her actions had carried her this far.

"I know you would stay longer, but we cannot. There is the spring planting to oversee, as well as the management of my parish affairs. In a week you will know me better and be ready to bid your parents farewell."

"I am prepared to do that now! Surely we should leave much sooner. As you say, there are your fields to oversee, and I know how troublesome tenants and peasants can be when their master is away."

"It's not as if they are unsupervised. I have left my bailiff and steward in charge."

"But still . . ."

"They are trustworthy men and can handle my affairs until we return. After all, how often does a man wed?"

"Indeed," she murmured.

Nicholas looked over the crowd. "Thomas! Here!" To Jessica he said, "I want you to meet my brother. Thomas, this is your new sister."

"Welcome, Lady Madeline," the young man said, giving Jessica a chaste kiss on her lips as befitted family and she gave a slight start at being addressed by her sister's name. "Such a beautiful bride has never been seen." His dark eyes raked over her as if he were claiming Nicholas' rights for his own.

"Thank you," she stammered. Something about the young man disconcerted her. He was very similar to Nicholas but a lesser man, as if all the family's fire had been inherited by his brother. While she was overwhelmed by Nicholas, she found Thomas lacking.

The last of the knitting cup was drained and Randolph motioned toward the door. "To the castle. We will feast the night through." His words were greeted by loud cheers and laughter.

"But not the entire night by us, my sweet," Nicholas whispered in Jessica's ear. "At least we will not feast on food alone."

Jessica moved away quickly. She longed to put him firmly in his place, but to do so would give her away. Instead she demurely smiled as Madeline would have and lowered her lashes coyly.

Again Nicholas offered her his arm, and together they led the revelers from the church. At the sight of the new couple the commoners on the steps and road cheered and waved their congratulations. Jessica, who had never been considered shy, leaned nearer to Nicholas' comforting bulk. He beamed at her encouragingly and she jumped away at once.

Surely, she thought as she walked beside him back to the castle, she would be alone at some point. She needed only a few minutes to run up to her room, change into the servant's dress, and be gone before she was missed. Standing in for Madeline had been a foolish mistake, and at the moment she wasn't really sure what she had intended. But she could still resort to her original plan. Now that Nicholas was a part of the family, he probably would not cause them as much trouble when he discovered his bride's disappearance as he might have had his bride backed out of the wedding at the last minute. She peered up at the strong line of his jaw and wondered if she were right. He looked awfully stubborn.

By the time they reached the castle the feast was ready. As many trestle tables as could be fitted into the hall had been set up and covered with long white damask cloths. Nicholas escorted her to the dais and placed her in her mother's armed chair. In honor of the occasion they were to use the formal chairs under the red brocade canopy.

Devona sat beside Jessica and said in a tight voice,

"Don't fret, Madeline, but your sister is nowhere to be found."

"What?"

"I saw her earlier when she went to look for you, but no one has seen her since."

Jessica jerked her head back to stare at the hall, away from her mother. "Surely," she lisped carefully, "she will be found soon."

"I almost hope not," Devona sighed. "At least when she is gone she cannot shame us, and since she disappeared before she was presented to Lord Nicholas, he does not even know she exists."

"Surely you wrong her, Mother," Jessica said more sharply than Madeline would have. "She is not so bad as all that."

"If only you knew it all," Devona sighed. "Jessica has been the bane of my life."

Jessica clamped her mouth shut on the words that nearly tumbled out. Hurt tears stung her eyes and she blinked to contain them.

"There now! I've upset you. Forgive me, Madeline, I know how you hate unpleasantness. Would that your sister were half as good as you." She leaned closer. "Madeline, you are most fortunate in your husband. He will give you strong sons. Mark my words. You'll see."

Jessica stared at her mother, then remembered to dip her head shyly. He would give her no son at all, for she would be well down the road before then.

The feast lasted for hours. Meat dishes were followed by fish, then fowl. Vegetables in sweet sauces as well as sour were brought by in a seemingly endless procession. Jessica shared a plate with her groom and he fed her the best morsels. She smiled with her lips closed and her eyes downcast until she felt as if her face would crack. How Madeline ever managed to maintain this farce, Jessica would never know.

She longed to run from the hall or speak without first weighing every word. If she could but have a few minutes of her usual outspokenness, she could set Nicholas back a few paces. He was speaking to her as if she were as simpleminded as she was forced to act. She risked a glance at him and found him studying her. Defiantly she continued to look upon him in a contest to stare him down. But soon she realized that time was losing its meaning. Hastily she looked away. She had to be gone from here as soon as possible, for he was mesmerizing her! And it was far from unpleasant.

At last the fruit was replaced by the marchpane extravagance, fashioned in the shape of a castle with fairy spires and a real drawbridge. Besieging the castle was a fearsome dragon that actually breathed smoke when the lever that moved its jaws was pressed.

Once the tables had been cleared and removed, the musicians high up in the music gallery began a dance tune. After so much food, Jessica longed only to go to sleep, but that meant bed, and she was prepared to dance all night to preclude that. Somehow she had to stall until she could slip away from everyone, change into the servant's dress, and escape.

Nicholas extended his hand and bowed before her. As Jessica let him lead her to the improvised dance floor, the tune swept into the stately strains of the pavane. Nicholas was an excellent dancer and Jessica found she was almost enjoying herself. He swept her in a graceful pirouette that belled her yellow-and-turquoise gown as if she were an inverted flower. When he brought her back to him in a salute of solemn turns, she smiled up at him with no ruse at all.

Nicholas felt a stirring inside every time her dewy lips parted, showing her gleaming white teeth. She was so beautiful, the model of felicity. Next to her graceful form he felt awkward and clumsy. All afternoon he had tried to hide this in sweet words, but he was no courtier and he had almost exhausted his store of compliments. When she looked at him with that special sparkle in her eyes, he could swear he was truly in love with her. There was a subdued liveliness within her that had ever been lacking in Lady Jane and in his mother, the only two ladies he had ever seen on a daily basis. That devilry gleaming in her eyes and the color in her cheeks could just as well belong to a buxom dairy wench. At once Nicholas felt ashamed of himself. His wife was a lady, born and bred. As such she was naturally of a gentle and delicate nature. The sparkle and bloom must be merely signs of her good health rather than indications of a passionate nature.

The band began playing a quicker tune and Jessica swung easily into the steps of the lavolta. Skipping and twirling, she matched Nicholas step for step. The candles had been lit against the quickening darkness, and he remembered to dance her away from the hanging light in the center of the room where the tallow might drip onto her gown and spoil it. He grinned at her with enjoyment. No other woman in the hall could equal her for grace and agility. Nicholas found himself wishing for the hour to be up so he could steal her away.

As the first galliard began, Devona watched her daughter closely. She had never seen Madeline look so radiant. Although she attributed the change to the fact that her daughter was now a married woman, a curious dread settled in her bones. Leaning toward her lady-in-waiting, she said, "Mistress Anne, what think you of Lady Madeline tonight?"

"Never has a bride been so beautiful," the older woman replied as she peered nearsightedly at the blue-and-yellow blur she knew to be the bride.

"Hummm," Devona murmured. Then shook her head at her thoughts. What a ridiculous notion. Of course that was Madeline. What bride wouldn't be more outgoing than usual when she was presented with such a perfect bridegroom, and him an earl in the bargain. Besides, if that was Jessica, then where was Madeline? She decided she was full of nerves from the strain of preparing for the wedding on top of her worry over Jessica.

Jessica and Nicholas spun and leapt in the wild steps of the galliard until she was breathless and near fainting from her tight lacings. As was the custom, she sang out, "This dance, it can go no further!" At her signal, Nicholas bowed and took her hand to lead her in the slowly revolving cushion dance. She couldn't recall ever enjoying herself so much, and she laughed up at him with her own natural candor.

"You are even more beautiful when your cheeks are flushed and your eyes sparkle like stars at twilight," Nicholas said.

Too late Jessica realized Madeline would never have danced so exuberantly nor have enjoyed herself so much, and she glanced around to see if her parents had noticed. Randolph was drinking with some of his cronies but Devona was watching her. Jessica lowered her eyes and tilted her head shyly. "You pay me too many compliments, my lord. My head will surely turn."

"I long to hear you call me by name. Do you realize you have yet to speak it?"

"Later," she hissed as Devona came toward them.

The last of the leaping couples began whirling in the reellike cushion dance, and after another refrain, the music ended.

Devona put her hand on Jessica's arm. "If I may, Lord Nicholas, I will steal away your bride."

Jessica's eyes widened in fear that she was found out, then realized Devona meant to prepare her for bed. Lowering her eyelashes, Jessica followed her mother obediently. Her heart was racing, however, and she realized she now had virtually no chance to get away.

"Madeline, dear," her mother said as they swept along the corridor toward the large chamber prepared for the bridal night. "What will happen tonight may be offensive to you, but it is the lot of all married women. It is but a small price to pay in compensation for a fine castle and title of your own." She paused at the doorway to the chamber. "Do you recall what I told you? About what will happen?"

"Yes, Mother," Jessica said dutifully. Tib, the maidservant, had filled her with knowledge of the sex act years before. Surely Devona's talk with Madeline couldn't have been more definitive.

Devona went in and Mistress Anne, along with several maids, followed closely. When the door was closed, the maids began undressing Jessica as Mistress Anne and Devona took Madeline's new nightgown and nightrail from the chest.

"Are all my clothes here?" Jessica asked.

"Yes, this will be your chamber for the next week or so until you leave for Wyndfell." Devona sighed. "How I wish I could see your new home. I would rest easier if I knew you would be well cared for."

Jessica looked away as she remembered that this loving mother to Madeline was the same woman who wanted to lock Jessica in a madman's cell for life. "I doubt I will be uncomfortable in an earl's castle, Mother," she replied in a honeyed voice.

Devona glanced at her sharply but Jessica made her expression sweetly simple. "Doubtless your father and I will journey to see you in good time."

Nodding, Jessica stepped into the hip bath of warm water and soaped her body clean. By the time her parents journeyed to Wyndfell she would be long gone. In fact, she hoped to slip out this very night after Nicholas fell asleep. The idea of roaming the castle's black corridors chilled her, but not so much that she had changed her mind. But by then she would have been properly bedded by her husband. A shiver ran over her. Could she possibly get away before then?

A rivulet of water coursed down her breasts and dripped into the soapy tub, causing her to be all too aware of her naked body. This man stirred her far too much. She couldn't look at him without feeling a pleasant warmth steal over her, yet she couldn't love him. Not so quickly. Even Tib had told her that love was a thing that grew between a couple as the years passed. Perhaps Tib had omitted something, for Jessica felt what could only be described as desire whenever he spoke to her. It was as if she had known him forever.

She stood, and one of the maids poured warm water over her to rinse away the soap. The water sluiced over her rosy skin and symbolically rinsed away the girl she had been in preparation for her becoming a woman. Jessica ran her hands over her waist and hips and enjoyed the sensation of cleanliness. Unlike Madeline, she had always loved to bathe. She stepped onto a linen towel while another maid dried her. The servants started bailing the water from the tub and tossing it out the window as Mistress Anne turned back the heavy bedcovers and fluffed the chaff-filled pillows. Jessica was dressed in the nightgown, a white one due to her youth and status as a bride. As she sat on a stool, her hair was freed of the wilting flowers and was brushed to burnished softness. Then she was led to the tall bed.

Putting her bare foot on the cushioned step, Jessica looked at her mother. Devona smiled encouragingly and put the lacy nightrail across the foot of the bed. "Don't be afraid, child. It lasts but a little time."

Jessica tried to look reassured, but couldn't. Perhaps this really was going to be as painful and as humiliating as she had heard. She wondered if there was a chance in the world of slipping out before Nicholas arrived. No, she decided with growing trepidation, there was none. Already he might be waiting outside the door.

Devona and the maids bid Jessica good night and left, but Mistress Anne lingered behind. "Here," the older woman said as she drew a vial from the pouch at her belt. "Never tell your mother I gave you this."

Jessica leaned forward to take it. "What is this?"

"A draft to calm you. I recall my own wedding night. I swore if I had a daughter live to marry, I would spare her the first night." She pressed the vial into Jessica's hand. "Put it in your wine," she said, nodding toward the two chalices on the chest. "Use only half and you will be spared tomorrow night as well."

"Thank you, Mistress Anne," Jessica said fervently.

"I must go before Lady Devona misses me. Be happy, Lady Madeline."

Jessica watched the woman leave and pull the door shut behind her. Quickly she rolled to the other side of the bed and dumped the entire contents of the vial into one of the cups. If the drug would work on her, it would also work on Nicholas. She stirred the deep red wine with her fingertip, then slid out of bed and went to the window.

In the courtyard she could hear the sounds of revelry and knew the castle would party well into the night. She tossed the empty vial out the window and turned back to the chamber. Sudden fear seized her at the enormity of what she had done. She had managed to dupe them all, with the help of the spiced wine consumed by her parents and the servants. But she couldn't hope to maintain the ruse for a week. She had to make good her escape.

She went back to the wine goblets and lifted one. As she drank to calm her fears, she noticed a peculiar aftertaste and peered suspiciously into the goblet. Surely she hadn't drunk from the wrong one, she thought in dawning horror. She took another sip to test it. "Oh, no!" she gasped. Already a warm fuzziness was creeping into her bones.

When Nicholas came to their chamber, he found his bride sound asleep. Her hair was spread upon the pillow and her cheek was cradled in her palm. Long dark lashes made a lace upon her rosy cheeks. She looked more desirable than any woman he had ever met. He recalled how she had laughed up at him and whirled in his arms to the music. He longed to hear her laugh again and vowed that she would before the night was out. As much as he wanted her, he wanted more to teach her to love him without fear or reservation. He undressed and put out all but the candle nearest the bed, then slid beneath the covers. "Madeline?" he said softly, running his hand over her shoulder.

His bride only sighed and snuggled more deeply

into the covers. He shook her gently but still there was no response. "Madeline?"

When he was unable to rouse her, Nicholas sat up and stared at her. He was positive she was asleep but he had never encountered anyone who could sleep so soundly. He took a taste from the nearly empty chalice. The drug was unmistakable. With a frown, he shook her more firmly, but she continued to sleep. "Who dared do this!" he growled, knowing full well that she had likely been party to the deed. Jessica curled into a ball and settled deeper into the covers.

He looked back at her, put down the chalice, and reached for his own. She must have been terribly shy to drug herself against his advances. To win her confidence might take longer than he expected. As he studied her placid features, his initial fury subsided, and he began gently to stroke her silken hair, watching it curl sensuously around his fingers. Thus had he hoped to teach her to respond to his touch.

Nicholas drank his own wine and lay down beside her. He had no desire to take her as she slept, and he had ridden hard to reach Hargrove Castle in time for the ceremony. The morning would be soon enough to consummate the marriage, when both were awake and rested. "This is neither how I planned nor hoped to spend this night, love," he said to her, "but perhaps by not taking you as would an animal, I will more easily win your affection." He patted the rounded curve of her hip and curled around her with his arm over her waist. In truth he was more tired than he would ever have admitted, and in moments he was asleep.

6

JESSICA WOKE SLOWLY and blinked her eyes open as sluggish awareness crept through her. This wasn't the small cubicle where she had awakened every morning of her life. Nor was that steady cadence of breathing she heard coming from Madeline.

She sat bolt upright and stared at the man lying beside her. He awoke with a start and was in the motion of grabbing his knife from the chest before he was fully conscious. Jessica clutched the sheet to her chin and jerked away from him to crouch on the edge of the bed as he looked around for the attacker.

"Are you going to kill me with that?" she asked fearfully.

Nicholas' eyes went from her to the knife and a slow grin lifted his lips. "Nay, my lady. I mean you no harm. I thought only to protect you from an intruder." To reassure her, he tossed the knife to the far end of the chest. "Did you sleep well?" His voice was teasing but gentle.

Jessica recalled drinking the drugged wine and she caught her breath. Had he taken her as she slept? A quick peep beneath the cover told her she was still clothed in her voluminous nightgown. Her cap had fallen off during the night and he was fingering it as he watched her. She tried to read his expression but couldn't. "I don't know. Did I sleep ... undisturbed?" Surely no man would be wretch enough to use a senseless woman!

Without answering, he stretched out his hand toward her and she flinched away. After a pause, he finished the gesture by brushing her hair back from her eyes. "Pray don't shrink away from me, love. I would never hurt you. I told you so last night."

Her eyes narrowed distrustfully. "I don't remember you coming to bed," she said as she glanced swiftly around. "The bed curtains are not drawn. Can it be you have only now come up?"

Nicholas sat up and the cover pooled across his lap. Hard muscles ridged his broad chest and even in a state of relaxation his stomach was lean and taut. "I have slept beside you all night. As for the curtains, I saw no need to draw them since the night was not cold and we had the chamber to ourselves."

"Where are your nightclothes?" Jessica demanded, unable to tear her eyes from his tanned skin. Everyone at Hargrove Castle slept covered.

"My castle is far from court and we have not kept up with fashion trends. My brothers and I have always slept the old way, as God made us." He again grinned in that manner she found so disconcerting. "Does it disturb you?"

"Yes," she said bluntly.

"You should try it. You might find you like it better than sleeping in a linen sack."

She glared at him. "Never!"

He chuckled low in his throat and put his arm around her.

She struck at him and pulled the cover tighter about her.

For a second he looked surprised, then laughed. "You are like a kitten spitting at a mastiff. Don't be afraid of me."

"Just stay away." She had to know if she was woman or girl so she dredged up the courage to haughtily ask, "Did you enjoy yourself last night, my lord?"

"Aye, that I did."

Anger flared in her dark blue eyes and she swatted away the arm that was around her shoulders. "You took me as I slept? Shame upon you! A ... a barbarian wouldn't do such a thing!"

Again he stared at her, then said, "I meant I enjoyed myself at the wedding party. I thought we both did. Your father's hospitality was perfect, the food plentiful, the dancing superb."

"Then I'm still a maiden?"

He frowned at her. "Do you take me for the sort of man who would use a virgin in her sleep? And who dared give you a sleeping potion on your wedding night?"

Her chin lifted defiantly. "I took it myself by mistake. The drink was meant for you." She clamped her mouth shut as she realized what she had said.

"For me! God's bones, woman, why?"

She made no answer but held firmly to the sheet.

Understanding cleared his face. She was still regarding him as if he were a hungry tiger. In a gentle voice he said, "Are you then so shy, love? You mustn't fear me."

"I fear no one."

"Then stop flinching away from me." He caught her hands in a quick move and looked at her fingers where only one ring caught and held the morning light. "Where is my betrothal ring?"

Jessica's eyes widened and she swallowed nervously as she lied, "I . . . I lost it."

He studied her with suspicion. "No matter, I will have it replaced." He leaned nearer and pulled her toward him. "The first ring pales in significance to the second." He kissed her forehead where her hairline dipped into a widow's peak. "Let no worries come between us. Especially not on this first day of our future." As he spoke, he left kisses along her skin and over the curve of her ear.

Warmth flowed through Jessica as his lips brushed her skin, and she tried to still her nerves against his gentle onslaught. Yet when she pulled away, he followed her move and she found herself all but lying in his arms as his lips moved sensuously over the curve of her throat. Despite her fear, she wanted him to continue kissing her and to feel his powerful arms tighten possessively about her.

Abruptly she sat up and forced herself to say, "My lord, you forget yourself. 'Tis morning and no time for night sport." Her breath was coming fast and she was curiously unwilling to end his caresses, though she knew she must.

"You're wrong, love. Anytime is right for loving, as you will soon see." He drew her back to him.

She caught her breath and tried to roll from under him. If he continued tempting her like this, she knew she could never prevent him from taking her, or, for that matter, keep herself from wanting him to do just that. Nicholas, however, laughed and rolled with her, as if he found her movements exciting.

Again his lips drew near and he tangled his fingers in her hair to guide her mouth to his. Except for chaste kisses and the unwelcome fumblings of Sir Edwin, Jessica had never been kissed at all. When his mouth closed over hers and began to move seductively, her eyes opened wide, then closed as a curious glow began to spread through her. She pushed against his shoulders and ribs but he appeared not to notice.

Gradually her protests weakened as the heady sensation drowned her objections. He kissed her expertly, deeply, as if he had all the day before him. His tongue traced the curve of her lips and she opened to him so that he could taste the sweetness of her mouth.

Her traitorous body was coming alive and Jessica fought to regain her senses. She couldn't give in to him. Not when she could still escape intact. She reached out toward the candlestick that sat atop the nearby chest. If her aim was good, he could be knocked unconscious in one blow. If everyone was still asleep from the night's revels, she could be gone before he regained consciousness. As she covertly stretched, her fingers touched the silver candlestick; then she drew it into her grip.

Slowly, knowing she had but one try, she drew it back. Nicholas opened his eyes as the candlestick descended, and grabbed her wrist before it reached him. Instinctively twisting her arm, he freed the weapon and it fell to the floor with a clatter. Anger leapt into his fierce eyes, but Jessica met it unflinchingly with her own.

A loud hammering at the door startled them both. Then it flew open, banging against the wall. Both Jessica and Nicholas jumped as four men rushed in.

"What is the meaning of this!" he demanded, putting his bulk between Jessica and the men as he covered himself. "You, Sir Oliver! Who gave you leave to come from Wyndfell?"

The man he addressed stepped forward and bowed abruptly. "Forgive me, my lord. I have ridden all day and all night to reach you. There is grave trouble at home."

"Trouble? What sort of trouble!" Nicholas looked from his dusty bailiff to the man's begrimed companions.

"Lady Jane lies dead."

Nicholas stared at the man. "Dead! How can this be?"

"In your absence, Sir James Swineford's men tried to seize Wyndfell. We held them at bay with no trouble, but a stray bullet hit Lady Jane. She died almost at once."

"Lady Jane is dead," Nicholas repeated as if to accustom himself to the words. A dark scowl hardened his features. "And the attackers?"

"Several were killed, my lord. Although none were recognized as being in Swineford's regular employ, they must have been, for who else would attack thus?"

"You didn't see Swineford?"

"No, my lord. Either he stayed hidden in the trees or he sent his men out to do his bidding. There can be no mistake."

"Were they wearing the Swineford livery?"

"No, my lord, but would he not severely jeopardize himself by being so obvious?"

"You're right, of course. But regardless of who it was that attacked Wyndfell, we must leave right away." It made no sense for Swineford to attack, Nicholas told himself. He had no way of knowing that Nicholas would be getting the wedding dowry to pay the debt that was owed against Wyndfell. No one had been told of the marriage, save for a trusted few. All Swineford had to do was wait for the payment's due date to pass, and claim the property. The attack must have come from someone else. As Nicholas motioned for the men to be gone, he said to Sir

Oliver, "Awaken Thomas and the others. Explain the situation to Lord Randolph and ask that he supply you with fresh mounts. We ride at once." The men hurried to do his bidding as Nicholas swung his legs to the floor.

Jessica moved uneasily and Nicholas stared at her as if he had forgotten she was there. "Dress quickly," he commanded. "We must leave right away."

"I . . . I will come later," she suggested eagerly. This would allow the ideal opportunity for her escape.

"No! You will ride with me." He leaned over her and she drew back warily. "You have much to explain to me, such as why you tried to brain me with a candlestick."

"I'll not rush away now," she affirmed, pushing toward him so that he in turn retreated. "My castle is filled with guests and it would shame my family for me to flit away like a servant girl eloping with a stableboy."

"Only last night you were anxious to leave. Now you insist that you stay. Has the excitement of our wedding left you addled? Your castle is now Wyndfell, and as your husband I command you to get dressed!" As he spoke, he rose and began pulling on his clothes.

"I will not." Jessica drew up her knees and clasped her arms around them. With Nicholas and his men out of the way, she could find a way to take a horse and be nearly halfway to London before anyone missed her.

Nicholas frowned down at the woman who had seemed so gentle and docile the day before. "You will dress or I will drag you out in your nightgown."

"That you'll never do!" Jessica grabbed one of the silver goblets and threw it at him in a burst of anger.

He caught it in midair, then tossed it to one side. In one motion he captured her wrist and hauled her from beneath the covers. She struggled wildly as he looped his arm around her waist. She thudded her elbow into his stomach and was glad to hear him grunt painfully before he pinned her arm against him.

Following a perfunctory knock on the door, it again opened. This time Devona and her ladies entered. "Lord Nicholas," she began, "I just heard the news and . . ."

As if by magic, Jessica froze, then softened in his arms. "Greetings, Mother," she said with sudden gentleness.

Nicholas released her and stared in surprise at her sweetly smiling face. He couldn't have been more startled if her skin had turned green.

"Forgive me for my intrusion at such an inopportune time," Devona said as she blushed. "Your bailiff's words led me to believe you both were dressed."

"My lady wife was about to do just that," Nicholas said with a smile toward Jessica. "I fear I know little about being a maid. I will leave that office to your ladies."

Devona was looking closely at Jessica, who had turned away slightly. "We will see to it, my lord," she said absently.

"I fear my wife and I must take leave of you today. As you know, there is trouble at home and my sister-in-law has been killed."

Devona jerked her head up "Must you both leave? Perhaps if you merely dispatched your men—"

"We must go," Nicholas said firmly. "I beg your pardon for seeming so churlish, but without me, Wyndfell is in danger. And surely you could not expect Lady Jane to be buried with no family member there to see it well done."

"He is right, Mother," Jessica lisped sweetly. She

had seen the look her mother gave her and knew she must leave with Nicholas or not at all. Even now it might be too late to escape Hargrove Castle and the upstairs cell.

"Perhaps you could go, Lord Nicholas, and Lady Madeline could follow later."

"Beseech me not, Mother," Jessica said softly. "My place is beside my husband."

Nicholas was still staring at her, but he nodded in agreement. "It might be weeks before I could return for her. No, she must come now."

Devona nodded submissively, and with another curious glance at Jessica said, "I will see to your provisions for the journey. My ladies will tend Lady Madeline."

Jessica held her breath until her mother and Lord Nicholas were gone. Then she dressed hurriedly as the maids packed the remainder of Madeline's belongings. When all was finished, she looked back at the bed. Jessica was almost positive that her mother had deduced that she wasn't Madeline, but she had no way of knowing what Devona might do. If her mother inspected the bed and found no stain on the sheets, she might claim the marriage was not consummated and retain her. Quickly Jessica went to the bed as if she had forgotten something. Holding her breath, she ran her finger over the rough base of the remaining silver goblet. A dark bead of blood welled to the surface. Pressing her hand into the rumpled sheets, Jessica pretended to straighten the covers. If her parents thought she had married and bedded the powerful earl, they might let her leave no matter who they thought she was. At least she hoped so. Now that she considered it, her chances of escape were better on the road, perhaps, than from here. Jessica had never traveled beyond the parish and had no idea where London was, but she knew she would be constantly watched here at the castle if Devona was suspicious.

Straightening, she said, "I'm ready. Have my chests carried down, please." Desperately she walked out into the corridor, hoping she would find Nicholas before Devona found her alone.

Nicholas and both her parents were waiting for her in the wide entry of the hall. Jessica checked her brisk pace and smoothed her wine-red kirtle over her cream underskirt. Madeline had spent weeks embroidering the vine design onto the kirtle, and Jessica felt strange wearing it, for Madeline would never have lent it to her. She adjusted the high-necked chemise that extended past the square neckline of her kirtle as befitted a married woman. Keeping her eyes on the floor a few yards ahead of her, Jessica assumed Madeline's gliding walk.

"Here she is now," Randolph said as Jessica joined them. "Good morrow, daughter."

"Good morning, Father. Are the horses ready?"

"The men are bringing them around now," Nicholas said as he watched her closely.

Jessica smiled, keeping her lips shut. Trying to stun him with the candlestick had been a bad idea. What if he mentioned it to her parents? Madeline wouldn't have done such a thing. Or would she? Jessica recalled the cat that had been drowned in the pail of milk. When angered, Madeline was capable of anything.

Again Devona was eyeing her daughter in a suspicious manner. To escape, Jessica said, "Might I beg leave to tell Mistress Anne farewell? I'll be but a moment."

"Of course," Nicholas agreed. "We are not in such a hurry as all that."

Jessica went to the winter parlor, where Mistress Anne was sure to be found. While she wasn't that fond of the woman, Madeline was, and Jessica was trying hard to do exactly what her sister would have done. "Mistress Anne?" she said as she glided into the room where the ladies had already gathered to start the day's work. "I have come to say good-bye."

"Lady Jessica?" the woman said. "No, how foolish of me. You are Lady Madeline, to be sure. You must forgive me. Your sister is much on everyone's mind today."

"Oh?" Jessica heard Devona's footsteps behind her, and her heart thudded against her ribs.

"She has run away, it seems," Devona supplied as she joined them.

"Surely she hasn't done that. Where could she go?" Jessica said with Madeline's note of mild interest. "Perhaps she is only hiding somewhere about the castle."

"We've looked everywhere," Mistress Anne said. "Her clothing is still in her room but she is nowhere to be found."

"Such a foolish child," Devona clucked impatiently. "She has been nothing but trouble since the day she was born. How can she possibly expect to survive with no man to protect her?"

"A woman alone would be fortunate to reach the next town," Mistress Anne agreed. "So much evil lurks along the roads these days."

"If she reached town, what would that benefit? She has no kin there, no money for food or shelter. She will have to beg for crusts of bread like the scurvy lot at our back gate, sleep in hay bins, endure God knows what."

"There's only one way for a woman to survive alone," Mistress Anne said with a grimace.

Devona jerked her head in agreement. "She'll become a common whore. That's no more than I could expect of her."

"Perhaps," Jessica said tartly, "she prefers whoredom to life in a madman's cell." Instantly she could have bitten her tongue, for Devona turned toward her sharply. With a sweet smile, Jessica said, "I must return to my husband. A good wife would not keep him waiting while she gossips. No doubt Jessica will turn up by dinnertime. Farewell, Mother, Mistress Anne. Ladies." She nodded to the other women who sat sewing across the room.

"Godspeed, Lady Madeline," Mistress Anne said as she kissed her cheek. "Fret not over your sister. Likely she will come home soon, just as you say. She may only be hiding to vex us and put a strain upon your wedding."

"Doubtless," Jessica agreed dryly. She hadn't realized she was disliked so much.

"Godspeed, daughter," Devona said, kissing Jessica with reserve. Before drawing back, she studied Jessica closely.

Jessica bobbed a quick curtsy and hurried away as fast as Madeline's gait could take her.

Nicholas escorted her out of the hall as he said farewell to Randolph. "Fear not for your daughter's happiness," he said as he put his arm around Jessica. "I will guard her as surely as I guard myself."

Randolph beamed at the couple. "I know you will, my lord. Lady Madeline is my pearl of great value, as the saying goes. In her I give you the best Hargrove Castle has to offer." Devona came to his side, and silently stared at Jessica.

Nicholas led her to a pretty gray jennet, and Jessica ran her hand over the mare's satiny neck. "Is she mine?"

"Yes. I meant to give her to you later today. Are you pleased?"

"Very much, my lord. Thank you." The animal looked swift, Jessica thought, and her deep chest promised stamina. Such an animal could carry her all the way to London. For now it was enough to get out of her mother's sight. She looked around for a groom to hand her up onto the sidesaddle, but instead Nicholas caught her waist and swung her up. Jessica tossed the voluminous skirt over the jennet's rump and hooked her leg firmly over the sidesaddle pommel, then thrust her feet into the stirrups.

For a moment their eyes met, his questioning, hers wary. Then he mounted his large bay and took the stirrup cup offered by one of the maids. When he had drunk, he handed it to Jessica and said to her parents, "Again I ask forgiveness for our hasty departure."

"No, no," Randolph protested with shakes of his head. "I fully understand. I would do as much myself. Fare ye well and come again when you may."

"Farewell," Devona said, speaking at last.

"Perhaps when the crops are in, you will come visit us," Nicholas said heartily.

"Or perhaps next spring"—Randolph grinned—"when we may bounce our first grandbabe on our knees."

Jessica grimaced before she realized Madeline would have blushed. But Nicholas' roaring laugh kept her parents' attention.

"Away!" he called, signaling toward his men. To cries of farewell and Godspeed they rode out of the courtyard.

Jessica kicked the willing horse into a trot and rode expertly toward the castle gate. The gray tossed her silver mane spiritedly and cantered after the others.

Nicholas had held back for her, and together they waved to her parents as they rode away. Jessica glanced up at Hargrove Castle for the last time and smiled. She was glad that she would never see her ancestral home again.

7

AFTER THEY PASSED the village fields and entered the wasteland, the road became progressively worse. Although by law it was to be fifty feet wide, it was only twelve feet at most with overhanging bushes that scraped the panniers of the packhorses. In the next parish the roads were in even worse condition and the horses were forced to ride in single file on the four-foot-wide path.

Conversation dwindled and Jessica noticed everyone was looking about constantly. Highwaymen were known to frequent stretches of woodlands, and even along the wolds, the high bushes could conceal a band of outlaws.

Thomas rode in the rear, his hand on the hilt of his sword and his eyes alert for trouble. Nicholas took the lead, his body tensed for battle as they passed thickets of heavy undergrowth. Jessica rode close to him, as he had insisted. Never having been attacked by a band of robbers, Jessica had no way of knowing the magnitude of danger they were in. Thus she felt little apprehension about their safety, and instead busied her mind with the more pleasant aspects of this new experience.

Although their progress was slow, she felt a quickening of excitement. Travel was thrilling! She was no longer caged by stone walls and had no parents to scold her every move. The blue sky arched overhead and each curve of the road brought sights she had never seen before. Never had she dreamed of the endless hills beyond her familiar village, or the numerous forests and streams. Larks sang over her head and her heart answered.

The road widened as they approached a village and Nicholas reined in beside her. "Take heart, my lady, we will soon reach the inn."

"How far is it to Wyndfell?" she asked eagerly.

"Another day's ride, I fear. I hope you are up to it."

"Of course I am," she breathed, forgetting for the moment that he was her enemy and she should be planning to escape. "I never imagined travel would be so exhilarating. No wonder our lady the queen takes so many progresses."

Nicholas looked at her curiously. "You're enjoying yourself?"

"Yes! There is so much to see."

"I thought ladies detested travel," he mused.

"Not me. I would travel forever after this taste of it."

She looked about her. The cumbersome carts of her belongings were left far behind already, the wheels being a poor match for the innumerable ruts and holes. Purple cranesbill and delicate pink yarrow bloomed profusely along the roadway. Wild strawberry plants, tangled in the sunshine, were dotted with tiny white flowers that would soon give way to berries. The flanking cornfields were lush and green, with heartsease nodding among the stalks. In the field opposite, fat brown cows grazed on grasses dotted with wild mustard and mayweeds as bright as daisies. All of England seemed to be bursting into bloom to welcome her.

"You continue to amaze me," Nicholas commented thoughtfully. "Have you never journeyed from your castle? Not even to visit London?"

Jessica shook her head. Her parents had taken Madeline to London, but never Jessica. Each time she was left behind, Jessica had been miffed. Had she then realized what she was missing, she would have been distraught. "No, I have never traveled anywhere. Will we go through London?"

"Only if we lose our way. London is behind us and we are riding north."

"Oh." Somehow she had assumed they would pass through the great city. She had planned to make her escape there. "Will we pass any other cities?"

"No, but we will see villages larger than the one by Hargrove Castle. Why? Are you worried about robbers?"

She remembered the tenseness she had noted in the men earlier. Now that they were in tilled fields and not in the heavy brush, everyone seemed more relaxed. "Should I be?"

"Not with my men so near. A group such as this may pass unmolested, whereas a lone rider would court disaster. The penalty for highway robbery is death, so the outlaws have no qualms about killing anyone who could identify them."

"I see." She gave up her idea of slipping away and riding alone to London. Surely there would be some other way.

They passed several villages as they wound their way north to Yorkshire. Some were composed of only a few mud-and-wattle huts that squatted beside sluggish streams. Others were large enough to be called towns, with a church and resident smithy and their own market squares. Having just arrived in one of these, Nicholas led the caravan into an enclosed inn yard:

"We will rest here at the Swan and Angel," he explained as Jessica looked about with interest. "Night is approaching and this is known to be a clean inn. It's frequented by others of our rank."

The inn, fashioned of stone and timber, was rambling in design, with two stories. A sign painted with the emblem of a swan and an angel gave the place its name, and a red lattice to one side of the door indicated that ale was sold there. On their arrival, the innkeeper came out of the door. At the sight of the impressive clothing and the size of the retinue, he beamed broadly and wiped his hands on his white apron.

"Good evening, my lord. Come in, come in."

"Have you chambers for the countess and myself and room for my men and maids?"

At the word "countess" both the landlord's and Jessica's eyes widened. She had not been called by her new title before now. "Certainly, my lord. Right this way." He bowed Nicholas and Jessica into the inn and Thomas followed as stableboys ran to take the horses to the barn.

The common room of the inn was clean-swept, with a large fireplace at one end. The walls were paneled in oak, and numerous long trestles stood in preparation for supper. Due to Nicholas' rank, the innkeeper himself showed them to the oak staircase built into the wall, and kept up a steady stream of pleasantries as he led them down a hallway and to a room. Jessica was aware of Thomas' eyes upon her back and she turned to see if he was about to speak to her. Instead, he merely met her gaze and looked as if he were thinking something unpleasant. She glanced away. No doubt he was dwelling on the death of his sister-in-law and was mourning her loss. She had caught drifts of conversation from all the men on the day's ride about what should be done to avenge the murder.

The innkeeper opened the door to a bedchamber and said, "I hope this pleases your lordship." He struck a light to the logs laid in the hearth.

"This will be quite suitable." Nicholas counted out six shillings for their room and for Thomas' and a shilling each for their horses' care. After being assured his men would be lodged in the two dormitory-type rooms nearby, and Jessica's maidservants in the next chamber beyond, Nicholas added two shillings for each of his retinue.

When the innkeeper left to show Thomas to his lodgings, Jessica said, "So much money for a night's rest?"

"His fee is high, but we may rest safely here. I have heard no tales of murder or robbery at the Swan and Angel. Also, my men will be nearby."

Jessica went to the latticed window and looked down into the yard, where the last of the horses was being led away by a boy in a blue jacket. "I have never stayed at an inn before, nor spoken to anyone who did." When her parents and Madeline visited London they made the journey in one day and stayed at the town home of her Aunt Catherine.

Nicholas came to her and put his hand on her shoulder. "Fear not. I will protect you."

"Fear?" she said in surprise. "Nay, rather a rare adventure! All I have seen this day is crowding about

in my head. Surely I will remember this forever!"
Her eyes sparkled with enjoyment.

Slowly Nicholas smiled and toyed with a strand of
her hair. "There will be no need to recall this journey forever. If you enjoy travel, we will see all of
England."

Instantly she was wary. "You tease me, my lord."

"Look not at me as if you were a hare and I a
trap." He laughed. "I, too, like to travel. I will take
you with me."

"You would do that?" she said uncertainly. "Even
to London?"

"Of course. Would you like to be presented to the
queen?"

"You could do that?"

"I am an earl and you are a countess. It is to be
expected for those of our rank."

"I have heard of wives who are of your rank who
never leave their castles. Their husbands go to London and other cities and never take them."

"I am not that kind. If it will please you, I will take
you with me."

A smile crept over Jessica's face and the elusive
dimple appeared. "Forsooth, my lord, I find I have
stumbled into a great fortune in you." She was rapidly changing her mind about Nicholas. So far he
had treated her more kindly than she had ever been
treated in her life. If he meant even half he said—and
she expected no more—she would lead a much better
life with him than she ever would as a London seamstress or lady-in-waiting. For a life of occasional travel
she might not even object too much to his nightly
use. Perhaps. She wondered if he meant his enticing
words.

They ate in their chamber, as was proper for their
rank, with two boys singing sweetly to the accompa-

niment of a lute and a viol throughout the meal. Jessica was so excited she could scarcely taste the heavily seasoned meat. So much had happened that day that she felt as if she would never be able to sleep. She glanced at the large oak bed and sudden worry made her food go tasteless. Something terrible would have to be endured before she slept. She peered at Nicholas from the corner of her eyes. He looked kind; he even treated her with deference. Perhaps he could be persuaded to leave her unmolested. She had heard stories of women who were so pious that their husbands respected their wishes and never forced them to their wifely duties. Would Nicholas believe she was a holy woman? No, she decided. He would never be that gullible after she had tried to crack his head with a candlestick.

His movements were bold and his voice deep and rather awesome. He looked as if he could break her in half as easily as he tore away a bite of bread. Yet although his eyes were dark, they were velvety in their expression rather than glittering as were his brother's.

She quickly looked down and studied his hands as he cut his meat. They were large and powerful, but looked as if they might be gentle, if he so chose. Again she felt a surge of trepidation. However gentle he might appear, he had complete ownership of her and could use her however he saw fit. She found it difficult to breathe for the fear in her heart and tried to make the meal last as long as possible. She had been foolish even to consider staying with him. He didn't love her and probably never would. Such was not to be hoped for. She wondered if she could somehow escape while still intact.

Eventually she could dawdle no longer. The servants carried away the food scraps and the innkeeper bowed into the chamber. "Is there aught else you require for the night?" he asked, checking to be sure that the lamps had ample oil and that the maid had filled the water pitcher. A cursory glance assured him that the basin was clean and not chipped. "Shall I draw off your boots or send in your valet?"

"No, thank you. We will need nothing until morning," Nicholas said in dismissal.

"Good night, my lord, my lady." The man bowed again and left.

Nicholas locked the door and laid the heavy key upon the table. Across the room Jessica stood stiffly looking out at the night and making wildly improbable plans to protect herself. He crossed to her and put his large hands on her upper arms. At once she grew rigid under his palms.

"Madeline," he said softly. "I promised you I wouldn't hurt you. Can you not believe me?"

She turned to him, her eyes wide and frightened. "I know better." She was recalling the way Sir Edwin Fairfax's bony fingers had pinched and bruised her. Surely the act of consummating the marriage would be much worse.

"How do you know better?" he asked with a frown.

"I have heard talk from the maids. They were forever telling how their husbands and lovers misused them. I know what you will do to me."

Understanding lit his face. "So that is why you tried to brain me with a candlestick this morning?"

"I planned only to knock you senseless so I might escape," she confessed, with a proud lift of her chin.

Nicholas stared at her. No woman made choices like that. "Did you not realize your father wouldn't harbor you against me? The law is against anyone doing so."

"My plan was to leave Hargrove Castle and journey to London," she said in defiance.

"Alone? You don't even know the way!"

"London is a rather large city, I hear. It shouldn't be so hard to find."

He was fascinated by her words and the calm way in which she stated them. "Once there, what did you plan to do? Go to relatives?"

"No, my aunt would have returned me at once. I planned to get a post with some household."

Nicholas, who knew the improbability of such a scheme, studied her with interest. "You would do all this to avoid me and my bed?"

Jessica hesitated, then answered, "Not only that, but to escape my parents. I know it's foolish of me, perhaps, to tell you all this, but I hope you will release me willingly if you know my true feelings."

"Your parents were cruel to you?" His eyes narrowed as if he were ready to leap to her defense. "Why?" He was ignoring the last half of her statement, for he had no intention of setting her free to run away on her own. Such a thing would be very dangerous for a young woman. But he was intrigued that she would want to.

"Ever since my childhood it has been so. I have no memory of a soft word from either of them."

Nicholas swore beneath his breath and drew her to him. "How could they be so unkind? Perhaps they longed for a son and heir, but a daughter is not to be blamed. 'Tis unnatural for parents to be so cruel to their only child."

Jessica glanced up at him but held her tongue. She had forgotten that he did not know she was a twin. This would make her deception all the easier if she decided to stay, and her trail harder to follow if she left. *When* she left.

"You look at me with the eyes of a trapped deer," he murmured, tracing his thumb along the firm line of her jaw.

"First a hare, now a deer." She laughed nervously. "What next, my lord?"

"I have no courtly phrases," he confessed. "Wyndfell is far from London and I was nurtured by an uncle at an even more remote castle. I never learned the art of pretty phrases to make a lady love me. I must seem awkward and barbaric to you. For that I ask your forgiveness."

Jessica forgot her fears long enough to truly hear him, and suddenly she understood. In his way he was as nervous and unsure as she was. His heartiness and blusterous ways were merely his mannerisms and not portents of callousness. Her heart went out to him, though tempered somewhat with caution. "Hush, my lord. No apology is necessary to me, for truly you are the finest knight I have ever seen, and the most lordly."

"Your father is richer than I," Nicholas admitted. "Let there be no lies between us. 'Twas your dowry I loved, and naught else."

"You speak bluntly," she said in surprise.

"Just as I said. How could I have loved you, having never seen you before? I had met only your father, and the countenance of an aging man scarcely foretells the beauty of his daughter."

"You find me beautiful?" she whispered. Although she and her sister were as much alike as two buttons, she had heard Madeline's beauty praised, but never her own.

"I find you more beautiful than the spring flowers. Your voice rivals the nightingale and your skin is like fine velvet. I can scarcely believe my good fortune."

His words were spoken hesitantly, as if he was afraid she would laugh. Instead she reached up to touch his soft beard and smiled shyly. "Your words fill my heart," she replied gently. "I begin to think that I, too, am fortunate." She had never considered that he might feel awkward around her. This surprising revelation altered her opinion of her situation. She could care for a man who was courageous enough to admit that he was unsure of himself.

Slowly Nicholas lowered his head and claimed her lips in a kiss that was almost shy. Then he grew more bold and the kiss deepened to passion. Jessica let the tide sweep her up and she found her arms around him, holding him close. She, who had never before kissed a man in desire, found her senses to be ample teachers and she returned his passion with her own.

Nicholas murmured at the unexpected responsiveness, then raised his head to gaze into the dusky blue of her eyes. He found no artifice there, yet she kissed with the ability of a leman. He had heard that all true ladies were cold to their core, yet no one could say that about the daughter of Hargrove Castle. Glorying in this unexpected boon, Nicholas grinned.

Jessica stiffened. "I did something wrong?" she demanded. She could not recall one time when she had not been scolded for behaving naturally. She mentally cursed herself for dropping Madeline's guise when Nicholas' opinion of her suddenly meant so much.

A deep chuckle rumbled through his chest. "You have done nothing wrong, love, but ever so right. I suspect you have a talent you might never have guessed."

Relieved that he wasn't laughing at her, Jessica let him draw her into another lingering kiss. This time she pressed her body against his, giving pressure for pressure, and ran her fingers through his thick hair. When he lifted his head, his eyes were as dark as midnight and seemed soft with longing. An unknown sense of power ran through Jessica at the way she could give him pleasure and receive that look in return.

"You wear too many clothes," he said softly.

"I shall call my maids to assist me," she said uncertainly as her fear began to return. Perhaps if he left to give her the privacy to disrobe, she could slip out.

"No, lass. I will be all the servant you require this night."

With practiced fingers he unlaced her kirtle and pulled it from her. Jessica allowed him to do so with no protest, but crossed her arms over her breasts to hide the thin lawn of her chemise. Moving slowly so as not to frighten her, Nicholas untied the points of her underskirt and let it drop, soon to be followed by her petticoats.

"My . . . my gown is in my travel chest," Jessica said as a furious blush colored her cheeks. "I'll get it."

"Stay, love. You'll not need it."

She regarded him uncertainly but held her ground. Gently he took her hands away from her breasts and showed her how to loosen his own clothing. He helped her undress him down to his nethergarments, then paused. Jessica's eyes were downcast in a rare burst of genuine timidity. Somehow she had not expected the touch of his skin to so unnerve her. He was every bit as virile and sensuous as she remembered from waking beside him that morning. Energy seemed to emanate from him as well as a maleness that she found all too exciting. Whatever knowledge she might lack, she knew ladies were not supposed to be so excited at the sight of a man. If he ever guessed that she wanted to look at him, to kiss that curve of muscle that barreled his chest, to run her hands over the hard warmth of his shoulders and arms, would he not chastise her? And if she ever revealed these wanton impulses, would he not fall upon her and ravish her unmercifully? Perhaps he was teasing her to make her fall into a trap so that he could derive some sort of satisfaction from her lack of experience. She felt her fear return twofold.

He put his finger beneath her chin and lifted her head. Laying his hand along her slender throat, he said, "Your heart is beating as fast as a bird's. Will you not trust me?"

"I have never known anyone who moves me as you do," she answered honestly. "When you look at me or speak to me, I feel something I cannot name. How can I trust you or even myself when I know not what is happening to me?" Then she realized she had admitted far too much and she said awkwardly, "Forgive me, my lord. I spoke before I thought."

In that moment Nicholas fell in love. Here was a lady who neither scoffed at his country ways nor acted as if her mind was far withdrawn from him. She had an intriguing, untouched quality about her, as if she had lived in a world where courtly intrigues and shallow flirtations had never existed. She was like a flower still in bud, awaiting his touch to open and bloom. Yet, beneath her innocence was a sensuality that was entirely devoid of pretense.

"You may trust me, love. I will teach you how." He untied the satin ribbon that secured her chemise and pulled the garment away from her throat and over her shoulders.

Jessica's breath quickened and her chin lifted as she allowed him to remove the last of her clothing.

The only protection she had ever had was her bravery. Even when she had been quaking inside, it had never shown, and she had often bluffed her way out of beatings from her parents simply by not letting them know how afraid she was.

Nicholas' eyes swept over her and his own pulse quickened. She was more beautiful than he had expected. Her fashionably tight bodice had flattened her breasts when she was dressed, but now they mounded full and proud. Her waist was slender without being thin and her hips were gracefully rounded. Bending, he swept her up and held her against the thunder of his heartbeat. Although she was light in his arms, her eyes widened as if he had accomplished a great feat.

She ran her hand shyly over his bulging arms and shoulders, then looked quickly at him as if she expected to be reproved. Her touch was like that of a butterfly, and Nicholas smiled encouragingly. He carried her to the bed and laid her on the sheets. Quickly stripping off his nethergarments, Nicholas lay down beside her.

"What thoughts are in your head?" he asked as he stroked her hair back from her forehead. "You look at me so imploringly."

"I was wishing I had the vial given to me by Mistress Anne to ease this night."

"You will have no need of ease," he reassured her. "I have much to teach you of the ways of a man and a woman."

Gently his mouth met hers and he kissed her lovingly before his tongue urged her lips to part. For a moment he thought she would refuse to open them, but then she did, and he licked over the moist inner lips that were softer than rose petals. When she began to respond to his kisses, Nicholas drew her closer to him so that her breasts brushed his chest, then mounded against him as her entire length met his. She drew her breath in sharply but didn't pull away.

When he smoothed his hand over her back and hip, she moved even closer, as if by instinct. He caressed her and whispered love words in her ear as his hand found her breast. He cupped it in his hand, feeling the warm fullness and how her nipple puckered eagerly. Jessica also quickened beneath his hand, and instead of easing away with maidenly shyness, she sighed with pleasure.

Never had she felt such ecstasy. His hands were gentle and knowing as they moved over her. Surely no other man knew how to touch a woman in this way so that her skin glowed from the inside out. The maids at Hargrove Castle had never mentioned this! His fingers toyed with her nipple and she tensed, remembering how Sir Edwin had hurt her, but there was no pain in Nicholas' lovemaking.

His head lowered, leaving a trail of kisses down her throat and chest, then her breast. Jessica held her breath as the soft brushing of his beard and the warmth of his lips neared his goal. When his lips covered the throbbing bud and he rolled his tongue over it, she moaned with exquisite pleasure. He chuckled softly and increased the movement of his tongue until she threaded her fingers in his black hair and arched toward him.

Nicholas loved first one breast, then the other, until she ached with a need she couldn't define. The curious glow had spread throughout her and all her senses seemed to have centered in her breasts and below the pit of her stomach.

"Does this please you?" Nicholas asked, already knowing her answer from the way she was responding.

"Yes. Oh, yes" She closed her eyes to savor the delicious things he was doing to her.

"Would you have drugged your body to dull this pleasure? I told you I would make our loving enjoyable for us both. Always believe in me, love. I will never hurt you."

"Yes," she whispered, her sapphire eyes meeting his, her voice soft with pleasure. "There is no hurt in the way you touch me."

He let his hand stroke over her slender stomach, dipping his finger into the shallow opening of her navel, circling it, then drifting lower. She let him part her legs and he touched the center of her womanhood, his fingers gentle. Expertly he probed and caressed, bringing her to even greater heights.

When she moved restlessly in her passion, he knelt between her legs. "There will be a moment of discomfort. Nothing worse," he promised.

Jessica nodded and reached up to pull him down to lie on her. As he did, she felt him enter her and her eyes flew open. At first she thought he was surely too large and her body would be unable to take him. Then he pushed past the barrier and she cried out.

At once Nicholas lay still and soothed her with honeyed words and loving caresses. At length Jessica began to respond again. Soon he had her at the same fever pitch as before. He began to move within her, pacing himself to draw as much pleasure for them both as possible. Jessica tensed, then relaxed when she found greater pleasure following his rhythmic motions. She moved with him as the fires burned more brightly within her.

He moved his hand between them to touch the seat of her femininity as her passion mounted. At his touch she felt a new desire leap to life, and all at once she seemed to be spiraling up a great bank of fiery clouds. When she reached the top she hovered for a breathless moment, then cried out in ecstasy as she experienced pure pleasure. Nicholas moaned in the hollow of her neck as he joined her in joyous release.

For what might have been aeons or moments, Jessica floated on the cloud of afterlove, cradled safely in Nicholas' strong arms. When he kissed her temple, she opened her eyes and met his smile with one of her own. Forever banished were all her thoughts of leaving him. In their place was a warm, tender emotion that she suspected might be budding love.

"Was it so bad?" he teased.

"It was wonderful. Why was I told such pleasure would hurt me?"

"Had I not prepared you, it would have been painful. All too often a man gets caught up in his own passion and forgets or cares not about his woman."

She studied his face dreamily as she stroked the midnight of his hair. "And now we will have a child."

"In time, little one. In time," he said with a grin. "That rarely happens the first night. Did your mother not tell you these things?"

"No, she didn't." Jessica blushed. "You must be my instructor, Nicholas. Will you mind?"

His breath caught at her first use of his name and he drew her to him. "I will not mind. I have a feeling they would have told you wrong anyhow." He released her slightly and looked lovingly into her eyes. "I'm glad to have you for my wife, Madeline."

A veil dropped behind her eyes and her expression became still. After a moment she said, "I am honored to have you for my husband, Nicholas."

She lay in his arms as sleep overtook him and

wondered what she should do now that she had decided to stay with him as his wife. If she told him the truth about who she was, would he not repudiate her and send her back to her parents? Yet if she did not, she would never again be called by her own name. And when he looked at her so lovingly, she wanted her name upon his lips and not her sister's. With a troubled sigh she closed her eyes. Better that she should lie in his arms as an imposter than be sent back to Leopold the Mad's bare cell. Feeling safer than she had in months, Jessica put her arm across Nicholas' hard-muscled stomach and went to sleep.

8

JESSICA'S FIRST VIEW of Wyndfell was breathtaking. Its massive stones seemed to rise in silver majesty from the encircling moat. "How beautiful!" she exclaimed.

Nicholas beamed proudly. "The keep dates back to the twelfth century. The motte it rests upon was raised under William the Conqueror. My great-great-grandfather built the towers in the curtain wall, added the present halls, and changed the course of a nearby stream to serve as the moat."

"He was a man of great vision. Wyndfell is the most beautiful castle I have ever seen. I like the way you have kept the stone natural rather than having it whitewashed as so many have done. It seems to have sprouted from the earth." With the exterior so magnificent, the interior would surely be three times as grand. Her decision to stay as Nicholas' wife had been a good one.

Nicholas glanced at her to see if she was teasing him, but she appeared to be quite serious. Although his preference was for the natural color of the stones, splotched here and there by russet and golden-hued lichen, he had been inclined to follow the fashion and have the castle whitewashed, but his lack of funds prevented it. However, since she was pleased with the result, he saw no harm in accepting the credit, and there was no need to explain any further. His problems with money were a source of great irritation.

"You should have seen it in my childhood," Thomas said, riding up to her. "There was no castle to equal it. Wyndfell Castle has been in our family for generations, and likely will always be."

"No thanks to Walter," Nicholas said shortly. Thomas' words had reminded Nicholas that the debt to Swineford was due. As soon as Lady Jane's funeral was done, he would have to send over the gold. It galled him that he might be paying her murderer, but if he didn't, Wyndfell would become the forfeit.

"Walter?" Jessica asked.

"Our brother, Walter, from whom Nicholas inherited this grand place and grand title. But be that as it may, I wanted to tell you that Wyndfell has never had as beautiful a mistress as you, Lady Madeline." Thomas bowed gallantly to Jessica.

Nicholas scowled at his brother's impudence. "I have an errand for you, Thomas. Since you have gamed so often with Swineford, you will be the one to take the payment to him."

"But what of the attack? Was that not Swineford's doing?"

"How can we know? But if it were, I'm sure you would have been spared. Once Lady Jane is laid to rest, you are to go, taking several guards with you to ensure that Swineford gets the money, and bring me a receipt." Without giving Thomas a chance to argue further, he spurred his horse forward, and motioned for Jessica to join him.

They rode over the blanket of wildflowers and up the hill that skirted the castle. The moat was cut deep and wide. Reed-mace lined the water's edge, while wild yellow irises grew in profusion on the sweeping banks. When they crossed the heavy timbers of the drawbridge that spanned the protective moat, the horses' hooves clopped hollowly on the planking.

The gatehouse, immediately ahead, was wide and shady with a raised portcullis at each end, signifying that the castle had been built in more turbulent times. Looking up, Jessica saw archer slits through which the castle's defenders could shoot back from a position of relative safety. Now only doves inhabited the narrow openings, their warbling coos sounding throughout the courtyard.

The cobbled yard was enclosed by the curtain wall which contained numerous outbuildings. People milled about, some wearing the usual blue of servants, others in green livery with the gold griffin of the Garrett coat of arms. Jessica looked at them more closely. While they were moderately clean, none wore a whole set of unmended clothes, and the outbuildings showed signs of neglect. This minor oversight could be easily corrected.

She dismounted at the castle steps and put her hand on Nicholas' wrist as they ascended to the main entry to the castle. As Jessica anxiously waited for Nicholas to open the massive wooden door, she noted that the large nails that studded the door to help repel attack were rusted and that the wood looked as if it had gone soft over the years. Nicholas shoved the door open with apparent ease and led her inside.

As her eyes adjusted to the dimmer interior, she found herself standing in the great hall rather than in an entry alcove as she had expected. The vast area was draped in black as befitted a house in mourning, but she could tell that the tapestries beneath the dark fabric at the windows were threadbare. She saw no painted cloths at all to cover the stone walls. She sniffed and poked at the rushes which had clearly been on the floor all winter, even though the fields were now full of sweet grasses. The trestle tables for dining were notched and gouged from long use, and a large cat lay sleeping on one.

Jessica picked the cat up in passing and stroked its broad yellow head before putting it down. While Nicholas was pointing out the many captured banners that hung from the vaulted ceiling, Jessica was looking at the rusting pikes that were mounted for display above the huge fireplace. In an alcove in the corner, she noticed that the steps that led to the chambers above were not a proper stairway at all, but rather were only hollowed stone steps built into the wall itself. Disappointment crowded in on her and she didn't know what to say. She couldn't remark on its beauty or its grace, for all she could think of was the work that needed to be done. Had she judged Nicholas wrong? Had Sir Raymond Chadwick told the truth when he said that Nicholas was miserly?

When Nicholas realized that she was unusually quiet, he sensed that she was not pleased with what she saw. For an instant he was hurt, for he was very proud of Wyndfell and wanted her to share his feelings. Realizing that she simply hadn't seen enough in order to make a fair judgment, he hurried her across the hall to the adjoining room.

The sheer beauty of the winter parlor drew her attention away from the evidences of poverty. The entire outside wall was made of colored glass that depicted St. George slaying the terrible dragon. Sunshine splashed vivid hues over the golden rushes and up the far wall. The large fireplace was graced by a mantel of inlaid teak and rosewood. Two real chairs with backs, arms, and padded velvet seats were drawn up to a gameboard. Although the walls were bare of any hangings, and the rushes needed to be changed, Jessica was captivated by this room. "It's lovely," she exclaimed with relief.

Nicholas nodded to her in appreciation for her compliment, but he was keenly aware that those were the first words she had uttered since she had entered the castle. "This was my sister-in-law's favorite room. She was wont to spend all her time here or in the gallery."

He looked back into the hall as if seeing the real condition of his home for the first time. It wasn't as he wanted it to be, but it would be, in time. Surely she could understand. After all, the lack of funds was not of his doing.

Seeing that the smile had again faded from her face, he chafed. Tapping his fingers on the back of one of the chairs, he said, "After Hargrove Castle you must think ill of the appointments here at Wyndfell." When she didn't answer, he continued, "You see, we have fallen on hard times here of late. My brother Walter had a taste for gambling and no head at all for making money."

On top of the disappointment she felt, Jessica was tired from the trip and the strain of her pretense to be Madeline. Without thinking, she acridly asked, "What of the contract money you received on our betrothal? Did you not see fit to use it on Wyndfell?"

Jessica's tone startled him. How dare she question him about money? In an equally hostile manner he responded, "I invested most of it in a ship bound for the Americas."

"You what!" Jessica had forgotten all her intentions to be a sweet and dutiful wife. Whoever had heard of risking money that was needed for the repair of a home? Certainly her parents had always put their castle first before any investments.

"It's a good ship. A caravel. If all goes well, she will return in a few months laden with gold and spices."

"Will she now?" Jessica said testily. "And what if she sinks or is pirated?"

"That is not likely to happen. I will quadruple the money I invested. Half the gain I will keep, and the rest will be invested in more ships. In ten years' time I will be richer than any of my ancestors dreamed of being."

"*If* the ship doesn't sink!" She paced the width of the room, her brow furrowed in concern. It had occurred to her, too late, that Madeline would not have engaged herself in an argument such as this. But what could she do? Then she realized that Nicholas wouldn't know the difference. Now that she was away from Hargrove Castle, she could be herself.

"Caravels are trustworthy and swift. She may be able to make two trips in the time it would take a larger ship to make one." He frowned at his new bride as if he weren't too sure what to make of her.

Without any reservation, Jessica said, "It sounds to me as if brother Walter wasn't the only Garrett with gambling in his blood. What of the repairs needed for your home? Your servants are verily in rags! What of the roofs? Are they whole?"

Nicholas glanced at the north tower through the leaded glass, then turned on her angrily. "I have no taste for leading a poor man's life. Who would, if he could prevent it? Shipping is a sound investment and one sure to restore my wealth."

"And what of your home, my lord? Will you let it fall to rack and ruin while you outfit ships for the Americas?"

"That is not a woman's concern!"

"It is a woman's gold!" she stormed, not bothering to keep her voice down.

Nicholas pulled her to him. "You forget yourself. You are my wife, and as such all your belongings are mine by right. You are not the first bride to be chosen for her wealth, nor will you be the last. Such is the way of the world."

She knew what he said was true. He had told her before that he had married her for her dowry. Yet she couldn't contain her surprise over the appearance of the castle. She had expected much more. "Did you invest all my gold in this ship? Is none left at all? Did you not think it important to ready the castle for your wife? Surely you must have known I would find it bare with no hangings or tapestries."

"You know not of what you speak. A great sum is owed upon Wyndfell and I must pay it or lose my home. Yet you prattle of new livery and tapestries."

"Lose your home! I was never told Wyndfell is in jeopardy."

"Now that we are wed, it is not. Such are a man's worries and not your own."

"I am your wife! If I'm about to lose my home, I want to know about it!"

"I have promised to care for you and to protect you. This I can and will do. Leave such matters to me."

Jessica gave him a measuring look. "You underestimate me, my lord husband. I am quite capable of being your helpmate."

"I seek only a wife," he retorted. "One with gold enough to repay my debt to Swineford and to set matters right with Wyndfell." His pride prevented him from mentioning that she had become more than a source of income to him.

She drew in her breath sharply. "Then all your desires have been met, it seems. I have brought you gold and I will serve as your wife. But bear in mind that the nights may be cold if there is naught else between us."

"What else can there be?" he demanded. He wasn't about to mention his love for her when she was speaking to him in such a manner. "Love is a ploy for a minstrel. In all the marriages to which I have been witness, never have I seen this ingredient called love. In faith, it must be rarer than a unicorn's horn."

"Aye," she answered heatedly. "And with good reason!"

Their voices had risen sharply with the exchange, and now they stood glaring at each other. Neither heard the man enter the room.

"My lord," the man said uneasily as he came near. "Welcome home."

"Greetings, Sir Richard," Nicholas said in a tight voice. "This is Wyndfell's new mistress, Lady Madeline." To Jessica he said, "My steward, Sir Richard Norwood."

She nodded a pleasant greeting at the man. "My lord husband was just instructing me in the ways of my new home."

Richard glanced from one to the other. He found it difficult to equate this smiling beauty with the high-tempered words he had heard on entering. Nicholas, who was his friend as well as his master, looked as if he were ready for combat. Having grown to adulthood with Nicholas, Richard knew all his friend's moods. Had fate been kinder, they would have been equals, but Richard's castle had been lost by his squandering father, and all the lands sold before he could inherit them. Only Nicholas' generosity and friendship had enabled Richard to come to Wyndfell as steward and still remain his master's friend. He studied his new mistress carefully. She was a rare beauty, but spirit lurked in her eyes and firm chin. This was no curds-and-whey woman such as Walter had married.

That reminded him of his errand. Respectfully he said, "Lady Jane lies in the chapel, my lord. I have arranged her funeral for today."

Nicholas swore under his breath. In his argument with Jessica he had forgotten the reason why they had returned so quickly. Even in death Jane remained unobtrusive. "We will go to the chapel now. Notify the vicar that we will arrive at the church within the hour."

"So soon?" Jessica asked.

"Now that we are here, there is no reason to delay."

Jessica followed Nicholas back outside and down the passageway to the wide stone steps that led up to the chapel. Lifting her skirts, she climbed to the outside landing. "There should be a rail here for safety's sake," she hissed as he opened the door. She wasn't over her anger yet and wasn't eager to let the discussion go.

"We at Wyndfell are not clumsy," he retorted as they entered.

The chapel was long and narrow, with tall windows of opaque green glass. At the altar was a bier and upon it lay a thin woman. Her plain face was waxen in death and her pale hands were clasped over her flat bosom as if she were in prayer.

Nicholas looked down at her sorrowfully before kneeling at the prayer rail. She had been a dutiful wife to Walter and had never crossed him, unlike Nicholas' own wife, who seemed to have a penchant for doing just that. He cast a glare at Jessica, who returned it. In fact Jane had been as quiet and calm as the stones most of the time. Her habit of fading into the background had made life smooth for her menfolk. Only when he had first brought Jessica into the hall had Nicholas noticed that his servants had become somewhat less respectful and lax in their duties. Even the rushes hadn't been changed in some time. Supervision of the household had been Lady Jane's one responsibility. He reflected for the first time that perhaps his sister-in-law had been too spiritual. Guilt washed over him, and he dropped to his knees and prayed for forgiveness for his ungenerous thoughts and for the safekeeping of Jane's soul. He also found himself praying that he wasn't about to find himself saddled with a shrew for a wife.

They remained thus until the menservants came to carry Jane's body to the hall. Nicholas put his hand under Jessica's elbow and lifted her from her kneeling position. He glanced at her to see if her unpredictable temper was under control, only to find that she seemed as gentle now as she had in front of her parents. She had two aspects, this wife of his, and he was puzzled.

In a short time, Lady Jane lay in state in the great hall. All the castle servants filed in, far more than could have entered the tiny chapel. The chaplain, a short and rotund man with red cheeks and wispy hair, solemnly closed the coffin after all had viewed her. He placed a large pot of wine on the lid and turned to face the gathered people.

"Lady Jane Garrett was a good woman," he intoned. "She was pious by nature, gentle always to her servants, and the perfect picture of wifely submission."

Jessica felt Nicholas looking at her rather pointedly and she met his eyes boldly. She had no intention of being submissive to him. Already she could see her duties were set out for her. If he wanted a wife who could manage a castle, he had one. All the servants she had seen thus far, with the exception of the steward, were deplorable. A woman's firm hand was sorely needed and she was going to see that it was applied. She had been foolish ever to think a man would marry a woman and expect to gain more from the arrangement than an overseer for his household. All marriages were thus.

Jessica glanced around the room to see who would be her ladies-in-waiting, but she found no one of rank at all, judging by their garments. Was she to be completely unattended? The thought was unbelievable. When her eyes fell on Thomas, he gave her a slight smile, and at once she felt better. Nicholas might be as rough-mannered as a soldier, but Thomas was gentler. She could talk to him, at least, and she had always wanted a brother.

For the next half hour the chaplain praised the dead woman's virtues and omitted her faults, making her seem a veritable saint. Jessica tried to listen attentively but she had never known the woman and her thoughts kept returning to the manner of Jane's death. She had been shot here in Wyndfell itself, through one of the windows. Nicholas seemed to know who had ordered the attack. Would he strike back? Life here might be far more interesting than at Hargrove Castle. She, however, wasn't eager to be caught in the middle of a feud, so she decided it was her place to talk sense into Nicholas to prevent him from launching a private war.

When the chaplain finished his eulogy, the wine was passed around as a loving cup, while the mourners filed by to lay a sprig of evergreen yew on the coffin. Sir Richard handed Nicholas a velvet bag and he solemnly gave a penny to all the children. Then Richard brought in a large box from which Nicholas took ribbons and scarves to give to all the adults. Thomas came forward to help distribute the gifts. When it was done, Thomas laid a bouquet of rosemary on the coffin. He broke off a bit to put in his hat and did the same for Nicholas and Jessica.

Because Jane had been all but a recluse the last years of her life, the procession was small. The castle folk paraded solemnly to the church, unaccompanied by any of the local guildsmen or professional mourners. The coffin, drawn by two black horses, was covered by the same pall that had sheltered Walter and his parents before him. The hearse, a black canopy carried over the coffin, was supported by Sir Richard, who was Jane's distant cousin, and by three other men.

As they entered the church, Jessica hesitated superstitiously. Surely bad luck would result from going into a church for a funeral so soon after her wedding. But she could not refuse, so she walked in on Nicholas' arm, aware that many of the stares were for her rather than the coffin.

The vicar read the burial service and the coffin was lowered into a grave made in the pavement of the chancel. The smell of fresh earth came to Jessica as she walked by and tossed a bit of evergreen into the opening. The grave was beside Walter's, his stern effigy already in place. Jessica studied it to see any resemblance to Nicholas, but there was none. The village stonemason was evidently not very talented at making true likenesses. But the stone figure was a well-carved depiction of a powerfully built man in full armor, with his palms pressed together in eternal prayer. When Jane's effigy was finished, it would no doubt show her in a similar posture. Centered on the wall between the graves was a stone tablet which warned against removal of the bodies, a necessary measure, as the graveyard and chancel had limited space.

When all was done, the granite slab was slid over the opening, hiding Jane's coffin forever. The grating of stone upon stone made Jessica shiver, and Nicholas put his arm around her. She gazed up at him. He had not been cruel to her, she reflected. Perhaps she should at least try to be more dutiful and quieter than was her nature. After all, he had rescued her from a living grave in Leopold's cell, whether he knew it or not.

She looked sweetly up at him, remembering to keep her lips closed as a lady should, then cast down her eyes. Nicholas frowned slightly as if he wondered what she was up to now. To reassure him, Jessica said, "Has the feast been prepared for the mourners?"

"Sir Richard will have arranged it."

"And the black gowns for the parish poor? Have they been distributed?"

"No gowns were ordered," he said. "You forget Wyndfell is not as richly endowed as your castle."

"Wyndfell now is my castle," she reminded him, "and a countess is due proper mourning. I will send for black stuff to sew into peasant garb and set the needlewomen to work at once."

Nicholas smiled at her warily. "Lady Jane will be honored."

"That was my intention," she answered as she smiled in return. Pleasing him wasn't so difficult.

Thomas joined them as they led the procession back to Wyndfell. "I have had little chance to talk to you since arriving at Wyndfell, my lady," he said with a bow. "You must think we Garretts have no gallantry at all."

"Nonsense, Brother Thomas. I find the Garrett men most noble." She flashed him her most dazzling smile.

Nicholas watched her closely. He wasn't certain he liked being lumped together with Thomas in that way. And she was smiling at his brother in a manner that would turn a stronger head than Thomas'. He decided that he'd better keep a close watch on his brother.

When they reached the castle, Jessica was still busily talking with Thomas, who was giving her his undivided attention. Nicholas' frown deepened. Heretofore, if a woman preferred one of his brothers to him, he shrugged it off in the sure knowledge that for that one woman there were two more waiting and willing. But this woman was his wife, and the jealousy he felt was a new emotion for him, one of which he was uncertain. He didn't want to react inappropriately and cause embarrassment for himself or his new wife.

Unable to cope with the frustration he was feeling, Nicholas turned his thoughts to a subject he could manage. As he strode into the hall, he bade his guests to begin the feast, but he motioned tersely to his bailiff. He led the man up to his closet and turned on him angrily. "Now, Sir Oliver. What say you about my sister-in-law's death?"

Sir Oliver looked at him warily, for Nicholas' temper was well-known. "As I have told you, my lord, it was an accident. The castle was attacked. We drew up the drawbridge and lowered the portcullis, both of them to be sure. I ordered the men-at-arms to the slits and we were giving as good as we got. It would have amounted to naught save a bloody skirmish except that the Lady Jane went to a window in the gallery."

"Why would she do such a damn-fool thing?" Nicholas demanded as if the fault were Sir Oliver Braeburn's own. Behind the bailiff, Nicholas saw Jessica enter the room, but he paid her no heed.

"I know not Lady Jane's reason," Sir Oliver said in his defense. "Mayhap she thought to watch the battle. There was no way the enemy could take Wyndfell, so I saw no reason to confine the womenfolk in the keep."

"You saw no reason," Nicholas snapped, his anger growing when Jessica remained in the room. Couldn't she see he was giving the bailiff a necessary upbraiding? Why didn't she return to the hall? "You saw no reason, and now Lady Jane is dead!"

"It was an accident!" Oliver protested. "A stray bullet."

"Or one intended for my kin!"

"My lord!" Jessica interrupted, stepping between the men. "He has said it was an accident!"

"This matter does not concern you!" Nicholas roared.

"But it does! I cannot see you besiege this poor man due to a matter over which he had no control." She recalled the countless times she had been accused and punished for Madeline's deeds. "Do you think Sir Oliver shot Lady Jane?"

"Of course not!"

"Then why ever are you railing at him thus?" To Sir Oliver she said, "You defended our castle and we are grateful for that. Go now and attend the feast."

Both men stared at her in amazement. Sir Oliver glanced uncertainly at his master but made no movement toward the door.

Ignoring his wife's interference, Nicholas turned his attention back to his bailiff. "Lady Jane's death must be avenged, but I know not who is responsible. You say that Swineford was behind the attack, yet you give me no proof!" With his jaw tightly clenched, Nicholas thought for a moment, then ordered Sir Oliver to dispatch a guard force from the men-at-arms. "Post them in the oak copse that borders Swineford's land. I cannot attack him in retaliation, for I am not positive of his guilt, but if any of his armed men fail to take heed of the warning not to cross the boundary into our parish, you will kill them."

"Lord Nicholas! That is illegal!" Jessica disputed, miffed at being ignored. "And uncivilized," she added. "There are laws to protect us."

"The Queen and her laws are in London. We are here, days away."

The confused bailiff stared from master to mistress and back again.

"Still you must appeal to Her Majesty, else you are also a lawbreaker."

Nicholas glared at her. "I fully intend to inform the Queen of Lady Jane's death and the circumstance of the attack. In the meantime"—he turned his angry countenance upon Sir Oliver—"you will guard the oak grove and protect against another attack. Is that clear?"

"Aye, my lord."

"But, Nicholas, you cannot send men out to do murder . . ." Jessica began.

"Out of my sight!" Nicholas ordered the bailiff. When Sir Oliver had all but run from the room, Nicholas wheeled upon Jessica. "Have you lost your senses!" he demanded. "You have no right to defend anyone against me, and especially one of my own men!"

"Should I stand by and see a man unjustly accused? I am, after all, the Countess of Wyndfell and not some strumpet off the road. I have a duty to my servants, and Sir Oliver is as much my bailiff as he is yours."

Nicholas closed the distance between them and jerked her to him. "You will not talk to me like this!"

Jessica shoved against his chest but found she couldn't break his clasp. "I will speak however I please!" She knew if she backed down now, he would always expect her to give in to him.

Bending, Nicholas threw her over his shoulder as if she were a sack of meal.

"Put me down!" Jessica demanded, hitting at his back.

Nicholas made no reply, but strode with her out of his closet and down the corridor toward their private wing. He met Sir Richard going toward the hall, and Nicholas nodded to him abruptly without speaking, and strode on.

Richard paused and nodded in return, and after they had passed him, he turned to stare at the sight of Nicholas' strange burden. A wide grin spread over his face.

Jessica glared at her steward's bemused expression and struck her husband again. "Put me down!" she hissed in fury.

Nicholas ignored her completely. At the end of the corridor he shoved open a heavily carved door and strode into a room well furnished with fancy chests and two painted chairs with arms. He didn't stop there, but passed through after kicking the door shut with a bang. He entered an inner chamber, also slamming that door, and dumped her on the bed.

"How dare you treat me thus!" she demanded, rolling to a sitting position and rubbing her stomach. "Sir Richard saw you! He will have lost respect for me!"

"On the other hand, as news spreads of your defense of Sir Oliver, I will gain face by having called you to task."

"Will you! No man calls me to heel as if I were a schoolboy!" Fire leapt in her stormy eyes and her hair seemed to crackle in temperament. "I am your wife!"

"As I well recall, and you apparently need reminding." He had removed his tippet and was yanking open the laces of his jerkin.

"What are you doing!" she demanded.

"What would you guess?" he growled.

"You can't! Not now! We have a hall full of guests that I must tend to."

"You should have thought of your wifely duties earlier." He stripped off his doublet and released the points that held up his trunk hose.

"I'm not staying here!" she announced firmly. "If you wish to lie abed, you will do it alone. I must see to my guests." She slid off the high bed and tried to flounce past him, but he caught her wrist.

"You're going nowhere, Madeline," he growled. "One would think you are two people, from your actions. Around your parents you are the soul of sweetness, but now you might pass as a village shrew."

"Turn me loose!"

"Nay, love. Not until I wipe the battle from your eye and have again my sweet wife."

"You can never keep me here that long," she retorted. "For men will ever be duped by silly grins and blushing glances, but I will have none of such games! You will have me as I am or not at all." She tried to pull free, but he caught her to him.

Her struggles were to no avail, and in no time he had stripped her to her chemise. Jessica cried out for help, though she knew no one would dare rescue her, even if anyone heard.

"Call all you like." Nicholas grinned spitefully. "None will hear you over the din in the hall, and if anyone did, he would never invade my chamber."

"You're no better than an animal!"

"And like an animal, I have mated in kind!" He pulled back the bedcovers and dumped her upon the sheet.

Jessica rolled away from him. "In kind? Nay! For I am more than match for you!"

His white teeth flashed in his broad grin as he came after her. "No lass may better me!" He pinned her easily and knelt astride her middle.

"You best me only in size!" she ground out. "What man would battle with a lady?"

"What *lady* would force him to?" His mouth came down on hers and when she tried to bite him, he caught her lip between his teeth.

Jessica freed one arm and clouted her fist against his ear.

With a growl, Nicholas again imprisoned her and with one hard yank ripped open her chemise. Jessica fought him wildly. "Would you rape me, my lord?" she asked scathingly.

"Only if you continue to fight me."

"Then rape me you must, for I will never give in to you now!"

"Won't you?" Nicholas grinned. Again his mouth closed over hers, forcing her to calm in order to breathe.

Jessica fought against him, but by merely shifting

his position, he could cut off her air. Her eyes narrowed and she pretended to give in. He chuckled softly at his easy victory and released her wrists. She waited until he was relaxed, then shoved against him as hard as she could.

With a startled yell, Nicholas tumbled to the floor. Jessica scrambled to the end of the bed and was almost to the door when his hand fastened around her ankle. She kicked against him but fell to the floor, only to be dragged back to him.

He pulled her beneath him on the bear rug before the hearth and glared down at her as he held her in an iron grip. "I will tame you!" he said between clenched teeth.

"Never!"

Her color was high and her golden hair waved about her face like a halo of light. Dark blue fire flashed in her eyes and her pink lips were parted, revealing her even teeth. Nicholas had never seen so beautiful a woman. He kissed her long and hard, willing her to submit to him. Instead she struggled and bit at his lip. He gave a strangled cry and lowered his mouth to the proud breasts that were bared beneath him.

Jessica tried to wriggle away, but he was not to be fooled a second time and he held her fast. His mouth sent fire through her rebellious body, and she cried out in frustration at not being able to oust him or to control herself. Still he licked and kissed her breasts, drawing her nipples into his mouth, one after the other, in such a way that she arched her back, not knowing if she still fought against him or if she struggled to give herself to him.

He entered her quickly and she cried out in surprise. Still holding her beneath him, he began a steady rhythm that excited her beyond belief. His lips found hers and she met his tongue, tasting his mouth as he tasted hers. The fires kindled higher and she matched his thrusts eagerly.

With a roll of her body, she changed positions so that she lay on top of him. His eyes widened but she lowered her face to kiss him as she continued the undulations of her hips. He moaned with pleasure and Jessica grinned, then pulled back so that only the tips of her breasts grazed his bare chest and he was drawn even deeper into her.

Nicholas wound her hair around his palm and pulled her back to his lips as a sudden release of passion thundered through them both. Their lips muffled their moans as both met their completion.

Jessica lay upon him, her rapid breathing matching his own, her heart beating its cadence with his. Slowly he stroked her tangled hair and kissed her forehead.

"There now, love," he said in his deep voice. "Was it so bad to submit to your husband?"

Jessica raised her head until her eyes met his. "I am on top, Nicholas. I would say you submitted to me." She gave him her sweetest smile before he tumbled her to the floor.

Nicholas was frowning as he pinned her unresisting hands to either side of her head.

"Shall we do it again?" she asked innocently. "This time you may be on top."

For a minute longer he glared at her; then a low laugh began deep in his chest. Laughter roared from him and after a moment she joined in. He rolled from her and lay on his back beside her, pulling her head to lie on his shoulder. Jessica watched him warily, but he made no move to punish her pert words, so she relaxed against him contentedly.

9

JESSICA'S BAGGAGE, CONTAINING the fine tapestries and wall cloths worked by Madeline's skillful fingers, came two days after her arrival at her new home, and she was all smiles as she unpacked the brightly stitched finery. Nicholas professed no concern in such womanly interests as tapestries and wall cloths, but he stayed in the hall, she noticed, and peered into chest after chest.

"Your parents must have hoped a long time for your marriage," he teased. "You have near enough needlework here to fit out all of Wyndfell."

Her hands faltered, and she glanced at him nervously. She well knew it was her own fault neither she nor her sister had been married years before. "I sew quickly," she said.

Nicholas held up an allegory which depicted a scene of a dragon battling a griffin. "This is the emblem for our family. How came you to fashion a griffin?"

"I saw a sketch done by a vendor that frequented Hargrove Castle. At the time I had no thought as to how appropriate it would be," she said as she smiled

at him winningly. "Will you hang it in your closet?
The window beside your bookshelf seemed drafty to
me."

"I'll take it gladly." He handed it to a maid, who
curtsied and carried it away to be hung.

"These painted cloths, we'll hang here in the hall,"
Jessica said decisively as she unfurled a long strip of
tempera-painted canvas, colorfully arrayed with summer flowers. "Also the ones with the falconry design.
The ones with unicorns and the ones with ivy vines
will be put in the winter parlor. If there are any left
over, I will hang them in the ladies' parlor."

Nicholas watched with amusement as she sent servants scampering for ladders and rushing about frantically to do her bidding. Thomas, too, had come to
see what her bridal chests contained, and was leaning against the doorway, a grin upon his lips as he
watched her. His gaze was directed more toward the
curve of her breasts and the slender span of her
waist than her needlework. Nicholas narrowed his
eyes. Since Jessica had come to Wyndfell he had felt
an uneasiness toward his unmarried brother. He glow-
ered at Thomas until the man gave him an infuriating grin and sauntered out of the hall.

Summoning a half-grown lad, Jessica called, "You,
boy! Start scrubbing down the trestle tables."

"Scrub, my lady?" the boy said doubtfully. "The
tables?"

"Yes, you heard me. And get that cat back into the
kitchen where it belongs," she added, pointing to the
big yellow ball of fur that dozed on the table.

"But Old Tess always sleeps there," the boy informed her. "She was a pet of Lady Jane's."

"Old Tess *used* to sleep there," she corrected. "Now
she sleeps in the kitchen." As the boy picked up the

cat and started to leave, she said, "Send in some other boys. These rushes are to be changed at once."

The boy stared at her, but bobbed his body in an awkward bow.

"You manage the servants as if they were a battalion and you the general," Nicholas observed in amusement.

"They but need clear instructions," she said with the confidence of a woman accustomed to being obeyed, though she'd never had such responsibility before. Her talent for this sort of thing was a natural one. "You! On the ladder! The cloth is hanging askew. Lift that side. There, you have it now." To Nicholas she said, "Meaning no disrespect, but I wonder that Lady Jane didn't see to all this. To look at the castle one would think no woman had been near it in ages."

"Lady Jane was of an ascetic turn. She would have been better suited for the convent than marriage. Her pleasures were in a psalm well-sung or in listening to a sermon, rather than in seeing to fresh rushes for the floor or painting canvas wall coverings." He helped her lift a large tapestry. "You'll find the chaplain well versed and his office carried out in perfect order."

"Unfortunately, guests care more about the hall's bareness and the smell of soured rushes than the proficiency of a chaplain," she pointed out. "No more tongues shall wag about Wyndfell's poor condition."

"You've heard ill about Wyndfell?"

"I never heard of this place at all before the betrothal," she said over her shoulder as she showed the menservants where to hang the tapestry.

"We may have fallen on hard times," Nicholas objected, "but surely you must have at least . . ."

"No, not a word," she assured him. "But we had

few visitors at Hargrove Castle." Then, "No, no, you're hanging it upside down." She hurried to the window to set the tapestry right.

Nicholas was thoughtful as he watched her. She might be fiery-tempered, but she certainly knew how to work wonders. Already the drab walls were brightened by long cloths, and several boys were starting to shovel out the noisome rushes. After having walked over them all winter, Nicholas hadn't noticed just how rank they had become until they were stirred. "Dickon," he said to a servant entering the hall, "take some men and gather fresh rushes for all the rooms. Mab, go to the herbal garden and pick rosemary and thyme to strew atop the rushes. Mayhap some fresh mint." They went to do his bidding and Nicholas walked over to Jessica.

"I had thought to put in a staircase," he said. "There, in that corner."

"A real staircase?" she asked eagerly. "But it should go over here by the outer wall."

"Why would I put it there," he asked, "when my closet is back nearer the corner?"

"Because," she said firmly, "the main corridor is over by the outer wall, as well as our bedchamber and the ladies' parlor."

"We will seldom go from hall to bedchamber, save once up and once down. I'm in and out of my closet all day."

"Then we will build a corridor to connect your closet with the stairway, or you may move your closet into another room." Her voice was silkily polite.

"That chamber has been the master's closet since this wing was built many yeas ago." His voice, too, was heavy with politeness.

"Then mayhap it's time for a change," she suggested.

"I am master here and I say the stairway goes in the back corner!"

"I am mistress and I say it does not!"

"We will see!"

"If you build one back there, Wyndfell will be the only castle in England to have two great stairways!"

He frowned down at her and she glared up at him. The trouble was, her argument made sense. A corridor connecting his closet to the private wing would be easily constructed. But he hated to give in. "We will paint the risers green and the railings yellow."

"The railings may be yellow," she conceded, "but the risers will look much better in red."

"Whoever heard of red risers?" he asked in exasperation.

"My Aunt Catherine has red ones and she lives in London. My mother has said they are most fetching."

"I care not for 'fetching' risers. Ours will be green, as is our livery."

Now that he mentioned it, the green and gold of Wyndfell's banner would look pretty on the stairs, but if she gave in too easily, would he not expect her to do so on all matters? "You may paint your stairs green. Mine will be red."

Before Nicholas could reply, a messenger wearing the Hargrove colors entered the hall and bowed deeply before them. "Lord Nicholas," he said. "My lady."

"Yes. What is it?" Nicholas growled as Jessica turned away from them both. He couldn't understand why she angered him so easily. Could she never be pliant as a lady should be?

"I bring greetings from my master and mistress of Hargrove Castle and their wishes of finding you and Lady Madeline well."

"Of course we're well," he snapped. For some reason Jessica had turned her face away and he couldn't catch her eye to see if she was truly upset with him. "We only left them a few days ago."

The messenger faltered at Nicholas' stormy reception, but he continued. "My master and mistress are on a progress to York Minister Cathedral. They beg leave to stop here for a few days to visit you and your lady wife."

"A progress so soon after a wedding?" To Jessica he quipped in a low voice, "It seems they were glad to be rid of you and are on a pilgrimage of thanksgiving."

She ignored him and put her hand nervously to her pale throat. "My parents? Here? When?" Her voice was filled with anxious anticipation.

"On the morrow, my lady, before sundown."

When her breath caught in her throat, Nicholas looked to her with curiosity, then turned back to the messenger. "You may leave us. Take a fresh horse from my stable and ride to tell your master that he and his lady wife are welcome at Wyndfell." When the man left, Nicholas said in a voice only Jessica could hear, "You seem overly eager to see your parents. One would think you were a child bride of fourteen instead of a grown woman of twenty."

"You mistake me," she said without thinking. "I dread their arrival most gravely." Hurrying away, she raised her voice to the servants. "Hang the blue drapery over that window and the yellow one over there. Hurry! There's much to be done. You! Nan, is it? Come show me to the guest chambers. I doubt not there is work to be done there."

Nicholas watched her go and his expression grew thoughtful. True, she had just left her parents and had had no time to miss them; then he recalled that she had told him of their cruelty to her, and he understood her dread. Why were they coming so soon? Their own guests from the wedding must only now have departed. Nicholas was full of curiosity as to what he might expect from her parents. Although he doubted they would do anything untoward during their visit, he was fully prepared to defend his wife, whatever might come. Nicholas stayed in the hall to supervise the hanging of the remaining cloths.

Devona and Randolph Hargrove were sighted on the road leading to Wyndfell the next afternoon, and Jessica was alerted as to their imminent arrival. All the Wyndfell servants were still in a state of high activity, finishing with last-minute details. Clean rushes lay on the floors of the hall and both parlors, their fresh scent dispelling the faint musty odor left by their predecessors. All the bright cloths of Madeline's bridal chest were in place and the pikes above the mantel in the hall were burnished to a high gleam, and the cobwebs had been struck from the captured battle banners that lined the ceiling.

Until her parents reached the drawbridge, Jessica had run about the castle in a flurry of last-minute orders. Now she stood on the steps beside her husband and Thomas, nervously clasping and unclasping her hands. As the first of the entourage entered the gates, Jessica felt a wave of nausea. She couldn't hope to pass herself as Madeline over a span of days, especially since she was certain that her mother was already suspicious.

"Why such a dither, love?" Nicholas asked, his dark eyes searching her face as if probing beyond whatever answer she would give. Surely, she must know he would protect her against her parents, if need be. What the matter could be, he couldn't guess, save for her feelings about the present condition of the castle. "Your household affairs are in order. Why, I've not seen Wyndfell look so good in years."

"Dither? What dither?" She adjusted her yellow brocade kirtle yet again and anxiously touched her hand to the French hood that concealed most of her hair. "I only want to impress my parents, that's all," she lied.

"You are a countess, sweetheart. That is impressive enough."

His face lit up encouragingly, but Jessica's concern kept her from responding in kind. Was she a countess? Or was she merely her sister's proxy? When her parents learned what she had done, who could tell what might happen to her? A new, most dreadful thought occurred to her. What if Madeline was with them?

"Pardon, my lord," she said faintly. "I recall something I've forgotten." She turned to flee, but Nicholas put his arm about her.

"It can wait. Here are your parents now."

Jessica glanced over her shoulder. Devona and Randolph were riding into the yard of milling people, their horses prancing at the unfamiliar surroundings. Behind them rode their personal servants. But not Madeline.

"Welcome to Wyndfell," Nicholas boomed, making an expansive gesture as if to offer them all his estate.

Jessica forced a smile to her lips and lowered her eyes demurely. "I welcome you, Mother, Father. Did you have a pleasant journey?"

Her parents dismounted and came up the steps, both of them staring at Jessica as they made a show of greeting her and her husband. "A pleasant journey. Yes," Randolph said absently as he studied her.

"The cook is preparing farsed chicken," she said,

"with lots of cherries. I know it's your favorite." She gave him her sweetest expression.

Randolph visibly relaxed and kissed her cheek. "Good, child. Good."

Jessica glanced at her mother, who was watching her as if she were a snake. "Mother, how good it is to see you so soon. Welcome to Wyndfell."

Nicholas had been watching his wife with great surprise. She was suddenly as sweet and gentle as she had been on their wedding day. Even her speech was different, with a hint of a lisp. He had almost begun to believe he had imagined that she had ever been so affable. "Come in," he welcomed as he led them into the hall. He looked around proudly at his castle's new splendor.

Tess, the big yellow cat, had slipped in during the flurry of arrival and taken her customary place on the table. Without breaking stride, Nicholas scooped the animal up before his guests could notice her. Jessica was being so cordial, he felt he should meet her halfway and lend a helping hand, though he knew the cat was cleaner than most of the men who shared the table with Tess.

"Your castle is magnificent," Randolph praised. "A skillful hand has prepared your needlework."

Devona, who naturally recognized every piece, nodded curtly. "Certainly so."

"My lord husband has replaced his other tapestries and hangings with these of mine in order to please me," Jessica spoke up. She had seen Nicholas take the cat from the table, and she was grateful.

Nicholas gestured with the hand that held the cat. "That one with the unicorn is my favorite." As he made another sweeping gesture, the cat merely blinked as if accustomed to being passed about in the air. "By next year I plan to have glass in all these windows."

"Glass?" Devona echoed. "I assumed . . ."

"Come see the winter parlor," Jessica said before her mother could affront Nicholas by saying every window in Hargrove Castle's more important rooms had glass. She swept past them and pushed open the door. The vivid hues of the large stained-glass window drew an approving murmur, even from Devona.

Randolph ran his hand over the closest chair and looked approvingly on his son-in-law. "A man who has chairs other than at his table is truly refined. I'll not worry for my daughter in so gentle a hand."

Nicholas looked at his wife and said, "Never fear for her at all, for she is safe with me."

"That does remind me of the reason for your hasty departure," Randolph said. "I was concerned that Madeline might be in danger of the same fate as that of your brother's late widow. Now that I've seen your castle, my mind is at ease."

"Wyndfell is well fortified. Lady Jane foolishly stepped into the line of fire. Now that I have returned, there will be no repetition of that unfortunate skirmish." His firm voice was as reassuring as Wyndfell's massive walls.

"Madeline," Devona said, "could you show me to our chambers? I am not accustomed to such long riding and would like to rest."

"Certainly," Jessica said contritely. Madeline would never have needed such prompting, she reminded herself. "In my gladness to see you, I have forgotten my manners." Keeping her eyes downcast, Jessica led Devona and her serving women up the tower stairs.

"You have no staircase?" Devona said, touching her fingertips to the damp wall.

"We plan to build one right away." Jessica was glad Devona hadn't seen Wyndfell in the state she had first seen it herself.

Devona, who harbored no fantasies as to why an earl would wish to marry the daughter of a rich viscount, made a doubtful sound.

"I have drawn a cartoon laying out a tapestry for this wall," Jessica said when her mother looked disapprovingly at the damp stones. "When the cloth vendor comes I will start it right away."

"Jessica was always clever at devising patterns," Devona mused aloud. "Who is your lady-in-waiting? Why have I not seen her?"

"Actually, I have none as yet. But there are many servants, and one is particularly amiable to me."

"A countess does not befriend her serving wenches," Devona reprimanded sharply.

Jessica bit her lip and kept her head averted. Another slip like that and her secret would be out, if it wasn't already. Since her mother had not directly accused her of duplicity, perhaps she didn't know. Jessica could only pray and be careful that she didn't give herself away. "Yes, Mother, I know," she said softly. "I never meant to make her my confidante."

"I should hope not. When we leave, I will ask one of my own women to stay with you."

"That won't be necessary," Jessica said hastily. All her mother's women knew both her and Madeline, of course, and would be all too happy to send word of the duplicity to Jessica's parents.

"Nonsense. No woman of your rank can manage without at least one noblewoman to attend her. Whom could you talk to?"

"Surely Nicholas has his own kin. I doubt not that a suitable companion has been sent for and has simply not yet arrived."

"What of this Lady Jane? Had she no women about her?"

"I understand she was of a contemplative turn and very religious. She neither required nor wanted female companionship, but rather busied herself with prayer."

"Rubbish. A man gets prayers from his chaplain and vicar. From his wife he expects gaiety."

"Yes, Mother," Jessica forced herself to say meekly.

They reached the wing set aside for guests and Jessica pushed open the door. Her worried glance perused the chamber. It wasn't nearly as grand as the suites at Hargrove Castle. On hearing Devona's disapproving sniff, Jessica knew that even with her thorough cleaning, the rooms were sorely lacking. "I plan to sew cloths for these rooms as well," she said defensively. "As you know, I have had no time."

"You will do nothing but ply a needle for a year's time if you cover all the bare walls I've seen thus far. Had there been no hangings at all?"

"As I've said, Lady Jane was religious and had no mind toward frivolities."

"She sounds perfectly deplorable. Thank goodness she is no longer here to influence you."

Sharply Jessica responded to her mother's goadings. "You speak of my dead sister-in-law. She was the Countess of Wyndfell and of higher rank by birth than either you or I."

Devona triumphantly wheeled to face her daughter. To her ladies she said briskly, "Leave us."

Horrified, Jessica stared at her mother, realizing too late that she had been tricked into revealing her true nature. When they were alone, Jessica went to the opposite door, hoping to hide her slip by changing the subject. "This doorway leads to the bedchamber of your ladies-in-waiting. Beyond is your bedchamber. I'm certain you and Father will be comfortable there. The mattresses are freshly turned and the bedding newly washed."

"Stop your prattle," Devona snapped. "You are not Madeline, but are Jessica!"

Feeling all the blood leave her face, Jessica forced herself to smile. "Do not tease me, Mother. How is Jessica? Why did she not come with you? Has she not yet been found?"

"No! You are Jessica!" Devona stared at her with widening eyes. "My God! What have you done with Madeline?"

Jessica dropped all pretense and faced her mother squarely. "I have done nothing at all with her. She ran away on the morn of her wedding. I took her place in order to save the family great embarrassment and shame."

"You fiend! How could you do such a thing?" Devona pressed her fingertips to her lips. "Madeline has run away? No! I don't believe it! Madeline—alone?"

"She isn't alone. Sir Raymond Chadwick was with her."

"I can't believe that!"

"It's true. You have always refused to believe ill of Madeline."

"I don't believe it now. You have done something terrible to her! Killed her even!" She stared with horror at her daughter. "You are mad!"

"No! I am not insane and never was. That claim goes to Madeline." Jessica glared at Devona and crossed her arms over her chest as she watched her mother pace the floor.

"You have done this . . . this hideous deed in order to escape the cell you so clearly deserve." Devona's voice was reedy and her skin seemed to stretch tautly across her cheekbones. "You have murdered your sister!"

"I have not! Think back. Did you see Sir Raymond at the wedding? Was his absence not marked by more than one?"

"Yes, but . . ."

"Surely you don't credit me with murdering him as well!"

Devona stared at Jessica as she groped blindly for a stool. "You're Jessica," she repeated as if to herself. "Where is my poor, sweet Madeline?"

The words tore at Jessica's heart and she knelt beside her mother's knee. "You never knew her as I did," she began.

"Not know my own daughter? Preposterous! I knew Madeline and I know you!" Devona jumped to her feet and hurried toward the door. "Randolph and Lord Nicholas must be told at once!"

"Stop!" Jessica ordered, running after Devona. She caught her at the door to the guest parlor. "Think what will happen if you tell Nicholas."

"You will be returned to Hargrove Castle and the mad cell as you should be," Devona ground out, "and we may start searching for Madeline. Or her body."

"I swear to you that Madeline was alive and well when I last saw her. If you think back, she left before the wedding. *I* married Lord Nicholas."

"No, no, it couldn't have been you."

"But it was. I am the lawful Countess of Wyndfell and Lord Nicholas Garrett's wife."

"Madeline was his betrothed!"

"Nevertheless, he married me!" Jessica lifted her head. "He also bedded me. Even now I may be carrying the future Earl of Wyndfell."

Devona stared at Jessica as if she couldn't comprehend what she was hearing.

"I took Madeline's place in order to save both our family name and myself," Jessica admitted. "Had I not done so, Lord Nicholas might have pulled down Hargrove Castle stone by stone. You know not what a fearsome temper he has." When Devona looked uncertain, Jessica elaborated. "Even the mildest disturbance is enough to send him into a rage. We all walk with caution and try not to upset him. Who knows what might happen if he thought he married the wrong sister?" She watched Devona carefully to see if she was believing all this.

"Do you mean he might become violent?"

"Who can tell? Besides, I married him in the village church before all our people and I have lived with him ever since. To take me away would cause more trouble than to leave me here. Especially if I carry his child."

"You can't know that! Not so soon!"

"No," she admitted, "but neither can I be sure that I am not. You have seen how he is. What would he think of having Papa take away his son? His rage would be ferocious."

Slowly Devona's hand dropped away from the door. "Yes. Yes, I can see that."

Far below, a trumpet blew, calling everyone to the table. Jessica reached out her hand to caress her mother's shoulder. "Fret not, Mama. Nicholas is not too cruel a man. I will fare quite well."

Devona jerked away as if burned by Jessica's touch. "Do you think I worry for you? Never! You have always been able to look after yourself. It's Madeline I fear for."

Jessica exchanged a long look with Devona and realized that from this moment on she would have no mother. And likely no father either as soon as Devona could get Randolph alone. Then, without a word, Jessica led Devona back through the corridor and down the steps to join the men.

Nicholas noted Jessica's strained expression with dismay. All wives placed too much value in a well-run and pleasingly appointed home, yet Wyndfell had fallen in disrepair under Walter's rule. Perhaps Devona had pointed this out to Jessica, or mayhap one of the servants, grown lax under Lady Jane's hand, had given offense. He wanted Jessica to smile and bubble with excitement as she had on the trip to the castle. Having seen her livelier nature, Nicholas found her meekness rather pallid. Yet such was proper and befitting in a lady. He had often said so himself. In time he hoped to subdue her quick temper, yet retain her happy exuberance and thus create the perfect wife. As a means to that end, Nicholas determined that he would do all in his power to make her parents' visit as pleasant as possible. He led Jessica into the hall, with Thomas, her parents, and their retainers close behind. His castle staff respectfully rose to their feet as Nicholas seated his wife in one of the great chairs beneath the canopy on the dais. The chaplain stood after everyone else was seated and asked God's blessings on food and Queen.

The meal was served efficiently, but without the finesse Nicholas had observed at Hargrove Castle. When the fowl was slow in arriving, he glared at the carver, causing the man to stumble and nearly drop the bird. Nicholas watched the man closely as he spoiled the hen and divided it for the honored guests. Had the man been drinking again? Nicholas had reprimanded him for drunkenness at mealtimes before. Yes, Nicholas thought, the man was unsteady on his feet.

After the chicken was eaten, the fish course was brought in. Nicholas dipped the point of his knife in the salt cellar, and as he sprinkled salt on his chined salmon, he wondered if the drunken carver would make it through the meal without mishap. Thus far Randolph seemed not to have noticed and Devona still appeared miffed over whatever had happened upstairs. So did Jessica, though she kept her face calm and her eyes downcast. Only the paleness of her cheeks gave her away.

Nicholas picked up a morsel of fish studded with almond slivers and was about to eat it when he caught its odor. Suspiciously he sniffed at the white dish. "Rancid!" he exclaimed with the good intention of informing the other diners, forgetting he was trying to impress his in-laws favorably. "The fish has gone rancid!"

The serving man flinched at his master's roar and stared down at the offending dish. Without pause, Nicholas put his fish and Jessica's back on the serving dish, then leaned over to do the same for her parents. Thomas watched him apprehensively.

"Take this back to the kitchens at once and bring the next course. Tell the cook I'll see to him later," he growled to the servant, then grinned to put his guests at ease.

Jessica was rubbing her forehead with her fingertips as if she had a headache. Devona was sitting bolt upright as though she might have been offended royalty, and Randolph was staring at the spot on his plate where the fish had recently lain.

"These things happen," Nicholas said to smooth matters over. "I once saw a venison brought in that must have been older than the man carrying it, to judge by its smell." He motioned for a servant to bring a bowl of water, then washed the fish juices from his hands as Thomas hid his smirk.

After a while the carver reappeared with a platter of veal. His step was even less steady than before, and his glassy eyes suggested he had tried to revive his spirits with a measure of malmsey. Nicholas fastened him with his eye, which made the man even more unsteady.

Holding his knife properly in his right hand, Nicholas cut a piece of veal and carried it with his left hand to his mouth. Below the salt, the menials might spear their food with their knives, but gentlefolk used their fingers. The veal was to his liking and Nicholas nodded curtly.

"All the more reason to employ a taster," Randolph observed. "I can't tell you how often meat too rancid for a gentle palate has been turned away by my chief yeoman while taking the say." He blithely ignored his wife's reproving glance at the slur upon her household management.

Nicholas nodded absently as he watched the carver. Jessica had been served, but as the man moved to Devona, his fingers fumbled and the veal's juice gushed from the platter into Devona's lap.

She shrieked and threw up her hands. Nicholas was on his feet and over the table before Randolph could comprehend what had happened. Nicholas shoved the platter toward a pageboy and bodily lifted the drunken carver. With one sweep he tossed the man toward the door. "Sober up, knave! And see that someone else is sent to do your serving."

The butler and the pantler dashed forward and dragged away the miserable carver. Nicholas nodded decisively and went back to the table. All the diners were frozen in place, staring at him. Nicholas spread his hands, palms-up, and gave them his most benevolent smile. "As you say, Lord Randolph, these things happen."

When Mistress Anne and the other ladies had finished cleaning the gravy from Devona's gown as best they could, dinner was again resumed. Jessica watched the stunned expressions on her parents' faces, then nodded appreciatively at her husband. "Thank you, Nicholas," she said as if all had been handled in a most gracious manner. "Will you have more malmsey?"

Nicholas, who had also perceived his guests' appalled stares, nodded. "Thank you, love."

Jessica refused to meet her parents' eyes and acted as if nothing at all had gone awry. Nicholas' gestures were rough and larger than necessary, but she found him all the more lovable in his lack of polish. All her life she had been on the outside of the family's circle and she could understand a person who lacked a courtly patina. Even if she hadn't been beginning to care for him as a man, she was his wife and she was loyal. Besides, though she had never minced words with him, he had not once struck her. As accustomed as she was to her father's blows, this alone warranted her fealty. So she pretended that it was normal and appropriate that Nicholas had thrown out his drunken servant in the midst of a meal and had snatched the rancid food from their guests' plates. By her supportive actions, she dared anyone to find fault with him.

When the meal was finished and the chaplain had given thanks, all rose to leave. At the door Nicholas bowed to Jessica. "If you will take your parents to the winter parlor, I will join you later. I must speak at once to the cook about the salmon and to the butler concerning the matter of the carver's deplorable condition."

"Of course, Nicholas." She dreaded being alone with her parents, but knew the scene was inevitable.

When Nicholas was gone, Randolph sighed with relief. "What have I done to you, sweet Madeline? I have married you to a barbarian, a savage!"

"Speak not so of my lord husband," Jessica retorted sharply. "Nicholas may not be as gently reared as some, but his heart is better than most."

"Madeline!" Randolph exclaimed. "Never have you spoken so irreverently before."

"Nor has Madeline now," Devona burst out. "Look well at her, Randolph. Do you not recognize Jessica?"

"Jessica?" he gasped. "How can that be?"

Before his daughter could speak, Devona answered, "The cunning wench changed places with our Madeline, just as they did as children. She has married Lord Nicholas in her sister's place!"

"No! Tell me you lie!" Randolph stared from one woman to the other.

"You see? She doesn't even try to deny it! Speak to your father, girl, and tell him of your evil deed."

"I did no evil, Papa," Jessica said in her defense. "Madeline ran off, presumably to elope with Sir Raymond, and I took her place. That is all."

"All! You've usurped your sister's husband and her title, and you say that is all?" Randolph's face was growing livid.

"She had already gone, Papa. Could I have let you be shamed when no bride appeared?"

"Jessica did it to save her own neck," Devona hissed. "She knew we planned to lock her away."

"Papa," Jessica whispered, "would you really have done that to me?"

"You're mad, child. Whether curse or prophecy, Leopold was right."

"I'm not mad!"

Randolph paced to the stained-glass window and gazed at the vivid colors without seeing them. Suddenly he turned and strode to Jessica. "If you're not Madeline, then where is she?"

"I told you, Papa. She has gone away with Sir Raymond. If you think back to the wedding day, you'll recall that two people were missing—Raymond Chadwick and Madeline, who everyone thought was I."

"I don't believe it!"

"Neither do I," Devona spoke up. "Our Madeline wouldn't lower herself so. The man is but a mere knight."

"You betrothed *me* to a knight," Jessica pointed out. "No one considered that demeaning to me."

"What have you done with Madeline?" Randolph demanded, his eyes wild. "Have you killed her and hidden her body?"

"Killed her! Never!" Jessica gasped.

"I thought that myself," Devona moaned. "My poor baby!"

"I haven't touched Madeline!"

Randolph grabbed her wrist and jerked her toward him as he raised his fist. "I'll beat the truth out of you!"

Jessica cried out and dodged, but before his fist could reach her, Nicholas appeared and grabbed Randolph's arm in a bone-crushing grip.

"What is going on here?" he demanded. "You would dare to strike the Countess of Wyndfell?"

"I dare to strike my daughter!" Randolph challenged.

"She is no longer your daughter, but my wife." Nicholas' voice was rimmed with steel and his eyes were fiercely steadfast. "Anyone who lays hand on her may consider himself my enemy. If I were you, I would think this over most carefully."

Randolph recoiled as if struck. Devona rushed to his side. "There has been a . . . a mistake, my lord," she said quickly. "You see, this girl is—"

"As my mother means to say," Jessica interrupted, "we had a family quarrel. It was all my fault and I do most humbly beg their pardon." She knelt quickly in a devout posture that would put even Madeline to shame. "Say no more about the matter, Mother," she said, throwing her parents a warning look. "As you can see, my husband is my lord now, and as such, he has total say over my whereabouts."

Nicholas drew her to her feet and put his arm around her. "A pretty apology indeed. Who would not forgive you after that? Come now, what was the problem?"

"They wished me to come away with them," Jessica said innocently. "I told them I could not. A wife's place is with her husband. Besides, one cannot know so soon, but I may be with child." Jessica stared defiantly at her father. She watched his stunned expression. She had never seen him at such a loss for words.

"What my lady wife says is true. I'm surprised at you, Lord Randolph. My wife stays here where she belongs." He looked from Randolph's stony face to Devona's crumpled one. "In time we will come for a visit. Perhaps we will bring with us a grandbabe for you to dote on."

Both parents looked at him sharply, but Jessica smiled. If they thought she could be carrying his babe, she was safe. "Let there be no more harsh words between us," she said. "I will stay, and that is that."

"Yes," Randolph answered slowly. "I would say the

two of you make a perfect match. Never have I seen a wife who so well deserved such a husband, nor a husband who was mated so well. I wish the two of you a life such as you both deserve."

Nicholas looked puzzled, but then grinned and slapped Randolph heartily on the back. "A father's blessing is always welcome. Let there be no ill will between us. Come, we'll go to the gardens and walk."

Jessica exchanged a leaden glance with her mother, then lifted her head regally. "Yes, we must show you all of Wyndfell quickly, as your visit is to be so short."

"You speak of leaving so soon?" Nicholas asked.

"We ride on the morrow. As you know, we journey to York. A personal matter and one we are not at liberty to discuss." Randolph gave Jessica a long look. "I bid you good-bye, daughter."

"Farewell, you mean," Nicholas corrected. "You will see her again. Besides, there is time enough for parting on the morrow. For now, let me show you where we plan a new knot garden in a 'passion-love' design."

Jessica went out by Nicholas' side. She understood quite well what her father had meant. He was glad to be rid of her. She would manage to find excuses when Nicholas suggested a visit. In spite of her sadness over what might have been, she felt a sense of freedom. Surely now that the truth was known to her parents, nothing would ever stand between her and the happiness she could find with Nicholas, so long as he never learned the truth.

10

MADELINE STRAIGHTENED HER back uncomfortably and wished once more that she had the comfort of traveling by litter instead of by sidesaddle. Still, their journey must be almost ended, as Raymond had said they would arrive by noonday and the sun had already passed that point. The sidesaddle necessitated riding in a curved position and the muscles in her lower back ached from the unaccustomed strain. Her right leg was numb all the way to her hip from the pressure of the leg brace, and her other ankle was cramping.

"We're nearly there, sweeting," Raymond called to her. "See? Yonder is our parish church."

Madeline nodded but made no effort to smile. What did she care for an unknown church in some small Yorkshire village? She only wanted to be off the horse.

Raymond rose in his stirrups and flexed his legs to ease his discomfort. Madeline kept the grimace from her face, but her lips tightened ever so slightly in a pout. When she had tricked Raymond into taking her away, the elopement had sounded like the most exciting of adventures. She had traveled to London several times with her parents and assumed all travelers paced themselves so as to arrive not too travel-worn. Raymond, however, rode as if she were a fellow knight and accustomed to sitting on a saddle from dawn to dusk.

The night before, they had stopped at an ale-house. Their room was small and not very clean, but their mutual passions had obliterated the minor discomforts. Madeline had never placed much stock in clean linens as long as they were free of insects, unlike her mother, who had insisted that the bed-clothes be changed once a month whether needed or not. Besides, she could overlook a great deal to lie in Raymond's exuberant embrace.

She narrowed her eyes and regarded him closely. Did she love him? Perhaps so. Never having felt that emotion for anyone or anything, she had nothing to serve as a basis for comparison. Certainly Raymond came closer than most to quenching the fires of passion that raged within her. She squirmed in the saddle. Merely looking at his muscled thighs made her hunger for him again. This must be love, she decided, this unquenchable desire that growled within her in defiance of her exhaustion.

"Look! There it is," Raymond exclaimed. "Pritchard Hall."

The drive wound up a low hill to a mansion, newly constructed of deep-red bricks. The park that skirted the house was spacious and well tended, the drive lined with young lime trees that would someday provide an imposing entrance.

The two-story house had been built in the shape of the letter E, with the three legs facing the front drive. Large square mullioned windows, graced the walls, along with elaborate cornices and ornamentation. Numerous gables and chimneys vied for roof space, creating a profile far different from the familiar one of Hargrove Castle. Ivy had been planted in the gardens surrounding the house, the first long green runners of which were creeping up the rough brick walls.

"As you can see, Sir James Swineford is loyal to Queen Elizabeth," Raymond said as he pointed out the shape of the building. "His family has always proved loyal to the crown."

"He must be very wealthy indeed," Madeline commented as she judged the cost of construction and maintenance of such a magnificent place.

"Although born on the wrong side of the blanket, he was his mother's only heir. She was a rich widow at the time of his birth."

"And his father?"

"His father is rumored to be the same who fathered your previously intended, Nicholas Garrett."

"Is it true?" she asked in surprise.

"Who knows, save his mother, and she is long since dead. Sir James believes it and that is all that really matters. Therein lies the source of the bad blood between the Swinefords and the Garretts."

"Why should that be? Bastards are scarcely rare. They generally are brought up to know their place and accept whatever is their lot by fate."

"Not Sir James. I've heard it said that his mother fed him rebellion along with her milk. Had his parents married, he would have been the firstborn son and heir of the Wyndfell estates as well. He never forgave his father for marrying another woman, nor accepted the natural loss of those lands, the castle, and the title."

"I see," she said slowly. "Is that why you fell in

love with me? To spite Lord Nicholas?" A pucker
was gathering on her brow.

Raymond looked at her quickly, then grinned. "Of
course not, sweeting. After seeing your beauty and
hearing your sweet voice, the motivation was all my
own. As I told you before, we have come to Pritchard Hall because this is the one place where we will
be safe from Lord Nicholas. I hope that since Sir
James and he are sworn enemies, Sir James will give
us protection to provoke the Garretts."

When Madeline continued to frown, Raymond
looked back at the house. In the past two days he
had seen a glimpse of a temper more fierce than any
he would have suspected from a woman. "Sir James
will be more than pleased at what we have done," he
said hastily. "Such is his hate for Lord Nicholas that
he will likely give me a pension with land and a
house of my own for poxing the wedding. When he
hears I actually stole away Garrett's bride, he may
give me a handsome amount of gold as well." He
rode closer so that his knee rubbed Madeline's. "You'd
like that, wouldn't you, poppet? A purse of gold
angels to buy you frills and gewgaws?"

Madeline smiled and the storm was averted. Her
lips curved sweetly, concealing her pearly teeth, and
her blue eyes lit with pleasure. Raymond hid his sigh
of relief. She must not guess he was actually in
Swineford's pay. When Madeline was happy, she was
the epitome of ladyhood, and radiant in her beauty.
He could still hardly believe she was the ardent lover
he knew her to be.

At the front steps a boy ran to fetch their horses.
Raymond helped Madeline dismount and steadied
her until she had her balance. Then she gave him
her hand, and he led her ceremoniously up the steps
and into a long passageway that was lined with the

offices necessary for the running of a household this size. The several petitioners who were waiting outside the steward's door stared in frank curiosity at the beautiful woman. Madeline looked through them with regal indifference and swept by as if she were the queen herself.

Raymond took her to the great hall and left her there while he went with a servant, ostensibly to discuss possible employment with Sir James. Madeline wandered about the oak-paneled room, gazing at its rich appointments. Here was the home of a man with great taste and discernment—a taste that matched her own. Beyond the front windows lay one of the two identical knot gardens that filled in the open spaces of the house's design. Certainly Sir James wasn't as near with his money as Raymond had said Lord Nicholas was. As new as it was, the house was already a showplace.

When Chadwick entered Swineford's chambers, the man greeted him with a dark scowl. "You fool! What have you to say for yourself?"

The self-satisfied grin wavered on Raymond's face, then melted. "Why, I did as I was bid. I ruined the match with Garrett."

"Then who is the bride Lord Nicholas brought home? All the parish is talking of her."

"I know not, but she isn't the Hargrove heiress."

"How can you be certain of that?" Swineford went to the window and looked east in the direction of Wyndfell.

"Because I have brought the bride here with me," Raymond stated proudly.

"You stole his bride? Then he will be upon us as soon as he traces her here!"

"No, no, I left with her before the wedding. She

came quite willingly once I told her of his crooked body, ugly face, and cruel ways."

"She believed all that?"

"Aye, my lord. Why would she not believe an eyewitness?" He winked at his master broadly. "She also believes that I've come here to ask for work and your protection."

"I see." Swineford reached in the slit pocket of his jerkin and took out three ryals, which he tossed in rapid succession to Raymond. "You have done well."

Raymond caught the coins and stared at them in his palm. "My lord, surely you recall your promise. I was to have a house and land, a yearly pension."

Swineford regarded him narrowly. "Yes," he agreed slowly, "I recall now. As yet I have made no arrangements, however. You must be patient for a while."

"Yes, my lord," Raymond agreed reluctantly. Every day of delay meant a greater possibility of losing Madeline.

"In the meantime, you may quarter with the other men-at-arms as you did before you were sent to Wyndfell, and I will see to the lady's comfort."

"Pardon, my lord," Raymond burst out, "but there is more of which you know not. The Lady Madeline is of a shy nature and views me as her sole protector. That was how I lured her away. In the past few days we have become . . . close."

"In other words, you are bedding her?"

"In a manner of speaking, yes."

"You, a mere knight, dared lay hands on a noble-woman?" Swineford demanded.

"No, no, it was not like that. I never forced her. You see, we have fallen in love. Because of our elopement, Lady Madeline is doubtlessly disowned and is therefore of no greater rank than am I."

Swineford stroked his dark beard thoughtfully,

feeling the coarse hairs bristle under his fingers. "Of course. I had not thought of that. She would be disowned, I imagine." And thus not worth a ransom, he finished silently.

"Of a certainty, my lord. She is now penniless, and as a knight I am sworn to protect her."

"Yes, yes. Of course." Swineford turned back to the window. "You stole her away before the wedding, you say?"

"Aye. She never laid eyes on Lord Nicholas."

"Then the news of his marriage must be empty servants' prattle. Well, Sir Raymond, you have served me well. The note on Wyndfell and its lands is due forthwith. When Garrett is unable to pay it the inheritance will be mine at last." A thin sneer narrowed his lips. "At last!"

"Sir James, I beg a boon," Raymond said, in a hurry to take advantage of his master's rare good nature.

"Yes? What is it."

"I beg leave to marry Lady Madeline."

"Marry her!"

"We both desire it. I asked her to marry me before we left her castle and she agreed. She will be ruined if I don't wed her." Raymond gestured helplessly.

"Very well," Swineford agreed impatiently. "You have my permission."

"Thank you, my lord," Raymond gushed gratefully. "Thank you! We both thank you."

"Now I must see this prize that has been snatched away from my rival."

Madeline heard voices from outside the room; then the double doors opened and a tall man entered with Raymond two steps behind.

Raymond stepped to Madeline's side and gestured

grandly. "May I present Lady Madeline Hargrove? My lady, this is Sir James Swineford. He has agreed to let me serve him here as we had hoped."

Madeline turned and was haloed by a beam of sunlight that turned her hair to golden silk and her skin to pale porcelain. She saw Sir James draw in his breath sharply in appreciation of her beauty, and she favored him with her most angelic expression. Since her earliest memories, she had loved being adored. Especially by men.

"Sir James," she said in a sweet lisp as she dipped into a graceful curtsy. "Forgive my appearance. I fear I am greatly travel-stained."

"Nonsense, Lady Madeline. I find you the image of perfection," Swineford said as he found his tongue. To Raymond he said, "Surely this is not the Hargrove bride of Lord Nicholas!"

"The very same," Raymond said with a smirk.

Swineford glanced from her to the knight and back again. "I am truly honored, my lady. But come, I forget my manners. You must be tired from your journey." He pulled a tasseled bell-pull to summon a servant. The door opened at once and he instructed the maid, "Take my lady up to the guest chamber and see to it that she is made comfortable. Sir Raymond and I have matters to discuss." He bowed Madeline out and closed the door.

Madeline inspected the anteroom and guest chamber as if deciding whether or not it was grand enough to suit her. The walls were block-paneled in light oak, with small tapestries hanging in the center of the raised wainscoting. Even Madeline's well-trained eye couldn't fault the needlework on the pale green bed hangings. Darker green cushions embroidered in floral patterns padded the stools, but there were no proper chairs. Nor were the window casements and chests carved, and there was no fireplace at all.

"It will do," Madeline said begrudgingly.

The maid bobbed a curtsy and turned to go, but Madeline stopped her. "Wait. Do you know how to dress a lady's hair? I am rather windblown from my journey."

The young maid looked at the woman's well-coiffed hair and nodded dubiously. "I done it afore, my lady."

Madeline sat on a stool and turned her back to the girl. "Brush my hair and be quick about it," she ordered.

The girl pawed through Madeline's small traveling chest, dusted with grime from the road, and found a silver-backed brush. With great trepidation she removed the ivory bodkins from Madeline's hair and uncoiled the heavy braid. When her hair hung in loose waves, she cautiously drew the brush through the tangles. She had helped the other maids on occasion, and had dressed her younger sisters before being placed as a maid at Pritchard Hall, but she had no idea how to dress a lady's hair in a stylish manner.

Madeline flinched and jerked to one side. "Careful! You'll pull me bald!"

"Pardon, my lady," the girl mumbled. Taking great pains, she eased the tangles from the hair and started to separate the strands so she could rebraid them.

Again the waving hair snarled and Madeline leapt to her feet. Her palm struck the maid's cheek with stinging force and the girl flinched away with a cry. Madeline once more raised her hand to strike, but the girl snatched up her long skirts and ran from the room before she was hit again.

Raymond entered as the maid fled. "Madeline, whatever is wrong?"

At once the fury left Madeline's face and she looked at him most piously. "That silly girl acted as if I meant to harm her," she said with feigned innocence. "I believe she is simpleminded. All I wanted was for her to brush my hair."

He went to her and lifted the shimmering strands in great admiration. "You're so beautiful. The sight of your loose hair excites me."

Madeline glanced at him from the corner of her eye. "Do I truly, Raymond?" Demurely she bent her head. "I must then confess that your nearness does the same thing to me."

Raymond grinned. This was one of Madeline's most exciting teases. At times he could swear she was a virgin, though he had ample reason to know differently. Madeline's sexual appetite was the reason the journey from Hargrove Castle had taken an extra day.

A hungry flame leapt in her cerulean eyes. "Come, Raymond," she said breathlessly. "Take me! Quickly!" She tore at her clothes in a white-hot urgency. The ever-present need within her was blazing intolerably. She had to have release at once. Otherwise she knew not what she might do.

When Raymond was slow in removing his clothes, Madeline began to rip at them with rabid impatience. Her breath came in short pants and the irises of her eyes were dilated so that the blue became black.

Naked, she threw herself on the bed and rolled over, her legs spread not in invitation, but demand. Raymond threw the last of his clothes across the room and hurried to her. She met Raymond's hard thrusts and groaned as her bestial need roared with engulfing proportions toward her completion.

Soon waves of culmination pounded through her,

coming so close, so desperately close to satisfying her. At last the consuming fire was banked again. At least for a while.

Raymond, spent from the unexpected effort, rolled off her and lay spread-eagled over most of the bed. Already his eyes were glazing into sleep.

"Wake up," Madeline demanded, shaking his bare arm.

"What?" he asked groggily.

"You cannot sleep now! What if someone comes in?" She slid off the bed and began to dress in modest haste.

"Madeline, sweeting, I . . ."

"Cover yourself!" She blushed as furiously as any virgin might have on seeing his limp member. "Really, Raymond! It is broad daylight."

Reluctantly he pulled on his tight netherstocks and held them up with one hand as he struggled to shrug into his shirt. He pulled on his petticote and tied the points of his upperstocks to it. Decently covered, he turned to Madeline. "But the idea was yours, my sweet."

"You mustn't talk to me of such low things," she scolded as she laced her kirtle.

He sighed and shook his head as he drew on his doublet. Ladies were a strange breed indeed. He never knew if Madeline would be a purring kitten or a raging lioness. Only moments ago she was as wildly insatiable as a harlot. Now she was virginally shy once more. He knelt to buckle the broad straps of his shoes.

Madeline brushed her hair, braided it, and coiled it over her head in a thick rope. "I must find a lady's maid right away. Will you ask Sir James for a woman to attend me?" She smiled at Raymond as if nothing out of line had just occurred between them. Turning her back on the rumpled bed, she nudged her toe against the small travel chest. "Also I must have some clothes at once. How often I've regretted not taking the time to pack properly."

"You couldn't, sweeting. You know that. Any delay would have ruined our plans."

For a moment Madeline looked blank, then nodded. "Of course. That's right."

Raymond surreptitiously straightened the bedclothes. Perhaps Madeline was too naive to know that anyone could tell from the bed's disarray that they had just made love there. Even the youngest servant girl would understand and comment on it in the kitchens. Raymond didn't want to upset Sir James any further on this issue, at least not until he and Madeline were wed.

That reminded him of his interview with his master and he pulled out the three coins. "Look, sweeting. Here's gold enough to buy a chest of gowns."

Madeline came nearer and took the coins he offered her. "You must be quite wealthy to give me so much. I didn't expect half so fine a gift."

Raymond, who hadn't expected her to take all three, shrugged. "I know gowns are important to a woman. Never let it be said that my wife wanted for aught."

"Wife?"

"That is my good news. Sir James has granted me permission to marry you. In no time, we will be wed and living in our own home, surrounded by our own land."

"How marvelous." She looked with excitement around the room. "I much prefer a house to a castle. No damp stone walls, no steps worn into crescents from centuries of use. Yes, Raymond! Let's have a house!"

He nodded thoughtfully. Surely she knew he meant a yeoman's cottage and not a great mansion such as Pritchard Hall. Of course she did! Any other assumption would be foolish. He smiled and drew her close. "Then we'll soon be wed?"

"Certainly, Raymond." She fluttered with shy dimples. "After all, you have had your way with me." She sighed and pouted prettily. "When I think where I might be now, I am all aquiver with fear."

"What do you mean?"

"Why, I would be the chattel of that cripple!" While she momentarily wondered about the novelty of being taken by a hideously deformed man, she shuddered at the notion of a steady diet of such fare. Besides, cripples were generally weak and she yearned for a strong man, one who could use her hard enough and often enough to slake this damnable fire in her loins.

Raymond glanced away and pretended to be adjusting the lacings of his jerkin. If they stayed in the area of Wyndfell, she would eventually hear a true description of Lord Nicholas or even see him for herself. He shuddered to think what a scene might follow.

Madeline went on as if Raymond had answered in agreement. "I wonder what took place when I was missed. I can see it now. Mother running about like a chicken with its head chopped off; Father bellowing at everyone." She giggled girlishly and pressed her fingers to her lips. "Somehow they will have fixed the blame on Jessica. I wonder what reason they will concoct." She spun about the room as if dancing to unheard music. "Perhaps they will tell it about that my poor crazed sister has murdered me."

"Madeline! Don't say so even in jest."

"What does it matter? Jessica was to be locked

away after the wedding anyway. Don't be so superstitious, Raymond." She whirled laughing into his arms. "I'm free! Free of all those dour fools who used to watch my every move. Free of Jessica's nagging and Mother's simpering and Father's stupid comments. But how I would have loved to see all their faces when there was no bride." She dissolved into helpless laughter and Raymond had to support her until she could collect herself.

Madeline and Raymond Chadwick were married in the chapel at Pritchard Hall the next morning. The bride had no time to sew a new gown, and Swineford and the house staff were the only witnesses. But the bride was so shy and beautiful that the small chapel might have been a great cathedral. The groom was glassy-eyed, as if he had had no sleep the night before, but he responded bawdily to the ribald innuendos that always accompanied a wedding.

Swineford watched the woman and found he was actually envying Sir Raymond. The woman was of good stock, as well as being incredibly beautiful. By the looks of her downcast eyes and innocent blushes, he suspected she might be too docile in bed for his liking, but what pleasurable times might be had in teaching her to sport!

As if she heard his thoughts, Madeline suddenly looked directly at him, and he saw her trace the tip of her pink tongue over her lips. The blatantly seductive gesture made him straighten in surprise. Then Madeline glanced away, again all daintily shy. Swineford blinked and wondered if he had possibly misinterpreted what he had seen.

Before he could move closer, a page approached him and bowed. "Some men to see you, my lord. It's Sir Thomas Garrett."

"Thomas? Here?" Swineford glanced at the newly married couple. Since Thomas couldn't possibly know about the wedding, Swineford thought he might as well let it remain secret a bit longer. In time such discretion might come in handy.

He went to the downstairs closet where he always entertained Thomas, and Walter before him. No doubt the young man had been sent as an emissary to plead more time on the note owed. Swineford smirked in anticipation of the refusal he had rehearsed over and over the night before. He didn't like Thomas any more than he did Thomas' brother.

"Thomas!" Swineford said in affectionate greeting as he entered the chamber. "How good to see you." He took note of the two armed guards that had accompanied Thomas, but made no comment. Warily he left the door open and kept it to his back.

"Am I interrupting something? It sounds as if a party is going on."

"No, no. One of my knights was married today. That's all. What can I do for you?" Though he covered his nervousness with a broad smile, he looked from Thomas to his men and back again. Placing his hand on the hilt of the knife he wore at his waist, Swineford waited for Thomas to speak.

"I come on a formal errand." Now that he was here, Thomas was glad to see that Sir James was as cordial as ever. Nicholas was obviously mistaken in thinking that the raid had been by Sir James' order.

"Oh? An errand? Yes, now I remember. The note on Wyndfell is due today, isn't it?"

Thomas nodded, then took a green velvet bag from his cloak. "Here is the gold. Full payment for Walter's gambling debts. I know you are as glad to receive it as we are to pay. It's quite an amount."

Swineford stared at the bag, then at Thomas. He

had been prepared to refuse an extension, and this unexpected payment threw him off, though it did explain why Thomas had brought guards with him. "You have the gold there?"

"Indeed. All gold ryals and angels. Nicholas says I am to count it out in front of you so there can be no saying we paid you short. He also instructed me to have you sign for it."

Swineford was silent until Thomas counted out the full amount. As he scrawled his signature on the paper Thomas presented him, he asked, "Where did your brother get the gold?"

"Did you not know he married an heiress? I would have expected the gossips to wag their tongues on both ends since we returned with her."

"I've heard nothing," Swineford lied, then continued lamely, "A bride? But . . ." His mind was swirling over this turn of events. How had Garrett managed to find and marry another heiress so quickly?

"A bride, indeed, and with a large dowry. Now that we are paid in full, I must go."

"Thomas. Thomas, you offend me," James soothed in mellowed tones. "Are we not friends? Here, I know your brother keeps you without money of your own. Take back a portion of these coins for yourself."

Thomas stared longingly at the glittering mound of gold, but shook his head. "Perhaps Walter would have been so foolish, James, but not I. Not when Wyndfell hangs in the balance. I may not be its lord, but it is my home."

With a resigned gesture, Swineford scooped the coins into the bag and carefully tied the silken cord in a knot. "Very well, Thomas. I had thought there was friendship between us. I suppose I was wrong."

"You say me false," Thomas objected, thinking

about the gold Swineford had offered. "Paying a debt is a way of proving friendship, not the opposite. I'll tell you what. On Thursday next, I'll meet you in the village at the Bear and Bull. We'll watch the baiting and I'll play you a game or two of primero. If luck is with me, I'll get back some of Walter's losings."

"Until Thursday," Swineford agreed with a forced smile as he thumped Thomas on the back. If that was truly Lady Madeline in the hall, where had Nicholas gotten the gold?

"In the meantime," Thomas was saying, "you must be missed at the revelry. My men and I will go now."

Swineford said farewell and tossed the bag of gold into the silver card bowl. Never had he been less pleased to see so much money. Before Thomas could reach the door, Swineford called out, "You forgot to tell me the name of this bride!"

"Lady Madeline of Hargrove Castle," Thomas called back, then waved good-bye.

Swineford watched after him until the outer door banged shut, then wheeled and strode toward the hall. He easily found Raymond and summoned him abruptly.

Raymond arrived with his smiling bride at his side. "Why such a serious face, my lord?"

"Thomas Garrett was just here. He brought the money to repay the debt on Wyndfell."

"No! How could that be?" Raymond gasped.

"Perhaps you could tell me. Thomas said Nicholas just married a wealthy heiress—Lady Madeline of Hargrove Castle."

Raymond looked dumbfounded and Madeline blanched. "She must have taken my place," she exclaimed to Raymond. "Jessica took my place!" All the pretty smiles disappeared along with the dimple, and anger stiffened her features, turning them hard and sharp. "How dare she do that! I had it all planned to embarrass Lord Nicholas and get revenge on my father for matching me to a poor cripple, and now Jessica has ruined it!"

"Madeline, calm yourself," Raymond soothed as Swineford stared at her.

"Don't touch me!" She slapped aside Raymond's hand. "Who do you think you are to lay your hand upon me?"

To Swineford Raymond explained hastily, "It's the shock, no doubt. It must have momentarily deranged her."

"Who is this Jessica she mentioned?" he demanded.

"Her twin, and as near her image as you can imagine. No doubt Lady Jessica was substituted in the guise of her sister in order to save trouble at the wedding."

"Take your wife to my closet," Swineford said stiffly. "I'll send a maid for rosewater. Then return to me. I have something to say to you."

Raymond led the protesting Madeline down the corridor to Swineford's study. "Compose yourself, sweeting," he pleaded. "This is your wedding day."

Madeline drew in her breath sharply as if she were about to scream. "Leave me, you oaf! Leave my sight at once!"

"I'll see what is keeping the maid with the rose-water," Raymond said hastily.

She slammed the door after him and paced like a caged beast in the confines of the closet. Jessica had married in her place and spoiled her revenge. How dare she? Then it struck her that she should not be angry at all. She should be pleased. With Jessica married to the penniless earl in her stead, her father would have no cause to look for her and try to force her to leave Sir Raymond for her betrothed. Then she began to laugh. She must have been crazed to get angry when she should have rejoiced. The thought jolted her and her laughter instantly ceased.

As a smile returned to her lips, she noticed a bowl of cards and decided to examine their design. But to get at the cards, she had to move a velvet bag that had been placed on top of them. At the unmistakable clink of coins, she paused. Cautiously Madeline opened the bag and looked in; then she began to beam with delight. Here was more money than she had ever seen at once!

Glancing toward the door to be sure she was alone, she took out a handful of the coins and slipped them into the tight bodice of her kirtle, between her chemise and her skin. Leaving enough coins to give the bag some weight and shape, she retied the cord. Some servant or other would be blamed and she would have money for a new wardrobe and hangings for her new house.

When Raymond and Swineford returned with the maid and the bowl of rosewater, they found Madeline completely restored to her sweet self. No one noticed the depleted bag of coins in the bowl.

11

APRIL DWINDLED AND May approached in a splash of sunshine and birdsong. Oxeye daisies waved above the shorter lady's slippers, and bees busied themselves gathering pollen from massive drifts of red clover. Along Wyndfell's moat and the stream that fed it, marsh marigolds gave way to ragged-robins and forget-me-nots. Wild irises spread a carpet of gold along the sloping banks of the moat, and orange-tipped butterflies hovered over pink lady's-smocks. With the songs of the cuckoos, spring had officially arrived.

Jessica watched the broad lawns and parks of Wyndfell greening and brightening daily and felt a corresponding stirring in her blood. Now that she no longer bothered to copy Madeline's demure behavior, her step was quick and light. Often she sang as she supervised the servants' work and tended those tasks of her own that kept Wyndfell running smoothly.

On the last day of April the servants went to the woods and cut flowering boughs of white thorn to adorn the doors and windows of the castle and the huts that mushroomed around it. All work came to an agreeable halt in preparation for May Day.

Jessica dressed in a bright pink kirtle, embroidered with lifelike wildflowers and bees, and joined the festivity of cutting greenery to decorate the castle. Nicholas, who had been riding through the fields to watch over the plowing, saw her at a distance, carrying a large wicker basket. She wore no head covering and the sun glinted in the web of her hair. Her feet scarcely seemed to touch the ground as she crossed the meadow and stepped beneath the boughs of the oaks at the edge of the forest.

Nicholas reined his horse to follow her. He, too, felt the siren call of spring and was glad to escape the winter confines of the castle.

The tall oaks shaded a parklike area where Nicholas' swine had fed on acorns the previous fall. Now the ground was thick with bluebells, and in the low-lying areas, cities of tiny mushrooms were scattered about. Nicholas dismounted and tied his horse within reach of the stream. Ahead he could see Jessica pulling bluebells for her basket. He stayed back for a bit, enjoying the picture she made.

His life had changed since she entered it, he reflected, and all for the better. For the first time since his mother's death the castle was well-run and the servants were properly disciplined. Somehow his new wife managed to accomplish this minor miracle without unpleasant scenes or undue fuss. He supposed that from childhood she had been taught to manage a castle and staff, and she had clearly learned her lessons well. She even seemed to enjoy the work that he would have found tedious in the extreme.

Before his marriage, Nicholas Garrett had been accustomed to living in whatever way seemed easiest. Not that he was lazy or uncaring, but by the time he

saw to the harvesting and heard the local grievances
between the village folk and looked over the castle's
accounts and saw to the care of his livestock and
horses, he had little time or energy left to see that
the bedding was aired or the rushes changed. His
sister-in-law had cared for little but the welfare of
her soul and her incessant prayers for Walter. Now
all was set right by a word from his wife. What did it
matter that she was as spirited as a Gypsy and rarely
docile? Nicholas found he actually enjoyed their spar-
ring at times.

"Madeline," he called to her.

Jessica jumped, looked about, then back at him.
Relief spread over her face when she realized he was
addressing her, then gladness. "Nicholas! I didn't
hear you ride up. You startled me." Jessica wondered whether she would ever hear her sister's name
without flinching.

"You were singing. What was the tune?"

" 'The Elfin Knight,' " she replied. "Have you never
heard it? It's about a man who comes to woo a young
maid and offers to wed her if she will but sew him a
seamless garment using no thread. She answers that
she will do so when he grows her a crop of corn on
the sea strand, harvests it in spring, threshes it in his
shoe, and brings it home dry over the sea. It's a very
pretty song."

"I had hoped you were singing of happy lovers.
Of a maid wooed and won by a mortal prince,
perhaps."

Jessica shook her head. "The maids in such songs
seem so boring. All they ever do is pine amid some
bower or ply their needles nonstop."

"I find such maids to be the picture of feminine
grace and domesticity."

"How long could a man stay interested in such

languid behavior? In a fortnight he would find her too dull to talk with. In a year he would be yearning for his lost freedom."

"You seem pretty sure of that."

"Did you ride out here to battle with me?" she asked testily. "I should think you get enough of that indoors."

"That I do," he retorted, forgetting that he had been thinking favorably on her temper. "And you would do well to remember it."

Jessica looked up at him in exasperation. He was the only problem that ruffled the surface of her new life. The servants needed a firm hand, and she knew well all that was required to run a castle. But Nicholas gave her trouble. He seemed, most times, to be determined to make her into one of those milksop ladies in a knightly fable rather than just accepting her as she really was and loving her for it. At times like these, she couldn't help but wonder if she would ever win his love.

"Let us not argue, I entreat you," she said in a softer voice. "I meant not to upset you."

Nicholas sighed, then smiled. "I never meant to say those hard words, but rather to tell you how beautiful you are. Here in the woods you could be an elf yourself."

"And you my elfin knight?" she teased. "Elves seem far too interested in humans to pay much heed to each other."

"Come, love, sing with me. Do you know 'Two Sisters'?"

"Not that one," Jessica said hastily. She was in no mood to sing of one jealous sister killing another.

"It seems we may not sing, then. Will you let me gather flowers with you?"

"These are your woods and therefore your flowers. How may I stop you?" Somehow her day had seemed brighter before Nicholas deigned to share it with her. She never knew how to talk to him and the day was too beautiful to spoil it with an argument.

"You could send me away with a word," he answered quietly.

Jessica saw the puzzled hurt in his dark eyes, and she looked away before the answering stab in her own could be seen. "I would not send you away," she replied in a low voice.

Nicholas took the basket of flowers and matched his step to hers. "It's rare we see each other alone," he commented after a while. "Always there are servants or yeomen or Thomas or tenant farmers who need an audience."

"Such is castle life," she said as she shrugged. "We are not commoners or even merchants, who may live alone in a tiny cottage. Nor would we want to be, if all were told. I like having the luxuries of tapestries and meat at every meal and more than one gown to my name. Is this not worth the lack of privacy?"

"Perhaps." At times, he had felt he would gladly trade it all for a cottage where the two of them could be alone. Yet she didn't seem to share the love he felt growing within him.

She turned to face him. "At least this is what I have always been told. Yet ..." She paused, then said, "There are times when I'm out in the dawning with the sky above me and a horse beneath me, when I wish I could follow the road, any road, just to see where it leads." Her voice trailed wistfully. "Or sometimes I see a farmer and his family going to market, and their only worry seems to be over selling their turnips and returning with all of their children still in tow."

"Surely your own worries cannot be so great,"

Nicholas remarked in surprise. "Do you not know that I will provide for you and protect you all your life?"

"Yes. Yes, of course." Jessica smiled up at him. He must never know of her ever-present fears of Madeline riding through the gate or of being somehow forced to return to Hargrove Castle and the mad cell. She bent to pick some buttery primroses so Nicholas wouldn't guess how deep her real worries lay.

In a like manner, he, too, gathered a handful of windflowers and put them in the basket. She had said she would like to ride away. That, of course, was idle dreaming, for what woman could ever do that, but he wondered if she was really happy at Wyndfell. The idea surprised him. Walter had never given a thought to whether Jane was happily settled in, nor had his father for his mother as far as Nicholas knew. They had just assumed a woman would be as happy here as anywhere else. After all, wasn't Wyndfell a castle such as anyone would be proud to call home? "Are you content here at Wyndfell?" he asked unexpectedly.

"I am well content," she answered as he tossed more windflowers into the basket. Jessica knew the delicate blooms wouldn't last long enough to weave into a garland for the door, but she didn't want to discourage his efforts.

"I didn't bring you here by force, you know."

"I know. I have said I am content." She reached out to stop him from picking a stalk of pink foxglove. "That one is poisonous," she explained.

"There is more to picking flowers than I had thought," he commented as he noted the windflowers were already wilting.

"Have you never gone gathering to celebate May?"

"Not since I was a boy. I used to run with my brothers through the woods in search of the maypole. Later I realized there was more than one meaning to that search, and then I understood why the older boys chose pretty girls to help them search."

"Naturally, you never did that," she teased.

"I find some village customs more appealing than others," he confessed with a grin. "But you'll notice I'm here and not galloping off with some yeoman's daughter."

"Luckily for you," she pointed out tersely.

His grin disappeared. "There! You're at it again! Do you not know that a man is his own master? If I wanted to hide in the hedgerow with a comely lass, I'd not need your permission."

"Nor would you find me later in your bed," she flared in response. "How would you feel if I spoke of heading for the woods with some young buck?"

"That's different! You're my wife."

"And you're my husband. And someday those young wenches will also be some men's wives. Where is the difference?"

Nicholas met her frown, then bent to grab a handful of bluebells. He threw them in the basket, roots and all. "Enough of this! We are here to gather flowers!" He yanked up a wad of primroses.

Jessica wasn't eager to be mollified. "Therein lies many a poor girl's despair," she said darkly. "A man expects his wife to be all meek and mousy and obedient, while he mates every skirt in the village. I'll not stand for such!"

"I have not touched one woman save yourself since our marriage," he roared. "And often babes are born to those 'meek' wives who bear no resemblance to either the mother or her husband!"

"What are you accusing me of!" she gasped. She

had merely been venting her opinion on unfaithful men, not indicting Nicholas. Now he was accusing her!

"Nothing!" he snapped.

"A pox on you!" she cried out in frustration. She threw the basket at him and lifted her skirts to run for the castle.

With a growling sound, Nicholas threw aside the basket and watched Jessica run over the green. She had brought more than order and beauty to Wyndfell. She had also delivered her share of jealousy and confusion. He couldn't remember ever being so vexed by a woman.

May Day dawned as fair as anyone could wish. Serving wenches and their lads, who had spent the entire night "searching for the maypole," straggled back to the castle and village. Nicholas and Jessica pretended not to notice the arrivals as they both knew the ancient pagan customs of the rites of Beltane went deeper than the vicar's teachings.

After a quick breakfast of bread, butter, and ale, Jessica and Nicholas walked with Thomas down to the village to watch the setting-up of the maypole. As they strolled, neither touching nor talking, Jessica glanced at him. This husband of hers was such a stubborn man. As a result of their silly argument, he had come to bed after he imagined her to be asleep and had lain on the far side of the bed, not touching her at all. Jessica, who had already forgiven him for his unfounded outburst, had been awake and eager to make up their differences. She was, however, much too proud to roll over and tell him so. He had started it and he could end it. When she finally fell asleep they were still back to back and on opposite sides of the bed.

A throstle called from the woods, and overhead two larks were diving and singing. Jessica watched their flight for a moment. "It's a lovely day," she said at last to no one in particular.

"Yes." Nicholas would have said more, but he was unsure how angry she might still be. He had wanted to set things right the night before, but when he finished the farm reports and went to bed, she was curled up on the far side. After listening to her breathing, he knew she was awake, but she never even bade him so much as a good night. Since the entire argument had been her fault, he decided to give her more time to come around. After all, what wife railed against her husband for being unfaithful— especially when he was innocent? Such things were ignored by ladies as being beneath their notice. Just the thought of Jessica's accusations brought back his frown. Besides, Thomas was waxing eloquent on the habits of larks and throstles, and Nicholas found the sound of his voice irritating. Evidently Jessica did not, for she was listening to him intently and had even laughed at one of his ridiculous sallies.

"Madeline—" Nicholas began.

"Don't call me that!" Jessica snapped without thinking, then tried to hide her slip by saying, "Must you call my name with every sentence you speak?"

"Pardon, my lady," Nicholas answered stiffly. "I didn't realize that doing thus was so great a transgression."

Jessica quickened her pace. She was embarrassed at her thoughtless retort. She had been trying to pacify him with her discussion about the birds, but obviously he was still angry and nursing a grudge. She scarcely paid any attention to Thomas, who was pointing out a particularly brilliant butterfly.

The maypole had been cut and a team of eighteen

oxen was hauling it out of the woods. Garlands of ivy and spring flowers were wound around the beasts' horns and draped over their brawny necks.

All around the team and maypole the villagers danced, and the younger and more exuberant even attempted the capriole or "goat's leap," flinging themselves high into the air and kicking their feet together before landing. Everyone was singing songs in praise of May, some of the tunes much older than the ancient village itself.

The oxen dragged the pole onto the green that stretched between Wyndfell's mighty bulk and the cobblestone of the village, and were stopped at exactly the same spot where the maypole had been traditionally set for more years than anyone remembered. Several young boys were playing tag among the benches under the pavilion that had already been set up adjacent to the pole site.

The Lord of Misrule, elected the Christmas before, along with his "court," made a great show of tying long streamers of brightly colored ribbons and cords of silver and gold thread, entwined with flowers, to the end of the pole that would be the top. Then the oxen were positioned and the lines were drawn taut as the broad base found the hole in the green. Everyone held his breath as the huge pole, stripped of leaf, limb, and bark, slowly rose from the earth. It shifted, then dropped with a dull thud into the hole. Cheers and cries of joy broke out as the music resumed with a flourish.

The womenfolk moved to the long tables that had been set up with platters and bowls of food, where they made last-minute preparations as the Lord of Misrule called for order.

Nicholas touched Jessica's elbow to guide her to the pavilion, but immediately drew his hand away.

The night before had been the first night since their marriage that she had not come willing to him, and he ached from wanting her. He wished now he had forced her to turn to him and that they could have erased this argument by loving the night away.

Jessica felt a tingle when he touched her, and she tried to convey to him her approval, but there was no way to do that with only her elbow. Besides, he released her as if he had been stung. Miffed at his stubbornness, she preceded him to the bench beneath the shady awning of greenery and sat down without waiting for his aid.

Thomas claimed the seat on her other side. With a smile, he turned to her and leaned companionably closer. "I had no opportunity to tell you earlier, but you look especially lovely today." Before she could respond, he said in a less circumspect tone, "Have you ever seen so fair a maypole?"

"Never," she confirmed. At least Thomas would talk to her, and after Nicholas' cold manner, she appreciated the compliment. She decided to simply ignore Nicholas until his anger was spent. "Nor have I ever seen such a lovely array of flowers, nor such a perfect day. Of course," she laughed, "I feel the same way each May Day. How pleasant it is to know winter is finally behind us."

Nicholas listened to the musical notes of her laughter joined with Thomas' baritone and his anger returned. Not twenty-four hours had passed and she was flirting with Thomas again! And in front of his very eyes!

Before he could speak, the mayor and other village officials shuffled in to be seated. As they crowded about, the clove scent from their pomanders and the floral fragrances of the various women's perfumes filled the tent.

Across the green was another pavilion where the Lord of Misrule, better known as the local wool merchant, gathered his court. All had been outfitted for the occasion in gaudy satins and velvets, with posies of flowers and ribbons and tinkling bells. In the center of the pavilion stood an elaborate throne, the same one that had been used every year for as long as the village had celebrated the May. Strewn with flowers and garlanded with vines of greenery, the mock throne awaited its queen.

Thomas again bent toward Jessica and said in a voice audible to Nicholas, "You should be the queen. No other lass can match your beauty."

"Fie, Thomas," she laughed. "You know the queen must be a maid." Still, she glowed with his kind words. Madeline had often been chosen a queen in her own village, but Jessica's reputation as a hoyden had always excluded her.

Nicholas stiffened and glared at his brother, who had turned back to the festivities and hadn't noticed. Jessica was still smiling at Thomas' sally. Nicholas wished he had turned such a compliment for her, but the idea hadn't occurred to him. Such courtly ways had always been foreign to his nature. Jessica was a rare beauty and he assumed she was knowledgeable of the fact and accustomed to it. Likening her to the Queen of May seemed like comparing a peacock to a lark.

The Lord of Misrule gave a signal and the parade began. First came "Robin Hood" and his men, all dressed in leather jerkins and carrying woodsmen's axes over their shoulders. Robin was distinguished from the rest by his green tunic trimmed boldly with gold braid, his blue-and-white hose, and the silver bugle he wore at his waist. His bow and a quiver of arrows were strung over his shoulders. Nicholas scarcely recognized him as the mayor's eldest son.

Behind the men pranced Maid Marian and her ladies-in-waiting, all dressed in blue gowns, with primroses in their hair. Silver bells jingled with their movements and their long hair billowed and furled in the breeze.

The archer guard followed, all in green tunics, with bows slung over their shoulders. The role of Little John was always portrayed by the blacksmith, as he was the largest man in the village. He walked with a ponderous step that could in no way be construed as dancing. Friar Tuck was evident in the russet priest's gown, which had been padded to a greater girth than the village apothecary normally boasted and was tied with a rope. Over his shoulder he carried a quarterstaff, and as he circled the pole, he bowed and waved to the onlookers.

Behind them came most of the daughters of the village merchants, dressed in orange kirtles, strewing handfuls of white flowers from the baskets they carried. The onlookers leaned forward expectantly to see the Queen of May—this year the butcher's second daughter. She wore a white gown with a train that swept the grasses, and her long curly black hair was adorned with brilliant flowers. A silver coronet embellished with bunches of violets sat atop her head. In her right hand she carried a silver scepter wound with gold silk cords. Her slender neck and fingers were covered with all the jewelry she could borrow from friends and relatives, and her narrow waist was circled by a gold-mesh belt set with semiprecious stones. As she was led to her throne by the Lord of Misrule, grinning and brightly blushing, the onlookers cheered as loudly as they could.

The parade circled the maypole and at the queen's

signal, each person took up the end of a waving cord or ribbon. When she called for them to begin, they started dancing about and weaving the streamers around the tall pole. Their dance recalled far more barbaric times, as did the songs they sang in unison with the music, calling up buried racial memories of May Day stretching far, far back to the beginnings of all festivals.

Noticing that Nicholas was engaged in conversation with the man seated next to him, Thomas eased himself closer to Jessica. "The symbol of the maypole is an old one," Thomas said to Jessica as he signaled for a serving boy to bring him a flagon of wine. "Its meaning is clear when you recall this was once a religious rite performed to trigger the fertilization of the fields and animals."

"I know. We understand symbols in Hargrove village as well as you do here at Wyndfell," Jessica answered quickly, hoping Thomas wouldn't elaborate further on the obviously phallic nature of the symbol. So far Nicholas seemed unaware of Thomas' inappropriate line of discussion and she was relieved. Nicholas was already upset with her and she didn't want him angered any further.

"I've heard it said that at one time the queen would have been raped by the men to further ensure a crop, or even sacrificed to whatever pagan gods were in favor at that time. Personally, I prefer the former."

"Personally I prefer the present," Jessica snapped, trying to make her point without drawing Nicholas' attention. Obviously this wasn't the first measure of wine Thomas had had that day, for his tongue had become much too familiar. In response, Thomas haughtily arched his eyebrows and turned back to watch the proceedings.

Men wearing hobbyhorse or dragon costumes about their waists pranced and gamboled into the crowd, stealing kisses from the women and earning good-natured blows from the men. When one came too near the queen, the Lord of Misrule rushed forward and tossed handfuls of meal at him to chase him away.

After a time, the food service began and the morris dancers started their ancient steps. The jingling of bells from Robin and the maids blended perfectly with the music as they moved through the traditional steps.

Having downed the wine and requested more, Thomas again began to speak to Jessica. "Later there will be music for dancing. Will you honor me with the first one?"

"That honor goes to my husband," Jessica replied, keeping her voice low. She was aware that some of her nearest neighbors had heard Thomas' earlier remarks and were straining to hear more. "You know that as well as I do."

"But he is sitting there like a great stone, ignoring you," Thomas pointed out. "Has he said a word to you since we left the castle? Why save the dance for him?"

"You forget yourself. Are you in your cups so early in the morning?" she scolded under her breath. If Nicholas heard this conversation he might be angry for weeks!

Thomas leaned nearer still and whispered, "Perhaps later I could show you another maypole."

"Oh!" Jessica exclaimed, forgetting to be discreet and turning on him furiously. "How dare you speak to me thus!"

At once Nicholas was on his feet and reaching

across her to grab Thomas, his fist knotted for the blow.

"No, no, Nicholas!" she cried out, realizing they were suddenly the center of attention. "Nothing is amiss!"

Nicholas glared at Thomas, who had paled and moved hastily away. "Something must be wrong for you to speak so," he said with a growl at Jessica.

"I but made a jest," Thomas said hurriedly. "Who would guess she would take it wrongly!"

Now Jessica glared at him as well. "Sit down, Nicholas. Everyone is looking at us," she murmured miserably. She was all too aware of the half-heard whispers and stares.

"Come," Nicholas said abruptly. Not giving her the chance to object, he took her hand and led her out of the pavilion. He drew her through the crowd and past the spot where the hobbyhorses and the dragons were planning their mock battle.

Jessica dared not struggle, but rather hurried to keep up. Too many eyes were following them already.

Nicholas was heading roughly in the direction of Wyndfell, but was cutting through the woods rather than taking the road. Jessica stumbled along in his grasp, trying to miss the roots and holes that would trip her. Unable to catch her breath because of her tight lacings, she suddenly hauled back. "Nicholas! Stop!"

Wheeling, he faced her and she saw the hurt and anger in his eyes. Realizing he must have heard everything Thomas had said, Jessica reached out to him. "Nicholas, I have no interest in Thomas. Please believe me."

He turned from her and went to lean his forearm against the gnarled and twisted boughs of a sweet chestnut. The tree had been split by lightning and broken into a hovering shape by some terrific storm. At the moment Nicholas wished he was no worse off than the battered tree. He felt as if his heart was breaking.

"I know," he said in a gruff voice, "that you had no say in this match; a woman rarely does. Mayhap after seeing Thomas and hearing his smooth words, you wished you had been given to the younger brother rather than the elder."

"Nicholas," she said softly, since the pain he was feeling was evident in his voice. "Speak not so."

"I ask myself how I would feel were I in your place, married to one, but desiring another. If it were me, I would set aside the unloved one and follow my heart, regardless of the consequences. But you are a woman and have not that freedom."

She came to him and put her hand on his arm. Beneath her fingers his muscles quivered as if he were undergoing a violent exertion. "I don't want that freedom."

He grunted his disbelief. "So I, too, would say if my mate were large enough to break me in half. I didn't expect to fall in love with you," he said defensively. "I thought to respect you and honor you, but love? Never."

"You truly love me?" she whispered.

"If I did not, would I put up with you? What man has ever been more sorely vexed?"

She hid her smile and let the warmth engendered by his words flow through her. Nicholas loved her!

He drew a deep breath. "I know not what to do. Should I cage you and forbid your happiness out of my selfishness, or should I turn my back and let you slip away with Thomas? No! I'll not give you up! You're my wife and here you'll stay. In time I will teach you to love me."

"Nicholas, you great fool," she laughed, forcefully pulling him around to face her. "I already love you. Would I come to you so willingly in the night if I did not?"

"It's a woman's duty," he muttered, unconvinced.

"Do I act as if it's merely a duty? It's this woman's pleasure," she corrected. "Look at me and listen to my words. I love you, Nicholas. Not your great castle or your title, but you. I wouldn't have Thomas, and I could box your ears for suggesting such a thing. You could turn your back, but I'd never go. No lock and key is needed to keep me by your side. I love you, such as you are—stubborn, wrongheaded, and rough. You are the substance of my dreams, the stuff of my future."

Nicholas' eyes searched hers for a hint of deceit, but she gazed up at him with no guile at all. Suddenly he swept her up and hugged her fiercely as her feet left the ground. Jessica felt as if her ribs would crack, but she returned his embrace.

After a long time Nicholas let her slide down his body until she again stood before him. He ran his curved forefinger under her chin and looked intently into her eyes. When she saw that his were suspiciously moist, she felt answering tears rise in her own.

"Let there be no more talk of parting between us, Nicholas," she said, "for surely it grieves me sore to hear you speak so."

"I must have been a fool," he replied. "The love in your eyes shines for all to see. Surely you could never look at me like this and care for another."

Jessica tiptoed up and pulled his head down for her kiss. "Never doubt me," she whispered. "How could you think ill of me?"

"You often fail to act as a wife should," he tried to

explain. "You refuse to fetch my ale or yield to me in all things. What else was I to think?"

"It might have occurred to you that I am not a serving wench and that I have a head of my own."

"But my brother's wife . . ."

"I am not your brother's wife. Lady Jane had her ways and I have mine. Did you think all women were made from the same mold?"

"Of course not," he said a little too quickly, "but I thought all wives—"

"Hush, love. The marriage ceremony doesn't make all the same, any more than does birth. However, I love you more, I think, than Lady Jane did Lord Walter. Often such blind obedience results in resentment that can taint those feelings of love."

"You are unlike any woman I have ever known," he said in confusion. "Will I ever understand you?"

"Only love me," she whispered. "Just love me."

He claimed her lips in kiss that began gently and quickly leapt to passion. "Madeline," he murmured against her lips. "Madeline, my love."

The sound of her sister's name on his lips, even though Jessica knew his feelings of love were for her, pierced her heart like icy daggers. She knew her eyes mirrored her hurt, so she closed them before he could see, and kissed him hungrily. "I love you," she whispered fiercely, having set aside her torment for the moment. "I want you."

Nicholas removed his cape and spread it beneath the bent limbs of the tree, the scarlet satin lining up. As his fingers released the frog closing at the waist of her gown, Jessica looked around. "Here?" she exclaimed.

"Why not?" He grinned daringly. "All the villagers are over at the green and will be until dark. No one will see us."

Jessica ducked under the lowest limb and rested her forearm and chin upon it. "Welcome to my bower, sir knight," she said in a teasing voice.

"You look as bewitching as Morgan le Fay herself. And as seductive." He slipped under the limb to join her. "Have you enchanted me?" he asked half-seriously. "First that I burn with jealousy as I never did before, then that I become as foolish as a young swain to do your bidding."

"The enchantment is not mine," she told him as her fingertips traced the line of his lips, "but that of love. I find I have fallen under the same spell. You teach me gentleness."

"Gentle? You?" He cocked his head to one side and looked at her with astonishment.

"It is all relative."

Their lips met and Jessica felt the earth sway beneath her. Even through his clothing she could feel the power of his muscles as well as his hunger for her. She felt him remove her gown and start to unlace her kirtle. The movements reminded her of the passion-filled nights in his arms, and she helped him with his own lacings.

Unfettered by clothing, they sat down upon Nicholas' cloak. The satin was smooth beneath her and cast a red glow on the curve of her hip and thigh. Nicholas gently stroked her cheek as their eyes met in love. She made no movement to stop him as he brushed her thick hair back from her shoulders, baring her full breasts. A sunbeam spangled her skin, casting minute rainbows on the pearly surface.

His eyes feasted on her luscious curves as his fingers drifted lower to touch the rounded globes with gentle reverence. Jessica sat perfectly still as he brushed his palm over her nipples, causing them to tighten eagerly. "You're so beautiful," he murmured.

She lifted her hand and let her fingers caress the muscled wall of his chest. The skin was olive-toned and tanned, his own nipples flat and bronze. "Never had I dreamed a man could be so handsome as you."

Again their eyes met and their souls touched. As slowly as new lovers, they drew closer until their lips fused in a lingering kiss.

Nicholas put his arm around her and drew her nearer until her peaked breasts grazed his hot skin. Tantalizingly they kept the distance, each teasing the other to desire.

With a groan, Nicholas laid her down and gazed at her in awe. Her golden hair was gleaming against the satin cloak and the rosy reflection glowed on her cheeks. Her eyes were darkened with loving passion until they took on the hue of summer storm clouds. Her lips, moist from his kisses, parted seductively. "I love you," he groaned. "I love you with all my heart."

He kissed her, enjoying the feel of her graceful body curving up to meet his and the way her arms encircled his neck to hold him lovingly. His hand smoothed over the swell of her hip and up the valley of her waist to cup her breast. Jessica murmured and shifted slightly to give him greater access. Already her nipple was turgid against his palm. Nicholas lost himself in his love for her. After knowing the charms of Jessica, all other women paled by comparison.

Jessica ran her hands over his back, feeling the swelling muscles and the indentation of his backbone. When her palms moved over the hard cage of his ribs, she detected the faint welt of an old scar, no doubt one that he had received as the victor in some fierce battle. Moving lower, she cupped his firm buttocks and pressed herself to him.

Leaving a trail of fire down her neck, Nicholas' lips moved lower over her shoulder and breast. For a moment he hesitated, licking her nipple teasingly until she moaned for release; then he covered it with his lips and drew it into his mouth. She cried out at the pleasurable sensation and laced her fingers in his black hair to guide him to her.

Loving first one bud, then the other, Nicholas stoked her body to flaming desire. With his fingers where his mouth had been, he rolled her nipple gently between his thumb and forefinger while his lips moved lower yet.

The flat plane of her stomach tensed with the tickle of his beard, then quickened with the warmth that spread from the caress of his lips and his tongue. Moving lower, he traced his tongue up the inner side of her thigh, and Jessica opened her legs to him, giving herself freely. Nicholas lay in the gateway of her love and stroked the fount of her desire with a skillful touch until she moved restlessly beneath his hand and cried out. When she could wait no longer, he put his tongue where his fingers had been and felt a sudden shock run through her as she reached her peak of ecstasy.

When she again lay quietly, Nicholas murmured love words as he guided himself into her. Jessica moved eagerly to accept him and Nicholas groaned with the pleasure he felt and the effort required for him to restrain himself.

Together they moved in the dance of love which was older than time, yet ever new. Again the physical hunger quickened within Jessica, and she matched his thrust with her own as her mind found his and joined it in an upward spiral. Both held back, keeping the passion blazing for a long as they could, then together they leapt into the golden lava flow that meant their completion. Waves swept through them, binding love to love, soul to soul. Slowly, ever so slowly, the gold melted to peace, and they lay content in their love.

Above them the ancient tree stood guard, its curved limbs sweeping downward as if to protect them from all harm. In its branches a bird sang lustily and all the world seemed in tune.

12

RAYMOND CHADWICK NUDGED his horse to a quicker
pace to overtake Swineford and Madeline, who were
riding beside the broad river, engaged in animated
conversation. Madeline wore a new gown of pink
linen trimmed in deep flounces of ecru lace. Broad
bands of rose embroidery decorated her sleeves and
skirt, and she looked as delectable as a marchpane
delicacy. She rode her sorrel palfrey with more grace
than skill and occasionally Swineford had to lean
forward to catch the animal's reins. Raymond scowled
with growing anger. They were being entirely too
friendly for his taste.

Madeline's servant carried Swineford's wedding gift
to her, a new peregrine tercel, whose leather hood
and jesses were dyed scarlet. Swineford's female peregrine, much larger than her male bird, rode on his
gauntleted arm. Raymond had thought the gift pre-
sumptuous from a lord to the wife of a knight, but
there had been nothing he could do about it. Especially since his plan to cheat Nicholas out of marrying a rich heiress had failed. Apparently the girl's
parents had merely substituted Jessica when Ray-

mond eloped with Madeline. Swineford, however, wasn't so philosophical and Raymond dared not offend him by having Madeline refuse his gift, even if Madeline could have been persuaded to do so. When they were alone, Raymond saw less and less of the docile lady he thought he had married.

At the horses' heels trotted two water dogs to fetch the ducks as they were taken. The kennel master rode near the dogs to keep them in control. Over his saddle were draped the canvas bags which would hold the prey. Raymond owned neither dog nor hawk since he was poor and not of the upper class of knighthood. Jealously Raymond noticed that Madeline seemed to know just how to discuss the falcons with Swineford, while he didn't know a varvel from the jesses.

Before long they heard the babble of a flock of ducks. The dogs pricked their ears expectantly and glanced from the kennel master to the river. All conversation ended as they rode nearer.

"Here," Swineford said in a hushed tone. "We will loose them here."

Madeline whipped the leather hood from her tercel as Swineford did the same to his bird. At once the falcons blinked, spread their wings, and flapped silently up to circle above the horses. When they were flying in lazy circles far above, the kennel master was signaled to send in the dogs.

Exuberantly the animals splashed through the tall reed-mace, scattering the flock of ducks into the sky.

"Look!" Madeline cried excitedly as one of the ducks flapped, frantically trying to outfly her tercel. The peregrine easily overtook the bird and swooped downward. His silver bells tinkling faintly, the peregrine struck the duck, breaking its neck with his beak. At once the duck dropped back toward the lake, the falcon in pursuit.

With a motion the kennel master sent one of the dogs to retrieve the duck as Madeline's serving man whistled for the tercel and lured it with a chunk of raw meat on a chain. The bird returned to the man's arm and received the morsel of meat as his reward.

"How wonderful!" Madeline gushed, her cheeks pink and her eyes sparkling. "How I do love hawking. I must admit that I enjoy all forms of the hunt."

By that time, Swineford's falcon had killed its prey, and he whistled for it to return as he twirled the meat lure. "I, too, enjoy it," he agreed as the bird settled on his gauntlet. "I think a man who doesn't keep at least one bird is no man at all."

"I couldn't agree more."

Raymond moved restlessly in the saddle. He was feeling more and more like an unwanted observer.

More ducks were sighted downstream and again the falcons were set upon them. By the end of the afternoon, the canvas bag was full of ducks, and everyone but Madeline was ready to return to Pritchard Hall. As they headed back, she spurred her horse forward to catch up with the kennel master. More ducks might be sighted on the way back to the manor, and she didn't want to waste the chance to prolong the hunt.

Beyond the river grew a hawthorn hedge, and past that lay a pasture. Swineford scowled at the hedge of snowy may blossoms as if the plants represented his enemy. He nodded toward it and said, "I cannot ride this way without seeing that hedge and regretting that it isn't mine, as well as that which lies beyond. By rights that should be mine now." he sharply reminded Chadwick.

"I had thought it would be," Raymond defended

himself. "I spirited away the bride. How was I to know another would be put in her place? From all I saw, the Lady Jessica wasn't favored by her family."

"Nevertheless, she is now the heiress. Tell me, are they so much alike that one could take the other's place?"

"They are remarkably similar, yet Lady Jessica was rumored to be insane."

"Is she?" Swineford asked with interest.

"She is willful to a fault," Raymond said with a shrug. "I know not whether she is mad."

"It's a well-known fact that a madwoman will be either sterile or her offspring will also be insane," Swineford mused thoughtfully. "Mayhap Nicholas will find himself without an heir." Then he scowled, "But by then I will be too old to inherit Wyndfell, even if Thomas were done in. No, I want it now, while I am in my prime and can enjoy it."

Raymond nodded in agreement. "I would feel the same way myself." He cleared his throat and said cautiously, "You mentioned a reward, I believe, for taking away Lady Madeline. A house and pension, as I recall." Hastily he added, "Not that I would try to rush you in your gift, but my lady wife is eager to have a place of her own."

"You think I would reward you for a mistake such as you made? The wedding took place and the debt was repaid."

"But I did as you ordered," Raymond said stubbornly. "I took away his bride. It isn't my fault that the plan failed."

"So you now expect a house and pension, do you?" Swineford sneered. "Here is your pension—find a way to get me Wyndfell. Otherwise I will turn you and your lady wife out on the roadway."

Raymond paled. "Surely you don't mean that, my

lord." The roads had been full of vagrants since the closing of the monasteries and convents a few years back. Those who had been put out had to beg their living or starve, for they had no way of supporting themselves.

"I would do exactly that," Swineford assured him coldly. "I will give you two months."

"Two months!" Raymond gasped. "God's bones! That's nigh impossible."

"Then perhaps you should get to it rather than spending your time sporting." Swineford kicked his horse to a gallop and left Raymond staring after him.

Never a quick-witted man, for the next few days Raymond puzzled over how to accomplish this herculean task. His talent as a knight lay in his ability to follow orders, but with no specific orders this time, his brain moved in sloggy circles and came up with no idea at all.

Madeline paced the bedchamber and glared at her husband. For nights on end he had sat there quaffing ale and staring into his tankard. He had made no effort to amuse her with conversation, and worst of all, he had not made love to her. She could not forgive him for the latter. Especially as he had actually turned her away the night before when she had insisted that he pleasure her.

The memory made her quicken her steps and caused her blood to pound in her temples. How did he dare to push her away? Her lineage was noble, whereas Raymond was only a knight due to his service under Swineford. He was only a commoner. He should be honored that the daughter of a viscount would deign to offer him her body. True, he was the only man she had ever found who could come close to satisfying the lust that never entirely left her, but that was helpful only if he would bed her.

Madeline paused and drew a deep, shuddering breath as she looked at him. He was so virile as he sat there. He wore his clothes well and the fabric was tight across his shoulders and chest. While Raymond wasn't a tall man, he had well-sculptured legs and a powerful physique. Just the thought of him naked and shoving into her made her breath come in quick pants.

Forcing a sweet smile to her lips, Madeline went to him and put her hand on his shoulder. "Come to bed," she urged in her most docile voice.

Raymond glanced at her and shook his head dismally. "Not yet, sweeting. You go to bed without me."

"Again?" She battled the strident note from her voice. "You look tired, Raymond." She ran her hand over his shoulder, letting her fingertips brush through the sandy hair at the nape of his neck. "Your muscles are all tight. Come to bed and let me soothe you."

"Not now. I have a problem that needs solving. Let me finish thinking it through."

She dipped her hand into his loose collar and over the furry breadth of his chest. "Whatever the problem is, surely it can wait." She kept her voice gentle and demure.

Raymond removed her hand and patted it. "I must work this through now. You know not its importance."

Madeline snatched away her hand. Standing absolutely rigid, she glared at the back of his head. A fanatical light flickered in her blue eyes and her skin was as pale and tight as ivory. He had pushed her aside again! Did he dare think he was her equal? Damn him! Her eyes darted about the room for a weapon. She was Lady Madeline Hargrove and was the vassal of no man!

She spied a heavy candlestick on the chest behind him, and eased quietly toward it. One blow, squarely on the top of his head, and he would never gainsay her again.

One hand curled around the cold brass candlestick, while the fingers of her other hand pinched out the candle's flame. The light from the other candles made the absence of that one indiscernible. She upended the weapon, sending drops of hot wax pouring to the floor. A surge not unlike a sexual need roared through her, causing her pulse to quicken and her stare to become intent. She licked her lips eagerly. Already she could almost feel the solid thud of the brass against his skull. He would never reject her again.

Suddenly there was a noise in the hall and Madeline's feral eyes glittered toward the door. Faintly she heard Swineford's voice giving an order to one of the servants. She tilted her head to one side as she thought. She didn't need Raymond to satisfy her body's demands. Not when Swineford looked at her with such obvious invitation at every meeting.

Madeline's lips curved up and her dimple appeared as her body relaxed visibly. Of course. She could simply go to Swineford. Whatever had she been thinking of? Calmly she relit the candle and placed the candlestick back on the chest. She crawled onto their bed and waited. In less than a half hour, Raymond's head began to droop to the tabletop. Minutes later, his snores signaled that he was sound asleep. Quietly Madeline left the room.

Night had fallen, and the corridor was deserted. In order to save candles, all the servants had gone to bed as soon after dark as possible, and already an eerie stillness lay over the large house. Madeline had always enjoyed the silence that meant she was the only one about in the night. It gave her a sense of power to know that no one suspected she was walking through the manor.

Her cloth shoes made no sound on the oak floor and her gliding walk prevented even the rustle of her gown. As silent as a shadow, she traversed the long hallway.

Swineford's suite of rooms was at the very end. Madeline waited at the door until all sounds from his antechamber had ceased. Then she eased open the door and made her way between the cots of his men-at-arms. Her heart pounded at her daring. She hesitated before letting herself into the next chamber, a long and narrow one whose far end extended over the manor's chapel so that Swineford could attend the service in private—or pretend that he did.

The next door was so heavy that Madeline thought at first it was bolted, but when she pushed harder, it swung open. Swineford was ready for bed and was climbing onto the piles of mattresses. When Madeline glided noiselessly into the room, he jumped and stared at her in near-fright. "Lady Madeline?" he asked at last. "Is it you?" She stood so still and her entrance had been so silent, he thought at first she might be a ghost.

"Yes, it is I," she said softly, wandering into a ray of moonlight. "Are you so surprised, my lord?"

Swineford glanced back at the door she had closed firmly behind her. "Are you alone? Why are you here?"

In answer, Madeline reached up and drew the bodkins from her luxurious hair, letting it tumble about her. Still not speaking, she started to loosen the laces that held the bodice of her gown. Pulling the fabric open to reveal the globes of her breasts, Madeline glided nearer. Running her fingers over her distended nipples, she said silkily, "I was lonely."

Realizing what she offered, Swineford grinned lasciviously.

"Then we must remedy that at once."

He pulled her to him, and Madeline laughed seductively as they tumbled onto the bed. For a moment he lay above her, still not quite believing she was there. Madeline's bright hair waved over the coverlet and a thick skein curled over her shoulders to nestle upon her breast. Hungrily James' eyes followed the silken strand; then he swept it aside to reveal the tight pink bud of her nipple.

Lowering his head, he nipped at the pouting treasure, and when Madeline moaned and arched toward him, he moved his mouth over her in greedy abandon. She writhed on the bed, her gown knotted about her hips, so he lifted her enough to thrust aside the encumbrance. She entwined her arms about his waist and wantonly pushed against him, her eyes glittering and as dark as the evening sky. James needed no further urging. He had lusted after her since the day he first saw her. Triumphantly he entered her and felt her fingernails rake his back in ecstasy.

James' movements were strong and sure, as though he were a master craftsman at the art of seduction. Madeline met him stroke for stroke, her quick words stoking him to greater urgency. With an effort he prolonged his completion until hers was done.

Madeline cried out as her body thrust against him, then trembled to a state as near to satisfaction as she had ever known. She closed her eyes tightly, trying to prolong the moment, to hang on to the exquisite pleasure. Slowly, as always, the sensation faded, and she opened her eyes against the faint but undeniable gnawing deep in her loins. The time she had almost reached that unnameable release. Almost.

For several minutes James lay over her, gasping for breath. As his heartbeat slowed, he smiled. Then, to her great amazement, he began kissing her as he moved within her once again. Madeline murmured with delight at the promise of perhaps at last quelling the demon within her. This time when he reached his satisfaction, she cried out and dug her fingers into his shoulder blades as a series of waves even stronger than the last roared through her.

As she tried to catch her breath, Madeline smiled and congratulated herself on finding this new and very pleasing diversion.

For days Raymond had struggled for an idea, even a poor one, of how to get Wyndfell away from Nicholas Garrett. Had the property gone to Thomas instead, there would have been little difficulty, as Thomas was as careless a gambler as his eldest brother, Walter. At last Raymond hit on a partial plan. If he met Thomas somewhere and they talked, perhaps an idea would present itself.

Raymond called in a son of one of the stablemen and gave the boy a copper ha'penny. "Go to Wyndfell," he instructed, "and tell Master Thomas Garrett that Sir Henry Rogan is to be at the Bear and Bull this afternoon and wishes to see him."

"Sir Henry Rogan?" the boy asked.

"Just give him the message, and if he asks, tell him that you work in Rogan's stable." Raymond knew Rogan was also a gambler and was a particular friend of Thomas'. Thomas was almost certain to agree to meet him at the inn.

Raymond walked along the corridor and paused at

the doorway to the ladies' parlor. Madeline sat upon a low stool, sewing prettily. A ray of sunlight from the window illumined her and glinted off her needle. As always her beauty caused Raymond to pause and stare. She looked like an angel come to earth, framed as she was in doorway and sunbeams. Her motions were smooth and deliberate, as if nothing could cause her to rush or become flustered. To look at her, no one would ever guess such a perfect lady could be so wild in bed, nor so shrewish when crossed. Though in the past few days she had again become the gentle woman Raymond had courted and won, he knew he would never understand her, but also that he would never stop loving her.

Of late he had been less attentive toward her and he felt a twinge of quilt. Madeline enjoyed bed sport more thoroughly than any woman he had ever encountered. At times he even suspected her appetite to be greater than his, if such were possible for a female, which he doubted. Yet the threat of being turned out on the road was dire enough to have temporarily erased any sexual longing on his part. Raymond made a silent vow that he would make up for lost time that very evening. By then, with any luck, he would have a plan to take Wyndfell.

Madeline lifted her head and smiled toward someone in the room who was beyond Raymond's line of vision. Raymond resolved to find a way to earn the house and pension from Swineford. Madeline must have her own home. She wasn't born to be second lady in a manor house, even though Swineford had no wife of his own. Madeline was still only the helpmeet of a humble knight. The quicker he gave her a hearth of her own and an armful of babies, the better.

Raymond saddled his horse and rode to the village situated between Wyndfell and Pritchard Hall. He rode slowly, planning how he would lay out his new farm and what crops he would raise. Although he was still young, he wasn't so young as to want to continue supporting himself entirely on his skills as a man-at-arms. This was the ideal time to build himself a small holding of his own. One he could pass on to his son as his own father had been unable to do.

By the time he reached the Bear and Bull, several hours had passed, as Raymond had intended, giving Thomas ample time to have arrived at the inn and have grown impatient for company.

He gave his horse to the boy on the doorstep and looked around the enclosed courtyard. A troupe of actors was busy setting up a stage and hanging the canvas backdrops for a performance later, but no one was paying any attention to who was coming or going.

Letting himself into the common room, Raymond looked around as if he had merely wandered in. Across the room he saw Thomas seated in one of the deep alcoves. Nonchalantly he strolled over and made a show of surprise on seeing Thomas face-to-face.

"Raymond Chadwick!" Thomas exclaimed. "Is it you?"

"Master Thomas! Upon my word! Fancy meeting you here. Are you alone?"

"Thus far. I was to meet Sir Henry Rogan but he has yet to show. Sit down. Sit down." When Raymond slid onto the opposite bench, Thomas said, "Where have you been? We were all worried about you."

Raymond looked at him in real surprise. Nicholas must not have gotten the note he left the day he took Madeline away. What must he have thought? Surely he had not learned of the switch and correctly concluded who was responsible for spiriting away his bride. Cautiously he offered, "As I said in the note I left for Lord Nicholas, I was called away suddenly. A family matter."

"It must have been a grave emergency for you to bolt before the wedding and not stay even long enough to clear your way with Nicholas. At first he was merely curious, for he could not make out your hand, but when you didn't return or send word, he grew angry with you. He feels you have let him down, and likely would not welcome your return."

"That is unfortunate, but it is just as well. As you know, I much preferred working for Lord Walter. And as it stands now, I am in the employ of kin and only here on business. But tell me, did the wedding go well?"

Thomas drained the glass of malmsey and motioned for more. By the glassy sheen in Thomas' eyes Raymond correctly assumed this wasn't his first glass of the day.

"The wedding was spectacular, the bride beautiful. The groom, unfortunately, was Nicholas."

"Oh? Raymond leaned forward eagerly. "Is he dissatisfied?"

"No. Oh no, who could be displeased to be married to Lady Madeline? But you know how rough he is. Nicholas can be as uncouth as a knave. He never took to polish as Walter and I did."

"You do remind me greatly of Lord Walter, bless him," Raymond agreed.

"Lady Madeline, however, came to us with the patina of a fine lady, though at times her patience wears thin at having to cope with Nicholas' demands."

"Theirs is not a peaceful union?"

"Not at all! Why I've heard more dissension between them in this month of their marriage than in the whole ten years of Walter's marriage to Jane." He scowled into his drink. "Would that I could rescue her."

Raymond's attention sharpened and he said, "Rescue her? From her lawful husband?"

"I know all too well that it cannot be done. Yet were it possible, I would leap to her defense, vanquish my brother, and ride away with her."

"Would she go, do you think?"

"Never. She is a lady born, not a tavern wench. Lady Madeline is far too perfect to run away with another man."

"Perhaps Lord Nicholas will set her aside?" Raymond suggested hopefully.

"Not a chance of it. He was enamored with her gold before he ever saw her. Were the nunneries still about so he could rid himself of her and keep her dowry, then perhaps, but they are gone." He drank down the wine as if it were water and added morosely, "Can you imagine Lady Madeline as a nun?"

"Never," Raymond said honestly. And her sister, Jessica, was even less likely a candidate, he thought. "But as you say, this country has set aside popish ways."

"Fortunately for my lady."

As if he were speaking to himself, Raymond said, " 'Tis a shame you weren't born ahead of Nicholas, for you would make a perfect Earl of Wyndfell. Think of it. The title, the wife you covet, the power."

Thomas stared at him in drunken seriousness, the last glass of malmsey having dulled his wits even further. "Thomas Garrett, Earl of Wyndfell," he mumbled, "and Lady Madeline Garrett, his countess. My, but it does have a sweet ring."

Raymond sipped at his own drink and said, "You

would likely even give me back my old position of man-at-arms, would you not?"

"Ask and it would be yours. Not so with my brother, though. He bears you ill will for your departure. Unprincipled, he called it."

"Such an unfeeling man to have sway over so large a parish," Raymond commiserated.

"What could I not do if I ruled my own parish? Nicholas lets his tenants grow lax. Any excuse they offer he accepts as reason for them to delay payment to the castle coffers. Our father was never so soft, nor was Walter."

"You would have made a good earl," Raymond repeated carefully.

"When Walter reached adulthood and was as healthy and hearty as they come, who would ever have guessed he would find an early grave? Now Nicholas is in his place—a man even as well and strong as our brother."

Raymond waited, scarcely breathing, to see if Thomas would make the leap from regret to revenge.

Thomas leaned low over the table and pointed his wavering finger at Raymond. "If aught were to happen to Nicholas, I would be earl."

"This is true." Raymond knew this was the time for great caution. Thomas must reach this conclusion for himself.

"If something tragic befell Nicholas, he would be dead. As dead as Walter. And I, Thomas, would be Earl of Wyndfell."

"Merely supposing something were to happen to him," Raymond mused aloud, "Lady Madeline would need a protector."

"That she would. And *I* would be there." Thomas sat back as if he had made a verbal checkmate.

"You're quite right. Tell me, Master Thomas. Does

your brother seem prone to accidents? A hunting accident, perhaps."

Thomas blinked and studied Raymond blankly. He was drunk, but he wasn't beyond reason. To say he would profit from Nicholas' death was one thing, but to discuss how it might happen was another.

"Lord Nicholas employs no taster," Raymond continued. "Something might enter his food. His food alone, mind, so that his lady wife is unharmed. Surely there is some dish or drink which he prefers that she always refuses?"

"Enough! Would you have me murder my brother?" Thomas asked thickly. "You take too great a liberty, indeed."

"I? All I did was agree with you on abstract matters," Raymond reminded him hastily. "We were only speaking in generalizations, were we not?"

"Aye," Thomas answered. "Generalizations. Of course."

Raymond stood to go. "By your leave, I must be on my way. Farewell, Master Thomas."

"Farewell," Thomas mumbled automatically.

As he drank another glass of malmsey, he wished Sir Raymond had kept his insinuations to himself. The thought of Nicholas dying hadn't seriously occurred to Thomas. The idea opened doors he almost wished had remained closed. But murder! No, the idea was unthinkable. Thomas motioned for the servant to refill his glass as his thoughts reeled longingly back to his brother's wife.

13

THROSTLES WERE SINGING from their perches high in
the beech trees as Nicholas rode out of Wyndfell. He
had always liked early morning. Dew silvered the
grass and the sky was an iridescent pale blue much
like that of an opal gemstone. His large horse
stretched his legs in a gallop that carried him beyond
the copse of trees and through the oak forest where
hirelings were pollarding trees. As they lopped the
long, straight branches off the gnarled burls from
past harvests, they tossed them onto wagons to be
carried to the village. In time the branches would be
used in the construction of mud-and-wattle cottages
or in a dozen other tasks that required supple and
straight wood.

The fields lay before him, green with the young
crops. Rye rippled in the breeze, and beyond he could
see the new field of hops that bordered the barley.
Nicholas rode slowly around the edge of the fields.
The seeds had been good this year. The grains were
abundant and there seemed to be fewer weeds than
usual. After the last harvest the sheep had, of course,
been turned into the field to graze on the stubble.

Unlike the previous years, however, Nicholas had ordered his people to leave the sheep droppings in the field, rather than gather them as fuel. Unless he was mistaken, this served as a better fertilizer than plowing leaves into the soil as he had always done before. Perhaps the idea hadn't been so farfetched after all, in spite of the derision from his yeomen.

As he circled back to Wyndfell, he met a tenant and his team of oxen heading for the fields. They exchanged a greeting and Nicholas rode on. All his fortune had changed of late. Even his tenants and hirelings seemed happier and more productive. Marrying had turned his luck for the better.

By noon he completed his rounds of the fields and returned to the castle. Jessica was waiting for him in the winter parlor. He paused at the door to gaze adoringly at her.

She sat in a splash of red and gold from the large stained-glass window and her dress was the green of new leaves. In her lap she held her sewing, but when he entered, her needle stilled. Her deep blue eyes met his and a quick smile sprang to her lips.

"Greetings, love," he said to her. "How have you spent your morning?"

"I have spent it thinking of you." Since he had returned early, she was glad she had seen to her chores already. The maids were dipping candles and working at the countless other jobs necessary to keep a castle fed and running properly. Only minutes before, Jessica had been notified of his arrival and had hurried to wash her face and hands and get to the parlor in order to present him with a picture of her in domestic calm. Such was part of her earliest training, for while a husband expected his wife to oversee all the household staff and to add her personal touch to herbal remedies and preserves and the like, no man wanted his wife to *look* as if she did these things. So Jessica always dusted off the grime of the buttery and cellars and washed away the vestiges of flour from her hands in time to reap his smile of approval.

"I asked that we be served here," she said, "since we have eaten in the hall twice this week."

"Good. I prefer that."

Jessica stood and walked to the window, peering through the clear glass along the sides of the colorful design. "It looks as if it might rain."

"Yes, but I've finished my ride." He came to stand behind her and wrap his arms about her.

"Look out there," Jessica mused. A lone woman was walking across the orchard, a basket looped over her arm. A man close by saw her and came to meet her. They hugged and sat on the damp grass to eat their meal.

Nicholas looked past her. "That's Kate from the village and her husband, Robin. Why do you mention them?"

"They look happy." She drew her slender finger over the glass. "I know it's a foolishness, but at times I wish we were merely yeomen or even tenants. I love Wyndfell, but we are rarely alone. I could never make a meal and carry it out to you so that we could eat it together on the grass. This Kate and her Robin have privacy that we will never see."

"No, love, that they don't. I know that family. They have several children, her mother, and his unmarried sister living with them. And all in a two-room cottage that would fit in this parlor."

"Are no lovers ever alone?" she asked wistfully.

"Seldom." His lips moved against her hair. "To be alone, their parents must be dead and their marriage barren. Who would wish that upon themselves? With no babes, who would see to a person in his old age? Besides, the extra hands make the work lighter."

"You're right of course. I'd not give up the luxuries of Wyndfell to live in a vassal's cottage. Not willingly. And anything larger would be impossible for us to tend to properly. Still," she added, "there are times when I want you all to myself."

He chuckled and nuzzled her ear. "I want you all to myself right now."

Jessica turned to him with a grin but stepped away as Thomas entered the room. He was pale and disgruntled and merely glared at Nicholas in greeting.

"Well, little brother," Nicholas boomed. "I see you have again joined the living. How do you feel?"

Thomas blinked and rubbed this throbbing head. "Not so loud," he complained weakly.

To Jessica, Nicholas said, "Our Thomas was down to the Bear and Bull last night."

"Did you see the play?" Jessica asked, "I was wondering if we might all go this afternoon."

"I saw no play." Thomas scowled. "I have no patience for watching actors rant and pace about."

"It seems young Thomas tried to follow the example of old George, Duke of Clarence, and drown himself in a butt of malmsey." Nicholas grinned with the enjoyment of a man who has no hangover surveying one who does.

"You wouldn't find it so amusing if you were in my shoes," Thomas protested. "On my honor, I think the wine was tainted."

Nicholas grinned, but made no comment as the servants arrived bearing their meal. A table was placed before the cold hearth, and he seated Jessica in one chair before he took the other. Thomas drew up a stool. Since the chaplain preferred to take his meals in the hall, they quickly blessed the food themselves and began to eat.

"We have good crops this year," Nicholas said to Jessica and Thomas. "I think it was from letting the sheep graze in the stubble and . . ."

"Please," Thomas groaned as he picked at his venison. "Spare me the details."

"Nicholas," Jessica said, "could we go to the play? It's *Gammer Gurton's Needle*."

"Yes, we can go. I've not seen a play since last fall." He turned to his brother. "Thomas, will you come with us?"

"Never! I couldn't face seeing even the outside of the Bear and Bull so soon."

"Were you alone in your dissipation?" Nicholas asked in amusement.

"I was told that Sir Henry Rogan wanted to meet me there."

"And did he?" Nicholas frowned. Rogan was one of the scoundrels who milked Thomas' pockets of gold as he had Walter's before him.

"No, more's the pity. I made the ride for nothing." Thomas braced his forearms on the table and looked over at Nicholas. "All was not wasted, however, for I cleared up a mystery. While I was waiting for Rogan I saw Sir Raymond Chadwick."

Jessica's reaction was instant. The wine she was sipping choked her and the rest spilled down her dress. Nicholas slapped her on the back and helped her sop up the rosy liquid.

"Chadwick, you say?" he said over his shoulder to Thomas. "Where has he been and what did he have to say for himself?"

Jessica's frantic eyes searched Thomas' face. Why did he hesitate so long before answering? Had Madeline been with Sir Raymond?

Finally Thomas said, "He's been in the employ of relatives. He said it was urgent business that had taken him from Hargrove Castle and that the note he left behind had said as much. The rest of which he spoke is of no interest to you."

Jessica met Thomas' eyes as she searched to see what he wasn't telling, for she knew he was holding something back. Then he looked away hastily, and Jessica stared at her plate. Did Thomas know about Madeline? He hadn't said so, but he could be withholding the truth as a weapon against her. Ever since May Day when Thomas had spoken to her so suggestively, Jessica had avoided him. She knew he had noticed and that he wasn't pleased. Blackmail had been used as a leverage for favors before this.

"A poor excuse. The man clearly had no loyalty. I should never have trusted him with so important a task as the wedding arrangements. We were lucky that he didn't botch that before he left. You say you spoke of nothing else?" Nicholas asked offhandedly.

"Nothing of importance that I recall." He glanced back at Jessica and found she was still staring at him, her eyes round and horrified. Thomas turned away with a guilty scowl. He knew that many women had the gift of seeing. What if she had divined that Chadwick had suggested that Thomas murder his brother? No, not suggested, but actually told him of a way to do so. Not daring to look at her again, he wondered what he should do if she told Nicholas.

That made the unwanted idea loom larger. It would be relatively easy, since Nicholas employed no taster. Thomas knew his brother had a fondness for tansy cake and that Jessica didn't like it. He was also the castle's primary consumer of canary wine. To poison a wine cask would be even simpler than bribing or outwitting a cook.

Thomas looked at his unsuspecting brother. If he used the right poison and in the correct way, no one would ever guess Nicholas hadn't contracted a wasting illness and died naturally. Suddenly he realized the exact nature of his thoughts and he mentally backed away. Kill his brother? Never! He couldn't do that.

Then he looked at Jessica's golden hair, piled high on her shapely head, the tapering curve of her slender neck, and the swell of her rounded bosom. And he thought that perhaps he could do the deed to win such a prize. Maybe.

Jessica and Nicholas rode down to the inn that afternoon and joined the crowd thronging the gates. Jessica put on her half-mask of black satin as had the other ladies of means before mixing with the mass of people. A man in a blue-and-yellow-striped hat was taking money, the charge being a shilling for the best seats and a penny for standing room. Nicholas gave the man two coins, and a boy led them to their seats.

The yard of the inn had been transformed. Beneath the sycamore tree was a painted canvas backdrop depicting a village house. Jessica leaned forward on the backless bench better to see the stage. Performers had fairly often come to Hargrove Castle and she always loved seeing a play. Beside her she felt Nicholas' eagerness and realized performances might be rare this far from a city.

People from the village and castle shuffled in and took their places according to their means. A couple of enterprising boys climbed the tree and tried to hide among the leaves to keep from paying their penny, but they were spotted by the man in the striped cap and charged a ha'penny for their lofty seats. Another boy, by arrangement with the inn, was selling apples and nuts to the crowd. As soon as they were seated, a number of the men lit their pipes. Within minutes a haze of tobacco smoke hovered over the improvised theater. Above them the sun beat down, adding to the press of bodies.

At last everyone was settled and an expectant hush fell over the audience as the group of players strolled onto the stage. Jessica, whose bench was practically on the stage itself, jumped at the power of the man's voice as he recited the prologue.

The actors portraying Hodge and Diccon came on stage and Hodge began bemoaning the sad state of his clothes, which sorely needed mending. From the other side came an old woman and her maid, played by two slightly built men. They made a great show of mourning a loss and disclosed that old Gammer Gurton had lost her only needle.

The audience shouted helpfully at the actors as they crawled about in search of the missing implement. The women in the crowd especially sympathized with the loss, as some of them could have little afforded to lose their own needles, the price being so dear. Not finding it, Gammer deduced the needle had been stolen by her neighbor, Dame Chat, and the audience howled in agreement. When the two actors engaged in a mock fight, the crowd began shouting, and one or two were on their way to the stage to help out their champion before their friends pulled them back. Jessica caught Nicholas' hand and held it tightly. The actors were long accustomed to such participation and played their parts with grimaces and gestures designed to heighten it.

Jessica tore her eyes from the stage for a moment to glance around the audience. Would there be a fight in reality? She had seen it happen more than once when the play was especially believable. Suddenly she saw a very familiar face at the opposite edge of the crowd. Raymond Chadwick was here, and he was looking directly at her! A deep chill settled over her. Her lips parted and her breath quickened in fear. Had he recognized her behind her mask? Of course he had, she thought immediately. What other blond woman would be seated beside Nicholas Garrett? Madeline was nowhere to be seen, thank goodness, but Raymond Chadwick was bad enough. A few words from him would be enough to shred her happiness and send her back to her parents and Leopold the Mad's cell.

"Madeline?" Nicholas asked in concern, causing her to start and look about frantically. "Are you feeling all right?"

"No, I'm not," she whispered. In truth she felt physically ill.

"Come. I'm taking you home." He stood and helped her to her feet.

Jessica made no protest. In fact she found she couldn't leave quickly enough. A glance told her that Raymond was still across the crowd but was watching her. Jessica stuffed her mask into her sleeve and walked faster.

All the way back to the castle, Jessica was nervous. She repeatedly glanced over her shoulder at the empty road. Fear that Raymond might overtake them and tell all to Nicholas made her unusually quiet.

"Did something frighten you?" Nicholas asked when she looked back yet again.

"Of course not! I merely felt ill. That's all. Possibly the venison we had for dinner had grown rank."

"It tasted fine to me."

"The fish then. At any rate, I'm feeling better now. Could we ride a bit faster?"

They were galloping by the time they reached Wyndfell and most of Jessica's color had returned. Thomas stepped out to meet them, a tankard of wine in his hand.

"Thomas, I see you've recovered," Nicholas observed dryly.

Thomas set the cup on the step in order to reach up and assist Jessica in dismounting. Shielded from Nicholas' view by the body of the horse, he let Jessica's body slide the length of his own. Her eyes widened in shock. "Aye, brother," he called out. "I've quite recovered and am finishing my cure with the hair of the dog."

As soon as Jessica's feet touched ground, she pushed Thomas away and glared at him warningly. Tonight of all nights she didn't want to parry his parlor assaults and try to cover them so Nicholas wouldn't see. She had too many other worries to fret over Nicholas' jealousy.

"You're home early," Thomas said to Jessica, his eyes stripping her. "Did you not enjoy the performance?"

"It was only average," Nicholas answered for her as a stableboy came to take their horses. "The crowd was making so much noise I could scarcely hear the lines."

"If I were Earl of Wyndfell I would have James Burbage and his troupe of actors out from London to perform for me."

Nicholas gave a short laugh. "You would fritter away all your money in a year's time. 'Tis fortunate that Wyndfell is my responsibility." He put his arm around Jessica's waist and they went up the steps to the door.

"Were many at the play?' Thomas asked, watching Jessica as he usually did.

"Most of the village and a number of our castle folk. The actors must have brought in over twelve pounds. I guess everyone believed them better at their craft than they proved to be."

Jessica glanced at Thomas and wondered again how much Raymond had told him. He was regarding her with an infuriating grin. He followed them into the winter parlor and lounged familiarly on a long bench beside the hearth. "Was there anyone there of importance?"

"None!" Jessica snapped. "I would rather not talk about it."

Both men stared at her in surprise and she put her fingertips to her forehead. "Forgive me. I have a fearsome headache."

Thomas sprang to his feet and helped her to the nearest of the two chairs, then called for a servant to bring a potion of rosewater.

Nicholas watched his actions, but his face was unreadable. "She admitted only to a headache, brother. You act as if she were in birth labor." He smiled to soften his words, but the expression never reached his eyes.

"If I had such a wife," Thomas retorted, "I would take better care of her."

Jessica looked from one brother to the other. Tension was almost beginning to crackle between them.

"First you say you would do thus and so if you were earl in my place, and now you assume husbandship over my wife." Nicholas retained his humorous countenance but his words were clipped. "Mayhap I should take you behind the stable and remind you of your place."

"My place!" Thomas spat out. "Where has my place ever been but behind my older brothers?"

"That is the way of things! When Walter became

earl, did I rant and rave and throw myself about? No! I gave him his due respect and went about my own business."

"But you were next in line and now the earldom belongs to you!"

"It belongs to me by right of birth!" Nicholas' voice rose to meet Thomas'. "Who may gainsay me that?"

Jessica looked from Thomas to Nicholas. Her pretended headache was becoming quite real.

Thomas wasn't angry enough to challenge Nicholas over an issue that he couldn't possibly win. Instead he pointed at Jessica. "How can you shout in her presence? No gentleman would treat a lady so."

"Your voice raised first!" Nicholas roared. "Don't presume to take me to task over my own wife."

"If she were mine, I would take better care of her. How do you know she isn't sickening of some disease?"

"She all but raced me home," he answered hotly. "A woman with a disease could hardly do that." Snapping his head around to Jessica, he demanded, "Tell me, my lady. Are you sick? Have you the plague? The sweating sickness?"

"I have but a headache," she replied cautiously.

"There! She has but a headache!" Nicholas glared at his brother. "I know my own wife. Were she sick, I would sense it in my bones. Her spirit and mine are one. She has only a headache."

The summoned servant appeared at the doorway, a basin of rosewater in his hands and a soft towel over his arm. He hovered just inside the chamber and looked fearfully at his betters.

"Abuse her, then," Thomas shouted. "Let her go unattended. In time you will destroy this good woman."

"Stop shouting over me!" Jessica burst out. "Why do you two go on so?"

Nicholas glared again at his brother and demanded of Jessica, "Am I not taking proper care of you? Do I not see to your every need?"

"Yes! But must you affirm so in such volume?" Her entire head was throbbing and she felt dizzy from the stress.

"Begging your pardon, my lord," the servant ventured. "Shall I go away?"

"No! Follow me!" Nicholas bent and swooped Jessica up in his arms. He did take proper care of her, he fumed to himself. Thomas must be insane to say that he didn't. Turning, he shouldered his way out of the room and strode for the stairs. The servant trotted to keep up with him.

"Nicholas, put me down," Jessica protested. "I can walk."

"Your head hurts," he snapped. "Allow me to take care of you."

Jessica sighed and buried her face in the muscles of Nicholas' throat. He was like the great bear in her childhood story that fell in love with a princess and was determined to protect her whether she willed it or not.

Nicholas kicked open the doors of their antechamber and bedchamber and carried her to the bed. With great care he laid her on the embroidered coverlet. To the servant he ordered, "Leave us!" The man placed the rosewater and towel on a chest and retreated hastily.

Nicholas wet the towel in the scented water, wrung it out, and folded it awkwardly across her forehead. Then he set about loosening her clothing.

"There really is no need to trouble yourself so,"

Jessica told him as he opened her laces. "I only have a headache."

He stopped and leaned over her, his arm crossing her middle. "Do I truly not attend you closely enough?" he asked in a concerned voice. "Thomas says—"

"I know, love. I know. But Thomas knows not what is between us." She reached up and stroked the black silk of his beard. "I am no Bartholomew baby that must be pampered and fed on cream and berries. Nor do I want that."

"He's right in part," Nicholas said gruffly. "My ways are coarse and I have no knowledge of how to please a lady with soft words and courtly deeds."

She smiled lovingly. "Dear Nicholas, you must stop saying that. How can I tell you how you content me? If you were as foppish as Thomas, I would never want you. Why, at times he seems more the lady than I do," she laughed.

Nicholas gazed down at her, wanting to believe her, yet not quite able to do so.

"Here," she said, sliding over to make room for him. "Lie beside me."

"Your headache," he said in token protest.

"My head will feel much better upon your shoulder than on this pillow."

Nicholas removed his boots and stretched out beside her. Jessica curled against his side and nestled into the curve of his arm. "There," she sighed. "That is much better."

He took the damp cloth from her forehead and stroked it over her cheeks. Although his movements weren't practiced, his intentions warmed her heart.

"I know such is not possible for a woman," he began slowly, "but *if* you had a choice, would you have chosen me?"

"Believe me, Nicholas. The choice was mine and I unwaveringly chose you. And I would do so again."

With a sigh he cuddled her close. She couldn't have really had a choice and he well knew it. A girl was betrothed to the man picked by her parents, and that was that. Still, if she thought she'd had a say in the matter, then was that not as fine a proof as if she truly had?

Jessica closed her eyes and enjoyed the way Nicholas soothed away her headache. Her thoughts drifted back to that day at Hargrove castle when she had decided to take Madeline's place. He could never know that the choice had, in fact, been solely hers, for he must never know she wasn't Madeline. Yet in a corner of her heart she ached to tell him. To hear him call her by her own name. To feel that, at last, he was solely hers as she unreservedly was his.

"I love you," he murmured in her ear. "Never doubt that."

"I never do," she answered. Nicholas wasn't a man to speak those words unless he meant them through and through. His unpolished manner proved his truth. She reached up and ran her fingers over the curve of his lips, then along his beard to trace his ear. "Do you ever doubt that I love you?"

"No. Sometimes I fear losing your love, but I never doubt it."

"My love is more constant than you give it credit."

He gazed at her and their souls met. Words too meaningful for speech were spoken and answered in their hearts. At last he kissed her, gently, with his full emotion in check. Jessica tasted his lips and ran her tongue over their inner softness.

Drawing back, he said, "Your headache . . ."

"My headache has gone," she said with a seductive tilt of her soft lips.

He tossed the damp cloth into the bowl of rosewater and drew her into his arms.

14

RAYMOND WAS HUMMING the melody to "Lord Randal" as he went into Swineford's closet. Swineford looked up from the papers he was perusing and speculatively eyed the younger man.

"You're in fine fettle today," he observed. "Does this mean you have devised a plan to get me Wyndfell?"

"That I have, my lord. I've not only devised it, I've set it in motion." Raymond beamed proudly and crossed his arms over his chest.

"Well?" Swineford finally prodded. "Might I be privy to your scheme?"

"The plan revolves about the fact that Master Thomas is as big a gambler as was his brother Walter."

"That earns us naught. Wyndfell belongs to Lord Nicholas."

"It does at the moment. But suppose," Raymond said smugly, "that Lord Nicholas were dead."

Swineford stared at him doubtfully.

"A vial of poison in his wine, or perhaps in his morning porridge. Some poisons are so deadly that they may even be used upon clothing to kill through the absorption of the skin. Our queen never accepts a gift of gloves because of it."

"Yes, yes. I know all that," Swineford said impatiently. "But how could you ever hope to gain access to his kitchens or his clothing? You are too well known and would be stopped before you ever entered the gate. It's a foolish plan " He turned back to his paperwork.

Raymond leaned closer. "I mean not to do the task myself. The murderer will be Thomas Garrett."

"Thomas! How do you think to accomplish that?"

"I have already done it. I met with him at the Bear and Bull and set the idea rolling in his head. I said what a shame it was that Nicholas and not Thomas had the accidental good fortune to be born first. Naturally he agreed with me."

"Of course. But there's a wide gap between that and murder."

"Fortunately for us there is another matter. Thomas is enamored of Nicholas' wife."

"Oh?" For the first time Swineford showed interest. A man might kill for love. Or even for lust.

"She is quite beautiful," Raymond continued. "The exact duplicate of my Madeline."

"Is she now? Perfect matches are rare." His mind wandered to the enticing fantasy of having both twins at once in his bed. If their appetites were also of a kind, that would be an experience to savor.

"I pointed out to Thomas that if his brother were dead, he would have the pleasant task of consoling the widow."

"Do you think he'll do it?"

"When I left him, he could talk of nothing else." Raymond hoped Thomas had not had a reversal of heart once he sobered up.

"You were careful, I assume, not to implicate me in any way."

"I never breathed your name. As far as Thomas knows, I was merely passing through the parish. He would never guess to find me here."

"Very good," Swineford admitted thoughtfully. "You've done well after all. If Thomas goes through with his work, Wyndfell is mine. I need not even gamble it away from him. I have only to accuse him of murdering his brother. After the execution I can buy Wyndfell, or simply claim my right to it as my father's eldest son."

Raymond straightened and turned to go. All at once he was hungry for his wife. The hours of thinking had paid off and his body wanted surcease. Taking leave of Swineford, he went up the broad stairway to his chamber.

"Madeline?" he called out. "Are you here?" A quick glance about the room told him she was not.

Where might she be? She had no reason to be in the kitchens or the cellars beneath the house. On the way to his chamber he had passed the ladies' parlor and seen that it was empty. Perhaps she had gone for a ride.

Still humming "Lord Randal," Raymond went back downstairs and out of the manor. On his way to the stables, he skirted the carefully clipped hedges of the privet garden and looked for Madeline as he passed. When he found no sign of her in that garden, nor among the roses, he felt sure he'd been right when he first concluded that she must have ridden out to enjoy the early-summer sunshine.

Raymond had the stable lad saddle his horse, and then he rode out after her. Madeline was fond of the park and the beech forest behind it, so Raymond thought it likely that she would have gone in that direction.

The large lime trees closed over him, making dark green spangles on the sun-washed grass. A bird was calling repetitively and was answered by another. Above the domes of leaves, the sky was brilliant azure with traces of clouds not yet heavy enough to rain. The day was perfect for a ride.

Raymond found Madeline in the beech woods beside a tumbling beck. She had dismounted and tied her horse to a bush so she could stroll by the water. When Raymond rode up, she looked at him with vague interest but not welcome. As a result of the past few nights, she had entirely switched her allegiance to Swineford, who had proved to be not only as lusty as Raymond but also less easily satiated.

"Good morrow, sweeting," Raymond greeted her, tying his horse to a bush near her own animal.

"What brings you out here?" she asked.

"I came to find you."

Madeline turned away and twirled a violet she held in her fingers. "I'm surprised you noticed I was gone. In the past week you have scarcely looked my way."

Raymond walked beside her and solicitously held aside a branch for her to pass. "All that is behind us now."

Almost absentmindedly Madeline nodded toward the north edge of the beech forest. "A band of Gypsies is camped over there in the meadow."

"Gypsies? I doubt Swineford knows that. He would never welcome them on his land."

"They looked harmless enough. I had an old woman read my fortune."

"You went among them? Alone? That was very foolhardy!"

Madeline shrugged. "There were only three wagons. She wasn't a very good fortune-teller. In fact, she refused to tell me much of anything."

"You shouldn't take chances like that. Harm might have come to you."

She glanced at him as if such an idea had never occurred to her, as indeed it had not.

"I have good news," he began. "I have devised a plan to dispose of Nicholas Garrett. Swineford is so pleased, he is certain to give us a house and a generous pension as well."

"That old cripple? Madeline scoffed. "If he is as ill-favored as you say, he will likely die before long anyway."

"Crippled? Ill-favored?" Raymond had forgotten the lie he used to win Madeline away. "Oh, yes. To be certain. But he is vengeful as well and has jealously eyed the considerable possessions of Sir James. He is an ever-present threat."

"Why doesn't Sir James simply send someone to kill the man?" she asked matter-of-factly.

Raymond frowned at her as he mulled over her curious comment. "It's not quite that simple to dispose of an enemy."

She sighed in a bored manner. "How hard could it be to murder a cripple? Have him poisoned. Surely there is a servant who could be bribed."

Hearing her so effortlessly seize upon the idea he himself had struggled over for days made the creases in Raymond's brow deepen. "Such talk is not for a lady. Come. Let us sit in the clover and talk of our house."

Madeline hesitated, then spread her skirts over the nodding shamrock-green leaves. She wasn't eager to leave Pritchard Hall, but she did want to have a similar manor of her own. In her mind, she was convinced that since Sir James was a wealthy knight, and Lord Garrett was a poor earl, rank had no bearing on prosperity.

"I already have a place in mind," Raymond said eagerly. "I plan to suggest it to Swineford as soon as news reaches us that Lord Nicholas is dead. There is a house near the river, down beside the road to Wakefield. It's in a copse of willows and within sight of the the water."

"I know of the willows," Madeline said as she shook her head in confusion. "There is naught there but a farmhouse." She rubbed her brow as if she had a headache, and frowned as she strained to concentrate.

"Yes, that's the place. I rode over to it yesterday. The roof is sound and its flooring intact. I could glass in the windows before autumn. Even the barn is still in good condition. I would judge that it hasn't been vacant for long and that the previous tenant was house-proud. He took very good care of the property."

"A farmhouse?" she asked incredulously. "You expect me to live in a farmhouse? A tenant's cottage?"

"A tenant's no longer. He has moved out. It would be all our own."

Madeline laughed uncertainly. "Tell me you're jesting. *Me*? Live in a farmer's house?" Surely he was leading her on to tease her. Raymond was a rich man. Nearly as wealthy as Sir James. Wasn't he? Madeline had completely forgotten that Raymond was in Sir James' hire.

"Where else did you think? A manor hall? I'm only a poor knight." Raymond was stung that she not only didn't like the cottage he wanted, but even scoffed at the idea. "I'm not as rich as Sir James, you know."

"Yes, but a farmhouse. Really! No, you can't be serious."

"I'm quite serious. This will mean security for us. We can't live forever on my skills as a man-at-arms. Someday I'll grow old and then where will we be?"

"Don't talk to me of growing old." Madeline turned her face away. "I hate the idea of becoming wrinkled and bent, like that old crone of a fortune-teller."

Raymond reached out and pulled her back into the clover. "You've a long road to travel before you need worry about that. Why, you're scarcely older than a child."

Madeline relented a bit and lay back.

Encouraged, Raymond ran his hand up her leg under her petticoat. "In truth you're the prettiest lady I've ever seen." He found the nest of curls he sought, but she kept her legs pressed together.

"Raymond, stop it. Don't paw me like that," she reprimanded petulantly.

"Come now, sweeting. You know you like this."

"Don't, Raymond. You're making me angry." She shoved at his searching hand.

With a chuckle, Raymond tossed her skirts upward and tried to pull her legs apart. "Open to me, sweeting. We have many nights to make up for."

"No! I don't want to." She kicked him back and rolled to her feet. "If you were any sort of a man, you would have tended to me before this. Now I don't want you!"

"Since when is a woman consulted in such matters?" Raymond snapped as he, too, stood up. "Should I mince about and ask permission to take my own wife? You belong to me!"

"Take care," she warned in a low voice. "Don't make me angry."

"Do you not care at all that I have been hard pressed of late? Do you imagine Swineford lets us live in his manor purely for the pleasure of our company?"

A curious smile tilted Madeline's lips. "Perhaps he does."

"No! he has hired me as a knight, and for days I've struggled to do my duty toward him. I've had no time to dally with you! A man must do what he must!"

Careful, Raymond," she said almost soothingly. Her eyes were darkening, beginning to glitter like a wild animal's. "Berate me not." First he jested her about living in a farmhouse and now he was pretending to be a hireling of Sir James. She was not amused. Fury was beginning to make her brain pound.

"Now I come to you and you push me away!" Raymond was fully angered and unable to stop his hot words even if he had wanted to. "You think you're such a fine lady. You're no more than the wife of a knight, and not even a wealthy knight at that. You should be thankful for a house of any sort."

Madeline circled him, her face pale and her flesh rigid. Her eyes were sharp and feral and her breath was coming quickly, as if she had been running. Her pink tongue darted out to wet her parted lips.

Raymond scoffed at her. "You take on such airs. You who could have been a countess."

"Stop, Raymond. Don't do this," she whispered.

He turned his back on her and reached to pick up his hat from the crushed clover. "And as for Lord Nicholas being a cripple, well, I can scarce believe you still swallow that. He's no more a cripple than I am."

Madeline reached down and picked up a stone the size of her fist. Almost dreamily she studied it in her palm. "Not a cripple, you say? You duped me?"

"He's as fair to look upon as a prince," Raymond crowed as he turned back to her.

Madeline's lips drew back from her teeth as she slammed the rock into Raymond's face. He cried out in pained shock and fell back. She was upon him at once, pounding him again and again with her weapon until his face was unrecognizable and he was long since dead.

Then she sat back and surveyed her work. Letting the stone roll from her fingers, she studied him sadly. "I told you to stop, Raymond," she said. "I warned you and you wouldn't listen. It's not good to make me angry."

For a minute she looked thoughtful; then her angelic smile appeared. Of course. Everyone would think the Gypsies had killed him. How perfect it was all working out.

Madeline stood and dusted the clover from her full skirts before strolling back to the horses. At the stream she paused and looked at her hands. Blood stained her palms and fingers. She knelt and washed herself clean, then untied the horses.

She rode past Raymond's crumpled body with no more than a passing glance. At the edge of the woods she paused to look across the meadow at the gaudily painted Gypsy wagons. Releasing Raymond's horse, she struck her riding crop across his rump, and the horse bolted forward. She had no doubts the Gypsies would take him. They were notorious for stealing everything in their path.

Madeline reined her horse around to return to Pritchard Hall by another route. In time someone would find Raymond. He was no longer any concern of hers.

*   *   *

Madeline sat in the main parlor of Pritchard Hall, strumming her fingers lightly across her lute. Supper had been served and taken away and the manor was settling into its quiet time before everyone went off to bed. Swineford looked fondly across the room at Madeline and she smiled back at him. Softly she began to sing a song of a knight who lay dying while his lady wept.

When the last note faded away, Swineford said, "Such a sad song to while away this calm night. What is the name of it?"

" 'Corpus Christi,' " she replied. "It's so named for the words on the tombstone in the last verse. As for its being sad, I considered it more thought-provoking than melancholy."

"Speaking of knights, where is yours?" Swineford tipped his cup to drain the last of the wine.

"I know not," she lied smoothly. "Mayhap he is down at the Bear and Bull again. He goes there often, I hear."

"Pah!" Swineford snorted. "What sort of man would go whoring when he had you at home?"

Madeline leered archly at him. "He no longer has me at home. You do."

Swineford laughed and reached out for her. "Come here, woman. We care not for that old maid you married."

With a giggle Madeline let him pull her into his lap and reach down the bodice of her dress to capture her breast. "Do you never tire of lusty sport?" she teased as she nibbled at his neck.

"Never. And neither do you." His other hand adroitly found its way beneath her skirt and she shifted her legs obligingly.

Neither heard the man at the doorway until he said for the second time, "Pardon, my lord."

"What?" Swineford said, hastily sliding Madeline to her feet. "Yes, what is it?"

The man shifted his weight uneasily from one foot to the other as he twisted his woolen cap.

"Well? Speak up or get out."

Glancing at Madeline and back again, he said, "Me and Wat was coming through the beech woods . . . and . . ."

"Yes?" Swineford prompted impatiently.

"Well, we seen . . . That is, we found something you ought to see. In the courtyard, my lord."

"Out with it, man! What are you talking about?"

The man drew a deep breath and braced himself. "It's a dead man, my lord. I . . . I think it may be Sir Raymond."

Madeline stepped forward as Swineford rose from his chair. "Raymond," she whispered, then fell toward Swineford in a faint.

He caught her and lifted her. To the man he said, "What do you mean by this! You know Sir Raymond as well as I do. Is it he or not?"

"It's hard to tell, my lord."

Swineford took Madeline to her chamber and laid her on the bed. Madeline's women hovered about her, and he could hear them speculating in hushed whispers as he left the chamber. As he followed the man down to the courtyard, his mind was racing. Only hours before, Sir Raymond had been alive and well. Surely no one would dare murder a man as near the manor as the beech woods. The yeoman must be mistaken. If he was, Swineford decided he would take it out of his hide.

Yet murder it was. The body lay on the rain-slicked cobblestones of the courtyard in a pale yellow circle of lantern light. Swineford took one look and turned away.

"We thought it best not to bring him in and him looking like this," the man called Wat said. "You can see it be no sight for the eyes of a lady. Especially being as she's his wife. Or was."

"Yes," Swineford said in a tight voice. "Yes, you did right. Wat, go rouse the carpenter and tell him I want a coffin." To the other man he said, "You'd better stay here with . . . him. I'll go get the chaplain."

When Raymond's remains had been blessed and placed in a coffin by the wide-eyed staff, Swineford went to Madeline's chamber.

She lay on the bed more or less as he had left her, yet he had the impression that she was aware of his entrance. After a pause, he went to her and sat on the bed. At once her eyes blinked open. He again had the uncanny sensation that all was not as it seemed.

"Raymond?" she asked in a husky voice. "Was it Raymond?"

Slowly he nodded, not taking his eyes from her face.

"Oh!" Her hands flew to her face and covered her lips. "He's dead then!" Her voice was stricken and tears gathered in the corners of her eyes, though her face didn't contort.

Swineford wiped away a tear that trickled over her temple. "Yes, he's dead."

After a moment Madeline spoke in a small voice. "I'm all alone then. Except for you, of course." Her big blue eyes found his. "I suppose now you will have to take care of me. Just as you said you wanted to last night. Do you remember? You said you wished it was only you and me in all the world." She waited until he nodded reluctantly. "And now it has come to pass," she finished softly.

Swineford took her in his arms and comforted her

as she cried silently. His own arms shook when he recalled what he had seen in the courtyard. Raymond had never been his friend, but he had known the man well for years and of late had depended on him. Only a monster could have done that to him. He wondered why Madeline hadn't asked how her husband had died. He wasn't sure he could break the news to her when she did.

Madeline clung to her lover and let tears flow effortlessly down her cheeks. It had certainly taken long enough for someone to find him. Tomorrow she would mention having seen the Gypsies in the meadow. Her eyes flicked around the chamber. She didn't want to continue living in this room. Perhaps James would let her move in with him, for with Raymond out of the way, they would surely marry. The first thing she would do would be to change the tapestries and order new bed hangings. Then she remembered to sob and felt his arms tighten protectively.

Across the night-shrouded lands the lights of Wyndfell still burned. Jessica raised her head suddenly as if she heard a noise. Nicholas looked at her with interest as he continued stroking the dog that sat beside him. "Is something wrong?"

"No," she said uncertainly. "I thought I heard something but I was mistaken." She looked about the room as if she still weren't sure.

"No one is around but us. Even if someone were, the guards would protect us."

"I know. I was just being foolish, I guess." Still the odd sensation lingered and she found herself wondering what Madeline was doing that night. All afternoon her twin had been on her mind. Perhaps because that very day she had received a terse and scarcely civil letter from her mother saying that Madeline had not yet been found, but that the search would continue until she or her dead body was located. Shaking her head, she stood up and went to the window. She pushed open the hinged glass and gazed out at the night.

A smattering of stars was struggling to peer through the clouds that smudged the sky, and the bright moon was low on the horizon. "Did you hear the maids' latest gossip?" she asked without turning. "They say a ghost has been seen in the gallery. A woman, they said, wearing a dark gown."

Nicholas paused before saying, "Yes. I've heard the same rumor from my valet and my steward."

"My maids say it was Lady Jane." Jessica ran her fingers over the thick stones that protected her from the outer elements. A thin film of water from the recent rain trickled down the casement. "They say they all recognized her."

"Don't let such talk frighten you. All castles are said to harbor ghosts. When I was a boy, Walter and I sat up many a night in wait for a certain monk that is said to frequent the buttery and solar."

"Did you ever see him?" Jessica asked, turning back to Nicholas.

"No, and I've not seen this ghost in the gallery, either. Until I do, I wouldn't believe it. Besides, if it is Jane, she will do no harm. She never had a harsh word for anybody."

Jessica came to him and put her hands on his shoulders. "Are you so certain? What if I dare you to go to the gallery and wait out the night?"

"Only if you come with me," he teased. "I've never made love in the gallery. Do you suppose ghosts blush?"

"Nicholas!" she scolded laughingly. "For shame."

He wrapped his arms about her waist and grinned up at her. "I would rather lay you on our soft bed, however, and love the night away there."

"I wouldn't object, my lord. Your wish is my command."

"It would be the first time," he retorted. "You never do anything I tell you to do."

"Nonsense, Nicholas. I do when I feel like it. Besides, we have more than enough servants to run to your beck and call."

" 'Tis a shame all the nunneries are shut down," he chided good-naturedly. "Perhaps we husbands could prevail upon the Queen to open one. It would be full to overflowing in a fortnight, all with disobedient wives.

"What a thing to say!" Jessica answered. "You could never find another woman so well suited to you."

"Couldn't I now?"

"Not if you searched the width and breadth of England. You aren't the easiest man to live with, you know."

"I'm not?" he asked with a mock frown.

"But you're the only one I will ever want." She stepped out of the circle of his arms. "Come, love. Come to bed with me."

As they walked hand in hand through the quiet castle, Jessica put aside her sense of unease. Madeline was goodness knew where and was no concern of hers. Perhaps her nervousness was due only to Thomas' poorly concealed infatuation and Nicholas' barely controlled jealousy. She decided to suggest on the morrow that they find Thomas a bride of his own.

15

A FINE MIST pearled the very early-morning air, making the trees in Wyndfell's park seem muted and vague as if viewed through gauze. Then the rising sun began to melt away the mist, and the fog that draped the hollows shimmered like gossamer silver.

Jessica ran to the window as she had every few minutes that morning, but this time her face brightened. "It's not even six yet, and it's clearing, Nicholas. It will be a fine day."

"Such a plather," he grumbled teasingly. " 'Tis but a fair."

"*But* a fair!" she rose to the bait. "There will not be another until harvest. Hurry and get ready or we'll miss the procession."

Nicholas, who was secretly as excited as she was, looped his heavy gold chain around his neck and over the red velvet of his doublet. Wrapping his cloak about his shoulders, he fastened the thick jeweled clasp and put on his wide-brimmed hat with the low crown. The hat's ostrich feather swept rakishly over his ear.

Jessica fitted her dark green French hood to the

back of her head and tied the narrow green ribbon under her chin. "Is my bongrace straight?" she asked her serving maid. As impatient as a child, she suffered the woman to smooth the draped veil that fell from the back of the bonnet to her shoulders. "How do I look?" she asked, twirling so Nicholas could admire her green gown and golden kirtle.

"As beautiful as a goddess," he responded fondly. "Calm yourself. You're not being presented to the Queen. You never get so excited over going to market."

"Market is once a week and can't possibly compare with a fair. You know the old saying, 'Three women and a goose make a market.' Are you ready yet?"

"What is the hurry?" he teased. "It will last six days."

Exasperated, Jessica caught his hand and led him out of the chamber. "How big will it be? As large as the one at Hargrove Castle?"

"At least, though not so grand as the fairs at Stourbridge or Bartholomew, of course."

They rode to the village and saw the procession about to leave town for the fairgrounds. No sooner had Jessica and Nicholas positioned themselves near the road than there was a burst of bell ringing and the town cannon fired. At once the musicians began to play and the gay entourage marched and danced out to the fairgrounds.

Tents and booths were already set up on the field and blue-coated apprentices were eyeing each other warily, as it was their responsibility to guard their masters' wares. One row of booths was given over to various jewelers, another to dealers of ribbons and inkles and other tapes. Another row sold cloth, and beyond that were the wood carvers with their tiny models of furniture. A bit separate from the stalls was a tent where several of the village merchants had gathered to hold the usual "court of pie-powder," whose purpose was to settle the disputes that commonly arose over money.

A great crowd had gathered and there were quite a few strangers. Unlike the market days, farmers and traders from outside the parish could sell their wares, and many had come in from surrounding towns.

Jessica and Nicholas tied their horses to a rail by a watering trough and wandered hand in hand down the rows of stalls. A man with a broad accent was striking a bargain for some pewterware with the wife of the village wool merchant. The daughter of the apothecary was placing an order for a new fire screen of inlaid woods.

"This is even grander than the fair at Hargrove Castle," Jessica exclaimed with her eyes sparkling. "I've never seen so many people in one place."

"I promise to take you to London," Nicholas said, "and show you a real crowd."

She smiled but secretly thought the streets of London couldn't be busier than the fairgrounds this day. As they moved through the press of bodies, she prudently kept her hand on the velvet bag she wore at her waist. Pickpockets would be everywhere on a fair day.

At a cloth stall Jessica bought enough midnight-blue plush to make Nicholas a cloak in the new Spanish design. Everywhere she saw new styles from London and even some as far away as the Continent. She let Nicholas buy her a new French hood of daring cut and a length of heavily embroidered gauze. Soon their attending servant was loaded with pomanders of perfumes Jessica couldn't make for herself, spools of laces and ribbons and braid, and several pairs of perfumed gloves.

Although Nicholas teased her for her curiosity, he paid a penny for them to see the six-legged calf, the snake with two heads, and the goat whose horns made two complete circles on either side of his head.

When they left the tent of wonders, the morris dancers were beginning their traditional steps. Jessica hummed along with the familiar tune as Nicholas studied the booth of German clocks. Soon he had ordered one that sported a marvelous picture of the moon and several planets that moved in unison with the clock's hands.

Men and women strolled about hawking wares from pushcarts such as they never would at a market. Jessica bought samples of foods until Nicholas assured her she would make herself sick. She noticed, however, that he ate everything she did.

At the edge of the field were the horses, oxen, and other livestock that were for sale. "Look, Nicholas," she said, nodding in that direction. "We should have told the stableman to look here for that mare you wish to replace."

He cast a practiced eye over the animals and shook his head. "I don't see one that interests me. The best fair to buy a horse is Harborough or at Ripon. It's worth the travel to get a really fine animal."

"Have you been to these places?" she asked. "And to London as well?"

"Next spring we make a journey," he promised. "Never have I seen a woman so eager for the privations of travel. Next year we will make a progress that would put the Queen to shame. By the end of it you'll be more than content to stay home at Wyndfell."

"I am content at Wyndfell now," she assured him. "But there are so many sights to see. Perhaps someday we could even sail on one of your ships. Think of it, Nicholas! Wouldn't you like to see a man with red skin such as they say live in the Americas?"

"I would have to see it to believe it," he said as he fingered the scarlet bonnet she held in her hand. "If you ask me, the sailors are telling tall tales again. I've also heard captains swear to having seen sea serpents and mermaids."

"Perhaps they did," Jessica marveled. "Imagine seeing a real mermaid!"

"Look," Nicholas said, pointing toward three gaudily painted wagons. "People like yourself. Mayhap you could join the Gypsy tribe and live in a house on wheels."

Jessica looked at the swarthy people with interest but said, "I only want to travel in fair season, not in snow and ice."

The Gypsies kept a bit apart from the booths. Two scruffy dogs were tied by ropes beneath the wagons, and behind were tied several horses. An ancient woman whose neck was swollen with a goiter was telling fortunes with a worn pack of tarot cards.

"Let's hear our fortune," Jessica suggested. "Wouldn't you like to know if your ship will come in laden heavily?"

Nicholas gave the woman a small silver coin and they sat down on the bench opposite her. The old woman looked at Jessica, did a double take, and pushed the tester back toward Nicholas. "No read," she mumbled in broken English. "No read cards."

"But why not?" Jessica asked. "Is our fortune so bad?"

The old crone's black eyes narrowed. "I have told all to you before. Will not read cards again."

"Before?" Nicholas broke in. "We have only just come here."

"No, no. Lady knows." The Gypsy gestured frantically and a big man with an impressive black mustache sidled near. "No read," she repeated firmly. "Leave now. Much bad luck."

The man bent forward quickly and put his hand beneath Jessica's elbow to help her rise. "Come. Look here. I have fine clothes pegs made of goat willow. See? There are no better ones in all of England."

Jessica let him lead her away, but she cast an almost frightened look back at the old woman.

As Nicholas started to rise to follow Jessica, the Gypsy stopped him by catching his arm. "Be careful!" she hissed. "Much, much bad luck!" Her narrow eyes stared after the woman whose palm she was certain she had read the day before. Murder had been written there. Murder and madness.

Nicholas pulled away and hurried after Jessica. "Daft old fool," he muttered. "She must be crazed."

But the woman's words had left a chill over Jessica. Everyone knew Gypsies were gifted with the sight. Unaccountably she found herself thinking of Raymond Chadwick and wondering where Madeline might be.

"I'm tired, Nicholas. Could we go back to Wyndfell? We can see the rest tomorrow."

Nicholas looked back toward the Gypsies with a frown. The village constable had ridden up with a stranger and, together, they were looking at the string of horses tied to the last wagon. The Gypsy man joined them and they began to wave their arms at a tall chestnut on the end. Nicholas shrugged. That the horse was probably stolen came as no surprise.

All the way back to Wyndfell, Nicholas pondered over the Gypsy woman's words. There could be no doubt that the woman had indeed been upset. Frightened, even. He glanced over at Jessica, who rode stiffly with her eyes staring straight ahead, in contrast to her usual relaxed manner. Although she had made no further comment, her face was still ashen and her eyes dark and round.

They crossed Wyndfell's thick drawbridge and the double gates. Passing from the shade of the gatehouse, they rode into the sunny courtyard. Nicholas helped Jessica dismount. Still she was unnaturally silent as she scooped up her dark green skirts. He climbed the steps beside her and pushed open the heavy door to the hall.

"What do you think she meant?" he burst out, unable to contain himself any longer.

Jessica jumped and stared up at him with the eyes of a startled fawn. "Who?"

"The Gypsy woman, of course," he replied with a puzzled look. "Why would she say she read your fortune when she had not?"

"How should I know?" Jessica turned away quickly. All the way home she had fretted over that herself. There was only one possible answer, assuming the old woman wasn't mad, and that was that Madeline must be in the vicinity. Possibly even at the fair! The very idea made her skin feel clammy and her stomach unsettled. Anyone might have seen Madeline! Perhaps even now someone was on his way to Wyndfell to tell Nicholas, or worse still, Madeline herself might ride into the courtyard.

Breathless with worry, Jessica glanced around the hall in exasperation. Two maids were cleaning the candle sconces, a boy was scrubbing down the long table though Old Tess still reclined on the far end, and through the doorway she saw more maids cleaning the stained-glassed windows in the winter parlor. "Is there nowhere we can be alone?" she asked with an edge to her voice.

Nicholas looked about as if he hadn't noticed the servants' presence. "Of course. This way, my lady."

She followed him up the narrow, twisting stairs in the far corner that led to the older portion of the castle. Jessica touched her fingertips to the damp wall in order to keep her balance, for the stone steps were hollowed deeply from generations of use.

Nicholas led her down a long gallery where vacant windows overlooked the formal gardens and the river. No tapestries or hangings softened the gray stone walls, and their footsteps sounded hollow in the cavernous room.

"Where are we?" she asked as she looked about.

"In the old gallery. This is the oldest section of Wyndfell." He pointed up at the hammer-beam roof where a multitude of doves cooed softly. "At one time this was used by my ancestors just as we use the one in the new wing. Then the castle was expanded, and this section fell into disuse. Since it faces north, it was never a pleasant room, so my grandfather built the present wing and this one was abandoned."

At the end of the room was another flight of steps that circled within one of the towers. On the level of the gallery was an antechamber that led to a solar. Nicholas opened the oak door and bowed Jessica into the room. "Welcome, my lady, to privacy."

"What a lovely chamber this must have been," Jessica exclaimed. It was round on three sides with numerous windows to let in air and light. Rectangles of lemon sunshine lay upon the oak floor. There were several odd stools standing about, along with assorted chests and old-fashioned candlesticks, as if the place had been used as a storeroom. A broad cot lay on the floor in the farthest rectangle of sunlight.

"This was the ladies' parlor when my ancestors lived in this wing. To my mind it was one of Wyndfell's finest rooms, but it's too far removed from the rest to be of use now." On the flat wall was a faint fresco depicting two white unicorns rearing and prancing in a most lifelike manner against a garland of faded spring flowers. "No one remembers who painted this or why he chose unicorns instead of the Garrett griffins."

"How odd," she marveled as she put her fingers to one chipped hoof. "Whoever would have thought of painting directly on the wall itself rather than on a hanging."

"As you can see, the idea wasn't a good one. The dampness has all but erased the painting." Nicholas nodded toward the cot. "My brother Walter and I came here as lads. He had one of the servants bring up the bedding so we could sleep here overnight."

"Whatever for?" The room was lovely but she couldn't see a reason to sleep here.

"You've heard me speak of the monk who haunts Wyndfell?"

"You said he is seen in the buttery," she corrected uneasily.

"There, too. He is said to materialize here in the solar and go down those steps just outside the solar door and thus to the buttery, where he disappears. Walter and I sat up here many a night to see him."

"And did you?"

"Not once. But we had some fine adventures while trying to catch sight of him." He went to the window and leaned his palms on the cold stone. Beyond the thick wall he could see the fairgrounds and the throngs of people that knotted among the booths. Thoughtfully he said, "I find myself still thinking of the Gypsy woman."

Jessica grew rigid and said, "What a bother about

nothing. The old woman must have been simple or addled by drink."

"She didn't seem so to me. She looked frightened. When you walked away she actually gave me a warning."

"A warning?" Jessica asked in a small voice. "About what?"

"She wasn't clear. Only that I was to beware."

"What nonsense. Who would want to do you harm?"

"A man always has enemies. There's Swineford, for one. I still think he may have been responsible for the attack on Wyndfell, though I have no proof."

"I had almost forgotten. That must have been what she was warning you of."

"I suppose it was."

Thankful that Nicholas had found a meaning to the Gypsy's words different from her own, Jessica went to him. "Hold me," she whispered. "Hold me close."

He turned and took her in his arms. "You're trembling, lass. I never meant to frighten you with talk of Swineford and that attack."

Jessica embraced him and breathed his warm, clean scent. If he thought she feared this Swineford, let him. At least he didn't suspect her terrible secret. She looked past his shoulder and out the window toward the fairgrounds. For all she knew, she could be looking straight at Madeline in the milling crowd and not even know it. She closed her eyes and shivered.

"Are you chilled? Come, let's go back to the parlor."

"No, no. I'm quite all right. Could we stay here for a bit? 'Tis rare for me to see you alone." She took his hand and led him to the cot. "Here. Sit with me in the sunshine and let's pretend there is no one else but us in the world."

"In the entire world?" he chided.

"In the castle, then. Please, I would have you to myself for a bit longer."

Nicholas unfastened his cape and spread it over the lumpy cot, then sat beside her. "You are quite unlike any woman I have ever known. All the others seem to pine for company, and I've heard friends say their wives expect an endless round of parties. Yet you seem to long for solitude."

"Not true solitude, for I would share it with you. And you are right in that I am not like most women." Her pansy-blue eyes darkened as she lowered her lashes in an unconsciously seductive manner. "My spirit has ever chafed against fetters. My parents could never understand that. In an effort to tame me, my father betrothed me to a doddering old knight in hopes of him serving to anchor me."

"You were betrothed to another man?" Nicholas asked in surprise. "I never knew that."

"It was long ago," Jessica lied hastily. "He died. You need not worry that he will show up and gainsay our marriage."

"I hadn't thought of that, only that I never heard you were betrothed before."

Jessica gave him a troubled glance. She had almost given herself away that time. Even with Nicholas she couldn't let go and be herself. "Will you kiss me?" she asked, trying to cover the unhappiness she felt.

"You'll never need ask me that twice," he answered with a grin. "I think, all of a sudden, I like this fascination you have for loneliness."

His lips covered hers and she swayed toward him. His breath was fresh and warm in her mouth and her lips parted eagerly. She circled his neck with her arms and threaded her fingers through his thick hair.

His large hands drew her nearer and she sensed the leashed power of his body. He was a big man and uncommonly strong, yet with her he was always gentle. Not once had he ever hurt her, though his strength was such that he could have cracked her ribs with a squeeze. Jessica marveled that this knowledge was like a heady wine to her rather than a frightening idea. She gloried in the love they shared that turned his might into gentleness.

Raising his head, he stared intently into the twin pools of her eyes. Their depths were a dusky blue so dark as to rival a twilight sky, and in them sparkled love. He felt awkwardly large next to her, yet he enjoyed her smallness. While she wasn't tiny, as women went, she was a wisp of femininity next to him. Her hand measured just over half his own, and when they were standing, her head fit neatly beneath his chin. While she wasn't as biddable as he might have wished, she was infinitely more arousing in bed than he could have expected.

"Do you love me true?" he surprised them both by asking. "I know all women say they do to their husbands, but do you really?"

"I would love you come what may. Were we unwed or even if we were wed to others, you would have my heart. At times I think the stars decreed us one for the other."

"At times I look into your eyes," he said with wonder, "and it's as if I have always known you, through all the long centuries, in other lands and climes."

"Who knows," she whispered. "Mayhap 'tis true. And by the same coin, perhaps we will always be together and loving for all the ages to come."

Slowly Nicholas lowered his head and deeply kissed her, with growing passion. Her response increased his excitement. Moving with teasing slowness, he gradually removed their clothing until Jessica lay naked upon the crumpled velvet of his cape. She stirred and the husk mattress crackled.

"I should order a feather mattress sent up here," he suggested with a grin. "Then when you crave time alone with me we will be more comfortable."

"I have no thoughts of comfort and mattresses. Only of your love." She traced the line of his close-cropped beard and ran her fingertip up the straight line of his nose. "You're so handsome, Nicholas. I'm the most fortunate of women."

Leaning back on his elbow, Nicholas stroked his hand down her slender neck where a pulse beat quickly, then over the warm silkiness of her shoulder and breast. The sunlight made her skin as translucent as fine porcelain and her erect nipples were the soft coral-pink of the roses that flourished in the garden below. He circled the firm bud and watched it pout to be touched and kissed. Slowly he lowered his head to oblige.

Drawing the morsel into his mouth, he felt Jessica arch toward him as she murmured with pleasure. After nipping her gently, he found her other nipple and rolled it between his thumb and forefinger. Her breasts were full and firm as he cupped them, and her eagerness triggered a response from deep within him.

She guided his lips back to her breast as his hands stroked over her waist, spanning it in a measuring of love, and lifting her toward him. Sensuously his hands moved, caressing the curve of her hip and the flat expanse where her navel dipped in. Then lower to ease her legs apart for his more intimate touch. When his fingers found her most secret place, Jessica called his name softly, yet urgently.

Her hands moved over his hard chest, her finger-nails gently tracing past his own nipples. Caressing the wall of muscle, she curved her hands over his shoulders and down his powerful arms, where a long vein stood out against his tanned skin. Easing herself beneath him, she opened herself for his advance.

"I want you, Nicholas," she whispered. "I need you."

Before he married Jessica, Nicholas had never known a lady to admit to having desires, but her words sent a white fire of passion through him. She wasn't properly meek and God knows she wasn't obedient, but this woman pleased him better than any he had ever known or imagined.

He entered her and heard the soft sigh that he knew meant she enjoyed the sensation as much as he did. As always he was momentarily amazed. This lady wife of his enjoyed bed sport as well as any tavern wench or dairymaid. Nay, better even. For with wenches he had always suspected his noble birth had a measure in their enjoyment. With Jessica he knew her passion was for himself, and the knowledge was heady.

Slowly he began to move within her, and felt her match his rhythm. She looped her slender leg over his hip to pull him deeper inside her as they lay on their sides with their arms entwined.

"I love you," she said in the husky voice that was a sure measure of her passion. Her hand slid over his skin in a way that made him see that she enjoyed touching him as much as she thrilled to his caresses of her.

"I love you," he replied softly. Her skin was warm and pliant beneath his fingers, and he covered her breast to feel her nipple strain against his palm.

Jessica curved her body to his and rolled so she lay

on her back with Nicholas poised above her. Their eyes met and held as their bodies rocked seductively. Her lips parted moistly to reveal the row of even teeth that were as white and unblemished as a child's. Their souls met and merged into a oneness.

Gradually the passion built within her but she held it at bay, trying to preserve this moment of delicious agony for as long as possible. Above her, Nicholas' black hair tumbled over his forehead and his eyes were as dark as midnight, fierce in his passion yet gentled by love. His strong arms were pillars to either side of her, and she ran her exploring hands over his ribs, chest, and back, enjoying the rippling of his muscles beneath her palms.

Then all at once the passion took control of her and she moaned as it grew relentlessly. Suddenly, release burst within her and she cried out at the overwhelming ecstasy. When she did, Nicholas gasped and then groaned as her completion called forth his own. Together they sailed on the surging tide of love.

After a time, Jessica smiled up at Nicholas with the unmistakable happiness of a satisfied lover. He gazed down at her with the same expression and brushed her damp hair back from her face. She cuddled into the safe curve of his arm and side and silently adored this man she had had the good fortune to marry. His own love echoed back to her and she heard it with her heart.

Across the room the door opened a mere crack. Beyond it, Thomas straightened, his face a mask of jealous fury. His grip tightened on the small jewel casket he had come to place in the storeroom, and his black eyes narrowed. So his noble brother took her here, did he? Like some kitchen slut that he could mate behind any bush?

She deserved better than a moldy mat on the floor of the storeroom! The sooner he rescued her from his oaf of a brother, the better. She bore her duty bravely enough, he recalled. She hadn't fought against Nicholas, nor even begged that he give her the respect that was due her as Countess of Wyndfell.

Thomas glanced in again and wet his lips. Her body was more glorious than a royal whore's. Her skin was pale as alabaster and her curves looked warm and enticing. Especially her breasts, which were fuller than he had suspected from her concealing and flattening kirtles. Her unbound hair was longer, falling in waves well below her hips. How he ached to mount her and show her how a real man could mate her.

Slowly he backed away. His own body was racked from having watched the two upon the cot. He needed surcease and he thought of a certain kitchen maid who was always willing for a threepence. Silently Thomas went back down the steep steps.

His mind recalled the night he had last talked with Raymond Chadwick. Perhaps he, Thomas, *should* be Earl of Wyndfell. After all why should he suffer from an accident of birth that made him last-born rather than first? He was the true gentleman of the two, and he would better know how to show it. Though the situation chafed him considerably, he could never commit murder for the title of earl nor for the estate of Wyndfell. But to see Madeline properly cared for, and to receive her love in return, no sin was too great. For love of her, he would even kill Nicholas.

When he finished with the kitchen lass, he decided, he would pay a visit to the buttery. In his chamber was a small vial of a potion strong enough to remedy this accident of birth. A mirthless grin creased his face, as he planned his brother's murder.

16

THE LOWER PORTION of the buttery was sunken into the ground, making the interior cool and cavelike. The arched windows were high and the walls splayed out and down to throw more light into the dim room. Large casks of wine and ale lined the walls and smaller ones lay in racks. Hard cider and perry from Wyndfell's orchards were ranged along one wall, flanked by claret, charneco, and muscadine from France, Spain, and the Canary Islands. Since coming into wealth from his marriage, Nicholas had kept the buttery well-stocked.

Leaning on a butt of malmsey, Thomas drew the plug and poured himself a draft. Downing it quickly, he stared into his empty cup. What he planned was so large a step that he all but shied from it. To wish Nicholas dead was one matter—even to bewail his fate while in his cups to a former man-at-arms. But to actually murder his brother was something else.

Thomas muttered an oath and turned to go. At the foot of the shadowy stairs he paused and looked up. Although the steps twisted and curved out of his sight, he imagined the top of the steps and the scene he had just witnessed. This memory drove him back to the malmsey, and he drew himself another measure.

By the time he had quaffed the heady wine, his thoughts were accompanied by a low buzz like a bee in a bottle. The memory of Jessica's shapely limbs and bare breasts, and the way her golden hair twined about her nakedness and pooled on the cot seared his loins. All that loveliness could be his. Only Nicholas stood in his way. He recalled the times he had seen Jessica's eyes light in anger at something Nicholas had said or done. Why, she might thank Thomas from the bottom of her heart for delivering her from her husband. Yes, he was certain she would.

Without further thought, Thomas hurried to his chamber and found the vial of poison. For a moment he held it up to the light and stared at it. The bottle was of thick blue-green glass and had a small cork stopper. The entire object fit in his hand or could be slipped unnoticed into the pocket of his jerkin. Yet he had been assured by the apothecary that this poison was strong enough to dispatch several large animals. Surely it would rid him of Nicholas.

Thomas returned to the buttery but paused at the door. Two menservants were there, drawing the wine for supper. Trying to look nonchalant, Thomas sauntered over to them. "Good day, Matt, Lachlán. Have you been to the fair?"

The two servants greeted him with familiar nods. To find Thomas Garrett in the wine cellars was no rare occurrence. Everyone in the castle knew he drank far more than the usual ration.

"Aye, Master Thomas," the one named Lachlan said. "We been to the fair, and a pretty one it is."

"Did you see the six-legged calf?" Matt asked. "I ain't never seen nothing so strange. How do you reckon he be able to walk?" As he spoke he leaned over to draw a pitcher of canary wine.

"Is that for the dais table?" Thomas asked off-handedly.

"To be sure." Lachlan nodded. "There be no guests tonight, so one pitcher is all that will be needed. Unless you'd rather I serve you malmsey or mead? Lord Nicholas has asked special for canary tonight, but I'd be glad to bring whatever it is that would please you, as well."

"No, no. Canary is fine." Behind his back, Thomas fingered the vial of poison. The wine was pale but the poison was colorless so there should be no way of detecting it. "Tell me, Lachlan. Does anyone else drink the same wine as the high table?"

"Lord, no. That wouldn't be fitting. We drew perry and ale for the others." He looked anxiously at Thomas to see if he had done right.

"Very good." Carefully he began to work the cork loose. "Tell me, what is in those vats down at the far end?"

Both servants turned to see where Thomas was pointing.

"Them?"Lachlan asked. "That be the alicante."

"No, no," Matt disputed. "The alicante is over yonder. Those are the metheglin."

While the men looked away, Thomas uncorked the vial and quickly poured the contents into the pitcher of canary, then thrust the vial into his sleeve.

"That's the metheglin?" Lachlan asked in a puzzled tone. "You're certain?"

"Aye. I stacked them in their cradles myself."

Lachlan turned back to Thomas. "I reckon it's metheglin. Matt is the one to oversee storing the butts. He ought to know."

"Perhaps we should sample that tomorrow," Thomas

said smoothly, trying not to look at the murderous pitcher of wine.

"Aye. We'll do it." Lachlan took up the pitcher and nodded to the other two. "I'd best be getting back to the kitchens. The meal is nearly ready to serve. Matt, you bring up the cask of ale."

"I'll do it."

Thomas couldn't help but stare at the pitcher as Lachlan turned to go.

"Have ye heard the gossip?" Matt asked as he shouldered a small keg of ale.

"Gossip?" Thomas asked absently. He was torn between feelings of elation and sharp anxiety. "What gossip?"

"Why, that about the Gypsies. The constable arrested one for murder this very day. Should have packed off the whole passel, if you ask me."

"Murder?" Thomas paled at the word and swung to face Matt.

"Aye. And do you know who the victim was? None other than Sir Raymond Chadwick! That's who."

"Sir Raymond!"

"Didn't nobody guess he was in these parts. Turns out he was working at Pritchard Hall for Sir James Swineford."

"Swineford! Are you certain?"

"As certain as saints in heaven." Matt glanced about cautiously, as Catholicism was no longer admitted openly. "Or at least that's the saying."

Thomas, who couldn't care less what religion the servant followed, repeated his question, "Sir Raymond was working for Swineford?"

"That he was. Living in the hall, even. I didn't never trust him for all that he was a knight. His eyes was too close together."

Thomas stared back at Lachlan who had reached

the steps and was already climbing out of sight. Chadwick and Swineford! Suddenly Thomas recalled the encounter at the Bear and Bull. Who had first suggested Nicholas' murder? Was it not Raymond? Yes! It had been! Thomas remembered the mild shock he had felt at the idea. Swineford must have sent Raymond to plant just such a scheme, for when Thomas had later questioned Sir Henry Rogan, his friend said he had sent no message to meet him at the inn.

Thomas paled and braced himself on the nearest wine barrel. All the malmsey fumes had cleared from his brain with this astounding revelation, and he saw it all in crystal clarity. If he could be duped into killing Nicholas, Sir James would be one step closer to owning Wyndfell. To remove the last obstacle, Swineford would need only to prove Thomas had killed Nicholas or he might simply have him murdered in turn. Thomas had never believed Swineford was behind either Walter's death or the attack on Wyndfell. Now he saw he had been wrong.

He took a step after Lachlan, but stopped in confusion. There was no excuse he could give to make the man pour out a full pitcher of good canary wine.

"Is aught wrong?" Matt asked.

"No. No, nothing's amiss. Go along with you."

He watched the servant follow after Lachlan as he leaned heavily against the barrel. What had possessed him to attempt this foolhardy thing? Everyone would wonder if Nicholas died suddenly. There was always talk of poison when a person died in his prime. Frequently the rumors were true.

Dimly Thomas heard the blare of the trumpet calling everyone to the table. His eyes searched upward in the direction of the hall. In a matter of minutes the meal would be served and Nicholas would fall dead.

Thomas started slowly for the stairs, but was soon running. He had to find some way of preventing the canary from being served. If Nicholas died, Thomas had signed his own death sentence.

Nicholas and Jessica were waiting for him in the vestibule. When the breathless Thomas hurried up to them, Nicholas said, "We were about to go in without you."

Jessica smiled and put her hand in Nicholas'. "Don't scold him," she said in gentled tones. "He wasn't so very late." She was in too mellow a mood to be upset with anyone. In truth they had almost been late themselves, for the solar was a long way from the hall.

Nicholas understood and returned her smile. "Come, love." He opened the door and escorted her to the chairs upon the dais. "You look especially lovely," he whispered as he seated her. "There is still a bedchamber glow upon your cheeks."

"Hush," she pretended to scold. "Everyone will hear you." But her eyes belied her words. She was gloriously happy and didn't care who knew it.

Nicholas leaned forward and looked at Thomas' frowning face. "Why so glum, brother? Are you ill? I noticed you were breathing hard when you joined us."

"I feel quite well," he snapped as he sat upon his stool. His eyes flicked toward the back door, where the meal would enter at any moment.

Sir Richard Norwood, the steward, leaned toward the dais table. Due to his high position in the castle, his seat was nearest the high table in the absence of ranking guests. "Perhaps Master Thomas has heard the rumor going about. The Gypsies were arrested at the fair."

Thomas sat bolt upright but Nicholas merely raised his eyebrows questioningly. "Arrested?"

"One of the men is accused of murder. And the victim was none other than Sir Raymond Chadwick."

A sharp gasp escaped Jessica as she gripped the edge of the table.

"Sir Raymond?" Nicholas asked in amazement. "He was here in the parish?"

He was found dead in some woods behind Pritchard Hall. They said one of the Gypsies did it to steal his horse.. The horse was there behind the wagon, so everyone is certain the man is guilty."

"Where exactly is Pritchard Hall?" Jessica asked in a choked voice.

"In the next parish, my lady. It's the home of Sir James Swineford, whom you must have heard mentioned," Sir Richard explained.

"Why so pale, love?" Nicholas asked as he reached for her hand. "You're safe here. The murderer has been arrested."

Jessica nodded and tried to smile, but her face felt stiff. If Raymond had been at Pritchard Hall, would Madeline not be with him? Again she recalled the Gypsy woman's refusal to read her fortune *again*. Madeline *was* nearby. Jessica was positive beyond any doubt.

In the kitchens the servants were hoisting the various dishes onto their shoulders. Lachlan, who had as keen an appetite for wine as Thomas did, surreptitiously eyed the pitcher of canary. Of all the wines, this was his favorite, and his mouth watered at the thought of its taste.

Cobb Raddly, the butler, noticed Lachlan's gaze and spoke sharply. "Be on your way. The lord and lady would doubtless prefer drink with their meal."

Lachlan nodded. No one was ever allowed to gainsay old Cobb, though the cellarer frequently grumbled audibly. Cobb had been managing the kitchen staff of Wyndfell since before most of the servants were out of swaddling clothes.

"And mind you don't sample the wine," Cobb reprimanded. You've served as drunk as a lord before, but you'll never do it again from this kitchen. One more mishap and you'll be turned out."

Lachlan grimaced but made no reply. There wasn't a butler born who could take that tone with him. As he passed through the serving corridor, he filched a cup, and when he was around the corner, he poured himself a generous portion of the pale wine. After a quick glance toward the kitchen, he downed it as if it were no stronger than watered ale. Licking his lips, he wiped his mouth on his sleeve. As canary went, this wasn't a good batch, judging by the rather unpleasant aftertaste.

Lachlan strode on toward the hall. Other servants began to pass him as he slowed to a crawl. For some reason the wine had gone straight to his head, for his muscles seemed weak all of a sudden. He stopped at the doorway and looked into the pitcher. One could scarcely tell any wine was missing. Surely one more glass would do no harm and might clear his head.

Through the doorway Thomas saw Lachlan pour wine into a cup. He half-rose as the man lifted the cup to his lips. Beads of sweat moistened his forehead and trickled down his back as Lachlan downed the wine and peered questioningly into the cup. Then he hung it at his belt and entered the room.

Nicholas cut a morsel of pheasant covered with a cold jelly of herbed giblets. When he saw Lachlan come in, his displeasure showed on his face. This was the same servant who had performed so poorly when Jessica's parents were visiting. By the man's unsteady gait, he had been at the wine again. Nicholas' frown deepened, and he laid down his knife to watch Lachlan.

The servant leaned against the table to steady himself as he poured Nicholas' wine. His face was clammy with sweat and his pupils were so dilated that his eyes looked as black as jet beads. Nicholas noted the man's breathing was ragged and his hands shook.

Lachlan moved to serve Jessica but suddenly he faltered. His mouth dropped open and he stared in astonishment at the wine. His eyes met Nicholas' as he made a garbled sound. All at once he pitched forward upon the table, sending plates and goblets flying. Jessica screamed and pushed away as Lachlan's hands knotted spastically in the tablecloth. Then he slowly crumpled to the floor.

Nicholas was over the table in a leap, kneeling beside the man. Already Lachlan's eyes were glazing and his swollen tongue was protruding from his mouth. "He's dead!"

Jessica pressed her hands to her mouth in horror. Thomas half-leaned on the table to stare at Lachlan and Nicholas.

Bending, Nicholas sniffed the dead man's mouth. "Poison!" he exclaimed. "The wine was poisoned!"

At once the unreal hush in the hall was shattered. Women cried out and men glared suspiciously at their own tankards. Stools and benches rattled as everyone crowded closer to gape at the dead servant.

"Get Cobb Raddly!" Nicholas commanded.

The butler, who was already hurrying to the hall, stopped to stare at Lachlan lying on the floor.

"Do you know aught of this?" Nicholas demanded. "Who could have poisoned the wine?"

"No one, my lord," the old man stammered.

"Obviously someone did. Who has access to the buttery?"

"Everyone." The butler's eyes were round with shock. "I would see anyone who entered by way of the kitchen, but there's the delivery entrance that lets into the kitchen yard."

"I saw something!" Thomas spoke in a rush. "Earlier today I saw two strangers in the yard."

"Strangers? Why wasn't I told?"

"On fair day the town is full of strangers," Thomas defended himself. "I assumed they had come to beg or seek shelter for the night."

"Strangers frequently come to our gate," Jessica agreed. "I oversee the giving of alms myself."

Nicholas scowled. "Why would two strangers try to poison our wine?"

"Now that I think on it," Thomas put in, "they weren't entirely unknown to me. I've seen them, I think, at the Bear and Bull." His eyes widened as if he suddenly recalled something. "I remember now! They were Swineford's men!"

"Swineford's men were here and I wasn't told?" Nicholas thundered as he menacingly advanced on his brother.

"I only now recalled who they were," Thomas said as he backed away.

Nicholas motioned to his knights. "I'm going to Pritchard Hall and see to it that James Swineford never troubles us again!"

"Wait!" Jessica cried out. She couldn't let him go to Pritchard Hall if Madeline was there. "Wait, I beg you!"

At the urgent note in her voice, Nicholas paused.

"Go not to Swineford," she pleaded. "This may be his trick."

"Trick? What do you mean?" he demanded.

Thinking fast, Jessica said, "He may have known you would suspect him and come to battle him. If you attack Pritchard Hall, you will appear to be the one in the wrong. Your lands could be forfeited, even your life."

Nicholas considered her words. "What you say is true."

"Appeal rather to the Queen. Call in the constable and have him witness that the servant was poisoned. Let him arrest Swineford and bring him to justice." Her eyes implored him to do as she asked, and her body ached from tension as she waited. "Please," she added softly.

Nicholas studied her. Never had she implored him to do anything. Her usual manner was to command. Besides, her words were sensible. Slowly he nodded and motioned to Sir Richard. "Fetch the constable. Thomas, find Ben Watson and have him ride to Hampton Court and tell the Queen what has happened."

Jessica rested her hands on the table and trembled with relief. Nicholas came to her and put his arms about her protectively.

"Come, love. Let me help you to our chamber. You must be sorely vexed over this."

She let him lead her away and was thankful that he thought her too shaken to walk alone, for in truth she was. Whatever she had to do, she knew she must prevent Nicholas from going to Pritchard Hall. As she went toward the steps, another wave of fear washed over her. What would Madeline do now that her lover was dead?

"They've arrested the Gypsy," Swineford informed Madeline. "He was at the fair in the next parish and not even bothering to hide. Those people are as bold as brass."

"Remarkable," she said as she tuned her lute. Then, remembering her role, she added, "Has he confessed?"

"No, but who in his right mind would when there were no witnesses? Raymond's horse was tied to the wagon, however, and there is no doubt that the man killed him."

"Will there be a trial, do you think?"

"Of course. He may be a Gypsy, but he is still a man." Swineford eyed her closely as she strummed the chord to "Young Beichan." "You're taking this awfully well, I must say," he commented dryly.

"Oh, Jamie! How can you say that?" She smoothed her hand over her dull black mourning garments. "I but try to busy my mind or I will fall apart from sorrow."

"Hmmm." He watched her reach for a difficult chord. "You weren't too disconsolate in my bed last night."

Madeline pouted and pushed the lute aside. "What would you wish me to do? Tear my hair out? Soot my face? Rend my garments? I mourn Raymond's death, but our marriage was not a happy one. He lied to me, you know," she said musingly.

"Lied? About what?" Swineford went to the door and summoned a servant.

"About Lord Nicholas Garrett. I was to marry him, you recall."

To the serving man Swineford said, "Bring us claret and a bowl of fruit." When the man was gone, he said, "You were saying?"

"Raymond told me that Lord Nicholas was crippled and ugly enough to repel any woman."

"Lord Nicholas? Sir Raymond must have been far more convincing than I guessed," Swineford laughed.

"Then it really isn't true?"

"Not a bit of it. My well-born brothers are as comely as angels."

"They are?" she asked in a low voice.

"It is said so. We shared a father, though their mother was wise enough to withhold her charms until after the marriage. Mine was not. It's said we resemble a great deal, though I saw it more in Walter than the other two."

Madeline studied her lover's face. If he did not have such a pinched expression as if he were always angry, Swineford would have been quite handsome. "And is his body as straight as yours?"

"Lord Nicholas is somewhat taller and some might say broader of shoulder."

A frown was gathering on Madeline's brow. She ignored the returning servant but took the cup of claret.

"It would seem you have been played the fool," Swineford returned as he sipped the wine. At once he spat it out. "Pah! This wine has gone to vinegar! Knave! Can you not even serve up a glass of proper wine?" He struck at the hapless servant, letting his pent-up anger lash out at the defenseless man. "Away with this and bring some more!" The man bowed out hastily.

"Tell me, Madeline, how does it feel to be the goat?" As always when he saw the opportunity, Swineford couldn't prevent himself from rubbing salt in a wound.

"Why did Raymond lie to me? Surely it was from love. He must have lied to keep me for himself."

Swineford chuckled harshly. "He did it for a purse of gold angels. I sent Sir Raymond to Hargrove Castle to foul the match between you and Lord Nicholas."

"You! But why?"

"Nicholas owed a large sum on Wyndfell, payable to me. If he couldn't raise the gold, the castle and all its lands would have been mine—as they should have been from the start. But when he married your sister and got your dowry, he paid what he owed and I lost what should have been mine. *I* was the eldest and I should have been my father's heir."

"But you're a bastard. You said so yourself."

"Don't use that term with me!" He crossed the room and slapped her, his face stiff with fury.

Madeline gasped and raised her hand to her reddened cheek. She was so startled she could only stare at him. No one had dared strike her since she was old enough to stitch a sampler.

As if he had no idea of the magnitude of what he had done, Swineford continued to pace the chamber. "I sent Sir Raymond to spoil the match however he could. I never expected him to spirit you physically away, much less to marry you. I can still scarce credit it—the daughter of a rich viscount marrying a poor knight. Why, Raymond's father was one of my yeoman!"

"And now you plan to marry me—also for my inheritance?"

"Marry you? Don't be daft. You have, no doubt, been disinherited and bring no more with you than a yeoman's daughter. No, when I wed, it will be to a wealthy bride. And she must be a virgin! I want no doubt as to whether or not her sons are mine."

"Don't do this," she whispered, still holding her cheek. "Don't make me angry, Jamie."

"Tell me, Madeline. Whose idea was it to elope? Yours or Raymond's?" He hadn't realized until now how much pent-up jealousy he harbored for the man who had first taken Madeline. Swineford longed to have been the first to taste her luscious charms, to teach her of lust's dalliance.

"I beg you, Jamie, leave it off. Anger me not!" Her voice had dropped to a low, flat note.

Thinking he heard submission in her voice, Swineford continued his attack. The idea of her cowering before him was strangely exciting, and he determined to reduce her to quivering supplication before taking her to bed. "What a fool you were, Madeline. Did you think him rich enough to set you up in a manor as fine as this one? Or mayhap you thought to live in the fields like a shepherd and shepherdess as in one of those romantic follies you sing."

The worried expression on Madeline's face was suddenly replaced by calm. She straightened, and as if in a dream, she crossed to the table where Swineford's dagger lay sheathed in its silken scabbard. Slowly, keeping her body between her tormentor and the table, she drew the knife, fascinated by the gleam of the long blade in the candlelight. Once her slender fingers closed over the silk-corded handle, her arm dropped to hide the weapon in the black folds of her skirt. "And you'll not marry me, Jamie?" she asked softly.

"No," Swineford answered. As he continued to pace with his back to her., he elaborated on Lord Nicholas' physical charms and her gullibility in believing Raymond's lies. Again she asked him in calm tones to quit his badgering, and again he ignored her.

Madeline watched him closely, like a hawk would track a sparrow. Her breath quickened with excitement as she recalled the last time Raymond had dared to cross her, and how good she had felt as she battered his head in with the stone. Her release had been more satisfying than any sexual pleasure.

In a quick stride she was behind him, the knife glittering in the light. "Jamie?" she said softly.

He turned, and his eyes widened as he saw the downward arch of the dagger. Then it was buried in his neck, and his lifeblood was pouring from him. Just at that instant the luckless servant returned with the wine. He stared at the tableau, too shocked to react.

Madeline yanked the knife from Swineford's neck as he crumpled to the floor. Swiftly she knocked the wine from the servant's hand and thrust the bloody knife at him. "Take it!" she commanded.

Automatically the man reached for the knife and she shoved him toward Swineford's body. Running out into the corridor, Madeline began screaming as loudly as she could.

Almost at once several men-at-arms and servants ran to see what was happening. She pointed into the chamber. "He's killed Sir James! He's murdered him!"

The servant threw away the incriminating dagger, but several of the men had already seen him standing over the body of their master with the gory blade in his hand.

"He killed Sir James," Madeline repeated hysterically. "They argued over the wine and the servant grabbed up the dagger and murdered him!" She was so convincing that she was beginning to believe her own lie. Real hysterics bubbled up in her, and she was glad to let her ladies surround her and offer her comfort. Over their shoulders she saw the struggling servant being dragged away.

She let the maids take her to her chambers—the ones she had shared with Raymond—and undress her. Madeline accepted a posset of mulled wine and let herself be soothed and petted. After a while she pleaded exhaustion and sent the maids away.

As soon as they were gone, she slid out of bed and strode to the window. A full moon silvered the fields and gave as much light as dawn. Beyond the woods and a rise of hills lay Wyndfell Castle. Madeline's hands knotted into fists as she thought what a fool she had been. Because of Raymond's lies she had been duped not only out of marriage to a comely man but also out of being a countess. Jessica now held that honor in her place!

Madeline's eyes narrowed as she wondered if Jessica had connived with Raymond to plan this. No, she decided, Jessica was much too direct for such subtlety.

She unclenched her fists, only to knot them again. She had no reason to stay here at Pritchard Hall. Swineford wasn't her husband, so she didn't stand to inherit so much as a tester of his estate. Nor did she have any interest in returning to her parents, for her freedom was too precious to lose. The man she decided she wanted was Nicholas Garrett, the one she should have had in the first place.

Thoughtfully she stared. Jessica had stood in for her before. On occasion, Jessica had successfully taken her place for an hour or even an afternoon while Madeline was dallying with one of the serving men at Hargrove Castle. Jessica had never wanted to do it, but Madeline had always been able to threaten or cajole her into it, especially since, if Madeline had been caught, Jessica would have been blamed. Madeline knew and could imitate her sister's voice and movements as well as Jessica could hers. And that had been with people who had known them from birth. Nicholas would never suspect the switch.

Madeline dressed in a dark garnet gown and let

herself quietly out of her room. Elsewhere in the castle she heard anxious voices and the sounds of maids keening over their master's death. She kept to the deeper shadows, and whenever footsteps drew near, she froze until they passed and faded away in the distance.

To move through the shadowy corridors and across the hushed chambers gave Madeline a sense of excitement and mystery, laced with a certain power. No one knew or even suspected she was about. At times she saw well-known servants pass a doorway before she reached it and never guess that she was near. She fancied that she had somehow become invisible, and with that came a conviction that she was also invincible.

In all the turmoil about the house, Madeline had no trouble slipping out to the garden. No one challenged her as she crossed the lawn and paused at the stable. Inside she saw the stableboys and grooms in the lamplight. She couldn't possibly take a horse without them seeing her and asking questions.

Resolutely she struck out on foot toward the woods, rationalizing that she preferred to walk anyway. Horses had always frightened her a bit. Keeping to the river, she followed its path to a bridge that arched over the water. The adjoining road would take her to the parish governed by Nicholas Garrett. After an exhausting walk through the unfamiliar dark countryside, she found the imposing structure that could only be Wyndfell.

Her fists clenched again, Even in the dark she could see this was a finer castle than Hargrove, although it wasn't properly whitewashed in spite of Jessica's—or rather her own—dowry gold. Madeline decided this would be one of her first orders as the mistress of Wyndfell.

Having sneaked in and out of Hargrove Castle on many occasions, Madeline knew to circle the walls until she found the back entrance. Used by servants and delivery carts, the bridge was narrow and not as firm as the great drawbridge in front of the imposing gatehouse. As silent as a shade, Madeline glided across the weathered planks and tested the door. Because these were times of peace, the door wasn't latched and she eased it open.

Ahead was the kitchen yard with its neat herb garden laid out in moon-washed rows. In the shadows was the darker rectangle of the door. Madeline closed the wall door and stepped lightly into the shadows of the castle.

Silently she let herself in and caught her breath as she waited for her eyes to adjust; then she started moving through the cavernous kitchen. The serving gallery was wide, and she trailed her fingers along the wall so as not to lose her way. She knew she had entered the hall when the cooler air of the huge room enveloped her.

Excitement was all but choking her as she followed the wall past the tapestries and wall cloths to the tower steps. Here she hesitated. The steps might lead to Jessica and the great bedchamber or they might lead to some collapsed wing full of rubble. Slowly Madeline climbed, holding her skirts back to avoid tripping. When she reached the landing she cautiously opened a door at random.

Moonlight faintly illumined the room and she glanced around to be certain it was empty. It appeared to be a guest chamber, for it had a bed at the far end of the two rooms of the suite. All at once Madeline realized how very tired she was, not only from the long walk but also from the physical drain of the dread act she had committed at Pritchard

Hall. Resolutely she refused to think of the deceitful Jamie.

She climbed on the bed and stretched out without bothering to undress. In moments she was asleep.

17

JESSICA HAD RISEN early. Midsummer Eve loomed near and all the castle servants were more eager for the celebration than for their tasks. She had set a group of maids to washing the huge bundles of soiled clothes and linens. Clean sheets billowed over bushes beside the river and an army of shifts and chemises draped the hedgerow in the warm sun. Another group of maids was melting the candle stubs accumulated during the past month to reform candles. Lye soap was boiling down in the kitchen yard.

She had just come from that odorous activity, and her face was still flushed from the fire's heat. She wasn't at all sure the lye from the hickory ashes had been strong enough, for the soap was refusing to set. Her thoughts were occupied with ways to coax the soap to harden into cakes as she crossed the winter parlor.

Automatically she glanced around to see if the room had been cleaned. Nicholas had invited friends over for the Midsummer Eve celebration and she wanted Wyndfell to do them proud. After the trauma of the previous evening, Jessica was more than a little worried about having guests at this particular time, but they had already been asked and were due to arrive the following day.

The impressive window in the winter parlor had been washed inside and out the day before by menservants and the old ashes cleared from the hearth. Jessica kicked the rushes and sniffed. More rosemary and thyme in the rushes would perfume the room. She made a mental note to see to that before dinner. By filling her mind with mundane tasks she was keeping her fearful thoughts at bay. Someone had tried to kill Nicholas and perhaps her as well, and while Nicholas suspected Swineford, they had no proof the would-be murderer wasn't someone there in Wyndfell.

Going into the great hall, she looked around critically as she scooped Tess off the table. The cat blinked her yellow eyes and purred as Jessica scratched beneath the furry chin. She noted that herbs were needed in these rushes as well. Lavender, she thought, would be a nice change.

She went to the door and put the lazy cat out into the sunny courtyard. Tess stretched and ambled off toward the barn for the next in her endless series of naps.

Jessica looked past the open gate to the green that surrounded her home. Somewhere past the swath of trees at the far side was the home of a man who hated her husband enough to kill him. The idea was terrifying. She closed the door and turned back, forcing her nervous thoughts out of her mind.

At first the movement in the shadows near the turret steps seemed to be a trick of the light. Then she discerned the shape of a woman, and she froze. With her eyes not yet adjusted from the sunlit courtyard, she could think only of the ghost that was being rumored to haunt the gallery, so silently did the figure move. Whether it was the gentle Lady Jane or not, Jessica had no desire to confront the apparition.

Madeline glided forward and out of the shadows. "Good day, sister," she greeted as if there were nothing untoward in her being there.

Jessica's mouth dropped open and she wished with all her heart that she was seeing only a harmless ghost. "Madeline," she whispered. After months of going by that name herself, the word seemed odd in her mouth.

"Did I startle you? Forgive me. I meant no harm." Madeline's voice was as sweetly gentle as the babble of water over smooth stones.

"Of course you startled me. What are you doing here?" Jessica stood in a stiff position, her hands clenched together at her waist.

"I'm a new widow," her sister said. "So tragic. My Raymond was cruelly murdered in the woods behind Pritchard Hall. By Gypsies, they say," she added.

"So you married Sir Raymond? I was sorry to hear of his death. We heard the news yesterday." Jessica glanced around and saw that they were miraculously alone. She walked quickly to her sister. "How did you get in here without my being told?"

"I walked in." She moved farther into the hall and looked up at the hangings. "How pretty my tapestries look here. Where did you put the painted cloths?"

"Madeline, lower your voice. No one must hear you."

Obligingly the woman glided back to the shadows with Jessica. "How terrible it is to be widowed so young," she murmured with no regret at all in her voice. "I have no one to look after me or to protect me."

"What of Swineford? If you and Raymond were living in Pritchard Hall, surely his master will offer protection to a woman in your position."

"Protection. Yes. He offered that and much more besides. Unfortunately, Sir James is also dead." When she heard Jessica's sharp gasp, she added, "By the hand of a servant. I was there and saw it all."

"What are you saying? Sir James Swineford was murdered?" A cold dread was creeping over Jessica.

"Yes, last night."

"Madeline, you didn't . . . That is, did you . . . ?"

Madeline raised her brows in a mild questioning stare. Jessica found she couldn't complete her query. To kill animals was bad enough, but for her sister to be a murderess was too unthinkable. She found she really couldn't bear to ask.

"So you see my quandary," Madeline continued. "First my husband, then my . . . protector murdered. Obviously I am being punished."

"What? How is that?" Jessica stared at her in confusion.

"Why, for not going through with my betrothed marriage as a dutiful daughter would. It was wicked of me to elope with Raymond and leave Lord Nicholas jilted at the altar."

"He wasn't jilted. I married him, as you must well know."

"Yes." Madeline's voice was silky but in the dim light Jessica noticed her smile never reached her eyes. "But I've come back to set that right."

All the blood drained from Jessica's face, and she felt as if someone had kicked the wind out of her. "What do you mean?" she whispered.

"As I see it, you married Lord Nicholas as my proxy. After all, you wed under my name and not your own. I've heard all about it, you see. Everyone believes you to be me."

"It was no proxy wedding! I am his wife."

Madeline shrugged. "So you bedded him by proxy as well. What of it? Tell me, sister, did I enjoy his bed sport?"

"Hold your tongue!" Jessica snapped. Her thoughts were tumbling about in her head in a roaring jumble. "What passes between my husband and myself is a private matter."

"Aye, but Lord Nicholas is really *my* husband," she affirmed, then glared maddeningly. Holding up her left hand, she let Jessica's gaze fall upon her betrothal ring. "Here is my proof of identity. Can you gainsay me?"

"I need not, for I wear his wedding ring," Jessica retorted.

"Without the betrothal you cannot be legally married. Even if he wed you in good faith and by your own name, the marriage would be invalid if it's proven he was spoken for in a previous match. Come, Jessica, you know this."

Jessica's eyes were large and haunted. She had thought this through many a long night. "Do you expect to merely step into my shoes? What of me?"

"You must return to our parents. In truth, they must be frantic over your disappearance. I will order you escorted there right away."

With an effort Jessica held her temper. "You have taken me greatly by surprise," she told her sister. "In faith I feel near to swooning. Suffer me patience, I beg you, to compose my thoughts." She glanced around. This place was much too public. "Come. Let us go somewhere more private so we may talk."

"Gladly. I would see more of my new home. Where do these steps go?"

"To the old gallery and solar. Come. I'll show it to you." Jessica's mind was churning to come up with some way out of this coil.

"Is there no proper stairway?" Madeline asked as she preceded Jessica up the hollowed stone steps.

"We plan to add one." Jessica stared at her twin's slender back and wondered what she could do to change this turn of fate. Her fingers were icy as dread crept into her bones.

They reached the gallery and walked along the empty length, each enveloped in her own thoughts.

"You must let me break this news gently to Nicholas," Jessica said as they neared the end of the long chamber. "He has had no reason to guess there are two of us, much less that he married the other twin. Such a shock might throw him into distraction."

"Oh? Is he of a weak mind, then?"

"No, no. Not that sort of distraction. But you can see what a jolt this will be."

"I suppose. Still, if he is an honorable man, I can only assume that he will be eager to right this grievous error. Will he not?"

"Yes. Yes, of course." Jessica peered questioningly at her sister. From all appearances Madeline seemed to have experienced no trauma at all, much less that of becoming a widow and having been witness to a murder only the night before.

"Tell me, Madeline. You say Swineford was killed by a servant? For what cause?"

"Jamie had upbraided him for bringing us a vinegary wine." He eyes became darker and veiled as she remembered. "At times Jamie could be most unreasonable. He even teased me about believing Raymond's lies about Nicholas. Can you credit that?" Her voice rose angrily. "He dared poke fun at me for believing Nicholas was lame and cruel of temper."

Her words came quickly, tumbling over each other as her resentment at Swineford became obvious. "He made me so angry!"

Jessica had noticed the familiar use of Swineford's given name. What had been going on over at Pritchard Hall? "And Sir Raymond?" Jessica asked cautiously. "Did he also make you angry?"

Like the sun breaking through the clouds, Madeline smiled. "Raymond? Make me angry? For shame to speak cruelly of the dead. Raymond was the best of husbands. Did you know he planned to move me from Pritchard Hall to a manor house of our own? How grand it was to have been." Her voice was now dreamy and tinged with sadness.

Staring at her, Jessica opened the door to the solar. Madeline swept by her and looked around the room with great interest. "How lovely. What is this chamber used for?"

"Nothing at the present. Madeline, you must give me time. I cannot go to Nicholas and blurt out all that has happened. I must have time to prepare him."

"I suppose. Was this the ladies' parlor? I think it must have been."

"Yes." Jessica glanced around the room at the sparse furnishings and the faded fresco on the cracked plaster wall. When Jessica had first seen this room, she had been able to imagine how fine it had once been, but Madeline seemed unaware of its deterioration from years of disuse. Perhaps she spoke so highly of it because of the abundant sunlight that streamed through the uncovered windows, a rarity for most castles. Or maybe she was losing touch with reality. "I want you to promise to give me a day or so to find a way to break this news to him."

"So long? How will you explain me in the meantime?"

Jessica drew a deep breath. "I have a thought. You could stay here, in the solar, and he will not know you're here until it is time."

"Stay here? All alone?"

"Not really. I will sit with you as much as I can. I will bring you food and drink and warm bedding. It will be like an adventure."

"Yes," Madeline said slowly. "It would be, wouldn't it?"

"Think of it. Time to yourself and no one else around to be constantly watching your every move. What woman has ever had such a privilege?"

"I've never really wanted to be alone," Madeline said doubtfully.

"I'll be here with you as much as possible."

"For only a day or two?"

"Perhaps two. Tomorrow is Midsummer Eve and Nicholas has invited guests to spend it with us. I can hardly tell him about this coil in front of company." Jessica waited and tried not to look as if she cared much one way or the other.

"An adventure, you say. I'd like that," Madeline responded, recalling the sense of power she had felt at being alone in the dark corridors of Pritchard Hall. This would be much the same.

"Good. Then 'tis settled. You'll stay here and I'll bring you the things you require. There's a bolt to the door if you want to draw it, but no one ever comes here." She glanced at the cot where she and Nicholas had made love. "At least not very often."

"Those steps outside the door. Where do they lead?"

"Down to the buttery. I'll answer all your questions

about Wyndfell. Just stay here and don't let anyone see you until St. John's Day."

"Two days. I agree." She sat on a stool and spread her garnet skirts primly. "Could you bring me cloth and some embroidery silk? I wish to spend my time productively, as Mother taught us."

Jessica nodded slowly as she took in this new change. Madeline had sounded almost childlike. "I will bring you needlework. I must go now before I am missed."

Madeline airily waved her a dismissal as if Jessica were no more than a servant. "See that you do, and don't forget."

Hastily Jessica left, closing the heavy door behind her. She was terrified and her thoughts skittered wildly. For a moment she touched the large key that rested in the lock. She should lock the door so that Madeline couldn't go to Nicholas before she had a chance to explain. But Nicholas might never understand. She had deceived him and would have to admit that. How would she be able to tell him?

Absently Jessica took a step away from the door. Madwoman. The word echoed in her mind. After seeing Madeline's swift changes of mood, there could be no doubt that she was now as mad as their uncle had been. She glanced back at the closed door and wondered what Madeline was doing in there. How had Leopold whiled away the years before death finally released him?

Unnoticed tears coursed over her cheeks. She couldn't lock Madeline away. There had to be some other recourse. She thought of her parents but rejected the idea. Had they not already known of the switch, she could have claimed that crazy Jessica had finally shown up, pretending to be Madeline.

She considered Nicholas for a moment. He would back her, she knew, but there was a chance he couldn't do so legally. What Madeline had said about being betrothed to one bride and marrying another was quite true. In the eyes of the law, Jessica might actually be a proxy wife. That would make Nicholas firmly married to Madeline who was physically sound and would be likely to live for years. Perhaps longer than Nicholas himself.

Not only that, but even if Madeline died, they probably could not get permission to wed, for if he was married to Madeline, then Jessica was legally his sister. Parliament might have been willing to marry Queen Elizabeth to her brother-in-law, Philip of Spain, but she was a queen. Jessica couldn't hope for so lenient a hearing.

She straightened and drew a deep breath. Unable to reason sensibly, she decided that only one course remained. She would have to keep Madeline hidden and hope she left on her own as she had from Hargrove Castle and Pritchard Hall. This didn't seem rational, but Madeline's previous actions had followed no apparent logic. Thus she might take it into her head to leave Wyndfell in the same way. In the meantime Jessica knew ways to keep Madeline amused and busy. As her sister was no longer of a strong mind, she would be easily diverted. Bolts of linen and silk needed to be embroidered, and Madeline could sit and sew for hours on end and never mark the passage of time.

Jessica dried the tear from her cheek. She would find a way to keep her secret from Nicholas, for she could never consider giving her place to Madeline. Whatever the law might be, Nicholas was Jessica's husband and she loved him deeply.

She stared at the door to the solar. For both Raymond and Swineford to be killed within days of one another was uncanny. Jessica realized it could have been chance, but if it weren't she and Nicholas might be in danger. No, she thought firmly, even Madeline wouldn't go so far as murder. The gloomy gallery was doubtless making her see goblins where there was only coincidence. Resolutely she headed for the steps that led to the hall.

By the time she reached the hall, she could hear the sound of hoofbeats in the cobbled courtyard. Jessica glanced out and cursed softly. The guests she had expected to arrive the following day had come early.

She called to a page and pointed toward the steps to Nicholas' closet. "Go get Lord Nicholas," she ordered. "And hurry."

As the boy ran to obey, she opened Wyndfell's massive double doors and stepped out into the sunshine to meet the first of several groups of visitors Nicholas had told her to expect during the fair-weather months. "Greetings, my lord, my lady. Welcome to Wyndfell."

The man swung his wife to the ground and handed their horses' reins to the attendant. Behind them their servants were dismounting and untying the bundles of clothes and linens from the packhorses. The man was of medium height and handsome. He wore elaborately embroidered silks and satins in shades of snuff and saffron. Even his shoes were saffron, Jessica noted as he removed his dusty riding boots at the door. His wife was petite and her coloring unremarkable. Her hair was brown and her eyes pale blue and round as if she were continually surprised. Her chin was weak and her teeth were small and already yellowing in spite of her youth.

"Good day, Countess," he greeted as he and his wife bowed. "At least I assume you to be the countess?"

Jessica glanced down and saw she still wore the

cloth about her waist from her morning chores. She untied it hastily and whipped it off. "Yes, I am Countess Madeline Garrett." She tripped over the name as she recalled the real owner of it was quite near.

"Enchanted. I am Sir Lowell Clayborne. This is my lady wife, Wilhelmina."

The woman bobbed another curtsy, then addressed Jessica. "We apologize for arriving early, but who would have guessed the roads to be so passable at this season? We made marvelous good time. No doubt our cart will arrive by dark."

"Come in, come in," Jessica urged. "A boy has been sent for Nicholas. Ah, here he is now."

Nicholas strode across the hall, his arms outstretched to greet his friend. "Welcome, Lowell," he boomed. They embraced fondly and Nicholas bowed to the small woman. "You're as beautiful as ever, Lady Wilhelmina."

She tittered coquettishly. "Lord Nicholas, how you do go on!"

"Wilhelmina was apologizing for arriving early," Lowell told Nicholas, "but in faith we should beg pardon for arriving so late. You must think us dreary friends to wait so long before coming to greet your bride."

"The fact is," Wilhelmina said in her soft voice, "I was in childbed and couldn't travel."

"You've a babe?" Jessica asked.

"My third. And another son it was." She glanced proudly at her husband. "Forsooth we seem able to make naught else."

Jessica could see that in spite of the woman's plain appearance, there was clearly love between her and her husband. "Have you the babe with you?"

"No, we were able to find a most reliable wet

nurse. The same girl we had with our oldest. I had no qualms about leaving young George in her care."

Nicholas' valet was motioning for the Clayborne servants to gather their traveling goods and follow him to the guest chamber. Jessica watched them with concern. The guest quarters were near the old wing and Madeline.

"Madeline?" Nicholas said, louder. "Are you daydreaming? Ring for ale for our guests."

With a start, she answered in a rather high-pitched voice, "Ale. Yes." Then, composing herself, she distractedly said, "Will you excuse me a moment? There is something I must attend." She started toward the steps, then tried to pretend that she had nothing weighing on her mind. "I will have ale, too, love. Just give me a moment."

Nicholas stared at her questioningly, but she gave him her brightest smile and hurried away. The door beyond the guest chamber opened into the old gallery. She had to be certain it was locked so the Claybornes didn't wander through it by mistake.

The servants were settling in with the usual amount of clatter and gossip. No one noticed her slip by and down the corridor. As with many of the doors in Wyndfell, the key was in the latch. She turned it and felt the bolts slide into place. Taking the key out of the lock, Jessica hid it in a painted jug in a wall niche. Now there was less chance of anyone wandering upon Madeline or of her wandering upon them.

Moving as quickly as she dared, Jessica went to the kitchens and gathered a loaf of bread, some cheese, and a thick slice of venison. Concealing the food in her apron, she tried to look as if she were merely passing through. At the butler's pantry she fetched a tinderbox and some candles. The bedding was more difficult to obtain, but the confusion of the guests' arrival helped cover her actions. Besides, no one would question the countess of the castle. She was glad for that.

Slipping down the kitchen steps to the buttery, Jessica ran across the cool room and up the older steps. Her heart was pounding as she opened the door to the solar.

Madeline sat more or less as Jessica had left her. She was humming softly and gazing out the thick-walled window. "You're back at last? I thought you had forgotten me."

"No, never. Company has arrived and I was detained. Here. I brought you food." She handed her sister the apron and bent to spread the blankets over the cot.

"This is all? No sweetmeats? No fruit?"

"I will bring you more later. In the meantime content yourself with this."

Madeline shrugged and drew her small knife from the satin sheath at her waist. Cutting off a sliver of cheese, she said, "I'll need tapestries, you know. I couldn't possibly sleep beneath open windows. The night air is poison."

"Yes, I'll see to it." Jessica cast about in her mind for a source of tapestries that wouldn't be missed. Getting them to the solar would also be a problem. She turned to go.

"You're leaving so soon? I thought you might stay a bit and talk to me."

"I can't. You heard me say that guests have arrived. I may already have trouble explaining my absence."

"Perhaps I should come with you. We can get the unpleasant explanations behind us and I will see to my guests."

"No, no. You promised. I must have time to prepare Nicholas. Especially since there are guests in the castle. Think how embarrassing this could be. They have already met me and know I live here with Nicholas. Would you want guests to know I sleep with your husband?" Jessica was thinking fast. "No, far better to merely switch places. Yes, that's it. You must stay here until I have time to tell you all about Wyndfell, Nicholas, and the servants."

"That could take days," Madeline protested.

"How else can you hope to pass as me?"

"Nay, 'tis the opposite. You are passing as *me*."

"Not in their eyes. Would you know Sir Richard, the steward, from Sir Oliver, the bailiff? No, you must stay hidden until I can teach you all I know."

"Very well. I suppose you have a point," Madeline agreed reluctantly. "But be quick about it."

"I will. Now, you stay here while I go see to my duties. Will you do it?"

Madeline carved a bite-sized chunk of meat. "I suppose. Yes, I'll do it."

Jessica left hurriedly and went down the worn steps as quickly as she dared. That had truly been an inspiration. She could string out telling of the castle and servants for days. Maybe weeks if she was skillful. By then Madeline might decide to leave or Jessica could possibly find a plan to vanquish her.

She almost rushed headlong into the buttery, but heard a noise in time. Cautiously she peeped around the corner and watched a servant drawing a measure of ale. Holding her breath, she waited until he plugged the cask and left the cellar. Jessica leaned against the wall and tried to get her breath. How could she dare this, she wondered. To succeed in hiding Madeline even for hours was nearly impossible. What was she going to do?

Drawing a deep breath, she lifted her chin. Having

a faint heart would never do. She would succeed because she knew she must. The alternative was her own banishment.

She calmed her features, then joined Nicholas and her guests in the winter parlor. Nichols looked at her curiously, but she gave no sign of having done anything out of the ordinary. "Forgive me for leaving you. I needed to tell the cook of your arrival."

"Sir Richard would have done that," Nicholas said.

"Yes, of course. How foolish of me." To Wilhelmina she said, "I've not yet grown accustomed to managing my household."

Nicholas stared frankly at her. She had always shown an unusual aptitude in handling the affairs of the castle.

Wilhelmina nodded. "No two castles are alike. When I married my Lowell, the castle was topsy-turvy for months. You will soon have it running to please you."

"We were just discussing Midsummer Eve and the superstition that prevails."

"Forsooth, Lowell, 'tis no superstition but the truth," Wilhelmina protested. "As a child I did try it, and the coming year the matter came to pass."

"Oh?" Jessica's mind was still on Madeline and what to do about her.

"Do you not have this belief in the parish where you come from?" she asked. "Here we fast and sit in the church porch on the Vigil of St. John. At the stroke of midnight, souls who will die in the coming year walk right up to the church door and knock upon it to be admitted. They even arrive in the order in which they will die!"

"I have often heard of this," Jessica answered, "but I have never tried it for myself."

"Shall we? Tomorrow?" Wilhelmina asked, leaning forward eagerly.

Suddenly a cold wave swept over Jessica and she shuddered. "I . . . I suddenly was chilled."

"Good heavens! That's an ill omen. Someone must have walked across your grave. Quickly say a prayer."

"I'm all right now. Perhaps it was merely a draft."

"Lowell teases me," Wilhelmina said, casting a coy glance at her husband, "but there is truth in these old tales, I think. Why else would they have survived?"

"For myself, I don't wish to know who will die," Lowell retorted. "It will be known all too quickly in real life. Besides, we don't live here and you wouldn't recognize any of the souls anyway."

"That's true," his wife agreed reluctantly. "Still, to see them would be interesting."

"I'm afraid you must count us out this time," Nicholas said with a grin. "Madeline is still a bride to me. She will be elsewhere come midnight."

Jessica blushed and lowered her eyes. Nicholas meant well but he was often more blunt than tactful.

"Nicholas," scolded Wilhelmina with the privilege of old friendship, "you have embarrassed your lady. For shame."

To Wilhelmina, Lowell said, "You might ask if I will let you roam from my bed, as well. Lady Madeline isn't the only one with reason to blush."

Wilhelmina swatted at him with her folded fan. "You two must stop that. Such lewd talk will drive us away."

Jessica listened to the banter but her thoughts continued to scatter like frightened geese. Whatever was she going to do? She remembered to laugh at her guests' sallies, but a deep worry remained within her.

18

MADELINE PACED THE round solar, her hands clasped behind her. Darkness had fallen behind the tapestries that Jessica had finally brought up to keep out the dangerous night air. By now all of Wyndfell's inhabitants must be settling down for the night. Even with guests, no one kept very late hours unless it was a festival or something of that sort. Candles were far too precious to be squandered.

She pushed aside a tapestry and stared out at the moon-silvered landscape. A few stars glimmered, but low clouds blanketed most of the sky. A light mist hovered in the air and pale lightning in the distance promised rain within the hour.

Madeline let the tapestry drape back over the window. If night air was harmful, wet night air might be disastrous. She had heard that the plague traveled on night vapors. She fingered the worn tapestry. Jessica could have brought her decent hangings. After all, she was the true Countess of Wyndfell.

With a mirthless smile, Madeline turned away from the window. She could scarce credit that Jessica had volunteered to teach her about Wyndfell. The woman had always been foolish, in Madeline's opinion. Did Jessica suppose she would simply be sent home with an armed escort to see after her safety? How ridiculous. Once Madeline took her rightful place, Jessica must be disposed of. Otherwise, she might return and cause trouble in the future.

Madeline went to the door and eased it open a crack to listen. Not a sound could be heard. Decisively she let herself out and stood for a moment on the landing. To her right were the steps leading to the buttery; ahead lay the gallery. As silent as the deep shadows, Madeline glided into the long room.

Designed as a place to walk on rainy days, the chamber was long and narrow. On either end were fireplaces that were cold and black. The outside wall was composed mostly of arched windows with no glass. In the winter, heavy tapestries would have been necessary to keep out the worst of the cold.

She tried to open the door which was halfway down the long wall, but it wouldn't give. Someone had locked it, she supposed, or the damp air had swollen it shut. She passed by it and went through the one she and Jessica had used earlier.

The steps she sought were invisible in the darkness, and for a moment Madeline hesitated. She could go back for a candle, but she hated to return for anything, for such was known to be bad luck. Instead, she felt for the walls on either side and slid her foot along to find the first step.

When she reached the bottom, her heart was racing. This was truly an adventure. To roam the deserted corridors of Hargrove Castle and Pritchard Hall had been heady, but this was laced with pure excitement. She knew nothing of the layout of Wyndfell, nor where each turn might take her.

Slowly she glided into the hall, thankful for the

pale moonlight that illumined her way. The servants of the lowest rank, as well as some of the guests' men had bunked down on the rushes in the huge room. Soft snores came to her ears as she walked down the very center of the room. The walls on either side displayed her tapestries, and she could see how pretty they looked, even in the dim light. She had put in long hours on each, aided by her mother and her mother's gentlewomen. Pride swelled in her to see them all hanging in such fine array.

She crossed to a doorway and paused. Who was beyond it? What might she find there? Gradually she pushed it open and saw the pantry that led to the kitchens. To one side was the tall ambry with its dim shapes of platters and ewers. Past that was the trencher board and surveying dresser, both empty in preparation for the next day's meals. Madeline went past them to the cupboards and felt in the darkness for the pierced tin candle box she knew must be there. When she found it, she took out several candles. All but one, she placed in the pocket of her kirtle. The last one she lit from the flint that sat beside the candle box.

Now that she could see better, she walked more quickly. The next door led to the corridor lined with pantries and cabinets used to store the vast amount of goods needed for the castle meals. Beyond that were the kitchens, where she had entered the night before.

Madeline helped herself to a square of nutterbrede and savored the sweet lemony sauce that flavored the delicacy. She also took some apples and pears for her breakfast, along with more bread and cheese. Jessica had been slow in answering Madeline's wants, and she saw no reason to starve because of it.

When lightning flashed outside the kitchen's windows, announcing the approach of the storm, Madeline's face and body were illuminated by its brilliance. Then it was gone, and thunder rolled over the hills. She tightened her lips in a grimace. She had always hated storms and had never understood why Jessica seemed to enjoy them. Ignoring the weather as best she could, Madeline continued her wanderings.

In a short time she had collected a pewter pitcher and a tankard and was headed for the buttery, which she reasoned must be nearby.

As her assumption proved to be correct, she soon found the door to the spacious wine cellar. Inside, she felt a vague uneasiness, as if ill deeds had been plotted here. Putting such fancies aside, she went to the first butt and tested the plug. It gave beneath her tugging and she bent to sniff it. Claret, she deduced. That would do. She pulled out the bung and let the liquid trickle down the sides of the pitcher. When it was full, she twisted the plug back into place and went to the other doorway.

Just inside the vaulted door space were steps. Madeline held the candle up higher and climbed them one by one. At the top she saw the familiar gallery and realized she had come full circle. Amazed at how easy her journey had been, she returned to the solar.

All about her hidden bower the inhabitants of Wyndfell slept. No one had seen her night stroll. No one even guessed at her presence here. Madeline threw back her head and laughed aloud.

In the newer wing Jessica curled closer to Nicholas and moved uneasily in her sleep.

By midmorning the following day, the rain had stopped. The newly washed grasses and leaves took on vivid hues under the sun, and gradually the clouds dissolved to mere puffs of buoyant cotton. The people of Wyndfell and the small village on its skirt all ran to the woods to pick flowers to garland the town wells. Hedgerows were plucked of dog rose and trails of honeysuckle; the pastures were robbed of marguerites and scarlet poppies.

Jessica, her arms full of daisies and poppies, laughed and challenged Nicholas and their guests to outdo her. Even Wilhelmina, who was of a calmer nature, joined in the fun and gathered bunches of yellow toadflax and bluebells. Singing rounds of songs to celebrate summer, they trooped back to the castle.

Beside the chapel stood Wyndfell's ancient well. Dedicated to St. Ruan, it had never accomplished any miracles so far as anyone remembered, but its water was always abundant and sweet. Using the honeysuckle as a twine, Jessica and Wilhelmina wove garlands over the oak upright and beam that held the bucket. The other flowers they made into nosegays to lodge in the lichen-covered old rocks.

"Do you think the fairies will be pleased?" Jessica playfully asked Nicholas.

"I wager this is the best-decorated well in the parish," he vowed loyally.

"It's frightfully old, isn't it?" Wilhelmina asked as she touched the weathered stones.

"Yes, it was here even before the castle. Some say there was a Roman camp here. Others say it was a Saxon stronghold. The well was dedicated to St. Ruan when the chapel was built, but so far as I know, the saint was never here."

"Our well is now called King's Well instead of St. Ethelred. With the dissolution of the Catholic houses and then the visit in the area of King Henry, this seemed like a wise choice," Lowell put in.

"I agree. After all, what's in a name?"

"Look," Jessica said, pointing toward the fair-grounds. "The bonfire is being built."

The wood, piled high the day before, was being added to by the exuberant villagers. Several smaller bonfires were being prepared by the village apprentices, the local schoolboys, and the members of the wool guild, who were of an independent turn.

"There will be many fires to watch tonight," Jessica told her guests. "I've ordered supper to be served on the green so we may watch them while we eat." In spite of her carefree tone, Jessica glanced up at the old turret that contained the solar and Madeline. She ached from forcing herself to laugh and be gay, but the effort seemed to have been convincing. Not even Nicholas seemed to suspect she was covering up a terrible secret.

"Let's go to the village and see if the musicale has started," Lowell suggested. "I do love a well-performed madrigal."

"There's something I must see to first," Jessica said. "I'll not be a minute." She turned and hurried into the castle before anyone could question her.

Rushing to her chamber, she gathered up the length of white silk she had planned to embroider as an altar cloth for the chapel and a handful of silk skeins. She carefully fastened one of her precious needles to the cloth so it wouldn't become lost.

Almost running, she sped to the solar and burst in breathlessly. "Good day, Madeline. Did you sleep well?"

"That cot isn't very comfortable, but I slept well enough. Why are you out of breath?" Madeline asked in a slow, sweet voice. "You know it isn't ladylike to race about the castle."

"I know, but I had to hurry before I was missed for too long. I brought you some silk and threads. I had intended this as an Easter cloth, but you may use it as you like. Here are threads of all colors, and the needle is here. Do you need anything else?"

"Only companionship. I find the hours tedious here alone." Madeline pouted prettily to lull Jessica into thinking she had stayed here all along. "You promised to while away the time with me and to teach me of Wyndfell."

"And so I will. But first I must see to my guests. It would never do to let someone suspect you're here before we are ready to switch places. Remember how we agreed?"

"Of course. Only I find it very dull up here all by myself."

"Busy yourself with this needlework. I'll try to come back before bedtime." When Madeline frowned, Jessica protested, "I'm doing the best that I can!"

"Very well. I suppose I can put up with it for a while longer." Madeline seated herself on a stool and began to spread the cloth over her lap to plan a pattern of embroidery.

As Jessica backed out of the room, she noticed that Madeline showed no protest. With a puzzled look, Jessica shut the door. She knew Madeline too well, and she was taking this too readily. The Madeline she knew would have railed against being shut up away from festivities. Had she really changed or was she up to something? Jessica was aware that the too-innocent tone of Madeline's voice was the same she had always used to manipulate their parents.

There was no time to wonder about it now, however, so Jessica rushed back downstairs and to her husband and guests. In her absence Thomas had joined them, and no one questioned her disappearance. Together the group walked down the green to the village. Jessica was so worried about her problems she didn't even notice that Thomas contrived to walk beside her and to talk to her far more than to anyone else.

In the village, impromptu rounds were being sung to the lutes, viols, and citterns. Madrigals sounded from the more proficient singers. Everywhere village children ran and romped in the rare interlude between chores. The butcher's apprentice had gathered a small crowd to watch him juggle brightly colored balls of wood, but his master, seeing the boy's idleness, bore down on him and dragged him back to work.

Thomas bought Jessica an apple from an old woman who was selling them from her doorstep. He daringly took the first bite, then handed it to her, his eyes meeting hers boldly. She had no choice but to take it or call attention to his overfamiliarity. Beyond Thomas' shoulder, Jessica saw Nicholas glaring at them, so she moved away quickly. Putting her hand in Nicholas', she offered him the next bite of apple as if the gesture on Thomas' part had meant nothing. Fortunately neither Wilhelmina nor Lowell had noticed the tense interchange. Jessica pointedly ignored Thomas as they wandered closer to inspect the bonfire.

Late in the afternoon, the party returned to Wyndfell, still singing snatches of the songs they had heard in the village. Tables had been carried out to the green, and long white cloths covered with snowy sanap were spread in readiness for the food. When Nicholas led Jessica to the two great chairs and seated her under the canopy that had also been brought out, the butler appeared carrying the ornate salt cellar. The meal began with the usual prayer for Queen and country and continued with the same rituals that would have been observed in the hall.

When the concluding prayer was said and the last dish had been carried away, they strolled over the grass in the deepening twilight and watched the fires being lighted in the village below—first the smaller ones that had been prepared by the apprentices and schoolboys, then the slightly larger one gathered by the wool guild. At last the largest pyre on the fairground was torched and a breath of awe sounded from the onlookers there and on Wyndfell's green. The flames licked higher and higher until the entire tower of wood was engulfed in leaping tongues of light.

As darkness became complete, more fires appeared as the villagers burned the dry heaps of compost and dung in their front yards and in their barnyards. The fires dotted the night, showing where each house and cottage stood. Behind them, Wyndfell's own compost heap was ignited.

The villagers could be seen dancing about the various fires. The boldest, or those intoxicated by too much ale, leapt the smaller blazes to impress their comrades and womenfolk.

"To watch the flames, I feel as if I have a link back in time," Jessica said dreamily. "Think how many hundreds of years we have celebrated Midsummer Eve. Thousands of times, perhaps."

"The vicars would like to see it stop," Wilhelmina said. "Ours is quite adamant that the bonfires are pagan. No one listens, though. The common folk will ever take a festival, even a pagan one, over solemn prayers and fasting. Who can blame them?"

Nicholas put his arm around Jessica's waist. "Such a display does prompt a person to pretend he might be back at the beginning of time. Before vicars. Even before castles."

Jessica glanced back at Wyndfell's reassuring bulk,

but the protective feeling she hoped the sight would engender was dashed to tiny bits. High up in the old wing was a light from the solar. Madeline stood clearly silhouetted at the window. Jessica watched, unable to wrest her eyes from the scene; then Madeline slowly let the tapestry drop back in place and the light was extinguished. Apprehension rose like bile in Jessica's throat. What if someone else had seen the light from the abandoned room and Madeline's form in the window? Fear knotted her stomach and she shivered. How could she ever hope to hide Madeline? She had no guarantee Madeline could be convinced to leave.

"Are you cold?" Thomas asked solicitously.

"The night seems quite warm to me," Nicholas stated gruffly as he moved closer to Jessica.

"Yes, yes, it is a pleasant night. I suppose I'm only tired."

"We are usually abed by this time of night," Lowell agreed. "I know I'm growing sleepy myself."

"The fires are beginning to burn low," Nicholas observed. "Perhaps we should end the night." He hugged Jessica.

Jessica sighed and returned his hug. He could use a measure more of tact, but she loved him. Besides, she also disliked the way Thomas had been looking at her. Tonight she had great need to be held in Nicholas' embrace. Who knew when she might be forever deprived of it? Risking a glance upward, she was relieved to see that the tapestry still covered the solar window. Nicholas would be certain to investigate a light from the unused room. "I, too, am tired. So must you be, Wilhelmina, and you so new from childbed." Jessica made a mental note to remind Madeline that candles were valuable and that she should use them only during the cloudy days when the solar would be too dark otherwise.

Together they strolled back to the drawbridge and into the courtyard. Jessica joined in the conversation as they entered the castle and climbed the steps, but her mind was on Madeline. She bid her guests good night at their chamber door.

Arm in arm she walked along the dim corridor with Nicholas. The servants had all but completed their preparation of the castle for night, and thus a hush had replaced the usual bustle and noise of the activity of so many people. Flambeaux cast a mellow, guttering light on the stone walls and floor, as black threads of smoke drifted up to add soot to the already blackened ceilings. Between the islands of light, the way was dark and shadowy, but Jessica felt no apprehension of the now familiar castle. Instead, her concerns centered on Madeline and the threat of her sister's mere presence.

Jessica's brow creased in dismay. Why had she thought of her sister in those terms? Madeline might ruin her own life, but Jessica had, for just a moment, actually felt bodily fear. Surely that was ridiculous. Or was it? Once again Jessica recalled that both Raymond and Swineford had died of violent causes. But they had been killed by other people, had they not?

"Nicholas," she asked as they turned toward their chamber, "what of the Gypsy man who is said to have killed Sir Raymond? Will he be tried soon?"

"I've not heard, but there will be no reciting of the Neck Verse for him."

"Neck Verse?"

"That's what the Psalm is called that entreats God's mercy and pardon. For years, if a priest or cleric was caught at a petty crime, he could recite the Neck Verse, and after being branded on the hand, he would be released. However, if he was caught again, he would be hanged. Of late, such lenience has been extended to secular folk, but not for a grievous crime such as murder. The Gypsy will have no recourse through the Psalm."

"Will he be found guilty?"

"Probably. Most people distrust all Gypsies, and with good reason. Their laws and customs are not ours, and they steal and lie by habit."

"Surely that is no reason to assume murder, though."

"Who else could be guilty? Sir Raymond's horse was in the Gypsy's string of mounts. That's evidence enough."

"When will we hear of his fate?"

"Soon. With no food, drink, or fire until the verdict is reached, trials are quick. Especially in cases where the accused is sure to be found guilty."

"Still, I wonder . . ."

"Are you taking up the law?" he asked with a chuckle. "Surely there will be no prettier solicitor in all of England."

"Nonsense." She smiled at his teasing. "I was only wondering. Somehow the man didn't look like a killer to me."

Nicholas shrugged. "What does a killer look like? They come in all sizes, shapes, and ranks." He opened the door to their antechamber and waved away his valet and Jessica's serving ladies. "We need nothing," he told them. "Go back to the fires."

When the servants bowed and left, he turned to Jessica. "Turn your mind from these doleful thoughts. I would have you smile and meet my loving with love."

"As if I could ever do aught else," she said. "In truth, you have bewitched me."

"Have I? And what of my brother?" The hurt in his eyes belied the light manner with which he spoke the words.

"Thomas is a fool," she replied. "He cants and poses and struts to his own audience."

"It seemed to me that he had a rapt audience in you."

"Would you have me be rude to your brother before our guests? Not only would that shame our family, but it would make our guests uncomfortable."

"You could put him in his place when there are no guests about. Or better yet, I could."

"Sweet Nicholas," she murmured as she stepped into his embrace, "would you have me give weight to that young popinjay's words? If I appear to take him seriously, we may find our troubles have just begun."

"Perhaps," he growled. "On the other hand, maybe I should take him behind the barn for a lesson on manners."

"You'll do nothing of the sort. Thomas is merely practicing courtly flirtations. It means nothing. We will soon find him a suitable bride, and he will find she more than occupies all his thoughts." She made her words believable in spite of the fact that she wasn't so sure herself of Thomas' motives. Unpracticed or not, his honeyed words seemed too familiar to her, as well. Still, it wouldn't do to force Thomas' hand at present. Not when she had so much else on her mind.

So she smiled to show Nicholas that she put no stock in Thomas' behavior, and started to unlace his doublet.

"I've never had so lovely a valet," Nicholas said as she pulled away the brocade covering.

"Nor one who loves you so dearly, I wager." She untied the strings at his wrist and neck so that his shirt hung loose, disclosing a wedge of his chest. She ran her fingertips over the firm skin and sighed contentedly.

Nicholas released the frog closure at her waist and removed the velvet gown. Reaching around her, he loosened the laces down the back of her kirtle and pulled it away. He removed the bodkins from her hair and let her tresses tumble free to her hips. "It's like a waterfall of gold," he said as he stroked her skein of hair. "Have you used these silken strands as a witch to bind up my heart? In truth I've not looked at another woman since I saw you in your wedding finery."

"No spells were needed, only my love. For caring for you as I do, could it help but breed more love?" She tiptoed and kissed him. "As we are, so we receive in return."

"Now you play the mystic. Is there no limit to the number of women I have married in this one body?" He loosened the ribbon at the neck of her chemise and let it drop to pool around her slim ankles.

Jessica untied the points that secured his nether-trunks and removed his shirt. Naked, they surveyed each other.

"How could I ever dream of any other man," she whispered, "when I have seen you thus? No man's jealousy has ever been more unfounded." Her earnest eyes told him she spoke the truth.

Nicholas stroked away the shimmering gold of her hair and let his fingers glide over her smooth skin. She stood motionless before him as his eyes drank their fill. His hand found her breast and teased the nipple of first one, then the other, to eager hardness.

Stepping closer, he let her breasts graze his chest as he bent to kiss her. She tilted her head up and her lips parted in welcome as her slender arms encircled his neck. His breath was warm on her cheek, and when he drew her to him, she sighed at the sensation of her flesh molding to his. For a long time he drank of her lips, until she felt dizzy from his nearness.

He led her to the bed in silence. The bedcovers had been folded back in preparation for the night by the maids. Jessica stepped onto the tapestried stool and sat on the bed while Nicholas went about the room extinguishing all the candles except the thick one beside the bed. Her hair draped over her breasts and onto her lap, giving her a most provocative concealment.

Nicholas climbed onto the billowing feather mattress and sat gazing at her. "Each time I come to you is like the first," he confessed softly. "I never tire of you or grow jaded with repetition. You are like many women all rolled into one."

"You taught me well," she answered. "I enjoy pleasing you and knowing that you will please me in return. How my mother could ever have referred to this as an onerous duty is beyond me."

"It's not like this with everyone. We are among the lucky ones. In faith, it's as if I've loved you forever."

"Perhaps we have. When I first saw you in the courtyard of Hargrove Castle, I somehow knew you. How else could I . . . ?" She broke off and her eyes grew round at what she had almost revealed.

"Have learned to love me?" he finished for her. "Once I had seen you I knew I could be happy with no one else."

"Kiss me," Jessica whispered. "Kiss me and hold me. Love me."

Nicholas drew her into his arms and cradled her against his chest. "Gladly, my lady." Again his lips covered hers and sent her soaring with need of him.

His fingers toyed with her breasts and urged her to greater heights.

Lying back on the feather pillows, Jessica moved against him, loving the feel of his manhood between their bodies as well as the sensations evoked by his fingers. Nicholas lowered his head, his lips replacing his hand as Jessica arched toward him with a moan of delight. His mouth and tongue sent hot flames racing through her. Soon her desire flared as brightly as St. John fires on the green.

She maneuvered herself so that he entered her effortlessly, and held herself still for a moment to enjoy the sensations of being filled by the man she loved. Then together they began moving in unison, their bodies tuned from other nights of remembered rapture.

In the candlelight she saw his face as ruggedly handsome as a fierce warrior of ancient Britain. His black eyes burned with desire for her and his hair fell forward in a crest of jet. His beard was as dark as the night against his bronzed skin. Hard muscles rippled and bunched in his shoulders as he loved her.

Wrapping her hair about him, she smoothed its glossy length over his taut back and arms. The urgency in his eyes deepened and a barbaric wildness thrilled her. Love of her made him gentle, but only to a degree. The idea of him ravishing her excited her even more.

Running her tongue enticingly over her upper lip, Jessica met his gaze with a challenge as old as mankind. Take me, her proud eyes dared. Match my fire with your own.

Nicholas read her look with primordial instinct and his strokes became quicker, harder. She lifted herself to brand her lips against his, and moved in excited response to his thrusts. With a lithe move Nicholas rolled over, carrying her with him. Jessica sat back, her desire for him racing within her. When her hair threatened to obscure her breasts, Nicholas brushed it savagely aside and wound it about his fist. His eyes devoured the rocking motion of her full breasts, and Jessica arched her back to tease him to greater heat.

Then, bending forward, she licked his hard nipples and scraped the tips of her nails tantalizingly over his rib cage. Taking his flesh into her mouth, she nipped him in love bites. Nicholas made a growling moan of ecstasy and rolled her beneath him.

Their eyes met and locked as sweat gleamed over their bodies. Harder and almost desperately they gave and received love. All at once, Jessica felt the surge that announced her completion. She fought it, trying to draw out the pleasure until she could bear it no longer.

Unbidden a cry escaped her lips and fulfillment crashed around and through her, hurling her to heights that were all but unbearable. Her completion triggered Nicholas' own, and he groaned with pleasure as his body matched and soared with hers. For what could have been an eternity or mere moments, they were aware only of each other and the overwhelming sense of their coming together as one.

Gradually the earth-shattering pulsations mellowed to a satisfied afterglow, and Nicholas rolled to his side, one leg resting over her hips to keep them together for as long as possible. Her breath still coming quickly, Jessica studied his face. Her love and determination were strengthened. No matter who was his legal wife, she would never give him up. Not even if it meant living in a cottage as his leman.

She was his in all the ways she could give herself to a man, and she felt an answering chord within him.

"Always remember I love you," she whispered. "Never, never forget it." Her eyes searched his for reassurance.

"Never," he murmured happily. "I will always love you, Madeline."

He didn't notice the saddened hurt that unwillingly sprang to her eyes as he cradled her head in the curve of his shoulder.

19

WILHELMINA SMILED AT Jessica as the last of the Clayborne linens were loaded onto the cart. "You have made our visit most enjoyable," she said as she took Jessica's hand. "Lord Nicholas is very fortunate in his choice of wife."

"I wish I could prevail upon you to stay longer. I feel we have scarce been able to visit, and now you are leaving."

Lowell came up to them in time to hear the last exchange and put his arm around his wife's waist. "Wilhelmina is like all mothers. Our brood drives her to distraction when they are underfoot, yet she cannot bear to be away from them. Even though her widowed aunt is in attendance to see that the children are well cared for, Wilhelmina is certain they are being starved or neglected if she isn't there."

Defending herself, Wilhelmina said to Jessica, "You'll see how it is when you have a babe of your own." A soft pride of motherhood crept into her pale eyes. "I've never been the sort of mother to hand a child of mine to some stranger to wet-nurse and not see it again for years. Nor is Lowell so cool a father, if the truth were known."

Jessica hugged her new friend. "God willing, I hope to know that soon for myself. Mayhap someday our babes will play together." She had recent reasons to hope that she might be carrying Nicholas' child, though it was too soon to know for certain. This gave her all the more reason to be quickly rid of Madeline.

After Nicholas had examined the packhorses to see that the loads were distributed properly, he walked over to join his wife and friends and slapped Lowell across the shoulder. "Take good care of your lady wife," he teased. "You're not likely to find another woman as good as Lady Wilhelmina. Tell my godsons that I send my love and that we hope to visit them soon."

"Our Hal will be as pleased to see you as we will be," Lowell assured him. "He and young Will were sorely vexed that they couldn't come with us."

"It's a long road for such young travelers," Nicholas agreed. "But assure them that we will come soon for a visit."

"Before Lammas," Wilhelmina urged. "I know how busy you'll be once the celebration of the beginning of harvest is over."

"We will visit before Lammas," Jessica promised. Surely by then she would have Madeline back with their parents or somehow under control. Also she would know for certain if she carried a babe. She put her hand in Nicholas' and imagined how pleased he would be when she told him.

Nicholas glanced past the milling retainers and horses to where a servant stood talking to the castle's blacksmith. Then he looked again. That was the same servant he had told Thomas to send to the

Queen with news of the attempt on his life. The man could never have traveled to Hampton Court and back in this length of time, nor would he have arrived without telling Nicholas of the outcome. A dark suspicion awoke in Nicholas and he looked over to where his brother was lounging against the stone wall watching Jessica, as usual.

Lowell led Wilhelmina to his white German horse. He mounted, then reached down to lift her up behind him in the pillion saddle. Wilhelmina waved and blew Jessica a kiss as Lowell reined the horse about. "Before Lammas, remember!" she called out.

"I'll not forget," Jessica replied with a wave. Although she had not wanted one of her mother's gentlewomen as a companion—who would recognize her in time and tell Nicholas—Jessica had been lonely for the sort of talk and gossip one woman would exchange with another.

She and Nicholas watched until the entourage was on its way; then he turned toward the castle. Jessica hung back. "I'll be in after a bit," she said. "I want to get some air." Tiptoeing, she kissed him and walked away toward the herb gardens.

The sun was warm, and while clouds were gathering beyond the far wheatfield, it would be several hours before rain was threatening. Larks skipped above the fields and yellow butterflies hovered over the rows of thyme and basil. Jessica decided to go for a ride.

She went to the stable and had the boy saddle her jennet. The horse whickered softly as she mounted from the block and reined him from the barn to the sunlight. In the past, Jessica had always found some respite from her problems by riding until her thoughts crystallized and she gained perspective. She nudged the horse into a canter and headed for the park, hoping that would happen now.

Tall lime trees bordered the riding path and ancient oaks and lindens with emerald-mossed trunks grew in the forest. The herd of fat white sheep kept the green carpet of grasses well-clipped. The thick leaves overhead dappled sunlight onto Jessica and her mount.

She had to tell Nicholas about Madeline. At every servant's entrance since her sister had arrived, at every message whispered discreetly to Nicholas, Jessica felt the dread of discovery. To hide Madeline in the solar at all had been foolhardy. To try to keep her there until she spontaneously decided to leave was absurd. Madeline was too single-minded to flit away, especially now that she wanted to become Countess of Wyndfell and take her place as Nicholas' wife. To expect her to agree to return to Hargrove Castle was unlikely as well. Jessica cursed herself for her shortsightedness. No, the only solution was to tell Nicholas. But how?

As she rode, Jessica tried several scenarios, none of which seemed likely to work out in her favor. The main problem was her uncertainty as to whether or not she was his wife by virtue of having lived with him, or if she had merely acted as Madeline's proxy. She might even be subject to some awful punishment for having occupied his bed, if he was really married to Madeline. She had no desire to face either branding or imprisonment.

A movement behind her caught her eye. Thomas was riding after her. The last thing Jessica wanted was an unchaperoned ride with Thomas. If Nicholas saw him out here with her, he would be furious. Besides, Jessica wanted to be alone.

She reined her horse toward the deeper woods. A

mossy log in a nest of ferns barred the way, but she knew her horse could jump it. As she signaled the horse, a fox suddenly darted out of the ferns and between the horse's legs. The large animal reared and plunged to one side. Jessica was caught unaware and cried out as she felt the horse leap from under her. She fell to the ground and then felt nothing.

Nicholas was in his closet finishing up some bookwork. He was experimenting with a new strain of barley and was recording its progress when Sir Richard Norwood came to the door. At his knock, Nicholas looked up from his papers. "Yes?"

"Pardon me for interrupting you," Richard said, "but a matter has come to my attention and I thought you should be told at once."

"What is it?"

"The constable's boy was by here, and he told me of a murder in the next parish."

"Do you mean Sir Raymond Chadwick? I know of that."

"No, my lord. I mean Sir James Swineford."

"Swineford!"

"Yes, my lord. He was murdered by a servant three days ago, it seems. The lad was vague, but I assume there is some reason to wonder if the man they are holding was indeed guilty. A woman is also missing. She was the wife of Sir Raymond and was also Swineford's leman."

"I didn't know Sir Raymond was married."

The steward shrugged. "Neither did I. Nor did anyone suspect he had connections at Pritchard Hall, for that matter."

"No doubt she is dead too," Nicholas surmised.

"It seems likely. That's why there is doubt about the servant being the killer, for he was taken at the scene. The constable of that parish seems to think the real murderer killed Swineford first, then later abducted his leman and killed her, as well, and hid her body before leaving for some other part of the country."

"One can only hope that he is taken soon. Swineford is dead! I never expected that." Nicholas stood up and went to the window. "Somehow one doesn't expect one's enemy to be swept away like this. For years I've wondered about Swineford's next move and tried to outguess him." He turned back to his steward. "There's no doubt?"

"None at all."

"This puts a different cap on matters. Rather than Swineford taking Wyndfell, I may buy Pritchard Hall. Look into it, Richard. Oh, and by the way. I saw Ben Watson in the courtyard at the smithy. Send him up, please."

When Sir Richard left, Nicholas crossed his arms over his chest and gazed out the window. What a strange coincidence, he pondered. First Raymond, now Swineford, murdered. And likely this woman they had shared, whoever she was. With a question in his mind as to whether the killer had indeed left the area, Nicholas decided to increase the guard on the gates.

"You sent for me, my lord?" a gravelly voice sounded from the doorway.

"Yes, Ben. I see you've returned. Why did you not report back to me, and how did you go to court and return so quickly?"

The man rumpled his wool cap and frowned in puzzlement. "Return, my lord? I've not been gone."

"Did Master Thomas not send you to Hampton Court with a message to the queen?" Nicholas countered.

"He never did that. I've been here since we brought your bride back from Hargrove Castle."

"Thomas never sent you?"

"No, my lord, and I'll say it again. To Hampton Court, you say? I'll be on my way there now, if you'll give me the message."

"Never mind, Ben." He looked back out the window and saw Thomas riding over the green toward the park. "You may go."

The man bowed and left. Nicholas scowled as his brother rode blithely into the sheltering trees. Grimly he strode from the closet and down the curving stone steps. As he went to the stables his temper rose. His brother had not done his bidding, and that bothered Nicholas. Had Swineford not met an untimely end, he might have made another attempt on Nicholas' life, thinking that the first attempt had not been attributed to him. The tainted canary wine had killed a servant instead of him but only by a stroke of fate. Thomas knew this as well as did Nicholas.

Quickly his horse was saddled and Nicholas set him toward the park. Thomas had some explaining to do, and his answers had better be convincing.

After a short ride, he spotted Thomas' horse, grazing with Jessica's jennet, their reins trailing in the grass. Anger flared even higher as Nicholas realized Jessica and Thomas must be walking together nearby. Almost at once he saw them.

Jessica lay on the ground in a bed of ferns beside a fallen tree. Thomas was kneeling beside her. Jealousy raged within Nicholas as he saw that his brother was unlacing the bodice and waist of Jessica's kirtle.

Jessica's hands fluttered and she reached up toward Thomas' face, then fell back. With an animallike growl Nicholas leapt off his horse and grabbed Thomas by the neck of his jerkin. Hauling him back,

Nicholas drew back his fist to begin pummeling Thomas for his transgression.

"No, Nicholas!" Thomas cried out, shielding himself as he twisted in his brother's grasp. "'Tis not what you think! Lady Madeline has been hurt!"

Nicholas blinked as the words registered; then he roughly shoved Thomas out of the way. He knelt beside Jessica and lifted her head. "Are you hurt, love? What happened?"

"She fell. A fox startled her horse and she fell to the ground."

Nicholas tugged at the laces to give Jessica more room to breathe. She gasped in a lungful of air and turned from pale to pink as she began to regain consciousness.

Looking up, she saw that this time it was indeed Nicholas, and she threw her arms around him. "I fell," she mumbled. "A fox."

"Don't fret. Can you move your legs? Do you hurt anywhere?"

She gingerly moved her legs with no ill effects. "I hurt everywhere."

"You took a bad fall, but you'll be all right." He helped her sit up and lifted her onto the log. "Are you better now?"

"Yes." She rubbed her middle with the flat of her palm. Now that air was available to her, she was feeling better rapidly.

Nicholas stood and stormed over to Thomas. "And what, may I ask, were you doing following my wife to the woods?"

"I was merely riding!" he objected.

"When have you ever ridden in any direction but to the Bear and Bull?"

"Nicholas . . ." Jessica tried halfheartedly to object.

"And what of the message I told you to send to the queen?" Nicholas demanded of his brother.

"I sent Ben Watson, just as you said." Thomas stepped back warily.

"You did not! I just talked to him myself and you never spoke to him at all!"

"I saw no reason to," Thomas flared in his defense.

"No reason! I was almost murdered at my own table and you saw no reason to report it to the queen?" His voice had risen to a thunderous roar.

"I tested the other wines on a goat," Thomas lied. "They were perfectly all right."

"I ordered you to send a message to court!"

"I'm not one of the servants to be ordered around! I'm next in line for your title!" Thomas bit back his words as if he had already said too much.

"I am the master of this castle," Nicholas declared, jabbing his finger at Thomas. "I am the ruler of whoever lives within its walls. When I say go, I expect you to go; when I bid come, I expect you to come. Otherwise, leave Wyndfell!"

"You can't make me go. Father made us all agree that Wyndfell would be our home forever. Walter wouldn't have gone against Father's wishes."

"Walter is dead. Father is dead. If you wish to remain at Wyndfell, you will do as I say. And you will keep away from my wife!"

Thomas glanced at Jessica, who still looked shaken and disoriented. For a moment when he was loosening her clothing she had reached up as if she meant to embrace him. Sullenly he said, "You can't send me away. You need me to spy on Swineford."

"No, I don't."

"Don't be so cocksure, brother. I saw him myself not so long ago. He was on this side of the river and

I doubt not he is hatching some new plot to take Wyndfell."

"Another lie!"

"It's true, I swear it! I saw him . . . yesterday. Yes. Yes, that's when it was."

"Then you saw a ghost. He was killed two days before."

"Killed! Swineford?" Thomas gasped.

Jessica also caught her breath and stared fearfully at Nicholas. Her heart was pounding and she was feeling faint again.

"Aye. He was murdered by a servant, it appears. But you lied to me yet again!" Nicholas grabbed Thomas and hauled him nearer. "You lied about sending the message to Queen Elizabeth and you lied about seeing Swineford. Is there no truth in your mouth at all?"

Thomas glared at him but dared not speak.

Jessica pushed herself up from the log and went to Nicholas. "Please," she said urgently. "Will you help me mount my horse? I must go back and lie down. In truth I feel quite faint."

At once Nicholas released Thomas and put his arm around her. To Thomas he snapped, "Fetch the horses." At first he wondered if his brother would obey, but he glared at him until Thomas turned to do his bidding.

Nicholas bent to Jessica. "You will be all right, love. You've had the wind knocked from you, and when that happens, a person always feels hurt and dizzy." Awkwardly he helped her relace her dress.

Jessica's thoughts were jumbled as she tried to gain her balance. If she was with child, would the fall cause her to lose it? Again she rubbed her flat stomach. If there was a babe, it was still very tiny. Perhaps her body had cushioned it from injury. Frantically she went over the instructions she had gleaned from pregnant servants. She should go to bed at once and stay there at least until tomorrow. An infusion must be brewed of lady's slipper, vervain, motherwort, and mistletoe. She would privately ask one of the maids to prepare it, for she didn't want Nicholas to know she might be pregnant. To learn she was with child, then see her lose it, would be a harsh blow for him. Better that she should bear this alone, if worse came to worst.

He lifted her carefully onto her horse, and her troubled eyes met his. "Don't fret," he repeated. "You're strong and healthy. You'll feel better soon." Ignoring Thomas, he mounted and led her horse back toward the castle.

Jessica tried to keep the animal's gait from jostling her any more than could be helped. Worry brought a frown to her brow.

When she was safely in the big bed she shared with Nicholas, she heaved a sigh of relief. As yet there was no sign of her losing the baby. When Nicholas was out of earshot, Jessica motioned for Meg, one of her most trusted servants, and told her what herbs she needed. The older woman's eyes grew round, and she nodded hastily. Meg was known for her quiet nature, and while that made her a dull companion, Jessica could trust her not to start a rumor throughout the castle. She lay back and waited for the infusion.

With nothing else to occupy her mind but worry, Jessica's thoughts seemed to dwell on how fiercely Nicholas had attacked Thomas. If she had not been there, Jessica was certain Nicholas would have struck him. She covered her eyes tiredly with her fingers and tried to rub away her encroaching headache.

"Feeling bad still?" Nicholas asked.

Jessica jumped. She had thought she was alone. Silently she nodded.

He came to the bed and sat on the edge. Awkwardly he smoothed her hair back from her face. Like all men who are never ailing, he was embarrassed and ill-at-ease by someone who was. "You have no broken bones," he consoled her, "or you could never have ridden home and undressed."

"No, my bones are sound," she said gently. He had insisted on carrying her up the steps and all the way to their chamber.

"Bruises mend quickly."

"Don't worry about me." She touched his arm and ran her fingers over the velvet of his sleeve, feeling the minute gold embroidery.

"Worry? Never!" he bluffed. "You'll be sound after you've rested. But Thomas—now, there's another matter." He scowled in recollection. "Can you credit him lying to me like that? Lying!"

Jessica's heart sank. Had she not done far worse in marrying him under another's name!

"I can still scarce believe it. Why, anyone with half a brain would realize I might notice Ben Watson was still here and not on his way to court. And then to lie about seeing Swineford! He could gain nothing by that."

"He was afraid you would send him away," Jessica replied.

"He also knows how I feel about people who are false in their manner or speech." He shook his head dolefully. "I tell you true, Madeline. Of all the faults a person may have, I count lying among the worst. Before I became earl I had precious little, but"—he punctuated his words by raising his finger demonstratively—"I had my good word. Any man in the parish, or woman, or child either, could ask me something and depend upon my word. Whether it was the promise of a goose for a peasant's pot or time off to harvest a threatened crop. I never went back on my word."

"That's not quite the same as a lie," Jessica ventured cautiously. "At times a lie is necessary ... almost," she added. His face still bore that same intense expression.

"Never. If a person has something to say to me, let him say it straight out. I may not like it, but better to displease me for the moment than to tell me a lie. Once the falsehood is discovered, trust is broken forever." Again he shook his head. "Thomas is too much like Walter."

Jessica closed her eyes and felt the pain in her head ramp up to rival her aching body. She couldn't tell Nicholas. Not ever. If he was this upset over Thomas' lies, he would be a hundred times more enraged to find out he was married to the wrong woman!

Meg entered the room and brought the infusion. Silently she came to the bed and held the bowl to Jessica's lips.

"What's that?" Nicholas asked.

"A simple potion, my lord," Meg answered. "A remedy to relax my lady and take away her soreness." Her calm eyes met Jessica's.

"Good," he responded. "No need to continue to ache when there's a remedy to hand. Well, love, I'll leave you to your rest." He bent over to kiss her gently.

Jessica managed a smile. When he was gone, Meg settled on a stool in the candlelight and took up her task of spinning yarn from a basket of combed wool. Her fingers were deft and silent as she spun the weight that carried the tread and twisted it expertly through her fingers. In the distance Jessica could hear the murmur of servants talking as they went about their usual tasks. Now and then a snatch of song would drift up or a clatter as something was dropped or overturned.

She let her muscles relax and felt perspiration wet her brow as the vervain took effect. Now and then Meg would pause and come to wipe the sweat away with her gentle hands. Soon Jessica saw the room through a gauzy haze and welcomed the relief from worry as the other herbs lulled her further.

As night fell, Jessica whispered to Meg, "Will I lose it, do you think?"

Meg shook her head. "There's no signs of miscarriage yet, my lady. I think we've saved it."

"Good," she sighed with profound relief. "Old King Henry himself never wanted a child as much as I long for this one." If Nicholas sent her away, she thought, at least she would have his child.

20

MADELINE LIT A candle and placed it in the holder.
Jessica had not come up as she had promised, so
Madeline had decided that she had no reason to
honor her agreement to stay in the solar. She opened
the door and went out into the shadowy gallery. As
before, all the castle's people were asleep and a pall
of quiet had fallen over the old stones. Madeline
glided down the long room and made her way onto
the winding steps. Her candle threw a faint glow on
the walls but did nothing to dispel the darker gloom.
Behind Madeline, her shadow stretched grotesquely
as it followed her down the steps.

When she reached the hall, Madeline paused as
one of the servants stirred in his sleep. When the
rattle of various snores continued on, she crossed to
the other steps that led to the newer wing. Ascend-
ing slowly, she listened for any sounds that would
warn of someone still stirring, but the silence was
undisturbed.

In the corridor a few of the rush lamps still gut-
tered fitfully with low, sputtering sounds. Madeline
kept to the far wall and moved silently, her dark

garnet dress appearing almost black in the somber light.

She came to a door and pushed it open as quietly as she could. Her heart was hammering at her daring as she went into the room. It was a bedchamber not unlike any other. A chest stood at the foot of the bed and another beside the wall. A woman's clothing hung on pegs, and her shoes stood by the bed.

Madeline drew nearer. Lifting her candle, she studied the woman's sleeping features. She was somewhat older than Madeline and her nightcap hid her hair, but Madeline guessed it to be dark by the woman's eyebrows and olive skin. She thought of the people Jessica had mentioned when she had come to the solar that morning. She had been in a rush to see to her guests' departure, but she had sat for a while and talked about the people in the castle.

By Jessica's description, and the fact that the sleeping woman wasn't required to share a room, Madeline surmised this to be Meg, Jessica's most trusted servant. Madeline tilted her head to one side as she studied her. In her opinion the woman looked rather pedantic. She would replace her with someone more lively when she took over Wyndfell.

Madeline backed out and pulled the door shut. In the next room, two rows of cots lined the walls and the air stirred with feminine snores and measured breathing. She had no idea who these people might be, although she assumed they were Jessica's maids, as they were lodged so far from the kitchens. She made a mental note to ask Jessica for names when they next talked. Silently she gazed at the women, memorizing each quiet face. One had red hair, another a black braid, one a curious mole on her cheek, the next curly brown hair.

Once more Madeline backed out into the corridor.

She skipped the next few doors, assuming this to be the women's wing. Excitement was racing through her at the idea of seeing these people who had no idea she was there. A surge of power almost overwhelmed her. Because they were sleeping, the people were completely defenseless. Madeline had the option of life or death over them all.

Beyond the sharp angle in the corridor, Madeline stopped to study one of the doors. Judging by the brass fittings and ornate carving, she correctly identified the bedchamber of Jessica and Nicholas. Madeline put her hand on the handle and felt the intricate design etched there. Curiosity was strong. She had seen Nicholas only through her solar window, and he had been too far away for her to make out much of his features. He was tall, she had noticed, and straight of limb, with broad shoulders and a narrow waist. For a moment she considered going in and getting her first really close look at his face, but then thought better of it and moved away from the door. Jessica would also be there, and Jessica was a light sleeper.

In the adjoining wing, Madeline chose another door at random and opened it. As with the first room she had entered, this one was large enough for only a single occupant. She lifted her candle higher to spread the light and stepped silently into the room.

When the figure on the bed stirred, she froze. The light from her candle glowed on the whitewashed walls and bright window coverings. The figure stirred again, so she lifted her hand to shield the light. As she did, her skirt rustled on the floor.

The man sat up and reached for his dagger in one movement. "Who's there!" he growled.

Madeline stared at him, too startled to move or speak.

"My lady! Forgive me," he stammered as he recognized her in the candlelight. "I didn't hear you call to me. Is aught amiss?"

Quickly surmising that he mistook her for Jessica, Madeline smiled. This was an element she hadn't considered in her game. Closing the door behind her, she glided to the small chest beside the bed and put down the candle.

"My lady? What's wrong?" the man queried as he stared from Madeline to the closed door and back again.

"Nothing is wrong," she answered as she deliberately unclasped the waist closure of her belt and curled it onto the chest.

"Why are you here?" he asked in incredulous tones.

Madeline reached behind her and unlaced her kirtle. "I was lonely." She pulled the garment off her shoulders and let it drop to the floor.

"Lonely?" he repeated in a choked voice. "My lady, I don't understand."

"Don't you?" Her eyes glittered with excitement as she untied the ribbon of her chemise and let it fall onto her kirtle. "Do you really not understand?" She stood naked in the candlelight, her face taunting him and her voice seductive. Slowly she raised her hands and unpinned her hair, letting it cascade down her back and shoulders to sweep about her hips. Sensuously she ambled over to the bed.

The man was slightly past his prime, with gray threading his hair, but his body looked firm beneath the sheets he clutched to his chest. Madeline leaned over and unknotted his fingers from the bedclothes and drew them slowly away. She leered and pointed downward. "It would seem your body understands."

"Forgive me, my lady . . . I . . . I . . . This must be a dream!"

"If it pleases you to think so." She sat beside him and drew his hand to her breast.

He snatched it away as if he'd been burned. "My lady! You be married to Lord Nicholas!"

"Yes, I am your mistress. And I command you to make love to me." She edged closer and replaced his hand on her pouting breast. "I command that you take me as hard as possible. Do you understand me?" Only a mere breath separated her lips from his.

The man's eyes were round with stunned shock. He could only nod.

Madeline squeezed his fingers over her flesh and her voice took on a note of urgency. "Do it! Now!" she hissed.

The man swallowed nervously and pulled her to him, kissing her lightly at first but more deeply as he felt Madeline's urging response. Her tongue flickered across his and she moved his hand from her breast along the tantalizing line of her body until he clasped her buttock. She turned and lay on her back beside him, guiding him on top of her, urging him into her with a passion the man had never before seen in a woman. When her legs clasped around him, he could not contain himself and he reached fulfillment as quickly as did Madeline.

An hour later Madeline dressed silently, a look of satisfaction curving her lips. The man lay propped in his bed, regarding her with disbelief. "Forgive me, Lady Madeline, that I'm no longer a young man who might lust until dawn." His breath was coming quickly.

"You have served me well enough." She clasped her belt about her slender waist and looked back at the man. "What is your name?"

"My name? Surely you know my name as well as your own," he said.

"I want to hear you say it."

"Sir Oliver Braeburn," he replied. "The bailiff of Wyndfell."

"Such a masculine name. I but wanted to hear it from your lips."

"My lady," he said as she turned to go. "What of tomorrow?"

"What of it?" she asked, pausing at the door.

"How will I be able to see you and not give any suggestion of what we have been to one another?"

"You will find a way," Madeline assured him as she thought of Jessica. "As I will."

"Surely you'll not tell Lord Nicholas," he protested with fear edging his voice.

"No. Not as long as you please me in every way and whenever I command you." She reached for the door handle.

"Wait, my lady! Will you return tomorrow night?"

"Perhaps. Perhaps not." She thought of the rows of doors here in the men's wing. She wouldn't mind the tedious days when she could pass the nights with such variety. In fact, she might let Jessica stall for as long as she pleased. Holding the candle against any chance of drafts, Madeline left with no word of farewell.

The bailiff had not had Raymond's animal urge or Jamie's finesse, but the novelty of the encounter had satisfied her. Madeline strolled along the corridor counting doors and fantasizing what delights each might hold.

The corridor curved to follow Wyndfell's walls and she found herself in the new gallery. Here there were bright tapestries over the windows and even rugs scattered about like colorful oases on the bare stones. At both ends were large fireplaces of carved black marble, with an even larger one halfway down on the inner wall. The entire wall was hung with allegorical needlework of knights battling dragons, and unicorns beside beautiful maidens.

Since no rush lights were burning here, Madeline had to hold her candle as high as she could reach in order to illumine the room's lovely appointments. The ceiling was vaulted and whitewashed, with bright garlands of flowers painted on the ribs and supports. All in all, it was a very pleasant room, Madeline decided.

She heard a noise and turned to see two young maids standing in the doorway. For a long moment the women stared at each other across the length of the gallery, the maids' faces stretched in horror. Then Madeline had the presence of mind to pinch out her candle. At once she was enveloped in concealing darkness.

The maids shrieked and ran, almost extinguishing the candle they shared as they crowded through the door. Their screams could be heard trailing away as they ran for the security of their own room.

Madeline hurried through the door at the far end and down the corridor to the steps. Not hesitating to look back, she walked swiftly back to the old wing and the safety of the solar.

"We seen her, my lady," one of the maids repeated earnestly. "Me and Ada both did. As plain as day!"

"It was Lady Jane," Ada agreed almost in unison with her friend. "She was in the gallery."

"What were you doing there?" Jessica asked. "You and Nell know you are to be in your room at that time of night."

Nell and Ada exchanged glances. Neither was far from childhood, and both were adventurous by nature. "We had heard tales of Lady Jane walking in the gallery and we wanted to see for ourselves," Ada ventured.

"It were her! As big as life," Nell spoke up. "In a manner of speakin'."

Jessica looked at them in disbelief but didn't dispute their claim. She wasn't so sure they hadn't seen Jane's ghost. "Did she speak to you?"

"No, my lady. She was there, at the far end. Right near where she died."

"And she looked right at us. I thought I would die of fright, I did. Do you think she put the evil eye on us?"

"From all I've heard of Lady Jane, she was a gentle and godly woman," Jessica replied. "She would mean you no harm. If she were indeed a ghost."

"Lord, there be no doubt of that," Nell affirmed. "As we was looking right at her, she disappeared."

Ada nodded vigorously. "One minute she was there and the next she was gone!" she said as she snapped her fingers. "Just like that."

"I could have sworn I smelled brimstone," Nell said solemnly.

"Nonsense," Jessica said with a smile. "If it was the Lady Jane, you would likely have smelled incense before brimstone."

"All the same," Nell argued, "I know I seen her disappear. I did as sure as I'm standing here!"

"Me too!"

"Very well. I'll look into it," Jessica promised. "Now you girls get back to work. Nell, you're to air the linens. Ada, the silver needs polishing."

The girls bobbed curtsies and went to do as they were bid, still whispering between themselves. Jessica sighed. In an hour's time everyone in the castle would know Lady Jane's ghost had been sighted again.

With reluctant steps Jessica went to the gallery and

stood where the maids had been the night before. She knew where the apparition had been sighted, for on her arrival at Wyndfell, several of the maids had been all too eager to point out the exact spot of the murder. It was marked, they all agreed, by a curious brown stain that couldn't be removed no matter how hard it was scrubbed. Jessica thought the stain looked a great deal like a natural discoloration of the stone, but the maids had all assured her it was the martyred lady's blood.

Jessica gazed down the long room. Certainly there were no signs of anything out of place. She saw a dribble of wax dots beside her feet from where the maids had jostled their own candle, and wondered if more dots might be found where the ghost had appeared. She still wasn't so sure another maid had not also come to the gallery in hopes of adventure— titillating or otherwise.

She walked to the rust-hued stone at the room's far end and knelt. There were no wax drippings that she could see. Still, if the person holding the candle had not tipped it as the maids had, the holder would have caught the drippings.

"My lady," she heard a man say, and looked up to see Sir Oliver Braeburn, the bailiff, coming toward her.

She stood and waited for him to come nearer. "Yes?"

He grinned at her in an oddly embarrassed fashion and said, "I heard you had come to the gallery and thought I would see if you needed anything." He winked and grinned broader.

"No, I need nothing." She peered at him to see if he had something in his eye, for he winked again. "Tell me, Sir Oliver, is this where Lady Jane was killed?"

"Aye. Right on this spot. The bullet come through the window. We had to send clear to London to patch the missing pane." Again he winked.

Jessica looked away. Perhaps the man was developing a facial tic and couldn't help himself. "I suppose you have heard that the lady's ghost has been sighted here. Do you know anything about this?"

"I've heard the rumor," he said, puffing his chest out and flexing his shoulder muscles. "But you've naught to worry over. I can well protect you against any foe. Even a ghost."

"Yes," she murmured, wondering what had come over the usually taciturn bailiff. "That's very comforting."

"Anytime you need me, you just let me know. God's bones, but I feel good today." He winked again.

"Sir Oliver, do you have something in your eye?"

"No, my lady," he chuckled. "Well, I'll be about my business. Remember now. *Anytime* you need me, I'm right here and willing."

"That's nice. Thank you." Jessica stared after him as the man swaggered away. With a shrug, she went to see to her daily tasks. She wanted to finish early in time to visit with Madeline again before supper.

Jessica's day was busy with the chores involved in running a castle. One of the kitchen wenches had been caught tippling the best Madeira and had to be chastised. A second cook was needed, so Jessica had had to choose one from the two women who applied for the job, both of whom were yeomen's wives and known to have hard feelings between them. She selected the more forthright of the two, feeling the woman would likely be more honest. The new cook agreed to work for the usual nineteen shillings a year, plus six shillings and eight pence to buy a blue servant's dress to replace her yeoman's russet. For good measure, Jessica also agreed to give her two loaves of brown bread each week for her family. She knew she was being overly generous, but she expected efficient work in return. Besides, like all the kitchen help, the woman would have stolen the bread anyway.

A tinker arrived at the back gate and Jessica bargained with him over the repair of two kettles and a pot. She informed him his prices were outrageous, and he told her no tinker in all of Britain could weld a dam as he could. Such banter was expected on both sides, and both would have felt cheated without it. At last she agreed to let him mend the cookware.

By then the beggars had arrived for their daily handout of kitchen scraps. Jessica cast a practiced eye over the lot. Most were people from the roadways who lived entirely on charity, some were holy men and women who had no homes, and some were common stock who were too old, crippled, or lazy to work. The lazy ones she chased away. The others she fed.

As she returned to the kitchen, Jessica noticed the thyme and rosemary were about to bolt, so she ordered two of the kitchen wenches to pinch back the flower buds and gather the herbs for drying.

By the time she had a chance to steal away to the solar, she was bone-tired. Madeline was patiently waiting, her fingers busy with the cloth she was embroidering.

"Look, Jessica," she said sweetly. "Have I not improved on your design?"

"It's lovely. You always did do finer work than I." Jessica sat on a stool opposite her sister and relaxed somewhat. It was almost refreshing to be addressed by her own name for a change. "I'm sorry I was unable to come up before now. Much has been happening today. Were you bored?"

"No. I slept quite late, in fact." Madeline smiled secretively. "How are things about the castle today?"

"The same as usual. My maids are all in a dither because two girls claim to have seen a ghost in the gallery last night."

"Oh?" Madeline glanced sharply at Jessica, but pretended to be studying the faded unicorn picture on the wall.

"You know how maids gossip, and these two have just recently entered service. They will grow out of it in time."

"Tell me of your maids. What are their names and which one has the red hair?"

"Mab is the one with red hair, but she wasn't . . . Wait a moment. Mab didn't report seeing the ghost. Why do you ask about a maid with red hair? I've never mentioned her to you. Where did you see her?" Jessica asked in surprise.

"I glimpsed her from the window," Madeline lied smoothly. "Tell me about them, what they look like and all. Also your menservants. I find I have a curiosity about all the people here."

Reluctantly Jessica described a few of the key servants and how they could be recognized. After a pause, she cautiously asked, "Madeline, have you considered going back to Hargrove Castle?"

"No." She laughed as if the idea were ridiculous. "Why ever would I?"

"Mama and Papa must be frantic with worry over you. They came here searching for you not long after the wedding."

"For me or for you?"

"Does it matter? The point is, you should go back and let them see you are safe."

"Why should I? They would only rant at me for eloping so I did."

"You're a widow now. Papa could give you my dowry and arrange for another, more suitable marriage for you."

"With *your* dowry as bait? I could expect no more than a knight."

"You settled for a knight in Sir Raymond," Jessica argued, though she kept her temper well in check. To have engaged Madeline as she wanted to do would have been disastrous.

"That was different. Besides, I have a husband. Lord Nicholas Garrett."

"I've been thinking of that," Jessica bluffed. "I think I am his true wife. After all, it was I who consummated the marriage."

"Who bedded with him, you mean. Until he beds me, the marriage hasn't been consummated at all."

"Then he could have it annulled!"

"Who would believe him? I have been with a man and would swear it was Lord Nicholas."

With an effort Jessica stayed calm. "You must realize it would be better to return to our parents and take another husband."

"And spend my life with your name, as you must live with mine? No, thank you." She looked up from her sewing and turned a threatening glance on Jessica. "Think not to rid yourself of me, sister. I am the Countess of Wyndfell, and the countess I will be."

Jessica tightened her lips to bite back the retort she felt rising. Without another word, she left Madeline to her needlework.

Nicholas sat in his closet, listening to the third grievance of the day. The first had involved a dispute over what furrow belonged to whom in the common field, the next was a family dispute between a tenant farmer and the man's second son. Both had been fairly resolved. The third claimant, however, was another matter.

The man stood before Nicholas in a half-crouched position, refusing to meet Nicholas' eyes. As Nicholas had never engendered fear in his tenants, he studied the man's behavior with great interest and some concern. The farmer's two sons had come with him.

Nicholas riffled through his papers until he found the family of Rutledge. "You owe one sack of barley grain. That shouldn't be difficult for you. You have your four acres as well as the two north furrows on the common field."

"We can raise the sack," the younger son spoke up. "But this morning we was told we were short by half a sack last harvest. That's not possible."

"An entire half?" Nicholas questioned as he consulted his records. "There is no mention of that here. Who told you so?"

"Master Thomas, my lord."

The father grimaced and made a hushing noise as if he were in mortal fear.

"Thomas? It's not his duty to collect the rents."

"Not only that, he said we must pay it now," the elder son continued. "He said if we didn't pay, he would take our cow."

"It's an old cow," the man whined. "Not worth the bother, but she's all we have for milk and cheese."

"Did you tell Thomas that?"

"Aye. And look what he did," the son said, pulling aside his father's loose shirt. The man's shoulders and chest were covered with blackening bruises. "He fell on Pa and beat him with his riding crop."

Nicholas motioned to his man-at-arms by the door. "Get Thomas!"

When his brother entered the room, Nicholas exposed the older man's chest and shoulders and glared at Thomas. "Did you do this?"

Thomas glanced at the man and shrugged. "I may have."

With a growl, Nicholas tossed the man a gold noble. "Go buy yourself a better cow." The farmers bowed and left hastily before their lord could repent his generosity. Wheeling on Thomas, Nicholas said, "What is the meaning of this?"

"I wanted money. The allowance you give me doesn't cover my needs."

"How many needs would you cover with the sale of an old cow?"

"Enough for an evening's ale at the Bear and Bull. As the old man said, the cow was practically no good at all."

"You beat him over this?" Nicholas was enraged not only at the act but also at Thomas' attitude. "I know the Rutledge family. They are hard workers, all of them."

"You're too lax. They could well afford two sacks of barley. If it were me—"

"It's not you! Nor will it ever be! I have no intention of shooting myself as Walter did, nor am I likely to be poisoned now that Swineford lies in his grave." He advanced menacingly on Thomas. "And I have a healthy wife who will doubtless fill this castle with sons to inherit after me." His eyes dared Thomas to take the bait.

"Will she now! And what if she refuses? It's well known that an unwilling woman may birth only daughters or have no child at all."

"Madeline is far from unwilling," Nicholas assured him.

"Are you so sure?" Thomas asked, recalling how Jessica had momentarily reached up to him when she was dazed from her fall. "If I were you, I would ask if I could discern between duty and willingness."

In one movement Nicholas collared Thomas and shoved him against the wall. Almost nose to nose, he confronted his brother. "This is my wife you speak of," he forced out through his clenched teeth.

"A wife has strayed before now, given enough cause."

"Are you accusing Madeline of being unfaithful? Explain yourself."

"Must I? For most men a hint would be enough," Thomas jeered.

A red haze veiled Nicholas' brain and he struck out, his knuckles landing solidly on Thomas' jaw. Thomas cried out as he fell across the room. At once he stumbled to his feet and lunged at Nicholas, clawing and kicking when his brother sidestepped to avoid a blow.

Nicholas clenched his fists together and brought them down on Thomas' neck. The younger man dropped to the floor and lay there in a daze. As he shook his head to clear it, Nicholas yanked him to his feet. "You'd do well to pay heed, brother," he snarled as he shook Thomas roughly to get his attention. "Madeline is my wife. If you so much as blink at her or ever even suggest she is thinking of playing me false, you'll be the sorriest man in all of Britain. Now go! Leave my sight before my temper bests me. And also leave my tenants alone!" He thrust Thomas from the room.

Thomas fell heavily against the corridor wall as Nicholas slammed the door after him. With a murderous scowl, Thomas straightened and pulled his jerkin and cloak into order. Perhaps he had gone too far in flaunting Jessica's preference, but Nicholas had asked for it. He rubbed his aching neck and jaw as hatred for his brother blossomed to fill him.

He thought back to the vial of poison that had almost served to rid him of Nicholas. He dared not go back to the apothecary for more, but there were herbs that would do as well. Belladonna grew in the woodlands, and its cousin, bittersweet, as well. Wakerobin was rare in these parts, but could be found by one who was intent, as could fool's parsley. Any of them could rid him of Nicholas as effectively as an apothecary's vial.

Thomas strode angrily down the corridor and around the curve toward the gallery. At an open doorway he hesitated. Jessica sat there with her ladies, their needles flying in their never-ending needlework. As they were gossiping happily, none of them noticed his presence outside the door. Jessica was wearing the same jonquil-hued gown she had worn on her wedding day. Her hair was coiled in a coronet about her head and was interlaced with a strand of seed pearls. Although she smiled at one of the women's jests, Thomas didn't think she looked very happy.

A new thought occurred to him, and he pondered it. Why should he kill Nicholas right away? To steal his wife's love first would be sweet revenge. He imagined the agony his brother would go through as he saw Jessica's love for him diminish as she turned her allegiance to himself. To see Nicholas burn with jealousy would be satisfying indeed. Then when Jessica was thoroughly his own, Thomas could dispatch Nicholas at his leisure. With his most captivating smile, Thomas sauntered into the chamber.

21

MADELINE FOUND HERSELF looking forward to night-time. With the large number of men living within the walls of Wyndfell, she had a vast array of diversions. True, some of the chambers housed a man and his wife, but she soon learned ways of opening doors so silently and of shielding her candle in such a way that no one ever guessed she was there. Sometimes she just stood in a room and watched them sleep, feeling such a surge of power over them that it was almost sexual in its nature. Then she would search out a lone male and satisfy her lusts.

During the week, she learned a great deal about Wyndfell's occupants, but she had carefully avoided the master chamber, for if Jessica found out what she was doing, the game would be over.

Each night after she'd had her pleasure, Madeline would ask the man's name. None failed to answer, but some were very curious that she seemed to have forgotten. The following day, Madeline would manage to get information from Jessica about her latest conquest.

A broad grin spread on Madeline's face as she

recalled how easily Jessica had fallen into her plan. Just because she was staying in the solar all day, Jessica seemed to think she had control over her.

Through the black corridors, Madeline again roamed in search of the chosen door for the night. This had become a game of skill in which she tried not to open the same door twice. Thoughtfully she wandered down to the hall and out the main entry door. As she had expected, a light glowed from the gatehouse.

She crossed the cobblestone-paved courtyard and went to the small door at the base of the guard-house. Lifting her skirts, she climbed the stair to the apartment she knew must belong to the steward. Jessica had told her so much about Sir Richard Norwood that Madeline felt she already knew him, but not as well as she planned to before the night was over.

At the top of the stairs, Madeline put her hand on the latch, and with keen anticipation she opened the door. As she had surmised by the light, Richard was working over his books, as was his wont. When she stepped into the chamber, he looked up in startled surprise.

"Good evening, Sir Richard," she greeted. He looked exactly as Jessica had described him.

"My lady! What is it? Why are you abroad so late at night?"

"I saw your light and recalled that you frequently work late. I thought I would come out and give you company." With a confident smile she blew out her candle and set it beside his lamp.

"Is Lord Nicholas with you?" he asked as he remembered at last to rise in a proper show of respect.

"No, he isn't."

"This is rather irregular, my lady, if you'll pardon

me for saying so." Puzzlement furrowed his brow and crinkled the corners of his eyes. "I had never expected you to come out here alone and at this hour of the night."

"Hadn't you? Did you never wish that I might?" She strolled toward him, her movements as sensuously lithe as a great cat's.

Richard unconsciously stepped back a bit. "Lady Madeline, you have me at a disadvantage."

"Oh? You even call me by my proper name. No matter. Everyone here does."

He looked confused and put his chair between them in unconscious self-defense. "Everyone at Wyndfell and the village knows your name. I don't understand your words."

"The village," she mused aloud. There was a whole new scope of adventure for her. With her smile deepening, she fixed her gaze with hypnotic intenseness upon Richard and began to remove the pins from her hair.

"What are you doing!" he exclaimed.

"Come now, Sir Richard. You sound like an untried girl about to be raped. Surely you can see what I'm doing." Her fingers began to loosen the laces of her bodice.

Suddenly Richard shoved the chair away and closed the space between them. His fingers bit into her arms and Madeline cried out in surprise as he spun her away from him. "Whatever your intentions, my lady, you'll not vent them here, mistress of Wyndfell or not. Lord Nicholas is my friend as well as my master and I'll not cuckold him." Still holding her by one hand, he relit her candle and thrust it at her. By reflex, she took it. Richard pushed her unceremoniously through the door and slammed it behind her. With a thud, the bolt slammed shut on the inside.

Madeline scowled darkly. How dare he insult her like this? As soon as she took over as countess, she would see to it that Sir Richard Norwood was replaced and thrown out to fend on the roadway. For an instant she considered setting fire to his door to be rid of him right away, but the door was solid oak and there were no rushes to ignite. Her revenge would have to wait.

She went down the stairs and out into the courtyard. Opposite Richard's set of rooms and separated by the gate passage and the linking room above was the other side of the gatehouse, where guards were posted by day and by night. The narrow windows there were also lit.

Madeline glanced contemptuously at the bailiff's windows and crossed over to the guardroom tower. Here, too, the door was unbolted. With Sir James Swineford dead and the countryside at peace, almost no one bothered to latch or bolt his door.

The guard was lazing in one of the broad window seats, looking out at the moon-washed green beyond the arrow loop. When he saw Madeline enter, he leapt to his feet.

She slammed the door shut and hoped the sound carried across the way to Richard. Placing her candle on a shelf, she yanked the ribbon lacing of her bodice. The guard stared at her with his mouth gaping. "Strip!" she ordered. She was no longer in the mood for subtleties.

"My lady?" he asked in a stunned voice as she shucked off her gown.

"You heard me. Strip off your clothes and prove to me there is a man in this gatehouse."

Her tone gave him no choice but to obey, and as so many of the others had done, he did as he was told with little reluctance.

Later Madeline dressed and turned her back on the exhausted guard. She still burned due to her anger, but he had slaked all he was able. When she had received his name, she took her candle and went as abruptly as she had come, leaving him staring after her.

She noticed Richard's lights still glowed, although the hour was now quite late. Madeline tossed her head indignantly, and hoped he lay sleepless all night after his treatment of her.

Letting herself back into the hall, she headed for the buttery. Her blood still boiled as fiercely as if she had not been with a man at all, and she hoped a stiff draft or two of canary would dull her needs.

As the cavelike coolness of the buttery eased her fevered skin, Madeline went familiarly to the cask she knew to contain the wine she sought and drew herself a full tankard. As she raised it to her lips, she heard the sound of footsteps, and she froze.

The doors to the kitchen opened and a lanky man came stumbling down the steps, two or three at a time. When he saw Madeline, he abruptly stopped, almost falling over himself. Then he grinned, "Good evening, my lady. I see you also have a taste for the grape." The servant came the rest of the way into the cellar and brazenly sauntered toward her. "I had no idea that anyone came here at midnight except myself."

Madeline stared at him in astonishment due to his cheeky greeting. Then he drew near enough that she could smell the strong aroma of Madeira on his breath. "Methinks you have been here more than once this night."

"Aye. I confess that I have. My intended has told me she loves another and will marry him after Lent. I hoped to drown my sorrow in a tankard of Madeira, but I found it insufficient. Therefore, I am back for more."

"Welcome," she said. "Will you try the canary this time? I recommend it."

"Whatever you suggest, my lady. I'm likely dreaming this anyway." He laughed and caught the wine coming out of the spigot. "Who would believe the Countess Madeline comes tippling to the buttery after all are abed?"

"Perhaps," Madeline suggested with her curiously angelic smile, "there is an even better way to forget your false sweetheart." She stepped nearer and began to unlace his jerkin.

In frustration, Jessica quit trying to engage Madeline in conversation and put her embroidery to one side. "What ails you these days?"

As she had of late, Madeline smirked secretively and shrugged. "I feel too drowsy to talk."

"Are you not sleeping well? Perhaps I could somehow slip a newer cot up here or a different mattress."

"The cot is comfortable enough."

"No doubt it's the lack of exercise. I become sluggish if I lie about too much." She took up the sleeve she was embroidering and critically examined the stitches.

Madeline's grin broadened and her dimple appeared but she made no comment. "Tell me, sister, how goes it in the castle today?"

"I've not seen anyone but my maids—and Nicholas, of course. We usually breakfast in the anteroom adjoining our chamber."

"Then you've not seen Sir Richard this morning?"

"No. Why do you ask?"

"No reason. I know he is your steward and I assumed he would report to you every morning."

"He usually sees Nicholas before Nicholas rides out to the fields." She filled in the petals of a flower with pale pink silk thread. "I understand we have an unusually good crop of hay. Harvesting will start soon."

"Faith!" Madeline snorted. "You sound like a farmer's wife. Do you never go to London or have exciting visitors?"

"Wyndfell is so far from London, or even York," Jessica protested. "Besides, the castle and lands were allowed to run down under Nicholas' elder brother, and we have had to work very hard to bring it all into shape."

"How excessively dull," Madeline complained as she painstakingly drew her thread through the cloth.

Jessica looked up hopefully. If Madeline was bored, perhaps she would leave. "Matters were different at Hargrove Castle," she baited carefully. "Mama and Papa took you to London at least once a year. And there were balls and pageants to attend."

"When I take over as countess, I will see to it that Wyndfell becomes a place of gaiety. Since we are so far into the countryside, I will encourage others to prolong their visits, and Nicholas and I will travel extensively to relieve the boredom. Surely a competent steward could be found to manage during Nicholas' absences."

Jessica frowned at Madeline's familiarity in speaking of Nicholas. "Sir Richard is competent. It's just that Nicholas and I prefer to see to the management of our castle and lands ourselves."

"You link yourself all too easily with him—remember, he is *my* husband."

Standing abruptly, Jessica folded her embroidery and thrust it in her pocket. "I must go. I have many chores waiting for me."

Madeline grinned sardonically as if she knew her barbed comment was causing Jessica's abrupt departure.

Jessica left through the doorway that led to the guest wing. If anyone saw her there, she could excuse her presence more easily that if she were seen leaving by the old gallery steps. As she walked, she passed her hand over her stomach as she had so often of late. She had not often been troubled by morning sickness, and as yet no outward sign of the baby showed, but she was certain the babe was there. She was racked over whether or not to tell Nicholas. If she told him, he would be pleased to no end. Yet if he had no choice but to be married to Madeline, would she not run the risk of having to give up her child to them at birth, especially if it was a boy child—the all-important son and heir to Wyndfell. The idea of Madeline raising her child made Jessica shudder. On the other hand, she couldn't keep something so important from Nicholas. Not when he wanted a child so keenly. Never had she been so irresolute.

She went down to the courtyard and crossed to one of the workrooms that lined the walls of the enclosure. The looms' click-clack of industrious laborers greeted her. Wives and the older daughters of yeomen, villagers, and tenant farmers were hired to work here at weaving and spinning. For each weaver there were nine spinners, as it took many hands to supply the fast-shuttling looms with thread.

Jessica walked among the women, checking the uniformity of the threads and seeing that the wool had been cleanly carded. Now and then she gave a word of praise or encouragement, but her mind was elsewhere. At times she felt overwhelmed and smothered by the enormity of her problems. With a last perusal of the cloth being formed on the looms, she went back outside.

A man she vaguely recognized as one of the guardsmen was waiting for her. "I seen you go in, my lady, so I tarried here."

Jessica curiously looked up at him and paused to hear his business, but he only grinned down at her. "Yes?" she finally prompted.

"Nice day, ain't it?"

She glanced at the heavy sky. "There's rain in the offing."

"Aye, but it's still a good day. For me, that is. And for you, too, I wager." He lounged casually against the wall of the building and was speaking to her as if she were a kitchen wench.

"Have you no more to do than stand about? Surely you should be in the guardroom seeing to your duties." Her voice was coolly firm to put him back in his place. It would never do to have her servants become so familiar with her.

"As ye well know, I had guard duty last night." He grinned. "And will have tonight as well." His eyes traveled over her as if he knew how she looked undressed.

"You forget yourself!" Jessica snapped. "As for my knowledge of your duties, I never trouble myself with such matters. Furthermore, I—" She was about to give him a tongue-lashing that would put him back where he belonged, but just at that moment Sir Richard came up to her and interrupted.

"My lady, I must see you about something."

She frowned at him. Before this he had always been the picture of politeness. "Can you not see that I'm busy?"

Richard jerked his head in dismissal at the guardsman, and after another grin the man ambled away.

"What did you do that for?" she demanded. "The man was insolent and deserved my wrath."

"No doubt," Richard said in cold tones. "You forget, Lady Madeline, that his guardroom is just opposite my apartments and that I worked late last night."

"What does that have to do with anything? And for that matter, your own manners need tending."

"Be that as it may," he answered with barely controlled anger, "I have a paper here that Lord Nicholas bid me have you sign. It has to do with a portion of your dowry." He held out a sheet of heavy parchment and pointed at the lines in question.

"Yes, yes. I know all about those lands mentioned here. I will tell him of their location when he returns from the fields." She wrote her name with the quill he offered and pushed the paper back toward him. "What is happening today? Half the men are openly insolent to me. They were not acting thus last week. Is there some troublemaker stirring them to revolt?"

"Certainly not. No need to play the coy maid with me." Richard rolled up the parchment and tied it with a red riboon.

"Is that the way you speak to your mistress?" she demanded.

For a moment Richard glared at her openly, then bowed stiffly. "It was wrong of me to so address my *countess*." Turning on his heel, he strode away, leaving Jessica staring after him.

What was wrong with everyone? Even while she stood there in the courtyard, a lackey, the falconer, and the bailiff walked by, and each gave her a wide grin and a wink. Their impertinence was infuriating. When she scowled at them, they merely chuckled and went on their way.

She circled around to the stables and ordered her horse saddled. To her relief, the boy leapt to obey

her and made no untoward signs as had the men
who lodged within the castle proper. Again she recalled the rampant rumors of Lady Jane's ghost and
for a tremulous moment she wondered if a spell had
been cast over the castle's men. No witches had been
seen in the area, but the luckless Gypsies might have
had reason to curse Wyndfell because one of their
own had been taken into custody by the constable.
Shaking herself, she drew upon her store of logic
and dismissed such ideas as improbable.

When her horse was brought around, Jessica
mounted and rode away toward the fields. The first
she crossed lay fallow, for it had been planted the
previous two years and was now being rested. Only
grasses battled for supremacy with purple thistles,
yellow buttercups, and crimson-budded clover.

She rode through the wooden gate set in the hedgerow on the far side of the field and skirted the
waving sea of rye. Nicholas was not far away and was
gesturing as he conversed with his hayward and two
yeomen. When Jessica rode up, the farm hands, all
of them men from the village, nodded in deference
and wiped their woolen caps from their heads. She
acknowledged them with a smile and waited for Nicholas to finish his business with them.

When his orders for the day were assigned, Nicholas mounted his large bay and they rode away down
the hedgerow that divided the field from the grazing
common.

"I'm glad you rode out," Nicholas said when they
were out of the workers' earshot. "You have been so
busy of late that we scarce see each other except at
mealtimes and in our bedchamber."

"I know, love, and I'm sorry for it. Lately there is
so much that I need to do." She thought of Madeline

and knew she should be spending this time placating her, instead of riding and talking with Nicholas.

"You work too much. You should get out and enjoy the summer. Already Lammas grows near. Then harvest will soon be upon us, and when winter comes, it will be too cold to enjoy being outside."

"Will we be able to visit Sir Lowell and Lady Wilhelmina before then as we had planned?"

"Yes, nothing will stop us. I forget the quicker life you led at Hargrove Castle. You must find the quietness of Wyndfell very tedious."

"Not at all," she laughed wryly. She almost wished for the opportunity to be bored, for that would mean Madeline and the threat she posed were somehow vanquished.

Nicholas' face lit with pride as he pointed to the neighboring field of wheat. "See what a fine crop we have? I planted rivet wheat, as the soil appeared too light to support pollard, and it seems I was right."

"Perhaps next year we may grow barley there."

"This field has always yielded wheat. I never heard of anyone switching crops around like that."

"Whatever you say. I know nothing of farming." They rode for a while in silence broken only by the soft plod of their horses' hooves, distant birdsong, and the soughing whisper of wind through the grain.

"The ship I provisioned should come in soon," Nicholas said. "She has had ample time to reach the New World and return."

"Surely not so quickly as this."

"With favorable winds, it might be home soon. Let us hope the venture was as profitable as I expect it to be."

Again they rode companionably in silence. Then Jessica, as nonchalantly as possible, voiced the thought that had sent her out to be with him. "Nicholas, have you noticed anything odd about the servants?"

"Odd? In what way? I've heard no rumors of plague or pox in the parish."

"No, not a sickness, but rather a lack of respect." Her brow was creased in concern.

Nicholas reined in and studied her thoughtfully. "Has someone been rude to you?"

"No," she evaded, "not exactly. But there's a strange feeling going about."

"A feeling?"

"Oh, I can't explain it. Perhaps it's only me."

Nicholas dismounted and lifted Jessica off her horse. "It's not like you to imagine slights. Are you certain you are telling me everything?" He lifted her chin so that she had to meet his eyes. "I feel there is something you are keeping from me."

Jessica had never had a talent for lying, so she took a deep breath and divulged the only secret she dared share. "Nicholas, we are going to have a baby."

For a moment he merely stared at her as the words soaked in. Then a broad grin spread over his face. "A babe! You're certain?"

She nodded vigorously as tears filmed her eyes.

"A baby!" Nicholas grabbed her up and spun her about.

"Nicholas!" she gasped as she laughed. "Put me down!"

"Did I hurt you?" he demanded in quick concern. "Do you feel all right?"

"Yes, yes, I'm fine. I was thinking what the field workers would say."

"Who cares at a time like this? Besides, there is an entire field between us and them." He took her in his arms and stroked her shining hair. "You're positive, you say? When will it be born?"

"Next spring. I'll have to consult a midwife and an astrologer to know the date more closely. About snowmelt, I would guess."

"A baby," he marveled in a gentler voice. "Imagine us as parents. Will it be a boy, do you think? We need a son, you know."

"I have no idea," she answered as she fondly smiled.

"Or it might be a girl. I confess I have longed for a daughter as well. One who looks exactly as you."

Jessica shifted uncomfortably. "I hope all our children take after your looks," she said fervently. "I would prefer to birth Garretts rather than Hargroves." She had heard once that a tendency toward madness seemed to follow some families. She and Madeline had taken after her father's branch and now Madeline was growing as daft as old Leopold. But others scoffed at the idea that anything like disease or madness could possibly be handed down from parent to child. She hoped the later line of thought proved to be true.

Nicholas sat down in the waving wheat and pulled her to his side. Experimentally he ran his hand over her slender waist. "There's no sign yet."

"It's too early. Just wait a few months and you'll see change enough."

"There will be no lacing until after the baby is born," he told her sternly.

"No lacing?" she laughed. "I'll look like a farmer's wife."

"The lower-class women have babies easily, while ladies of rank sometimes have great difficulties. Mayhap the reason is lacings."

"That seems rather farfetched."

"Nevertheless, I insist upon it. Promise me."

"Very well. Once the babe starts to show, I will

leave off my lacings. But don't be surprised when none of my gowns fits."

"I will hire a new seamstress."

"You're so good to me."

"I love you," he replied gruffly. "Someone has to take care of you. Otherwise you'd cinch yourself in until the babe had no room to grow. We want lusty children, not puling weaklings."

"I have a feeling any babe of ours will be lusty enough to satisfy any father."

He laid her back in the waving wheat and fit his long body beside her. "I so love you," he said seriously. "I couldn't bear to lose you."

"Do you truly mean that?" she whispered as she searched his dark eyes.

"Of course I mean it. I would rather have you than any babe."

She knew how important he thought it was to have an heir and how much he longed to fill Wyndfell with children. "In truth, you must indeed love me dearly."

"More than you will ever know. Had I seen you in a crowd, I would have picked you for my own. I think my heart somehow knew you before we met. Is that possible?"

"The astrologers would tell us so. I feel the same way about you." She pillowed her head on his arm and traced the line of his beard with her fingertips. "I want to give you a son." Then she remembered that to do so might mean never seeing that child grow up. "Nicholas, if aught should ever come between us, you'd not send me far away, would you?"

"I would never send you further than the next room," he said as he smiled at what he believed to be the foolish fancy of a breeding woman. "And even then, I doubt you'd go. You have a rare gift for not heeding my commands."

This was as close as she dared come to getting reassurance, so she simply returned his smile. "When all your servants desert you and you are unable to see to your own needs, then will I fetch for you. In the meantime, you must resolve yourself to my disobedience."

"I find it a remarkably light lask," he admitted. "You are nothing like I would have expected you to be, but I find the surprise rewarding." To tease her, he added, "Now that I am accustomed to it."

Jessica ruffled his thick hair playfully. "You would soon have detested a mealymouthed wench."

"No doubt you're right"—he grinned—"but at times I wonder."

Jessica swatted him, and he grabbed her wrist to pin her arms to either side. "You're saucy for a mother-to-be," he observed. "I had thought such a condition would calm you down, rather than the opposite." Laughter sparkled in his eyes, though he kept his voice mildly reproving.

"Very well," she said in remarkably meek tones. "I will become as you wish—docile and fully obedient."

"Well spoken, love. Now give me a kiss."

Jessica complied, putting no fire or sensuality into her actions. Nicholas drew back with a frown, then saw her mischievous eyes.

"Insolent wench! Do you dare taunt your lord husband?"

"I?" she asked in thickly coated innocence. "I but did as you told me."

He made a growling sound and swatted her on her buttocks through the many layers of cloth. "You have made your point. A fainthearted lass would warm no man's arms."

"See? I told you so." She wrapped her arms about his neck and kissed him exuberantly.

"But in the hall, one might not be so bad," he said with pretended consideration.

Jessica rolled him over and swung her leg over his middle to sit astride him. Placing her hands on his chest, she said, "Take that back, my lord, or you may get what you wish for and learn you don't want that, either."

He drew her down so that she lay upon him. "Nay, love. I'd not change you. As much as you sometimes try my patience, I find you are worth it." Before she could object, he sealed her lips with his.

Jessica felt the familiar swirl that his kisses always engendered. Love for him swelled within her and she returned his kisses with growing passion. The warm sun enveloped them and the sweet scent of wheat encircled them as their embrace became more heated.

"Have we ever made love in a wheatfield?" Nicholas murmured in her ear.

"You cannot remember and must ask?" she chided, then seriously added, "We couldn't possibly. The workers."

"They have been sent to the rye field for the day. We're alone." He ran the tip of his tongue over the curve of her ear.

Jessica murmured happily and began to help him undress. "Then I suppose you might convince me."

With a chuckle, Nicholas began unlacing her kirtle. In moments the sun washed over their naked bodies as they lay on a pallet of discarded clothing. Nicholas broke off a stalk of wheat and drew the green bead over her tender skin. Jessica laughed and wriggled as he stroked the sensitive spot on her neck and ribs, then lay still and savored the sensation as he drew it in ever-diminishing circles around her nipple.

Nicholas tossed away the grain and his mouth fastened upon her luscious breast as Jessica arched toward him with a sigh of desire. Already her nipples were turgid, and as his tongue and teeth brought them to tight buds of passion, she felt a surge of ecstasy.

The wind played over their skin, adding a new sensation to their loving. Jessica threaded her fingers in his ruffling hair and guided his lips to the parts of her that ached for his caress. He put his hand beneath her waist and lifted her in an arch to give him better access to her twin treasures. Jessica felt as if molten flames were glowing throughout her body and centering deep in her womanhood.

When he entered her, she murmured with pleasure. Together they urged each other to greater heights and more intense loving. At last neither could bear to wait any longer, and they soared together in love's release.

After a while the world reformed out of the golden cloud of afterlove and they gazed adoringly into the other's eyes. "I do love you most dearly," Nicholas vowed softly.

"And I love you," she whispered in return. Surely he would never send her away. Surely not.

22

MADELINE DRESSED HERSELF with care for her nocturnal games. Jessica had brought her two day dresses, but they were light-colored and Madeline preferred her own garnet velvet for concealment in the shadows. She consulted the small mirror she wore at her waist and concluded she looked as beautiful as ever. Pinching her cheeks to make them pinker, she left the solar.

By now the way was so familiar she hardly bothered to walk quietly or carefully. She knew the dank gallery carried no sound, nor did the curving steps. The hall was another matter, though, as its floor was strewn with rushes and the menservants who slept there. Though she had to thread her way with care to avoid stepping on the bodies, the crackling of the rushes from her footsteps was usually muffled by the men's incessant snores.

Since her encounter with the inquisitive maids in the gallery, she had avoided that room, lest others of the same ilk might again be watching for that ghost Jessica had mentioned. Also she had pretty well explored the wing where Nicholas and Jessica slept.

This night she chose to climb yet another flight of steps to see what she'd find. At the top she passed through a door and out onto the sentry walk. Because there was no threat of trouble, the wide walk was deserted. Parapets walled both sides, making a safe walkway from one section of the castle to another. Unlike Hargrove Castle, the walkway didn't require lead sheets to cover the floor, since the stones had been carefully laid so that they were smooth enough to walk upon without tripping.

A full moon sailed above the bank of clouds, casting them in a pale silver. The moonlight rimmed the castle and lands and gave off enough light to enable Madeline to find her way, even without a candle. She lifted her face and let the austere light illuminate her features. Moonlight caused madness, she had heard, and she wondered briefly if that was what had happened to her Uncle Leopold. Strange, she mused, she hadn't thought of him in quite a long time. The recollection reminded her of Jessica. As she crossed the walkway high above the ground, Madeline wondered if perhaps her sister was dangerously mad yet. Whenever Jessica came to the solar, she seemed sane, but Madeline knew she might be smart enough to feign normalcy. For everyone's good as well as her own, Jessica needed to be locked away. Father had said so.

She reached the far tower and let herself into the sentry room, and without hesitation headed down the flight of steps there. At the bottom she looked around and then realized that this wing was almost like the other one, only reversed, like an image in a mirror. Madeline went to the nearest door and pushed it open.

For an instant she thought she was face to face

with Nicholas. Then the man moved and she realized it must be his younger brother, Thomas.

"Madeline? Is that you?" he asked in amazement.

She nodded silently, her eyes glittering in the candlelight.

"Does anyone know you're here? No one saw you?"

Slowly she shook her head.

Thomas came to her and closed the door to shut out the castle and to close in their voices. He stared at her as if he could scarcely believe his good fortune.

"Are you surprised?"

"No. I've expected you."

She raised her arched brows in question.

"Every since your fall in the forest, I've expected you to come to me. I saw you reach up to me before weakness prevented you."

Madeline had no idea what he was talking about, but she smiled nevertheless. Perhaps Jessica had a game of her own going. "And now I'm here."

"I have a flagon of mead. May I pour you some? I fear there is only one cup, but we may share it. Surely honey wine will taste even sweeter with your lips upon my cup."

"What pretty words. One would think you were nurtured at court by your turn of phrase."

"No, I've never even been presented to the queen, curse my brothers. Walter was always too busy gaming to spare my expenses. Now Nicholas says we can't afford it. Someday, however, I will journey to London and try my fortune there. I have a talent for primero, you know."

"I didn't come her to discuss cards," Madeline said as she let down her golden hair.

Thomas swallowed and stared down at her. "If Nicholas ever found out . . ."

"I will never tell him. Will you?" Her eyes taunted him and she ran her pink tongue eagerly over her lips. Playing her suspicions, she added, "I know you have wanted me for ever so long."

"God's bones, yes!" His voice was thick with longing.

"Well," she said silkily as she began undressing, "I'm here and as hungry for you as you are for me."

Thomas didn't question her for fear of driving her away. Instead he pulled her to him and kissed her with bruising force. Madeline moved seductively against him and bit his lip as she chuckled throatily.

Dawn was spreading across the eastern sky when Madeline finally retraced her way over the sentry walk. A smile tilted her lips and her eyes were brilliant with satiation. Not since the early days with Raymond had she felt so nearly satisfied. Thomas was like an animal in bed and almost as unquenchable as herself. If his brother proved to be his equal or better, Madeline would greatly enjoy being a countess. The wife of one brother and the leman of the other. Between the Garrett men she hoped to at last quench the fires within herself. At least for a while.

When she reached the solar she disrobed and ran her hand over her still-tender flesh. Already a couple of faint bruises marked blue shadows on her breasts. She touched them with a fond recollection of her pleasure. Thomas was a forceful lover.

She poured water from her pitcher into the metal basin and slowly washed herself from head to foot. Today was going to be a turning point. She could feel it coursing through her. Being with Thomas had strengthened her. Now that she had made contact with a family member and her identity wasn't questioned, there was no need to remain in the solar.

When she dried herself on the linen towel, she put

on the clean chemise and lay down on the cot. Plans were bubbling through her head, and after a bit of consideration, she chose one to follow.

Jessica was more reluctant than usual to visit Madeline. Twice she started to go to the solar, but both times she stopped. A nameless dread filled her whenever she considered climbing the steps. As far as she knew, her fears were unfounded. Madeline had been very biddable all along, and while she still refused to leave, she also seemed content to stay in her repository.

Not for the first time, Jessica wished she had gone to Nicholas with the truth as soon as Madeline had arrived. Covering her sister's presence made her seem guilty of even more than she really was. Now, however, Madeline had been so long in the solar that Jessica was afraid to tell him. And since he was pleased about their coming baby, she had no real fears that he would send her away. If worse came to worst, he would install her in a house somewhere— maybe Pritchard Hall, which he was buying—and see her as often as possible. She would rather live in Wyndfell as his wife, but she would bear the distance in order to see him at all.

Jessica crossed the hall and absently paused to stroke the head of the large dog that padded after her. The lurcher had singled her out for his affections and of late went with her everywhere.

She gazed out the window toward the gardens. Four men worked on the tennis court, trimming the grass and stringing the rope to quivering tautness. Nicholas and Sir Richard had planned a game for the following day. Both preferred to eschew rackets and play barehanded, so they were an even match. Jessica always enjoyed watching the sport, but she still wondered at Richard's unreasonable animosity.

Especially since he was the soul of courtesy in front of Nicholas.

With a sigh she tried to accept the fact that he simple didn't like her. In a more populated area, where he would be a steward and nothing else, she could have overlooked this, but here in the country, Richard was also Nicholas' friend. She didn't want to be the cause of a rift between them. She thought longingly for a moment of the iron-clad hierarchy of Castle Hargrove, where a steward was a steward and nothing more.

Nicholas had ridden to the larger town of Wakefield to hire harvesters for the coming season and would be gone until near dark. Jessica had missed him all day. While he was usually in the fields or down at the village, she knew he was nearby, and he always managed to return and eat dinner with her. Today she had eaten alone in her parlor and had felt guilty that she wasn't amusing Madeline while she had so much unsupervised time.

All afternoon Jessica had managed to stay busy and had almost convinced herself that this necessary activity was the reason she was avoiding the solar. At last, however, the sun dipped toward the tops of the beech woods and she could delay her visit no longer.

From the kitchen, Jessica stole an ample supply of food, which she wrapped in a linen towel. She had become quite adept at the theft of food lately. Anyone who might have seen her evidently assumed she was taking it to some farmhouse where there was sickness. At any rate, no one ever mentioned her odd behavior.

Reluctantly she glanced around the empty hall to be certain no one was about, then climbed the steps. As she crossed the gallery, her courage flagged. A deep dread settled in her bones and made her reluctant to move forward. Jessica drew a deep breath and forced herself onward as she silently chided herself for paying heed to what must be merely the capriciousness of pregnancy.

She opened the solar and forced herself to look cheerful, though she didn't feel that way. "Madeline? Forgive me for being so late in coming." She glanced around at the empty room. A sinking sensation grew in the pit of her stomach. "Madeline?" she called uneasily.

Madeline stepped from behind the door and shoved Jessica as hard as she could. Jessica cried out and fell against the cot. Not waiting to see if her sister was hurt, Madeline ran out of the solar and slammed the door. Leaning her weight against it, she fumbled with the key.

Jessica staggered to her feet and ran across the room just as she heard the key grate in the lock. Throwing her body against the unyielding door, she beat on the wood with her palms. "Madeline! Open this door at once!"

"I cannot do that, Jessica," Madeline replied in dulcet tones. "It's time for us to switch places."

"No!" Jessica tried to force reason back into her voice. Nothing else would ever convince Madeline to open the door. "You don't know enough about Wyndfell. Not yet. Open the door and I'll tell you what you need to know."

"Do you take me for a fool?" Madeline's sweetness was replaced by a sneer. "If I were to open the door, you'd run out and be gone. It might take hours for my servants to recapture you. Do you not recall the troubles we had when Leopold the Mad escaped betimes?"

"Let me out, Madeline!"

"I cannot. As it is, you have enjoyed more freedom than was your due. Do you not recall that our parents planned to shut you away after my wedding?"

"I'm not mad!"

"You must be," the sweet voice sounded again with the logic of insanity. "One of us is, according to the prophecy. And it certainly isn't me."

"Madeline!" Jessica clawed at the door but it wouldn't budge. "You can't leave me here! I'll starve!"

"Nonsense. I saw the bundle of food you carried. Eat sparingly. Who knows when I will be able to come back?" Her voice was drawing away.

"Wait! Don't leave me!"

"Good-bye, Jessica." Already Madeline's voice was faint, as if she were well down the gallery.

Jessica leaned faintly against the door and fought a rising wave of claustrophobia. She was locked in! All her old nightmares came crowding back to smother her. Frantically she rushed to the window and pushed aside the tapestry to gulp fresh air. When she stopped shaking, she knotted her fists on the deep stone window and leaned as far into the narrow opening as she could force herself. She could see the rolling green and the village and a portion of the rye field, but the courtyard was invisible. She reached her arm out and tried to stretch her hand past the wall, but the stones were much too thick.

Again panic threatened to engulf her, and she had to fight hard to overcome her hysteria. When she could control her voice she began to shout for help as loudly as she could. After a while, she was too hoarse to continue and had concluded that no one would be able to hear her anyway.

Numbly she sank to the floor and wrapped her arms about herself.

*   *   *

Madeline strolled through the castle, humming to herself. After seeing Wyndfell only in deep shadow and by the light of a single candle, she found daylight gave it the clarity of reality. The colors were much brighter than she had realized, especially in the winter parlor. She stood before the huge stained-glass window and stared at it in awe, as prisms of red, blue, and gold washed over her.

The ladies' parlor was also a surprise. What she had thought were dark stone walls were actually stones that had been painted a deep green with a scalloped gold border of flowers, stars, and angels up very near the ceiling. Everywhere she looked there were carvings or painted ornamentation, even in the long corridors. Oak paneling that Madeline had thought to be blackened from ancient lamp smoke proved to be the tint of well-waxed wood. Wyndfell was even more beautiful than she had believed.

Making her way back to the hall, Madeline looked up at the row of enemy pennants captured by Garrett ancestors in battles past. Some bore devices that labeled them as French or Spanish, and some were from other English lords. Judging by the number of gaudy colored banners, the Garretts were fierce fighters.

"Pardon, my lady," a woman said as Madeline backed down the room.

"Yes?" she said as she stared blankly for a moment.

"The kitchen wenches are through with gathering the candle stubs. Should I tell them to begin melting them down or do you wish to let it wait until the morning?"

"Let them begin now. An extra hour's work cannot harm them."

The woman gave her a surprised look, but Madeline ignored it. Kitchen servants were always lazy and Jessica was no doubt too lenient.

When she was again alone, Madeline strolled to the courtyard. In the distance, lightning flickered from a bank of sooty clouds; then Madeline heard the ominous boom of thunder. She shivered. Storms always made her so nervous. She looked toward the gatehouse, where the sky was still clear.

Sunset was casting a dull glow on the stones that reared high in Wyndfell's protection. Madeline frowned at their bare appearance. The first order she planned for the morrow would be to have the castle whitewashed. It was a disgrace to leave it unpainted, as if they couldn't afford its upkeep.

Her eyes fell on the suite of rooms occupied by Sir Richard. In the very near future she planned to have Nicholas hire a new steward—one who wasn't quite so full of himself.

She walked through the shady gatehouse and out onto the drawbridge. Hargrove Castle had had no moat, nor had Pritchard Hall. As she gazed down at the glassy water, she felt a dizzying sensation, as if her world had turned topsy-turvy. Then she righted herself and saw it was, after all, only a reflection. For a moment she imagined she had seen . . . What? Her death? Madeline shivered and moved away from the edge of the bridge. The shadowy, half-formed image she had thought she had seen was only a trick of the shifting twilight combined with her nervousness over the approaching storm.

Down the road she saw a group of riders cantering toward the castle. As she strained to make out if they were of Wyndfell or guests, the one in front waved. Automatically she lifted her hand in answer. It was Nicholas. Her breath quickened until her heart pounded in her throat. Here was her true test. If

Nicholas accepted her, none could gainsay her right as countess.

With her hands clasped nervously in front of her, Madeline waited on the bridge for the men. Only when they drew near enough for her to recognize both Nicholas and Richard did she retreat to the courtyard.

Nicholas dismounted as his horse was still clattering to a stop on the cobblestones, and caught Madeline up in a bear hug. "You'll never guess what I learned in Wakefield!"

"What?" Madeline gasped breathlessly as she saw Thomas' glowering face over Nicholas' shoulder.

"The ship is in! Even now it's anchored in London. And the holds are full to overflowing!" Again he spun her around. "I talked to a merchant who had the report by post. No doubt the messenger will reach us by tomorrow with all the details."

"How wonderful. What ship is that?"

Nicholas laughed as he said, "Have we so many that you lose count? *The* ship! The one I financed with the remains of your dowry. You see? I told you it was a wise gamble."

"Yes, my lord," she replied sweetly. "Now I remember."

"What's for supper? I wager I could eat a live boar. An inn's fare never compares with home."

Madeline tried to recall the aromas from the kitchen. "Cabbage with marrow, I think, and perhaps galantine pie. I've been so busy I haven't looked in on Cook."

"No matter. Whatever it is, I'm ready for it." He looked about in boisterous good humor. With news such as he had received he was even feeling more amiable toward Thomas. To show this he whacked his brother companionably on the back. "Even

Thomas enjoyed himself, though he tried to be a slugabed. We were near an hour late leaving here this morning." Nicholas had insisted Thomas accompany him rather than leave him with Jessica. "What say, Thomas? Was the ale not finer at Wakefield's Golden Ram than at the Bear and Bull?"

Thomas turned his eyes on Madeline and she blushed prettily before dropping her gaze in a show of great modesty. "I wager none is so good as the heady brew found at Wyndfell," Thomas vowed. Madeline blushed deeper.

Nicholas looked up at the lowering clouds. "It looks as if we reached Wyndfell just in time. We're in for a fierce storm."

Madeline followed his nod and stepped back as if the storm were a beast from which she wished to escape. "Mayhap it will blow around us," she said hopefully.

"Not a chance of it. We're in for a big one, and no doubt about it." He grinned at her and winked, for he knew his wife enjoyed, most of all, to make love during a storm. He had never seen her quake, not even when it seemed the walls must crack from the storm's raging. "I wager it will last the entire night by the looks of those clouds."

"Don't even think it." Madeline shuddered. "Come in, come in. What am I thinking of to leave you standing here with no cup of ale to greet you?"

As Nicholas stared after her, she hurried away to fetch him a tankard of Wyndfell's best ale. She gave it to him and he continued to stare for a moment, then threw back his head in a laugh. "By God's bones! You seem to have missed me greatly. Mayhap I should ride out every day."

Thomas scowled and took his own tankard from a servant that came in to serve them.

News of the master's arrival spread to the kitchens and the horn was sounded to announce the meal. Nicholas handed Madeline to the chair and sat on one side of her while Thomas took his usual place on her other side. The lurcher stepped toward her, stopped in confusion, and retreated to the other side of Nicholas.

Madeline looked down the two long tables that were set at right angles to the head table. Many of the men were familiar to her, though she had never seen them dressed and in the daylight. A couple of them grinned at her when Nicholas' head was turned, and one even dared to wink. Madeline lowered her lashes coquettishly. To see so many of her conquests eating at the same board thrilled her. Only one, Sir Richard Norwood, gave her a disapproving look. She ignored him completely.

When the first dish was served, a farsed pheasant stuffed with spiced apples and oats, the carver knelt to rear it, then placed a portion on their pewter plates. Madeline poked at the meat and said, "This fowl is baked dry. Can the cook do no better than this?"

The carver looked at her apprehensively. "I'll see that she is more careful, my lady."

"Do that." She flicked her fingers at him as if he were a fly.

Nicholas was looking at her in surprise. He had never heard her speak sharply to a servant. Perhaps she hadn't been feeling well, what with the growing babe and all.

The second course was to her liking, but the third one drew another frown. "The luce wafer is too heavy," Madeline complained as she tasted the fish cake. "And the cabbage with marrow was underdone."

"I thought it was delicious," Nicholas said as he

watched her with growing curiosity. "Mayhap it's due to your condition that the food tastes not to your liking."

At once her frown smoothed and she said in the most gentle of tones, "I know not of what you speak, my lord husband. I am not ailing." To Thomas she said, "Was the meal agreeable to you?"

Thomas, who was more accustomed to bare civility from the woman in front of her husband, nearly choked. "It was quite acceptable." He noticed Nicholas' darkening expression and hoped Madeline wouldn't give any sign of what had transpired between them the night before.

"Tell me, Thomas," she continued, "do you think you could best me at a game of trump? I fear primero has never been my game and I know of your expertise there."

As thunder sounded throughout the hall, Madeline looked around nervously. Ignoring the storm, Nicholas said, "I didn't know you enjoyed cards."

"Of course I do. If Thomas can't be persuaded, perhaps you will play me?"

"I had hoped to see an early bed," he said pointedly.

"With such a storm raging? I could never sleep." Lightning glared in the windows, and she took a quick gulp of Madeira. Nervousness was making her too talkative, but she couldn't seem to still her tongue.

"Sir Oliver," she addressed the man opposite Sir Richard, "was the pheasant too dry, do you think?"

The bailiff looked exceedingly uncomfortable at being singled out, and he muttered something no one heard or could understand.

"And you, Sir Richard?" she asked with a saccharine smile. "Was it to your liking? But no, I suppose you fancy your tastes are too refined for anything less than curried swan."

Nicholas stood abruptly and drew Madeline to her feet. "The wine seems to have gone to your head," he said in a low voice. "Let us retire to the parlor."

With a show of meekness, Madeline curtsied and preceded him out of the hall. As she passed the lurcher, the dog growled softly and padded away. Her curiously gliding walk scarcely made her skirt sway as she went to the winter parlor.

Nicholas opened a window and sat her on the window seat. She stood up as the thunder crashed and rain pelted against the glass and onto the sill.

"Breathe deeply," he suggested. "It will clear your head."

Realizing she had committed some blunder, Madeline fell back on her armor of feminine helplessness. "Forgive me, husband. I fear the wine has besotted me."

"Fret not. No harm was done. I do wonder though about your flirtation with Thomas. I wouldn't have thought you had drunk enough wine to render you so thoughtless."

Madeline had no idea how to answer this. From Thomas' words the night before she had assumed he and Jessica were quite close. Then in the courtyard Nicholas had acted as if Thomas were firmly in his good graces.

"I gather by your silence you are contrite. Nevertheless, be more careful in the future."

"I will," she promised. "Have I offended you in some other way? If you but tell me, I will go to any lengths to please you."

Nicholas was regarding her with a wary expression. "You would?"

"Of course. Are you not my lord and master? It is a husband's place to command and a wife's to obey."

"Perhaps you should breathe a bit more fresh air," he suggested.

"No, the storm frightens me," she said with wide eyes as lightning flared against the window and thunder immediately rattled the panes. "Dear husband, if it please you, close the window."

After a brief hesitation, Nicholas shut the window and latched it. He couldn't understand what was wrong with his wife. She was usually so fond of storms that he had teased her about being a fairy. Not only that, she was actually being subservient. After longing for exactly that on many occasions, Nicholas suddenly found he didn't care for it.

Before he could question her, Thomas joined them and took down from the mantel the silver bowl of dice and cards. "Are you still for a game of trump?" he asked her.

"Let's play gleek instead so we may all join in," Madeline suggested.

"Cards have never interested me," Nicholas said. He could have sworn she knew that after all he had told her of Walter's gambling. "Tables is my game."

"Very well." She took the backgammon board from its shelf and laid it upon the game table. "Where are the pieces?"

Silently Nicholas pulled open a drawer set in the table and began taking out round pieces of ivory and jade that matched the inlaid board. He was positive that she knew where the pieces were kept.

Madeline sat opposite and began setting up the board for the game. "I fear only two may play, Thomas," she apologized, "but draw up your stool and cheer us on."

Thomas looked as if that was the last thing he wanted, but he did as she suggested.

In no time Nicholas not only had won four games

in a row but also had gammoned her twice. Madeline couldn't have played worse if she had downed the entire vat of Madeira.

"The storm is lessening," he said. "It seems it will soon be over. Are you ready to go to our chamber?"

Madeline stifled a yawn behind her fingers. "Yes. I find I am amazingly tired tonight." When she smiled at Thomas, he shifted uncomfortably.

Nicholas took her hand when she offered it in a curiously formal gesture and led her from the room. "Did I not tell you to keep a distance with Thomas? What are you doing?"

"I was only being polite," she replied with innocently wide eyes. "Surely there is no harm in that." She batted her eyelashes at him winningly.

Nicholas watched her curiously as he followed her up the steps. When had his wife ever smiled with her lips closed? He vaguely remembered her doing that during her parents' visit, but never since. And hadn't her gait altered? She seemed to float as if on wheels.

She caught him trying to catch a glimpse of her feet, and he straightened as if he had been found in the wrong. When they reached the ornately carved door that led to their chamber, Madeline hesitated until Nicholas opened it for her. As she glided through the newly furnished antechamber, she looked about as if she were seeing it for the first time, though she said nothing.

The maids were turning back the covers and doing the last-minute chores before retiring. Madeline scarcely glanced at Meg and went instead to a large-boned woman who had recently been striving to supplant Jessica's favorite. As usual, Meg made no comment or small talk, but Nicholas saw she withdrew from the slight.

Madeline did not realize the slip in protocol she

had made. Her actions would lead anyone to think this servant was the one she always chose to loosen her laces.

Nicholas waved away his valet and pretended to be busy perusing a document as he watched Madeline. When she was undressed, she went to his chest, not hers, for her nightgown. Though she covered her mistake by pretending to see if his green jerkin had been folded away properly, he wasn't fooled. Nor did she know where to find her hairbrush. He could make no sense of this at all. She looked and sounded like his wife, yet everything else was altered.

When she was attired for the night and the maids had gone, he came to her and sat beside her on the bed. She had gone to the wrong side, he noticed. "What is wrong, sweetheart?" he asked with concern.

"Wrong?" she laughed. "Why, nothing at all."

He studied her face. The well-beloved features were the same. Her lips were as pink and her cheeks as creamy. Her eyes were the deep blue of cupid's flowers, but in them he saw no shadings of love such as he had come to expect. Rather, she was regarding him in an almost predatory fashion.

"Nothing is wrong?" he repeated.

"Not unless you consider that my husband is fully clothed and I am not," she lisped coyly.

Nicholas stared at her.

With a laugh, Madeline lay back on the billowing feather mattress. "In faith, this bed is comfortable." She sighed contentedly and thought of Jessica sleeping on the narrow cot in the solar. "Will you not undress?" She pouted prettily. "Do you need to be coaxed?"

As strange as it seemed, Nicholas felt extremely uneasy. His wife had never played the coy with him.

"Let me be your valet," Madeline suggested as she

slid off the bed and knelt at his feet. "But command me, my lord. I am yours."

Roughly Nicholas pulled her to her feet and against his body. He knotted his hand in her hair and stared at her before lowering his head to claim her lips.

Madeline made a purring sound and opened her mouth to thrust her tongue deep into his as she ground her lips against him in a hungry kiss.

Nicholas yanked her away and held her at arm's length. Then he thrust her from him and strode from the room. Whoever the woman was, she wasn't his wife! Yet all his senses told him she *had* to be. Who else could have that form and know the castle and its servants? Or did she? She had not known her way about her own bedchamber and had insulted Meg by taking her laces to another woman. Nor had she played tables with a competitive effort to win. Nicholas was certain this woman had let him triumph over her.

This woman? What was he thinking?

Not knowing what else to do, Nicholas went back downstairs and out into the rainy courtyard. Richard's light was still burning, so he crossed to the gatehouse and went up the stairs. To his surprise he found the door to Richard's antechamber locked. He beat upon it until Richard called out.

"It's me, Nicholas. Open up."

Richard opened the door and stepped back as Nicholas entered. He watched him as if he wasn't certain whether this visit pleased him or not.

"Have you taken to locking you door?" Nicholas teased his friend. "Are we at war and I wasn't told?"

"A mere precaution," the steward said warily. "What brings you out this soggy night?"

Nicholas surveyed the man as if he wasn't quite

sure how to answer. "Have you noticed aught odd about Lady Madeline?" he asked bluntly.

Richard looked away. "I know not what you mean," he replied stiffly.

"Don't give me that, man. You saw how she was at the table. Did something go awry while I was gone?"

"Not to my knowledge."

Nicholas sat on a chest and shook the raindrops from his hair. "I've known you a long time, Richard, and I've never had you lie to me before." His black eyes forced truth from the man. "What has happened?"

Richard drew a deep breath and let it out. "Your lady wife has been acting strangely for some time now," he hedged.

"In what way?" Nicholas' voice brooked no evasions.

"There's talk among the men," Richard said reluctantly.

"What sort of talk?"

"That she comes to their chambers at night," Richard blurted out.

Nicholas sprang up and grabbed him by the jerkin. "Who dares say this!" he growled. "Who spreads such lies about her?"

"It's true!" Richard shrugged free and retreated a few steps. "It's true, Nicholas. She came here as well."

"*Here?*"

Richard nodded. "That's why my door was locked. I had no wish to have to send her away again."

Nicholas let himself drop numbly back onto the chest. "How can this be true when she sleeps beside me every night?"

"Are you awake all night, every night, to prove this? Nay, don't glower at me so. If I were not a true friend, I'd not tell you such news."

"A friend or an enemy must bear news like this,"

Nicholas mused, "and you have never been my enemy."

"Nor will I ever be," Richard affirmed. "I know not what has happened, for she wasn't like this when she first came to Wyndfell."

"No, she wasn't. Tonight I saw a stranger garbed in my wife's flesh." Nicholas peered at his steward. "Could it be a sickness?"

"Perhaps one of the mind that will soon pass," Richard said hopefully. "I have heard of such."

"Let us pray this is the case. I love Madeline and would not lose her." He stood and left as abruptly as he had arrived. The rain enveloped him as he strode meaningfully across the courtyard. He would not lose her, he vowed as he mounted the steps of the castle. Somehow he would find a way to bring back the woman he loved. In the meantime, he couldn't quite bring himself to share their bed. He mounted the steps and turned down the corridor toward the guest chamber.

Alone in the abandoned solar, Jessica curled up on the narrow cot and tried to compose herself enough for sleep. At every sound of the sighing wind and at every furl of the tapestries, she thought of the ghostly monk and shuddered. Sleep was a long time in coming.

23

BY MORNING NICHOLAS still had not returned to the bedchamber and Madeline was miffed. She allowed the maids to dress her in Jessica's jonquil-hued kirtle and comb her hair into a thick coronet braid. As she had the night before, Madeline gave special attention to the maid she assumed to be Meg. The woman beamed under her good graces.

Leaving the maids to straighten her chamber, Madeline went in search of Nicholas. She was too proud to ask if anyone had seen him, for to do so might let on that he had slept elsewhere. She was filled with curiosity about his unexpected departure. Was this normal between Jessica and him? He appeared very masculine and had kissed her with great expertise at first, but it might be possible that he was the sort of man who preferred boys. She hoped not, for that would be a pity, indeed. At least she had Thomas to rely upon for sexual satisfaction, and all the men of Wyndfell for variety.

In the winter parlor she found Sir Richard waiting for her. In his hand he held a sheet of vellum. Before she had time to leave, he called out to her.

"Pardon, my lady." His eyes reflected his distaste. "Yesterday when I had you sign the paper dealing with your dowry lands, I omitted a sheet. Will you write your name here?" He held out the paper and a pen.

"Very well," she agreed with a sigh that indicated her displeasure with him. Putting the paper on the game table, she quickly wrote her name.

"Thank you," Richard said as he took the vellum and looked at her signature. His brow wrinkled noticeably.

"Is something amiss?" Madeline snapped impatiently.

"No. No, nothing at all." He rolled the paper and gave her a brief bow as he left the room.

"Stupid upstart," Madeline muttered beneath her breath. "I'll be glad to see the last of him."

An hour later she found Nicholas in the orchard, talking to the head gardener. As she waited impatiently for them to finish discussing the harvest of the pears, she looked about. The orchard was planted on the northeast side of the formal gardens as was common in order that it would serve as a windbreak for the fragile flowers. The paths between the trees were graveled and the grass about the trunks was neatly trimmed. Apples and pears abounded, along with a few walnut and hazelnut trees. The newly imported apricot, peach, and rare orange trees were closest to the flower garden, in a more sheltered spot.

All in all, Madeline approved of her new home, in spite of its lack of paint. The eldest brother might have let it fall on hard times as Swineford had said, but certainly Nicholas was recovering it well.

When the gardener tugged his cap respectfully

and left. Nicholas turned to her. "Good morning," he said warily.

Madeline put on her prettiest smile and said, "Good morning, my lord." She lowered her lashes before saying, "I missed you in my bed last night and wished you had seen fit to stay. No doubt you found solace where you usually do." She waited for him to affirm or deny her broad suggestion.

He stared at her for a long moment before speaking. "I slept in the guest chamber."

She shrugged. "A man has a right to a mistress, or several if he's of a mind. I don't question you. I only meant that I was lonely."

"Madeline, what's come over you?" His voice sounded strained and he looked as if he had had very little sleep.

"Why, nothing," she replied innocently. No doubt Jessica had railed at him for keeping a mistress, but Madeline was too smart for that. She fell in beside him, and they walked back through the garden.

She knew he was watching her from the corner of his eye, so she kept her gaze demurely downcast toward the ground the proper six paces ahead. As they rounded the sundial with its French inscription, Madeline looked up at Wyndfell. "Lord Nicholas, if it please you, I would like to have the castle stones whitewashed."

"You would?" he asked in surprise.

"I've not mentioned it before, but I have always liked a neat appearance in a castle. If we don't keep up Wyndfell, how can we expect our underlings to do the same for their cottages? The village could soon become a pigsty."

"You want to whitewash the castle," he repeated as if he had never heard of such a thing.

"Of course. All the better ones are, you know.

Why, London fairly gleams with the White Tower and Whitehall Palace. You can't imagine how impressive that is."

"You speak as if you've seen them firsthand."

"Well, I have," she laughed. "My father might have been only a country viscount, but we traveled frequently to London. I have an aunt who lives there. Surely I must have mentioned her."

"Yes, I think I recall your doing that," he said thoughtfully. "As for whitewashing Wyndfell, I thought you preferred the stones a natural color."

"Where would you get that idea?" She smiled up at him pleasantly, determined to patch up whatever rift kept him from her bed. Looking at the way he moved and how he watched her, she couldn't believe he would rather dally with boys.

"I'll consider it."

"Thank you, my lord." She tiptoed up and kissed him, keeping her lips demurely closed. "I must go back and see to the servants. If I don't stay after them they will do nothing at all." She turned and hurried away with her oddly sliding walk.

Nicholas rubbed his beard and stared after her. By morning he had almost convinced himself that he was being foolish in doubting her. After all, she was the perfect image of the woman he had lived with for months. Now he wasn't at all sure. Here in the sunlight, he noticed a minor difference in the curve of her cheek. Not one that an acquaintance might note, but one that he, as her lover, questioned. And there was an indefinable change in her eyes. The color and shape were the same, but the expression was altered. Until yesterday he had always had the sensation of losing himself in her eyes. Now they regarded him with the shallow gaze of a stranger.

Avoiding the castle, he circled around to the chapel

and went through it to the courtyard. He needed to talk to Richard.

He found the door to the steward's office open and went in. "She's not the same," he announced without preamble. "Could she be bewitched?"

"There are no sorcerers about that I've heard of, nor witches for that matter."

Nicholas sat on the chest and struck his leg with his fist. "I don't understand it. Surely no disease of the mind could strike so quickly. Do you suppose she's had a fall and hurt her head?"

"Not so that I am aware. According to the rumors, this change happened over a week ago. Her night wanderings, you know?" Richard said as delicately as possible.

"You need not remind me," Nicholas growled.

"Look at this. Yesterday I had her sign a paper dealing with the deposition of her dower lands. To-day I had her sign another." He handed the papers to Nicholas.

"So? I know she can sign her name and even read a bit. What of it?"

"Look at the signatures. One would never guess they were done by the same hand."

Nicholas stared at the papers. On one was the pointed script he had witnessed on their marriage certificate. The other was a childish scrawl with a blot of ink below it. "What can this mean?"

"I know not. Surely a disease of the mind would not be reflected in the handwriting so clearly. Or would it? I'm no physician and have no way of knowing."

Nicholas stood to go. "I will watch her closely and you do the same. Tell no one else of this until we unravel this coil."

Richard nodded. "You can trust me."

*   *   *

Madeline set the maids to work and approved the day's menu. She had the girl called Ada distribute the scraps to the poor at the gate, and then Madeline went in search of Thomas.

He was in the winter parlor, tossing dice in a bored manner. When she came in, he frowned at her petulantly. "You didn't come to me last night. I expected you."

"I wasn't able." She had been afraid to leave the chamber for fear Nicholas would return and find her gone. Thomas would have to wait until she learned her husband's nocturnal habits.

"I can guess why," he said sulkily.

"Why, Thomas! Are you jealous?"

"Who wouldn't be? Do you think I like to lie in my bed and imagine my brother pawing you?"

Madeline smiled. "Dear Thomas. You know I am yours in my heart." She felt a rare stirring of what she thought might be love, but she was so unfamiliar with such an emotion that she was not sure. He was almost as handsome as Nicholas, though of a smaller build, and she had no doubt he loved her.

"I want your body to belong to me as well," he protested.

"How can that be? I will come to you as often as I can. We must be content with that."

"No! I've been giving this much thought. You could run away with me."

"Leave Wyndfell?" She laughed.

"Hear me out." He pulled her nearer so he could speak in a voice no one could overhear. Since she had come to him willingly, he felt he could trust her completely. "I have long had it in my mind to rid myself of Nicholas. My plan is this. You and I will run away together. As soon as we reach a place of safety, London for instance, I will hire a scoundrel to come to Wyndfell and kill Nicholas."

"Kill him?" Her eyes glinted in the light from the window. "In what way?"

"Poison. I have a key to the back gate where the beggars gather. The guards never bother with it other than to lock it. From there the man can find his way to the buttery and poison the wine. Nicholas is fond of canary. Eventually, it will kill him."

"Would a knife not be more sure?"

Thomas smiled to see how readily she fell in with his plan. "He is a powerful man. There is too great a chance of him overpowering the hired killer. Poison is better. As you recall, there was the earlier attempt."

She looked at him blankly, but he didn't notice.

"After one try, everyone will assume there was another poisoned barrel that was undetected. We can hardly fail if we choose our man with care."

"How can we know if the man is capable of doing this?" she asked eagerly. As with Swineford and Raymond, the idea of violent death made her breath quicken with excitement.

"I have ways of finding someone, don't worry about that. We have only to get to the safety of London. Are you with me?"

She nodded. Once Nicholas was dead, she could marry Thomas—whom she preferred—and still have Wyndfell and her title. "When will we leave?"

"Tomorrow, early."

Madeline walked to the window and gazed through its multicolored panes at the garden. She liked the idea, but such a haphazard plan seemed likely to fail. "I fear the poisoned wine will be detected before he drinks it," she said. "Especially if there has already been a threat of poisoning."

"What else can we do? If we try to have him

stabbed or shot, he may capture the hireling and learn we sent him."

"We could do it ourselves," she suggested.

"Us? Overpower Nicholas?" he scoffed. "You must be mad!"

A veil dropped behind Madeline's eyes. Of all the words he could have chosen, he had picked the only one that would turn her against him. "Mad?" she asked coldly.

"We could never do it. The idea is insane."

Madeline's hands knotted into fists, though her expression never changed. So Thomas thought her mad, did he? She would get revenge for that. Perhaps he had been playing her for a fool all along! Perhaps he was in Nicholas' employ to trap her into making a mistake! Her eyes squinted dangerously. They would see. She made no mistakes!

Turning to him with her sweetest smile, Madeline said, "You're right, dear Thomas, as always. How could I ever have questioned you?" She went to him and stood so near that he put his arms about her. "We must be careful. Tomorrow morning, come to the solar in the old tower. I will be waiting there for you."

"In the old wing? Why there?"

"Please, Thomas. Humor me this once. No one will overhear us there and we can make plans as to where we will stay in London." She smiled up at him in a way that made his heart pound. "Will you do that?"

"Of course, sweeting," he said, not knowing that had been Raymond's pet endearment for her.

With an effort Madeline kept the hate out of her eyes. Had Thomas been in league with Raymond as well? She knew he had come at least once to Pritchard Hall. How else could he have known what Raymond called her? "And, Thomas, you know how weak we women are. Perchance by the morrow I may grow fainthearted."

"I will win you over again," he promised.

"Even if I pretend not to recall this conversation—for such is sometimes my whim when I grow frightened—listen not. For I promise you, I do truly want to leave with you, no matter what I may foolishly say at that time." She lowered her lashes and stroked the velvet of his jerkin. "Will you whisk me away even in the face of my objections?"

"Without a moment's pause," he assured her. "Fear not. Will you, nil you, we will be in London before the week is out."

With a smile, Madeline put her arms around his neck. "I know I can depend upon you." She thought of Jessica and almost laughed to think how neatly she had contrived to dispose of her.

Thomas tightened his embrace and bent his head to her inviting lips. Madeline kissed him passionately. For a moment she had a twinge of doubt as to the rightness of her plan. He was truly magnificent in bed, and so far Nicholas had shown no interest in her at all.

Suddenly they were thrust apart as Nicholas pinned Thomas against the wall. Madeline staggered from the force in which she had been shoved back, but regained her feet. Nicholas' face was contorted with rage and Thomas' was deathly pale.

"What say you to this!" Nicholas ground out, his nose almost touching Thomas' as he half-lifted him off the floor.

"I. . .It was not as it seems," Thomas struggled to explain. "Tell him, Madeline! It was not as it seems!"

"In truth it wasn't" she blurted out. "Thomas. . . Thomas forced me!"

Thomas stared at her, then back at Nicholas. "It's not true! Believe your own brother when I say 'tis a lie!"

Nicholas growled and shook Thomas as a terrier would worry a rat. "Would I believe either of you?" He looked as if he were trying hard not to kill Thomas on the spot. "You have played me false for the last time, brother. Wyndfell is no longer your home, nor are you any longer my next of kin. I disown you! I should have done so long ago!"

"But, Nicholas, you—"

"Beg me not! You will take what personal belongings you wish and you will be gone from Wyndfell by dusk tomorrow!"

"Where will I go?"

"To hell, for all I care!" He shoved Thomas so roughly that the man sprawled across the floor. For a long moment Nicholas glared at Madeline. At last he said, "What I have to say to you is for your ears alone. As my countess I owe you that!" He stepped over Thomas and strode toward the door.

Madeline knelt briefly by Thomas and whispered, "Forgive me! It was the only way!"

"Come!" Nicholas bellowed, and she hastily got to her feet and hurried to obey.

Madeline had to run to keep up with Nicholas' long stride, yet she was too afraid of him to ask him to slack his speed. Nor would it have done any good, by the looks of him.

He led her to their chamber, and when the startled maids stared at his angry countenance, he shouted, "Out!" After they had scattered like a flock of chickens, he grabbed Madeline's wrist and pulled her roughly into the bedchamber and kicked the door shut with a bang. To his amazement, she dropped to her knees and quailed before him.

"A thousand pardons, my lord," she cried from behind her hands. "I would never be false to you! Thomas forced me to kiss him. I swear it on my honor!"

He stared down at her as she covered her face and wept brokenly. He had fully expected her to yell back at him and challenge him as she always did in an argument—not to cower at his feet.

"I swear by all I hold holy," Madeline sobbed, "he forced me. Had you not come in, God knows what he might have done!"

"You were kissing him back!"

"I was struggling to get free!"

"I find it hard to believe even Thomas would take it upon himself to rape my wife in the parlor in broad daylight! Do you take me for a fool?"

"Never, my lord! Never!" Madeline lifted her tear-stained face and held her hands up beseechingly. "Say you believe me! Tell me you love me still." Her blue eyes were filled with agony and were glistening with unshed tears.

Nicholas felt a sickness tighten in his belly. This was his wife, the woman he loved beyond all else in the world. How could he doubt her? He pulled her roughly to her feet and held her tightly as she sobbed in hysterics. He had never seen Jessica cry like this, and he could only assume it was proof of her innocence. "There now, love," he managed to say, though the words came out harshly. "I know how you feel about Thomas." He felt her stiffen and added, "I believe you. Yet surely you can see why I'm so distraught."

"Oh, yes, my lord," she cried. "Any other man would have beaten me by now! Surely you are the best of husbands."

"I love you." He looked down at her and saw to his

bewilderment that her tear-spangled eyes still held no depth of emotion he could define as love, only fear. "Stay away from Thomas," he warned her. "I'll see that he is served his meals in his rooms so that you are not forced to share bread with him. By dark tomorrow we will be rid of him."

"Yes, Nicholas," she murmured obediently. "Whatever you say."

He released her and strode toward the door. There he hesitated and looked back as if he were about to speak, then shook his head and left.

Madeline wiped her tears away with the palm of her hands and drew a deep breath as the small smile returned to her lips. That had been a narrow escape. Only her superb acting ability—perfected over the years with her parents—had proved her innocence. As she patted the last of her tears dry, her smile widened. Any man worth his salt would have beaten her senseless or at least have struck her. She had seen her father beat Jessica for even minor infractions when she was younger and at a time when he still had hopes of curbing her. No, Nicholas was weak, and tears were the key to controlling him, she was certain.

She went to the antechamber and seated herself at the writing desk. There was no way of knowing if she would be alone again before morning, and there was something she must do. She had no doubts that Thomas would take Jessica away, whether she protested or not. Thomas was quite forceful and he had given his word. But there was still an outside chance that Jessica would somehow contrive to return to Wyndfell and try to oust her.

Madeline took a sheet of parchment and laboriously wrote Nicholas a letter. Although she wasn't nearly as good at writing as Jessica, she knew enough to make a legible note. In it she confessed that she was a twin named Jessica and that she was the very image of his Madeline. She wrote that she had come to Wyndfell the day before and had imprisoned Madeline in the solar in the old tower. However, she had repented of her wrong to her sister and had departed, never to return. Madeline signed Jessica's name and dusted the ink with sand. As soon as Thomas had had time to spirit Jessica away, Madeline would leave the letter where Nicholas was sure to find it, then go to the solar, lock herself in, and wait to be rescued. Nothing could be simpler. Even if Jessica returned, she would never be able to convince Nicholas of her identity, since he himself would have freed the imprisoned Madeline.

Madeline had barely finished the letter, folded it, and sealed it with wax when her maids returned. They stared at her with round eyes, but she only smiled as if nothing untoward had happened. She beckoned to the one she still assumed to be Meg and said, "I want you to do me a great service. Here is a noble for you," she said as she handed her a coin. "Tomorrow I want you to give this letter to Lord Nicholas at noon. Can you read?"

The maid shook her head from side to side, her eyes wide at the amount of the coin.

"Give it to him at dinner—not before, mind you. No doubt he will give you another reward when he reads it. Can I trust you?"

"Yes, my lady. Tomorrow at dinner."

Madeline smiled. Life was so easy to arrange and manipulate when one only tried.

Jessica ate sparingly of her remaining food. Dusk was falling and Madeline had not come back to bring more. Fortunately, the pitcher was nearly full of water and she hadn't suffered for drink, but the water wouldn't last forever.

Nor would the candle. Only one was left of the several she had brought up. Jessica had thought there would be enough to last another week. Evidently Madeline had been keeping late hours, though she would have thought it so dull up here that her sister would have welcomed sleep.

Jessica pulled the tapestries back from the windows and lit the candle in hopes that someone tarrying late on the green would see. She sat on the cot and leaned back against the wall. Everyone would be at supper by now. Afterward, they would all disperse to their chambers and no one would be out to see her light, unless a courting couple happened to seek the privacy of the out-of-doors.

She closed her eyes against the painful idea of Madeline and Nicholas in the bedchamber. One night had already passed. Had he noticed the difference in the woman he must think to be his wife? Madeline was very cunning and their own parents had been fooled on many an occasion. Could Nicholas be duped as well? The night before, Jessica had been too frightened to think much about what might be happening in the master chamber, but tonight her imagination was working overtime. She had once overheard two stableboys say that all women were alike in the dark. Having bedded but one man, she didn't have any way of knowing if all lovers were the same. If it were true, she might languish here forever while Madeline stepped into her place. The idea of Madeline in Nicholas' arms made her groan.

She had to do something, so she banged on the thick door with the metal washbowl. Although the noise was loud inside her room, she couldn't tell if it was being heard by anyone in the castle. Soon she grew tired and quit. No one had come to see about the commotion.

Closing her eyes, she tried not to cry. Even with no one to see her, she hated to give in to tears.

Unbidden, the thought of Swineford and Raymond came to mind. Cruelly murdered, the reports had said. One by a Gypsy, the other by a servant. But after seeing Madeline's mercurial mood swings and hearing her talk of the two men, Jessica wasn't at all sure the guilty party had been caught or even suspected. She was growing more and more certain that the killer was Madeline. There had been a couple of tiny flaws in her story, a slip that might have gone unnoticed had she appeared more normal. If it were Madeline, a killer was now loose in Wyndfell. And she was sleeping with Nicholas, who would not be on his guard since he must think her to be his wife.

With renewed vigor, Jessica returned to the window and banged the battered pan on the stones as hard as she could. The noise floated out over the deserted courtyard and the empty green and died away into the night.

Nicholas ate little at supper, for he was concentrating on the woman beside him. Now that his suspicions were aroused, he saw a dozen little things that said she wasn't who she claimed to be. A disease of the mind might alter her personality, but would it make her acquire a liking for eel when she had abhorred it before? Or cause her to affect a coy lisp when she was trying hardest to please him? In all the cases he knew of, madness resulted in wilder, more chaotic behavior, rather than the opposite.

His eyes met Richard's and he shrugged. The puzzle seemed to have no solution. For if this wasn't his wife, where was she? A double might have been found and tutored in the names of the servants, but to what end?

When the meal finally ended, he was glad to escape the table. Through its duration, he had been aware that some of the men had been ogling Madeline. Some of it might have been Nicholas' imagination, but not all of it. He had even intercepted a wink from Sir Oliver, his bailiff! Surely she hadn't . . . He couldn't even finish the thought.

He had no stomach for games that night, and when Madeline suggested they retire to the winter parlor, he shook his head. She gave him that peculiar smile that was so unlike the one he knew, and preceded him to their chamber.

At the door to their bedchamber he hesitated. As ridiculous as it seemed, he couldn't bring himself to enter it. Not with her. "Let us sit for a while and talk," he suggested as he motioned for the servants to leave.

"Whatever you say, my lord." She seated herself on a low stool and took up her embroidery.

"Are you feeling well?"

"Of course," she said in surprise. "Why would I not feel well?"

"In your condition, it's not uncommon to feel poorly from time to time."

Madeline's eyes widened. Jessica was pregnant? She had not thought of that. "I. . .I feel quite well, all things considered, I meant to say." She would have to fake a miscarriage, she thought frantically. What else had Jessica not mentioned?

"Good." He was gazing at her intently.

"I must start sewing the babe's clothes," she babbled on. "Mayhap my mother could attend me when my time comes. You'd not object, would you?" she asked when she saw his surprised look.

"No, no. I have no objection. I was just thinking. I believe I'll send for the midwife tomorrow. She can examine you and tell more exactly when the babe is due." A look alike was one thing, but he knew no one could supply one that was also pregnant. "You wouldn't object, would you?"

"No, no. Of course not." She concentrated on the sewing she held, but she didn't see it. Somehow she had to have her "miscarriage" before the midwife arrived and determined she wasn't pregnant.

"Excellent. Then I will send for her tomorrow afternoon. I'll be busy in the fields until noon."

"Good," she sighed. "That you are sending for the midwife, that is." That would give Thomas plenty of time to take Jessica away and for Madeline to take her place in the solar.

"Well, it's been a long day," he said almost cheerfully as he stood up. "I need to sleep and I'm sure you do too. That scene over Thomas must have taxed you."

Madeline looked up hopefully. "You'll come to bed with me then?"

"In your condition? We cannot chance a loss of the child. No, we will wait a bit longer. If the midwife gives her blessing, then I will return to your bed. Not until." He smiled at her and let himself out.

As he went down the corridor to the guest chamber, he was deep in thought. This wasn't the woman he had married; he could almost swear to it. And if she weren't, then who was she, and more important, where was his wife?

24

JESSICA LAY CURLED on the cot, trying to ignore her growling stomach and to think of some way to escape the solar. The sun had come up, and sunshine glowed around the edges of the tapestries. Rolling off the narrow bed, Jessica went to a window and expectantly drew the tapestry back to look outside. Surely someone would be out and about this time. But again, no one was within sight, and she had to fight down her rising panic. Over the past two nights she had become fairly adept at controlling her anxiety, and soon had herself calmed enough to think.

She looked at the windows and sighed. While the width of the window on the inside was wider than her shoulders, the outside was much too narrow for her to squeeze through. This tower had been built when windows served more as archer slits than as openings to let in light.

She fingered the frayed tapestry distractedly; then her eyes darted back to the window. Why hadn't she thought of this before!

She pulled down the tapestry, then rushed back to the cot and began tearing the sheet into strips. In a few minutes' time she had fashioned a rope from the cloth and had tied the bright-colored tapestry to one end. Then she went to the window and tossed the unwieldy mass at the outside opening, eight feet beyond her reach. At last the wadded tapestry fell through.

Before an hour had passed, she heard footsteps and sat up expectantly. She got to her feet as the key scraped in the lock, and ran to the door as it opened, practically throwing herself into the man's arms.

"Thomas! Oh, Thomas, you can't know how good you look to me," she exclaimed as he drew her to him and hugged her to his chest.

"How long have you been here?" he murmured as she returned his hug with near-desperation.

"It seems forever. Come. Take me away from this dreadful place."

"Of course, sweeting."

In her relief at being rescued, she ignored his familiarity, and they walked briskly down the gallery. Jessica ached to know what had happened in the two days she had been locked away, but she dared not ask Thomas. She was fearful of giving away some secret that Madeline might not have told. Although she had been locked away for only two days, Jessica knew she would indeed go mad if she had to endure such as this for any length of time again.

"Where's Nicholas?" she asked.

"In the fields. There's no one about the castle but servants. I have our horses ready, and we have only to mount them."

Jessica was still too distraught to see anything odd in this. Her only thought was to ride out to Nicholas and let him soothe away the horror of her ordeal. She was light-headed and dizzy from shock and relief. Later she would feel better, she told herself.

Later she would be in better control. For now, all that was important was for her to reach Nicholas.

She hurried with Thomas to the stable, and he held her jennet while she mounted, then swung up onto his own horse. Tears were starting to well up in her eyes as she realized how close she had come to being forgotten and left to starve. Her hands trembled on the reins, and she kicked her horse to a gallop as Thomas did the same.

As they clattered over the cobblestones of the courtyard, she glanced up with a shudder to the flag she had improvised. She hoped never to see that room again. They crossed the wide drawbridge and rode across the green as if devils pursued them.

From the sentry's walk high above them, Madeline watched them leave with a self-satisfied curl of her lips. Thomas had done his work well, she surmised, for Jessica appeared to be riding with him of her own choice. Perhaps, she thought, there had been more between them than she had guessed.

She made her way across the walkway and into the tower. Her fingers caressed the cool stones as she carefully descended the steps. Wyndfell was truly hers now.

Madeline went down the curving corridor and into the long gallery. She no longer noticed the bare walls and cold hearths. In fact she felt almost fond of the dank place, for it had been her first introduction to Wyndfell.

At the solar she hesitated. In her effort to set this up, she had forgotten the difficulty of locking herself in. For a minute she pondered the situation, then knelt to examine the lower part of the door. Over the years the wood at the bottom had been gnawed away by mice and weathered by the elements blowing in the open windows. There was enough space between the door and the stones to push the key back out.

Without further hesitation, she entered the round room and pulled the door shut. Putting the key in the large lock, she forced it to turn. Kneeling, she pushed the key as far under the door as she could, then took a bodkin from her hair and shoved it further. Satisfied that all had been done, she composed herself to wait until Nicholas returned from the fields to rescue her.

She looked around the room and shook her head in dismay at the mess Jessica had made. The sheets had been ripped off the bed and torn into strips. If she had doubted Jessica's madness before, this was certainly proof. One end of the sheet was tied to the foot of the cot and then to a tapestry, then to the rest that had been hung out the window. The mattress was now a pile of straw heaped upon the pad that covered the rope base. With a sigh, Madeline drew the makeshift rope back into the room. Jessica must have thought she could squeeze out the window and climb down. The notion was pathetic. How foolish. How insane. Still, the rope was too noticeable a sign, so she began unknotting the tapestries. Madeline wanted no one but Nicholas to rescue her and see that she was truly locked in.

Nicholas finished inspecting the crop of barley and remounted his horse. Though it was an exceptionally good crop, he could take no pleasure in it for worry over matters in the castle. Not only was there the problem with Madeline; he now had Thomas to fret over as well. He didn't regret ordering Thomas to leave Wyndfell, but if Thomas chose to stay, he would have to throw him out, bodily. Not that Nicholas objected to a good fight, but this one would create bitterness that might endure for generations. He had known of family feuds like this. Some lasted long after the original combatants had died and returned to dust and no one even remembered why they had fought. He thought of his unborn child and sighed. Nicholas wanted to leave his children wealth, not a feud. And he knew Thomas would never forgive him.

He slowly rode back to Wyndfell. As always he felt a rise of family pride as he viewed the massive curtain wall and the crenellated castle within. His ancestors had fought and some of them had died to preserve this castle and these lands. Nicholas loved Wyndfell second only to his wife. Whatever befell the world, Wyndfell would remain. But what of his wife's erratic behavior?

He rode into the courtyard and pitched his reins to the stableboy. He was back early but he wanted to talk to Madeline to see if he could iron out whatever was disturbing her so.

She wasn't in the winter parlor or the ladies' parlor. After he looked in their bedchamber, he went in search of Meg. "Have you seen Lady Madeline?" he asked when he located the women in the rose garden.

"Not I, my lord," Meg answered stiffly. Meg was still miffed over the slight Madeline had committed in favoring her rival over her.

"I have, Lord Nicholas." The bigger woman spoke up with importance. "At least I have a message from her."

"Well, what is it?"

"She told me to give it to you at noon and not before. She was real plain about that."

"Give it to me." His dark eyes fixed upon her until she squirmed.

Pulling the sealed paper from her sleeve, the woman handed it to her master and made a bobbing curtsy.

With great concern clouding his face, Nicholas broke open the seal and unfolded the parchment to read the scrawl that was so unlike what he'd seen from her before. Suddenly he crumpled the paper and strode toward the castle.

He could hardly make sense of what he had read. His wife was a twin? That certainly explained the odd behavior he had seen. Taking the steps two at a time, he entered the castle and hurried across the hall to the rarely used old steps. He ran up them and strode the length of the gallery with fewer paces than ever before.

Nicholas found the key to the solar on the floor and called out to Madeline as he fitted it in the lock. He heard her muffled reply as the metal grated against metal; then he pulled the door open.

"Nicholas!" Madeline cried out and fell into his arms. "You've rescued me! I was so afraid."

"There, love, there. Don't cry." He held her in a fierce embrace as if he could squeeze out all the fearful moments she must have endured. "What happened? How did this come about?"

"Oh, Nicholas, it was terrible! I have a sister named Jessica. A perfect twin to myself," she sobbed. "I thought her still at Hargrove Castle with my parents and locked in a mad cell, for she's insane."

Nicholas gripped her tighter. That very well described the woman he had seen for the last two days.

"You can imagine my horror when I realized Jessica had somehow escaped and followed me here! She plans to step into my place as Countess of Wyndfell! I think she planned to leave me here to die!"

"Hush, love. You're safe now. I'll let no one harm you," he said with all the love in his soul.

"How did you know where to find me?" Madeline asked pitiably.

"The wretch left me a note. She has gone, or I would see that she is locked away where she could never escape." He buried his face in Madeline's hair. "You can't know how I felt, seeing such a change come over you. I thought *you* had gone mad."

Madeline stiffened and pulled away. Dabbing at her tears, she said, "Let's leave this place. You can't imagine how it distresses me to see that room, even from out here."

Nicholas put his arm around her and they walked down the gallery. "I'll see to it that the room is permanently locked. Although there have been a few good memories there," he said in an effort to coax a smile from her.

"There? Never!"

He thought back to the day he and Jessica had made such passionate love in that room. In her distress, she must have forgotten.

Jessica reined in her horse as they approached the village. "Why are we riding this way? The fields are yonder."

"So they are, but London is in this direction," Thomas said.

"London? I'm not going to London!"

"Of course we are, sweeting. You aren't changing your mind, are you?"

"I never agreed to go to London with you! Have you lost your senses?"

"So you plead forgetfulness, do you? Never mind. I remember my promise to take you whether you

will or won't go in peace." He reached out his hand
to catch her horse's bridle.

Jessica yanked back on the reins, causing her horse
to rear out of his reach. "Touch this horse and
Nicholas will have your skin!"

"What more can he do?" Thomas sneered. "Already I've been disowned and cast out of my ancestral home for you. Come! We must reach London
and hire a blackguard to kill him as we planned,
before he has time to legally strike me off as his next
of kin."

Her eyes grew large as she stared at him. "Mother
of God!" she gasped almost soundlessly. "What has
Madeline done!" Clapping her heels against her horse,
she sent the animal plunging away from Thomas
and back toward Wyndfell.

She took a circuitous route so that she could check
most the fields, but caught no glimpse of Nicholas.
Realizing he must have returned to the castle, she
galloped toward the drawbridge, with Thomas in
quick pursuit.

Nicholas held Madeline's elbow to steady her as they
descended the steep steps. Her tears had ended and
she walked quietly beside him.

"It's over now, this nightmare," she sighed as they
reached the hall. "Jessica is gone and I'm where I
should always have been."

"You'll never know what misery she caused me,"
Nicholas said as he watched her glide across the
rush-strewn floor.

"Misery?"

When he noted her closed-lip smile, his brows
knitted. "Aye. I found the harlot kissing Thomas in
the winter parlor. Sir Richard tells me she lay with

half the men in the castle, and the slut would have lain with him too if he hadn't thrown her out."

"Harlot?" Madeline said, her sweetness turning instantly to vinegar. "Slut!"

Watching her closely, Nicholas said, "What else am I to call a woman who has less scruples than a bitch in heat?"

"You dare speak to me so?" Madeline stepped toward him threateningly. Then realized she was taking the wrong tack and reversed her behavior to give him her most demure smile. "Forgive me for raising my voice, my lord. I have been sorely tried of late."

He pulled her to him and searched her shallow eyes. To further verify his suspicions, he lowered his head to kiss her.

Suddenly the door burst open, flooding the dim hall with light and causing the rush lamps to gutter. "Nicholas!" Jessica cried out as she ran to him.

"Nicholas, save me!" Madeline screamed as Thomas also ran into the hall. " 'Tis my mad sister come back to murder us both!"

Nicholas stared from one woman to the other. "My God," he murmured. "The two of you *are* exactly alike!"

Jessica stumbled over the rushes and caught his hand before Thomas could restrain her. "Hear me, love! This other woman is an impostor."

"Madeline?" he asked in confusion as he reached for Jessica.

"No, no! I'm Jessica."

"There!" Madeline screamed. "You hear her admit it!"

"But I'm the one you married!" Jessica cried out desperately. "Madeline eloped with Sir Raymond and I took her place before our wedding. *I* am your wife!"

Nicholas stared from one to the other, unable to comprehend exactly what was going on.

"You promised to come away with me!" Thomas shouted as he looked from one woman to the other, then back again.

Jessica's eyes begged Nicholas to recognize her as Thomas lunged for her arm to drag her away. Jessica jerked back and fell against Nicholas.

With a shrill scream Madeline grabbed a torch from the wall sconce and threw it at Jessica, shouting, "She will kill us all!"

The torch missed its mark but landed on the rushes. With a whooshing sound the flooring caught fire and almost at once spread several feet.

With a hoarse cry, Thomas grabbed the twin nearest him and dragged her away toward the door. Shouting for help, Nicholas tossed the other woman over his shoulder and did likewise.

The smoke was thick and acrid, stinging their eyes and congesting their lungs. Nicholas lowered his head and charged toward the door, unable to see through the choking fumes. Flames leapt and caught the tapestries and painted cloths, sending a conflagration up the walls to reach for the battle pennants and wooden ceiling above.

Nicholas' hand touched stone, and as he gripped the woman tightly, he frantically felt around for the opening. Already the heat was nearly unbearable and he felt his hair starting to singe. Just as he began to think he was going the wrong way, his fingers brushed the oak door.

He staggered, choking and coughing, out into the courtyard and unceremoniously dumped his burden onto the cobbles. The woman had obviously fainted, for she didn't move from where he left her.

Nicholas ran toward the door, determined to find

the other two and bring them to safety, as the court-yard filled with shouting and screaming servants. A human chain was set up from the castle to St. Ruan's well and buckets were tossed from hand to hand in an effort to douse the fire before it destroyed the castle.

"Madeline!" Nicholas bellowed as Richard and two other men forcefully restrained him from diving back into the inferno. "Thomas!" his eyes were wild as he strained against his captors. He caught a glimpse of a jonquil skirt as the flames separated her from his sight, and he raged against his men to save her, though he knew she was already lost.

Because fire was an ever-present hazard, the bucket brigade knew their work well. Letting the hall and the gallery and solar above go up in flames, they fought to keep the fire from spreading to the rest of the castle. Villagers had come running to help and to gawk, and the courtyard was soon overrun.

Until the fire slackened and began to isolate itself to feed on the last of the solar floor and fallen timbers in the hall, Nicholas fought to be free. Then the roof caved in with a resounding crash that smoth-ered most of the flames and sent up a roiling cloud of smoke and cinders.

Suddenly Nicholas quit fighting and stared at the window where he had last seen the woman. Sound-lessly his lips moved in her name as if he might recall her if he tried hard enough. Richard, his face grim in empathy, slapped Nicholas on the shoulder and gave him a masculine hug.

"We couldn't save her," he said gruffly. "If you had tried, you would have died too."

Nicholas could only stare in shock at the smolder-ing wing of his castle. "Do you think they got out the back way?" he asked in a choked voice.

"No." Richard could think of no way to soften the blow, and to give him hope would be too cruel. "She and Thomas are gone."

Nicholas remained staring at the smoking shell as people milled around him. At first he didn't feel the woman's hand on his arm. Not until she tugged at him did he pull his eyes away to look at her.

Soot marked her face and her hair was disheveled and half-down from her coil. Her eyes were as stunned as his and were round and dark with shock. "Nicholas?" she said, shaking her head uncertainly as if reality were not entirely solid with her as yet.

Slowly he turned to face her, his eyes searching her face. She looked so much like his beloved wife that he wanted to believe that he had been wrong in which twin he had grabbed. In all the confusion, maybe he had made a mistake. He couldn't bear to ask her name, and after the scene in the hall, he wasn't entirely sure which name went with which twin, anyway. As he stared at the woman before him, confusion twisted his mind and distorted his senses. He couldn't bear the thought that his Madeline had died in the fire. Building his hope with each passing moment, he decided that he must know her name. Reluctantly he asked, "Are you my Madeline?"

"Before I answer that question, I must tell you that I am your true wife. The other woman is the impostor." She knew that she needed to handle this carefully. Lovingly she smiled up at his beleaguered face. "My name is Jessica, but—"

"Dear God," he interrupted with a bellow as he looked back toward his fire-gutted home. "Will I never know the truth? You say you are my wife, yet you tell me your name is that of your twin sister. My throat is as parched as my heart. If the kitchen still stands, woman, fetch me some ale."

Unable to contain herself any further, Jessica burst out, "I have all but died in a fire and you send me for ale? Get it yourself! I had thought you would be glad I was saved, not send me on errands as if I were your servant!"

A sudden awareness of the truth lit his face, and he stepped forward to grab her as she began to flounce away. "Madeline!" he cried joyfully. "My wife! You're alive!"

As he caught her up and spun her around, she hugged him as if she would never let him go. "Yes. I am your wife, but my name is Jessica!" she protested, torn between laughing and crying.

"Jessica!" he boomed in unbounded happiness.

The surrounding crowd watched the couple's odd behavior, then shook their heads in wonder. The master had been so out of his head over losing his hall that he seemed not to know his wife was safe beside him. Not only that, he was calling her by another woman's name and she was laughing as tears streamed down her face. People could be strange in the head after a shock. Soon the crowd began to disperse to spread the gossip of the catastrophe at Wyndfell Castle.